OUT THERE

AARON BEACH

PAGE PUBLISHING, INC.
Conneaut Lake, PA

First originally published by Page Publishing 2021

ISBN 978-1-64628-947-9 (pbk)
ISBN 978-1-64628-948-6 (digital)

Printed in the United States of America

CHAPTER

1

Milo Webster, a reluctant bagman, sat gazing through the back seat passenger-side window at the early majestic purple heavens, which had yet to begin its fade to blue. As the checkered cab pulled up to the Los Angeles International Airport, the driver's judgmental lip turned up in a sneer, as he watched the massive man in the back seat struggle to adjust his girth and redirect his energy in an attempt to haul his obese frame from the motionless vehicle.

Checking his Timex, Milo realized he had around thirty minutes to make his six o'clock flight. The low tick, tick, tick of the car engine reminded him of a bomb just before its detonation. The heavyset man labored, contorting his entire body in order to place one of his enormous forearms through the passenger's side window to pay the driver. As the juggernaut waddled away, the driver noticed him set his suitcase down, move his backpack from one shoulder to the other, and then place both hands on his lower back as if an attempt to adjust his back fat. The cabdriver shook his head while wondering how someone his passenger's age could look so awkward and uncomfortable in his own skin.

Moving as fast as his stubby legs would carry him, the large male approached the South West Airlines counter, wiped off his sweaty hand on his pant leg, and then reached into his inside jacket pocket for his wallet. He removed his ID, handed it to the attendant, and placed his bag on the small shelf between the break in the counter, directly in front of the conveyor belt.

The attendant asked him a few questions regarding his bag's previous whereabouts as she attached a tiny card with an elastic string to the suitcase's handle and then placed it on the conveyor. The gentle giant watched as his luggage disappeared behind a severed plastic curtain while he awaited his boarding pass and baggage claim check. In a daze, he noticed the woman's lips move but was unaware of what she had actually said. However, he politely smiled, grabbed his paperwork, wished the attendant a good day, and shuffled off in search of Gate C-22.

Thousands of early morning travelers swarmed in every direction, each with separate agendas and each seeming to be in more of a rush than the last. Multitudes of conversations blended into a single buzz of indistinguishable noise. Pulling himself up the stairs with use of the handrail, Milo noticed the preboarding checkpoint and instantly began to break out in a cold sweat. Before he could take another step, he felt a slight tug on the back of his purple polyester suit jacket. Turning around, he realized it was the love of his life. Her brown eyes were all red and puffy from a long night of crying; her hair looked tattered and uncombed. She wore a baggy gray Cal State-Fullerton sweatshirt, a pair of faded acid-washed jeans, and black flip-flops, which forced her heels to slightly hang over the edge. Without a word, she grabbed his hand and led him back down the stairs.

"I don't have time for this. My plane is boarding in fifteen minutes. Besides, we went through this last night," said the huge man in the electric-purple suit.

"I know," she replied as tears began to pour down her young face once again. "But I've seen it, and you've seen it, too, Milo. We both know how this ends. Please tell me, why are you going through with it anyway?"

Snatching his wrist away, he noticed the indentation her fingers left on his arm.

"I have to," he blurted out. "I don't have a choice. Now, go home! I promise everything will be all right."

Milo quickly turned and made his strenuous journey back up the two flights of stairs to the checkpoint.

At the top of the stairs, he chose the center line because it had fewer people. However, all three were equally long. At the head of each line stood a glass case with a metal doorway standing inside it. Every line had an x-ray machine attached to a conveyor belt that scanned passenger's carry-on bags with two TSA agents dressed in sharply pressed bluish-gray shirts with matching pants. One agent sat in a chair viewing the contents of the luggage on a small monitor, while the other watched the travelers as they passed through the metal detector entryway. Two additional agents walked back and forth on the outer rows, "randomly" selecting individuals for full-body searches.

For the first few minutes standing in line, Milo could not seem to get enough air. He felt as if he was suffocating. He inhaled huge lung-filling gasps of air, but it did not help. He was sure that he would pass out before reaching the front of the line.

Worried that his uncontrolled perspiration would draw unwanted attention, he drew in small gulps of air through his nose, held it for five seconds, and exhaled slowly through his slightly dried lips. Internally, he tried to calm himself by singing "Jingle Bells"; it had always worked as a kid when he was nervous or scared. Next, he visualized himself sitting comfortably on the plane, halfway to his destination.

Channeling his terrible fear, the man stepped forward, picked up his bag, placed it on the squeaky black conveyor belt, and began removing everything from his skintight pockets and placing it in a clear plastic container. First, he threw in his keys, then his watch and wallet and a handful of change. The container received it with what almost sounded like a baby crying noise. Bending over, he struggled to keep his balance as he nearly toppled over a couple of times while attempting to remove his black Stacy Adams wing tips.

He held his breath as he followed a short, stout blue-haired woman wearing a miniature top hat through the metal detector. His thickness was nearly equal to the width of the doorway, so the man turned sideways and proceeded through with trepidation bursting from his pores.

A screaming alert siren and a flashing red light accompanied him into the booth. Once again, sweat began to pour down the large man's face. The TSA agent stepped to the man and asked him to spread his legs and hold his arms out by his side as he waved a gray metallic wand up and down his body. The wand gave an accusing squeal as it passed the man's bulging midsection.

"Please step back through the gate, remove your belt, place it on the conveyor belt, and step through the entryway again for me, sir, if you would," said the man in the uniform in a very monotone voice.

Without a reply, Milo did as he was told. His second attempt to pass through was successful. The big man nodded to the agent, smiled, and said, "Glad I don't have to go more than a few steps without my trusty belt 'cause my pants would be down around my ankles in no time at all. And I don't think anyone in here wants to see that."

The TSA employee did not return his smile or his humility. Instead, he studied the man's facial expression and movements as Milo acquired his belt and the tub with his belongings. Slowly, the large man tottered to the closest bench where he struggled to put on his shoes.

Once again, the huge bear of a man looked at his wristwatch, realizing that time was still of the essence. Milo looked up for the sign directing him toward Gate C-22 then humped off in that direction. The glossy tile floors provided little traction for Milo as he rushed with his backpack slung over his shoulder. He stumbled and slipped repeatedly while attempting to avoid oncoming traffic, but his determination fueled his progression.

Finally, after running for several minutes in what felt like a never-ending hall, the gate showed itself. Within seconds of seeing his destination, he heard the trumpeting call over the intercom for flight 4307 to Columbus, which was now boarding at Gate C-22.

A quick rapid survey of the gate floor was enough for Milo to realize he had arrived just in time to blend into the middle of the line that was gathering to board the soon-to-be departing flight.

The drone of the loud intercom announcement that there was no waiting in the green section being repeated every three minutes was being mimicked by two little kids a few places ahead of Milo. He soon noticed a perversely overweight blond woman attempting to settle down the two unruly children. One of her girls refused to stand patiently in line. She would skip around her mother every time the line moved. Each time she got behind her mother, she would make a funny face at the huge man in the purple suit.

The flower-patterned dress blossomed with vivid colors, which exploded off the woman's huge frame. Snickering to himself, Milo jokingly prayed that they were not sitting on the same side of the plane.

The roar of the line quieted to a minimal hush as travelers began to disappear into a hallway, which led to the Boeing 727. The line in front of the man shrank as he approached the turnstile headed by a woman in a South West Airlines uniform taking passengers' tickets.

As the big man advanced forward and reached into his inside jacket pocket to remove his ticket, he heard a sudden scampering of feet and a rumbling of keys from behind him. Turning to identify the commotion, he saw three TSA agents quickly moving toward him, headed by the man who told him to remove his belt back at the metal detector. Turning forward, he noticed two more agents, a man and a woman, coming out of the boarding hallway en route to his position.

He stood still, waiting for their response.

"Mr. Webster, would you please step out of line and follow me? We have some discrepancies with your identification that we need you to clarify for us," said a burly and rather sour officer, as he pointed back in the direction from which they had just come.

"For what? I haven't done anything wrong," Milo said.

Without responding to his statement, the well-built agent eagerly removed his baton and sternly told Milo that this was not a request.

With that, the huge purple figure was escorted around the corner where he vanished into a side hallway. As Milo was ushered down the vacant corridor toward the only door in a vacuum of walls, he pondered on the events that had led him to this point in time.

CHAPTER

2

To most onlookers, six-year-old Andre Brown looked like your average first grader. However, after closer inspection, it was obvious that was not the case. His face was slim and jovial, not happy, with childish excitement beaming with wisdom beyond his years. Despite his youth, two slightly underlined pools, which would bloom into full-fledged bags by his twenty-fifth birthday, set below his eyes. His reddish-brown hair was tightly braided and stretched to the nape of his neck. His speech was slow and deliberate. He sometimes displayed certain mannerisms that made people think he was an old man trapped in the body of a child. Even his posture resembled that of a senior citizen losing a lengthy bout with gravity. The only thing childlike about Andre was his pip-squeak voice.

On his favorite day of the week, Friday, Andre sat with his face pressed against the window of the Fayette County school bus. He dressed in white high-top Converse sneakers, jeans, a blue T-shirt, and a green Kimberly Elementary windbreaker. He rode patiently with his knees pressed against the back of the forward seat. In his little hands, he held a crushed bag of Ruffles chips and a school library book titled *Glue Fingers*.

During the twenty-minute ride, his eyes never strayed from the window; he never spoke to anyone, never joked, laughed, or even pestered his sister as most brothers often do. For the first part of the ride, Andre simply attempted to count each yellow reflector down the middle of the road. The afternoon sun felt as if it was melting his sweat-drenched face to the window. His new challenge became to maintain his eye on a certain faraway object outside and not lose it through the course of the bumpy ride.

The library book he held in his hands was now covered in crumbs from his potato chips, and a dark grease stain outlined the outstretched hand of a boy attempting to catch a football with another boy draped on his back. His lap was now buried under flakes of chips, which had leaked from the corner of the crunched blue and white bag during the bumpy excursion.

From Route 60, the bus would make a right turn onto Carter Lane, a cloud-creating dirt road, which swung pass the post office and over the railroad tracks. There, a young bully-in-training by the name of Jimmy Newsome would get dropped off each day, as well as his on-again, off-again best friend, John-John Patino, and his two sisters, Reese and Stacey. With two more labored left turns, the bus would return to the pothole-filled Route 60, leaving a ten-minute ride until his stop.

In just sixteen more hours, Andre would be watching his favorite Saturday morning cartoon, *The Young Sentinels*, eating a Jethro-size bowl of Capt'N Crunch with Crunch Berries and a big cup of cherry Kool-Aid to chase down his often-burned whole wheat toast. In just two more weeks, school would be no more than a bad memory for the glorious days of summer awaiting him.

As the bus came to a stop, the hot leather seat squeaked and perspired as seventy-five pounds of pure energy sprang from its restraint. A blur down the aisle like the Flash in the stairwell waiting for Ms. Jabber-Jaw Jones, as he referred to her, to open the doors and release him to the outside world.

Andre loved the hollow and its wild woods. When he moved here, he heard tales that brown bear had once made these woods home. Wild boar tracks could be seen in your front yard, and the deer population was out of control. At least the beautiful hills and valleys, the multitudes of trees, and assorted brush with endless winding paths for a youngster to explore had been unaffected by the slow crawl of modernization to the wild and wonderful mountains of West "By God" Virginia.

Up the hill, across the tracks and down the dusty lane, Andre sprinted, attempting to leave his older sister. The left sleeve of his green Kimberly Elementary School windbreaker dragged the ground, forming a small dust storm behind his fleeting white high-top Converse All-Stars.

"Wait up, Dre! Ma told me to hold your hand before you crossed the road."

"What? You don't have to. I'm old enough to cross the road by myself."

"If you do, I'm gonna tell Ma, and she is gonna whup your little yellow butt!"

"Tell, smell, go to hell. Hang yo britches on a rusty nail."

"I'ma tell! You said a cuss word," his sister screamed out while she panted violently, attempting to keep pace with her younger brother.

Latice Brown was a thin, wiry caramel-complexioned seven-year-old girl. Her eyes were so slanted that she appeared to be a dark-skinned Asian to some. Her only imperfection was a slight touch of reoccurring eczema between her light brown eyes and around her little nose. (It often took on the appearance of little dried mushroom.) Her biggest joy was tormenting and pestering her younger sibling every chance she got.

The low growl of a Mac truck grew like ragweed after the rain. The closer the dump truck got, the angrier the growl grew. Although Andre was certain the truck was still several houses away, he had planned to time the crossing of the road in his mind's eye and never look at the beast. As he stepped over the tracks and down a slight decline, the breath of the beast exploded and the stench of diesel fluid smacked the boy in the face. Still, he never looked up. Picturing the monster in his mind, he guessed the red and black behemoth to be at Mrs. McLemore's house. Step-by-step, Andre's courage increased. With his head down and confidence up, the boy stepped forward and heard the blare of a thousand trombones accompanied by a small bony hand on his shoulder yanking him backward.

"I told you to wait, you little dummy. Are you trying to kill your stupid self?" his sister asked. "Now hold my hand!"

"I don't have to," Andre replied. "You're not the boss of me!"

The rusty latch on the old gate screeched as it released hold of the end post connecting the silver Fence City link fence surrounding an acre and a half of prime coal mine country. The house was a late-twenties A-frame 1,100-square-foot, two-bedroom catastrophe. The outer siding was a pink-and-silver-speckled shingle-like material covering the entire front of the house, while the rear was covered in two-by-two plywood particleboard, which was starting to warp from years of weathering. The deteriorating boards housed a kitchen and utility room, which appeared to be sinking into the foundation. To the east and rear, the property line was greeted by Armstrong Creek, a meandering sewage-polluted stream, which reeked of neighbors' past meals in summer months and threatened to flooded its banks and invade homes close to its shores every spring.

Faster than the speed of thought, Andre blew around his sister and flew over the first two steps, exploding upward toward the lazy gray porch. His upward progress was cut short by his big toe on his left foot clipping the third step. His grounding was met by white-hot pain, which shot through his shin and lower knee. To make matters worse, there was now a hole in his good school pants. The only thing that kept him from crying was that if he did, Latice would make fun of him. Once, when they were playing in their grandmother's room with their Fisher Price multicolored bowling set, Andre had bowled a strike and while celebrating, Latice pushed him down on a small brown electric heater. He remembered the searing pain and the tears, which followed. He sustained third-degree burns from his left elbow up to his shoulder. Any four-year-old would have cried, and he did. Those tears would torment him for the next year. At every opportunity, his pain would be revisited and magnified in the butt of his sister's every joke, which always ended in "And he cried like a little baby girl."

No, he would not cry. He would never cry again if he could help it.

While fighting to hold back the threat of a tear in the corner of his eye, a yellow glimmer caught the eye of the boy sprawled out on the concrete. Andre thought the aluminum screen door shined

11

with the brilliance of a supernova in the late May sun. As the boy shaded his eyes, he noticed a yellow piece of paper tucked between the screen and the metal casing of the screen door. Apparently, Latice had noticed it, too, because as he lifted himself off the porch, he felt a hand on his back, forcing him back toward the gray concrete.

"It's a note from Ma," she said. "She wants us to go over Mrs. Judy's house until she gets home this evening."

CHAPTER

3

Virginia Brown's girlfriend had been one of those women who seemingly began training her children in the womb that good manners and respect for their elders was the path to righteousness and the grace of God. In fact, the only thing Mrs. Judy liked more than a well-mannered child was a well-mannered child who attended church three or four times a week, which, of course, her boys did.

"The idle mind of a child is Satan's playground" was one of her favorite sayings.

Mrs. Judy lived just two houses down, right next to the Mount Zion Baptist Church. The location served perfectly for she was one of the first ladies of the church. Everywhere she went, she made it known her husband was a pillar in the community as well as first deacon to the good Reverend Daniels. If Judy Lyn Harris had a mantra, it would have been to create the perfect, loyal, God-fearing family man. Her boys, all six of them, were raised to be model Christians with upstanding morals. These morals were instilled in a manner of ways, including preaching, praying, ministering, and occasionally bashing, if necessary.

These lessons were delivered in an assortment of manners starting with Sunday school at nine o'clock, followed by morning service at ten, usually lasting until about twelve thirty, at which time they would rush home to have a quick lunch. They would enjoy a few minutes of television combined with organized bathroom breaks, leaving just enough time to get back to the house of worship for the afternoon session, which lasted until 4:00 p.m. At this time, many parishioners would leave, but the faithful few would stay for the evening service, which ended at 6:00 p.m.

Sometimes, the congregation would gather in the basement for a dinner prepared by the sisters upon the service's end. This happened probably two Sundays a month. Days with dinner totaled about nine and a half hours on the church's property, and that was just Sunday. Mondays were an off day.

On Tuesdays, after school, they had to go to youth ministries for two hours and promptly report their assessment of the day's lessons to Mrs. Judy.

On Wednesdays, there was prayer meeting. Prayer meetings were usually reserved for the senior members of the congregation who would gather to pray for specific church members and their particular ailment or problem, usually financial. As far as Mrs. Judy was concerned, learning the art of prayer was the most important thing any child of God could know. So therefore, the entire Harris clan was there, including little Eric, who had been attending the gatherings since he was a toddler.

Thursday was another service-free day for the boys.

The Friday night ritual consisted of a light ministry, cookies, punch, and a movie, usually about the rapture or the pitfalls of living in sin.

On this particular Friday night, the Harrises' traditional trek across their lawn to the Mount Zion Baptist would be postponed because of the arrival of two unannounced guest.

Normally, Mrs. Judy would simply take her company to church with them, but she knew that the kids' grandmother, Ms. Lucy, was a devout member of the Kimberly Church of Holiness. Although they were friends, the two had words on more than one occasion about their choice of venues for worship. The last confrontation had nearly led to a knockdown drag out, and she had no intentions on putting herself in that position again.

Judy inched down the stairs and around the corner into the kitchen where her youngest of five boys pushed a red 1967 Corvette

Stingray hot wheel's car back and forth across an immaculate white linoleum floor.

"Mine popped a wheelie," said Eric, as he stood up a green Army man who looked ready to throw a grenade.

"I bet you can't knock him down in three tries, Dre."

"Eric Nathaniel Harris, if you don't get your narrow behind up and stop scuffing up my clean floor this instant, I am going to beat the black off of you!"

"Yes, ma'am. I'm sorry, I was just playing."

"Well, playtime is over, mister. Dinner is almost ready, so go wash up and tell your brothers to get ready for dinner."

"Yes, ma'am," the boy said. "Come on, Dre. I'll race you to the bathroom."

After dinner, the family sat in the front room and watched TV, a floor-model Zenith color television with radio, an eight-track tape player, and stereo all-in-one. It stretched six feet in length. Its exterior was brown oak with sliding cabinet doors, which hid the screen, transforming the appliance from visual aid to visual eyesore in a matter of seconds. A mahogany backdrop of paneling covered the entire room. The walls were covered with an assortment of black velvet oil-based paintings of black Jesus and his disciples. Each had a brown oak frame that matched both the TV set and the trim of the paneling.

As a result of Mr. Harris's oral compulsive disorder (the smoking of Moore Menthol 100s one after another, four and five cigarettes consecutively), the room had a breath of its own, a sweet, poignant tobacco aroma that was somewhat pleasing to your senses at first, until it attached itself to your clothes and, eventually, your underlying skin.

"Judy, can you fix that damned TV? That damn running is fucking driving me crazy! How can you just sit there on your ass? Never mind," Mr. Harris said as he flipped the last cigarette out and crumbled up the package.

"Bucky, would you adjust the vertical hold on the tube for your dear old dad?"

"No problem, Pops," Bucky said as he rolled over and pulled his Sears tough skins from the crack of his behind while simultaneously tuning the television.

"Ooh, Bucky's got a wedge!" Timmy snickered.

"So what? You still pee the bed and you are almost nine!" Bucky replied.

His twin, Tommy, attempted to cover his mouth as he laughed in agreement.

"I do not!" Timmy said and leaped up, punching at his older brother's head and crying.

"Mama! Tell Timmy to stop before I hurt him!" Bucky yelled.

But before Mrs. Harris could even utter the word, a wild left hook thrown from nine o'clock connected with Bucky's jaw, producing a popping sound similar to that of a bottle of Dom Perignon at a New Year's Eve party. A combination of spit and blood flew across the room, on the TV screen, the wall, and onto Mrs. Judy's all-time favorite painting, black Jesus walking on water.

In the midst of everything going on, the fighting, the screaming, the smoking, and of course, the television going full blast (an episode of *Sanford and Son* where Aunt Ester comes to stay with Fred because Lamont was out of town), the occupants of the room were suddenly jilted back into a semblance of sanity by a bellowing ring from the telephone.

At first, an eerie silence covered the room (except for the voice of Red Foxx screaming, "Elizabeth, I'm coming to join you, honey!") and everyone looked at one another in amazement as if each were hearing a phone for the first time. Even Mr. Harris appeared to have frozen midpuff. The cherry on the end of his slender long brown cigarette was glowing bright red with tiny swirls of smoke, appearing to stand motionless in midair.

The only person who was not mesmerized by the ring of the phone was Andre. Andre was preoccupied with the fact that time had seemingly stopped or perhaps paused momentarily. Suddenly, an odd clarity covered the youth, and he realized that time had not stopped; his point of consciousness had changed. (He did not understand it to be that at the time, but this is how he would come to understand it in the future.) It almost seemed to him as if he was watching the events of the room from a distance, and participating in them at the same time. He was somehow dual. It was like watching a VHS tape of *Sanford and Son* in super slow motion, except it was not the wise-cracking Fred calling Lamont a big dummy; it was the Harris family circus without the big top.

The room's dull brown surroundings had gradually blurred into a gray-blue haze devoid of both sound and spectacle. There was only a funny falling sensation in his body and an odd buzz in his head reminiscent to that given off by high-powered electric wires entering a transformer. That was all. There was no Harris family, no Zenith, and no smoke-filled room. In fact, young Andre was unsure if he was still in the Harris home at all. Suddenly, he remembered an episode of the *Twilight Zone* where a devious misunderstood boy with god-like powers banished his smart-mouthed sister to the cornfields. Had Latice somehow accomplished the same feat? If not, then where was he and what was going on?

The first thing Andre noticed was his throat had grown extremely dry, while his skin felt clammy and prickly. Then there was the smell of perfume, not overbearing, just a faint trace of Charlie, and then he was overcome with the feeling of being watched. The same feeling you get when you were doing something you knew you had no business doing. Only after all these things registered did his mind's eye put together a fleeting picture of its own. Perhaps picture was not the best way to describe it. It was the combination of sight, smell, sound, touch, and even tastes blossoming into a cornucopia of love and compassion. It was his Grandmother Lucy. He never knew why he was so nervous around his grandma. She had only wanted to make him to be an articulate, well-spoken young man.

"Speak up clearly and stop squeaking," she would tell him.

Somehow, he knew that he would never get a chance to not be nervous around her again. Already, he had begun to miss her.

The phone rang for a second time, reviving everyone from a catatonic-like state. Latice nearly fell from the old fifties-style bar-stool when Andre spun himself around 180 degrees on his butt and stopped, facing the telephone with his hands clasped, fingers intertwined on his lap like a little Buddha.

"It's about Grandmother! She's gone. Her soul has passed on," he said with his tiny, distraught voice.

His eyes wrestled to hold back tears when Mrs. Judy threw the boy a dagger of a look.

"Don't you play like that! You shut your mouth this instant! Only the Lord can say when that time has come."

She murmured under her breath, shaking her head almost singing as she answered the phone, "Jesus forgive him, for he knows not what he says."

Her voice quickly changed when she picked up the phone.

"Hello, Harris residence."

The expression on Judy's face was the look of someone who had just taken a bite of a sour Granny Smiths apple and found only half a worm.

"Judy, you okay?" Charles Lee (pronounced "Cha-lee" to family and friends) asked.

She stared vacantly through her husband and hung the phone's headset sideways on the hook, causing it to slide off onto the oak table and subsequently to the brown carpet below. Judy's Maybelline mascara left dark trails down her flushed cheeks. The forty-six-year-old wobbled like a toddler struggling to make it back to the couch. She pulled her hair back with one hand and wiped tears away with the other.

"I knew Ms. Lucy was sick but had no idea it was that serious."

Lucy Mac Broom was ill indeed, but in an old person sort of way. Nothing of itself should have been seriously life-threatening if properly treated. However, the combination of sugar diabetes mixed with high blood pressure proved to be more than a formidable foe when Ms. Lucy's common cold turned into a case of walking pneumonia morphing into full-fledged pneumonia, landing her in the Montgomery General Hospital.

Dr. Nitin Shaw had called Virginia Brown at noon to inform her of her mother's deteriorating condition. The Pakistani-born physician asked Ms. Brown to hold, then he made a half-hearted attempt to cover the receiver.

"Put this one on ice and wash it down until… This one's got as much chance as an iceberg on the Arabian Desert." He displayed the bedside manner more suitable for a field surgeon than that of Montgomery General's finest. The internist cleared his throat and raised the phone to his mouth, oblivious to his lack of tact.

"If your mother's temperature continues to spike, we will be forced to give her an ice bath and a continual bombardment of fresh fluids intravenously until her temperature drops back down."

Virginia tried to hold her tongue, but the doctor's cold, callous demeanor sickened her to her stomach and inflamed her troubled soul.

"The next time, if you don't intend for everyone to hear your brilliant prognosis, cover the phone better, you inconsiderate bastard!"

The young doctor stood stunned and motionless. Before he could put together a verbal response, his ear was greeted by a loud clack followed by a dial tone.

Virginia trotted across the living room to the hall closet and almost tripped in haste. She grabbed a silver key chain housing a wide array of keys and a florescent pink crab with the word *cancer* embroidered down its back and dropped them into a gray leather purse. As she reached to grab her bag, she thought of her mother's voice.

"No matter what you wear, always make sure that your shoes and handbag are nice."

In her discombobulated state, she was only aware of two things. One was she had to get to the hospital as quick as humanly possible. And two, make arrangements for the kids who'd be home soon.

Life in Kimberly was very simple. To begin with, there was only one road, Route 60. It was flanked on both sides with houses and trailers as it twisted deep into the Appalachian Mountains. A railroad track ran parallel west of the road, both terminating at the Appalachian Coal Company stockyard. A regimen of red and black Mack dump trucks patrolled Route 60 from dawn to dusk. (That road and those trucks smashed the life right out of lot of darn good dogs, and a few cats, too, for that matter.) Andre lost four that he remembered. The noise of the coal trucks was only drowned out by the bustle of the trains, which chugged in and out four times a day, and occasionally at night.

There were only 347 people in the entire town, half of whom were related to one another in some way, shape, or form. Everyone was either an Aunt What's Her Name or Uncle What's His Face. He never knew it was merely a way to give permission to some neighbors and his mom's closer friends to punish him as they thought fit if they showed out publicly. There was only his mom, Latice, and himself in Grandmother's old house. This did not include his mom's first marriage; he also had two half brothers and four half sisters that lived in the state of Ohio with his stepdad. He never really understood the concept of half because they all seemed whole to him. As far as other relatives were concerned, they must have been in other states or something because he had only met a few and they had lived in New York City.

CHAPTER

4

One day in late June, a bunch of his friends were playing Wiffle ball in the lane. The field boundaries were always the same no matter what games they played. The start of old Ms. Mary Terry's fence was where home plate lined up. In football, it was the beginning of the end zone, and her gate marked out-of-bounds line. The meeting of Aunt Mable's and Mr. Major's fences marked the home run line at about 130 feet from home plate. That same barrier marked the beginning of the end zone for many two-hand touch football games as well. Basically, those three houses formed the boundaries for nearly every game they played.

On this particular day, Tina Terry (no relation to old Ms. Mary Terry); Ceddy Major, the second son of Junior Major (whose house the majority of activities took place in front of); Freddy Brooms (the neighborhood tough guy who would one day be placed on the FBI's most wanted list for attempting to blow up a retired Kanawha County sheriff's house with C-4); Jenae Terry (Tina's little sister who would blossom into a Kanawha County beauty queen for three consecutive years. Her accolades also included state runner-up for Ms. West Virginia, an appearance on *Star Search*, and a failed acting career landing her flat on her back in a number of pornographic sexcapades like *The Buttman Adventures*, where she donned the screen name Kimberly Canyons.); Shawndra Collins; little June-Bug McGee, L-Ray Barton; and Andre made up two four-man teams.

Anyone who has played Wiffle ball knows the laws of physics and motion do not apply to this sport. The actions of a plastic ball filled with holes are at the mercy of every conceivable element, especially the wind. This was a lesson in physics young Andre would have to learn the hard way.

He was pitching to Freddy, who was no doubt the best athlete in the bunch, when he connected with his "Rolley Fingers three-quarter side arm" curveball. It appeared to be a pop-up to the one position. It seemed to go a mile straight up in the air, as if filled with helium. What started as an easy field pop-fly quickly turned into a catch that would be worthy of the highlight reel on ESPN's *SportsCenter*.

He spun in the lane, stopping with his Chucks facing east. Neck back at forty-five degrees spying the rotating spear, he pivoted to the right and then sprinted full speed toward home plate out of the lane and into a slick patch of grass leading up to Ms. Mary Terry's three-foot cinder block wall. Andre suddenly realized the ball's backspin was carrying it over Ms. "Terrible" Terry's fence and into her safari of a yard, patrolled by a giant sticky briar monster. He tried to stop, but he was too close. Andre braced his midsection for the impact when an explosion of red-hot pain erupted in both kneecaps, sending aftershocks of agony down to his bony ankles and back up to his tiny pecker. Suddenly the world was inverted, and the air in his lungs was being forced out by what seemed to be a concrete sledgehammer. Millions of outstretched green tentacles congratulated his upturned body with razor-sharp hugs, pats on the back, kisses to his cheeks, and forehead for his 110 percent effort.

Andre lay screaming internally. Internally because his pride would not allow him to look like a baby in front of his friends, especially the girl of his dreams. Internally because of a fear of alarming the horrid old witch who was believed to hate salesmen, pets, and the noisy, unruly, disrespectful ingrates that came from the bumping of uglies.

He found himself thinking about the story he'd heard about Ms. Terry putting a hex on a Hoover vacuum cleaner salesman, causing him to fall down her steps and break his left arm, left leg, left ankle, and a couple of ribs on that same side.

He lay partially on his side with his left arm twisted back behind his right hip. His face rested on a wet, moldy brown paper bag that read, KROGER, LET'S GO KROGERING! Andre could hear a stampede of feet, laughter, and giggling. However, he also heard a concerned voice.

"It's not funny, you guys. He could be hurt or dead or something!"

The bag had reminded him of the cat stories he had heard his sister, Latice, tell many times.

According to Latice, neighborhood cats had chosen Ms. Terry's yard as their hunting grounds, consequently ending the harmony of her bird sanctuary, which was frequented by the likes of cardinals, blue jays, and her favorite of all the graceful masters of the mid-air ballet, the hummingbird. Those days were long gone. Only the remains graced her sanctuary now. Occasionally, she would find tiny skeletons picked clean. Other times, she'd find what looked like slimy fur balls. However, instead of fur balls, it would be a glob of bloody regurgitated feathers. Lately, it seemed that the hunting parties only left the heads (which resembled marbles of all colors and sizes) on her porch as a token of their gratitude for the use of her yard.

Latice said that the neighbor's cats started disappearing one by one, only to turn up weeks later on the side of the road in plastic bags skinned with their claws and teeth removed. Bags were supposedly found from Powelton five miles north of her home to Deep Water twelve miles southeast and as far as Boomer seventeen miles away on the north shore of the Kanawha River. It was believed that the cats had been poisoned. Allegedly, they had been fed Little Frisky's cat food laced with d-Con. People whispered, and some even suspected their hermit-like neighbor of their pets' disappearance. But the fact remained that Ms. Mary suffered from rheumatoid arthritis and could no longer drive. Hell, she could barely tend to her own primary needs. But who needed mobility to scare the bejesus out of the neighborhood kids.

"Hey, squeaks, you just gonna lie around all day, or are you going to get your sorry butt up, grab the ball, and finish the game?"

Andre's kneecaps throbbed with excruciating pain, and he could already see huge raspberries forming on both knees. He guessed that he wouldn't be able to wear long pants for the next two weeks.

"Whatever, L-Ray, if you were me, you'd be running home crying to Mrs. Barton right now!"

This was probably true, and everyone knew it too. Leonard had a reputation for being a crybaby and a bit of a wuss.

"You all right, Dre? You took a pretty hard spill there. Do you need mouth-to-mouth or what? TT would be glad to give it to you if you do," Ceddy said with a huge smirk on his face.

"Uh-uh! If anybody's going to give it to him, it's going to be you, stupid!"

Even on Tina's sun-browned skin, the young girl's nervous blushing was obvious.

"I'm all right," Andre said as he peeled the slimy bag away from his sweaty face and willed himself to a sitting position. He attempted to chuckle off the pain and tough it out. "Did any of you see where the stupid ball went?" Man, I looked like Charlie Hustle on that play. I bet if the wall hadn't been in my way, I would have snagged that one."

"Ah, Dre!" Ceddy's voice cracked with anxious tension and fear, causing him to stammer, "Ma-ma-Mrs. Te-Te Terr—"

But before he could even finish his sentence, a creepy screeching of a screen door triggered an explosion of feet in flight away from Ms. Mary Terry's wall.

Fear gripped the youth. He wanted to turn around and look, but he dared not. His neck hairs quickly stood up, and his little teeth trembled in conjunction with his panic-stricken body. Andre mustered all the courage he could, but he still could not cache in the remaining endorphins to stand and face the terror behind him. The worst thing of all was he didn't know if he could run even if he had to.

Andre's mind barked off orders to his wobbly legs and cemented feet, commands that his muscles wouldn't oblige. Maybe they couldn't! His neck started to grow an uncontrollable crook. He had to look back. The only part of his body which still felt fully operable was the only part that he did not feel in total control of. He had an irrepressible desire to crane his neck 180 degrees, creating excruciating pain just north of his shoulder blades. Sort of like the unpleasant sensation experienced when you try to look two ways at once and tweak your neck. The back of his head, neck, and back were now burning from the stare, which willed him to turn around. Andre began to recite the Lord's Prayer as his aching body began to pirouette as if on a string.

Tears momentarily blurred his vision. Maybe he would not have to look upon the horrid face of the old witch after all. Unfortunately, he would not be so lucky because as new tears flushed away the old, a shimmering rainbow of colors yielded to a pair of ashy brown feet. They looked rough and patchy like an old leather belt suffering from years of wear. The feet were housed by two run-down and dilapidated pink bedroom slippers, the kind that allowed the toes to stick out in the front. The big toes sported an overly calcified thick brownish-yellow growth, which resembled eagle talons. The tiny feet were connected to two softball-size ankles, which grew into two skinny meatless calves. The boy wondered how such tiny feet and legs could support such a big woman. Ms. Terry's calves retreated under a huge dirty pink housecoat with embroidered flowers of all colors growing out of the tattered terry cloth material. The body under the coat was a mystery, but what was profoundly obvious was a round barrel-shaped belly supporting two breasts, each as large as his head if not bigger.

There was no neck, just a flab of meat connected to another flab joined by an egg of a chin with three or four gray hairs growing out of it. Her lips looked like two gigantic inverted snails, which leaped from a plate of escargot right onto her face. The nose was broad and bold, held high in the air like the noblest of regency. Her eyes were deep and dark! The two black pearls seemed to look into and extract his young soul. Her salt-and-pepper hair stood on end, one side platted and dancing to the sky. The other side sat in contrast, matted and tight to her scalp. Old Lady Terry examined the boy, and her desiccated lips curled up on one side like a question mark, and she then faded into her dark doorway like a shadow followed by an audible click from her screen door.

Suddenly young Andre's legs sprang into action, launching him over the concrete wall, speeding him across the lane over the railroad tracks, down the hill, and right into the middle of Route 60 where he was nearly smashed by a passing Appalachian coal truck. He lay there motionless momentarily on the side of the road, in the same place his German shepherd, a police dog named Shawn, had lain, gasping for air bleeding from her mouth, nose, and rectum nearly two years before. Once again, he began to sob. This time, it was not for himself; it was because of the vivid memory triggered by the event.

Young Andre had just returned from Baltimore with his mother and childhood best friend. He had often traveled back and forth from Maryland to West Virginia, but this was the first time he was allowed to bring his best friend, Shawn. The two had shared many meals together on numerous occasions and a couple right out of Shawn's dog food bowl. Even after being scolded by his mother, the boy did not understand why he was allowed to share his food with his dog but not vice versa. He had begged his mother many times to permit him to bring his dog with him to Grandmother Lucy's house, but she never would. She would always say there was not enough room for the two of them back there. When, on the contrary, it was the country with an abundance of space. After all, his grandmother had a huge backyard, probably three times the space she had here in the city. Maybe she had known something that her son had not.

Ms. Lucy was amazed at the relationship her grandson and his pet had shared. She had always said that they shared a bond, which bound them hand and paw. And one day, that bond would be the death of the other. He had never quite understood what she meant, but he assumed it was just another one of those old folks' sayings, which she had a million of.

A week had passed since arriving in Kimberly, and Dre had never enjoyed himself this much while staying with his grandmother. His dog had never seemed as happy and full of life as now. Perhaps, it was the wide-open space available for her to run until her soul was at ease, or maybe it was the wild deer she loved to chase each morning. They roamed the hills just west of the creek bordering the property line. Maybe it was that this summer was being spent with her best

OUT THERE

friend, instead of all alone, fenced in, in the backyard of her forty-by-forty Hillsdale prison. There, she would see someone at least twice a day, at feeding times, but usually that was it. The only companionship she had was barking at the neighborhood dogs, which she had never seen. Yep, Shawn was happy and enjoying life. This was where a full-grown German shepherd should be, with her master and best friend, free to run until her heart was content.

The morning had passed, and Latice and Andre had planned to go to the fair in Smithers with Ceddy Major and his older sisters. Latice had already gone across the road and was playing in the lane with the other kids, but Andre had not finished his daily chores. The chores included emptying and lining all the trash cans in the house with newspaper, cleaning the bathroom, and tidying up any messes, which Shawn may have made during the night. On this particular day, Andre made haste in finishing his work because he could not wait to get to the carnival. The cotton candy, the midway, his friends, and the unlimited pleasure he got out of smashing Latice senseless in the bumper cars. This was going to be a great day. But first, he had to finish the rest of his daily responsibilities. Then he could join the others in the lane.

There was just one more thing that he needed to do. However, Andre dallied in a fog. He wrestled with a stubborn case of amnesia for what seemed like hours. Unfortunately, the harder he tried, the further it slipped from his grasp. What was it? Finally, he caved to one of his mother's old sayings, "If you can't remember it, it must not be all that important."

But it was important. Probably the most important thing he would ever forget to do in his short life.

With everything done, he was good to go. He only needed to grab his jacket, go to his stash spot, and grab his cash. As he reached to pull his shoebox from under his dust-cluttered bed, he felt a familiar tug on his shoe. It was Shawn. Somehow, she had gotten back into the house and was playfully attempting to get the youth's attention. Again and again, Andre twisted his leg in attempt to free his foot from her grip. She nibbled around the boy's ankle, down to his Chucks (leaving a glistening trail of saliva) systematically locking her teeth into the laces and tugging her head from side to side until she pulled the bows loose.

"Stop, Shawn. I gotta go," he said as he pushed her away with a powerful shove from his right leg, causing the shepherd to yelp and scuttle away. Andre proceeded to remove a worn black silk sock from an old Buster-Brown shoebox. He marveled, as he always had a hundred times before, how much the boy on the box and his dog looked alike. Heck, they even smiled alike. It always left him with an eerie feeling.

The youngster counted his money, made sure all seventeen big ones were there, and darted toward the front porch with a chorus of "Later, alligator" and "After-a-while, crocodiles." He slammed the screen door, jumped off the porch, and floated toward the grassy lawn. With effortless fluency, he unlatched, stepped through, and re-latched the link fence. Andre's ears recognized the thunderous roar of what could only be a red and black Appalachian coal destroyer without even looking. It was about seven houses up, probably in front of Mrs. McGee's house.

Old Tommy Joe Jenkins was making double time to finish his twelve-and-a-half-hour day to and from the Hole, as he liked to refer to that darn blasted mine.

"The night Chicago died, da na-na-na-na-na, night Chicago died," by Paper Lace crooned on the radio. One more drop and he was free to shit, shower, and shave. What had started out as an extra P and D had turned into the pulling of a whole half of a shift on top of his original eight hours. His back hurt like a son of a bitch. And despite six mugs of Jake, two Cokes, and several mega blasts, he could still barely hold his collapsing eyelids to his wrinkled brow. A mega blast was a mixture of Stand-Back and No Doze. The No Doze was supposed to help to stay awake and Stand-Back to kill the headache the NDs gave him.

Sleep would have to wait because today was the morning he had received a visit from a certain police officer's wife for the past five months running ever since he found her thirteen-year-old chocolate Lab stretched out across Route 60 painting the asphalt red. Incidentally, it was his Mac truck that laid claim to the tragedy.

Originally, TJ had planned to apologize and explain what had happened, how he came out of Old Mill's turn to find the lab licking at some roadkill right smack in the middle of the road.

Shit, it was not his fault. The stupid mutt had it coming! What was he supposed to do? Stomp his breaks and jackknife his rig on that curve? TJ did not think so. However, after seeing the paralyzing reaction from Mrs. Crabtree to her lifeless Dexter, a mild faint, followed by hyperventilation, a trembling attack, and another small faint, made old Tommy Joe change his tune completely. When all was said and done, the chivalrous Jenkins had done everything except give the faltering Labrador mouth-to-mouth in attempt to save him. This had landed the lonely and devastated wife of the most compulsive working state patrolman in West Virginia into his arms for the first time.

As he struggled to keep his eyes open, the smell of her perfume filled his membranes and the thought of her firm cone-shaped breasts made his mouth water. Soon, very soon, his weekly rendezvous with the sexy Larissa Crabtree would end his tedious traveling and start him on a cruise of carnal pleasure, crashing him into a silent comatose-like state for the next six hours. Then he would get up and eat his standard meal, two soft scrambled eggs, white toast, a mug of black joe, and start the whole process all over again. TJ noticed a blur dashing across the street a few houses up but gave it little thought; it was too far away for him to concern himself. He kept his pedal smashed and slid back into the fantasy that awaited him at 4237 Blue Ridge Way.

There was nothing coming the other way, so Andre decided to make a dash for it. As he crossed the yellow line in the middle of the road, he knew that he was out of the truck's reach and guessed it would now be only three houses away in front of Mr. Botley's. It was then that he heard the familiar jingly sound that Shawn's choker collar made. His best friend had jumped the fence and was now running into the road after her master. Before he could turn and yell to Shawn to go back, he heard the painfully loud sound of the truck's horn, the screech of concrete burning tires, and a breathtaking thud that produced a choking feeling in the young boy's throat.

The shepherd took the blunt of the massive vehicle squarely behind her front quarters. Her ribs and front legs were shattered instantly. The force of the impact sent the animal flying fifteen feet, half through the air and the other half head over tail tumbling across the road and into the gully, snapping the dog's neck and breaking her spine. Somehow, she still managed to drag herself backward with just the use of her hindquarters. Slowly, she dragged her trodden frame across the road and into the driveway of Grandmother Lucy's.

Blood gushed from her muzzle as Andre slid his fingers under her limp, motionless neck.

"Shawn, I'm sorry. Please don't die. You're my best bud!"

Tommy Joe opened the door and jumped out of the truck.

"That darn dog just leaped right out in front of me! If you'd people learn to keep yer damn dogs tied up like you suppose to, we wouldn't have this ole bloodstained road!"

Tears poured from the youth's troubled eyes onto the canine's bloody coat, creating warm, gooey knots that made it difficult to pass his fingers through her thick luscious coat. Shawn's glassy brown eyes (now drowning in a blue hazy film) searched the heavens with hopeless frustration, seeking the comfort of her friend's eyes, only to fall short before sharing his gaze. All she wanted was to be fed.

Traffic crawled past the sprawled-out kid lying aside the road, but his reality was lost in the past. Ceddy slithered across the road between the stopped vehicles to check on his friend. Andre pulled his twisted leg from beneath him, plucking a sharp tiny piece of gravel from his knee. As he looked up, he heard a faint collection of voices from his friends down the lane creeping to ensure that their friend was okay, but keeping a watchful eye out for the old witch.

"Dang, Dre, that's the fastest I've ever seen you move! You could have even beaten Conlif in a race if you moved like that," Ceddy said. "So, do you still want to play or what?"

"Naw, man," he replied. "I think I'm done for the day. That was way too close. I'm going in. I'll catch you guys later."

In the small bathroom, the white toilet and pink bathtub, with the bottom covered in slip-resistant green frogs and lily pads, stood in close proximity to the off-white washbasin housing a shriveled-up blue-green bar of Zest soap covered with tiny black hairs resting in a slimy white soap dish. Andre stood in front of the bathtub brushing his teeth. Looking in the mirror, the boy wondered where his wide nose and tiny lips had come from. They did not resemble his mother's at all. Deep down, he questioned why he had never met his actual father. Was he such a repulsive, unlovable abomination that not even nature's powerful paternal instinct could hold him accountable? The thought saddened him and nearly brought tears to his eyes. Often, he marveled if his mother would one day find his repellent qualities contagious and flee from his presence as well.

The night was humid, and even with his window open, there was no breeze circulating. Thunder crashed against the heavens like two armor-clad titans locked in battle. From the window at the north corner of their bedroom, he could see the steady dim flash of lighting over the hills behind his house. Each burst seemed to grow hungrier, eating up more sky as it gradually drew nearer. The distant trees produced embellished faces on the sky with each strike of lightning. The weatherman had predicted thunderstorms for the next three days, but something seemed different about this storm. It seemed dejected and angry, eager to drench the dry, sultry earth and everything else in its path.

Sweat beads exploded from Latice's brow, and her heart banged in her chest. She had always been scared of thunder.

Poppa had said, "Never fear God's work because within his work, lies your ultimate salvation."

Latice lay with a wool green lint-covered blanket up to her neck even though she was suffocating in the room's stagnation. Her eyes popped from her sockets like the aluminum cover on a cooking pan of Jiffy-Pop popcorn. She compulsively popped her knuckles one by one until each finger had been popped three times, once for each according knuckle. Then she popped her thumbs. She also had a nervous habit of sucking her top lip with her bottom lip. This had caused a light brown circle to appear around her mouth. Between the sucking and the popping, she pleaded with Andre to come sleep with her. Andre continually ignored her request as he gazed out the window.

"Please come and lay with me until it stops," she begged. "I'll give you my Silly Putty and my Slinky if you do."

Suddenly, the room was illuminated by a bright flash followed by a bull whip's crack about seven seconds later. This sent the terror-stricken girl's head under the cover like a turtle into its shell.

"Please, Dre," she sobbed. "I can't breathe. Help me or I am going to die."

Finally, the young boy's gaze left the night sky and trained on his sister's fear-filled cries.

"Okay, but don't be hugging up to me and get rid of that stupid blanket," he said sternly. "It's too hot in here for that. I'm going to lie at the foot of the bed, so I can watch the lightning. And move your corn chips over there, okay?" he said while pointing to an area of the room far away from him.

"Okay," she replied. "But don't be tickling my feet, or you'll end up on the floor crying."

"Hey, who's doing who the favor here? You'd better be nice, or you will be sleeping alone."

As he lay staring into the midnight sky, his mind began to wander to a place far beyond the clouds, beyond our atmosphere, and into the deep regions of space where stars met the everlasting night and temperatures zoomed far below zero. Somehow, he knew but not in the way that you would like to believe that those x-ray glasses ads in "Believe it or Not" comics actually worked. This belief originated in a region that lies somewhere between your heart and solar plexus—a region of knowing he would someday journey to the far reaches of the universe.

Suddenly, his fleeting thoughts were interrupted by his sister.

"Dre, did you say your prayers? You know what grandmother used to say about little kids who didn't say their prayers before they went to sleep."

"No."

"Let's say them together like we used to, all right?"

In deep slumber, the youngster dreamed of the activities of the day. Playing in the Terrys' backyard playhouse and trying to find the perfect time to get his first kiss. The yummy crunchy fish sticks and tater tots he had for lunch at Freddie Broom's house. He could even recall the perfect sweetness of the lime green Kool-Aid his sister, Barbra, had made. The dream seemed as vivid as any he had ever dreamed, right up until the Ms. Mary Terry incident, right down to the paralysis.

Once again, the boy was frozen, unable to move a limb, staring into the eyes of the bruja but that is where the dream changed. No longer was the sun shining and the birds singing. The sky grew angry and dark; the wind danced, and thunder boomed. He grew dizzy as he vertically swirled. Suddenly, he realized that he was no longer standing in Ms. Terry's yard looking at her. He was horizontal. In fact, he was lying on Latice's bed with her feet right in his face.

At the foot of the bed, she stood, still wearing her tattered pink robe and a half head of plats reaching for the sky. As she leaned over, she reached out as if to grab the boy by his corncob of a neck. Her image flickered in and out like an old black-and-white movie reel. Unable to move, he attempted to wake up from his nightmare. Squeezing his eyelids as hard as he could, he forced his lazy eyes open. To his surprise, she was still there reaching out for him and flickering, still uttering her wordless sermon. Once again, he closed his eyes, but she was still there. There was no escaping. Eyes opened or closed, she had come to collect her prize, the intolerable little ingrate from across the road. His breathing grew difficult, and his heartbeat raced out of control. He felt as if at any second, his little heart would burst right out of his chest.

Her parched lips moved rhythmically in slow motion, dropping ash-like dandruff each time they rubbed together. Her eyes shined with unbridled passion, upon an expression, which pleaded for the boy's compassion. Sitting up, he slowly reached forward, attempting to touch the phasing holographic image. No longer was the figure menacing. Suddenly, the old hag Mary Terry was not a hag at all, simply a lonely old lady. Once he accepted this fact, his fear began to subside and was replaced with a warm, fuzzy sensation. He recognized it as love. As his fear dissipated, the flickering slowly stopped, and her words gradually gained volume.

Ms. Terry told a story of feeling alone and abandoned after her husband's untimely death at the age of thirty. She spoke of how he had taken her away from her family in her homeland of Haiti for mere fifty American dollars when she was but seventeen summers old.

Raleigh was a dirt-poor sharecropper; a father of twelve who had no problem giving his eldest daughter away. After all, no man in the village would have the evil cow after her first marriage at fourteen soured upon her failure to consummate. In an attempt to be patient with his new bride, Abdula tried to teach his wife the ways of oral copulation which led to the near removal of his genitals by her unwilling mouth. Yes, old Raleigh St. Jean had removed the family's albatrosses and gained nearly a half a year's wage in one swift move.

The message she conveyed to the boy was one of sorrow and pain. The youngster both heard her story and experienced it. Tears flooded his eyes as if he had lived it himself. Finally, after seven years of trying to conceive, her prayers had been answered, and something good had happened in her life. However, even that was short-lived. Unfortunately, Ms. Terry miscarried and lost her baby in the third week of her third trimester. This was exactly one week and a day before the untimely death of Mr. Terry. Ironically, this was the same day that her child was due. The causes of his death read undetermined on his death certificate; however, it was her belief that he died of a broken heart.

The first morning's light was greeted by Mr. Botley's rooster Spurs's nonstop crowing. The sky had changed from dark purple to light gray, but the clouds still sagged like soggy diapers waiting to leak. Andre rolled over, and pushed Latice's leg off his chest and eased onto the linoleum-covered floor. His dream sat dormant on his mind. He never even thought of Ms. Terry as he went about his morning ritual of cereal and the *New Zoo Review*.

In the refrigerator, he was greeted with no milk to go with the bowl of cornflakes he had just poured and put sugar on, and there was no butter for his toast as well. The lad could handle dry toast but could not stomach the thought of milkless cornflakes. As he pondered mixing Carnation evaporated milk and water, he heard his mother getting ready for work. Maybe he would have her blend it for him because he could never get the mixture just right; either it was too thick or too watery. Forget the cereal, he thought. He would just eat his toast with grape jelly and be done with it.

Virginia Brown's perfume lit up the room like a hundred-watt light bulb even before she entered. Andre looked up at his mom from the floor with adoration. To him, she was so beautiful and elegant, more suited for big-city lights than the dull daily rigmarole afforded by country life. Somehow, even as a child, he knew that the little town of Kimberly would not keep his mother content for very long.

"Boy, get your behind up and give your mom some sugar, so I can get out of here," she said as she walked into the room.

Andre pushed himself up from the circular pine-green throw rug and rushed to hug his mother. As she leaned over to embrace her son, she nibbled at his earlobe, causing him to laugh uncontrollably as his heart filled with delight. When she released him, he followed her out on the porch, intending to ask her to bring home a Gino's cheese pizza for dinner. It was then that they both noticed the red swirling globe of an ambulance parked in the lane in front of the Major house.

"Oh, I hope that nothing has happened to Liz," Virginia uttered, holding her breath as she stepped off the porch. "Call me at work and let me know what happened, okay?"

"All right, Ma. I will."

Sitting in the lawn chair on the porch, he wondered what was happening in the Major house and whom it had happened to. His mind contrived mastermind plots, which would allow him to visit his friend Ceddy with no one suspecting him of cat-killing curiosity. Plan after plan, his mind bounced off his body, but none motivated his legs to actually cross the road and follow up on his ideas. Somewhere deep inside, he knew that it was wrong to exploit the pain of others for self-satisfaction.

Finally, twenty minutes later, he decided to go back inside and watch TV. The youngster popped up, reaching for the screen door latch, when he caught movement out of the corner of his right eye. To his surprise, it was not coming from the Major house as he had suspected. Two light-haired paramedics wearing dark blue kakis and short-sleeved white collared shirts were attempting to negotiate the steep steps of Ms. Terry's porch with a vinyl-looking black body bag strapped to a gurney. Trailing the two was a short man with a receding hairline and black horned rimmed glasses. He carried a black doctor's bag and a briefcase of the same color.

Andre watched the paramedics carefully navigate the gurney down the steps and through the muddy puddle-filled lane right up to the back of the ambulance. The taller of the two had a mime painted smile smeared across his face as he pushed a lever on the side of the gurney, which caused the legs to buckle. And in unison, the two men lifted Ms. Terry's dead body into the ambulance. After closing the back door of the ambulance, the tall man removed his plastic gloves, ran his fingers through his thinning hair, and proceeded to walk over and hand the little man in the dark suit a clipboard, which he appeared to sign and promptly gave back. The paramedic's painted-on smile never wavered. They shook hands, exchanged pleasantries, and parted ways. Andre watched as the small man crossed the road and walked up to a black Crown Victoria with a Montgomery City Coroner insignia on the door parked in the Mount Zion Church parking lot.

It was then that his dream crept into his memory. Her pleading words began to haunt him. Was it a dream, or did the friendless woman from across the road really visit him? He wondered if she was alive, already dead, or in the act of dying when she came to him. Why had she come to him? The boy stood there contemplating these and many other questions when Latice screamed at him to either come inside or close the door. It would have been her preference for him to remain outside. Whether it was a dream or not he was not sure, but he was sure that he would never tell anyone about the experience because he knew that he would be labeled either as crazy or a weirdo for the remainder of his life.

CHAPTER
5

In the middle of the Mohave Desert, coyotes howl in anticipation of thirst-quenching rain. Wind gusts blow a convoy of tumbleweeds north across Old Sierra Highway, past a sign designated for antelopes. Although rain was in the forecast and the night sky appeared to agree with both the weatherman and the coyotes, the clouds themselves were a different story. They refused to release its trapped moisture. The Paiutes had a name for this. They called it scorned clouds. It was almost 1:00 a.m., and the spring night was still a blazing ninety-two degrees Fahrenheit outside.

In a little three-bedroom stucco house in East Rosemond, California, a second-generation Frenchman falls in love with his beautiful first-generation Columbian wife and begins raising a lovely family. One day, he hoped that his adoration and undying love for Margarita would be matched or even exceeded by her love. Up until now, their marriage had been a sham, a way to keep her from having to leave school and return to Bogota a pregnant disgrace to both herself and family.

Thirteen years later, not much had changed. Richard Jokinen still loved his bride unconditionally and worshiped the ground she walked on. She, on the other hand, had felt cheated and imprisoned. A free spirit forced into a straitjacket of nuptials and life of marital confinement. As much as she had despised Richard for impregnating her and trapping her in this domestic detention center, she had grown to love him even more for the four beautiful seeds they had produced together.

In the bedroom across from their parents slept the twins, Trevor and Tanya. The two were alike in birthday and last name alone. Trevor was slim with hair like night and eyes as dark as pencil lead. He was handsome, dark complexioned with traditional Columbian features. Tanya took after her father. She was chunky and uncomfortably built. At birth, her hair was blonde, but by her seventh birthday, it had begun to darken a little. Her skin was as fair as milk, with eyes of pale blue. If anything, she could have been her dad's twin because she resembled him far more than she did her brother.

The third bedroom was actually a converted den for the eldest daughter when the twins arrived. Eileen was a stunning beauty even at the age of thirteen. One day, she would be the full package—striking good looks with the heart of an angel. Richard had fallen in love with her the first time she smiled at him, as would many men after him. She shared her room with her youngest sibling, Michelle. Like her sister, Michelle shared their mom's attractive features. Both had copper-toned complexions with flowing auburn locks. One day, they would both inherit Margarita's ample bosom as well. The most obvious feature shared by the two girls was a beauty mark just left of their top lip, half an inch below their nose. The resemblance between the two was simply amazing.

Looks was just the beginning. Michelle idolized her older sister and modeled herself in her fashion. Her clothing, hairstyles, shoes, mannerisms, and even her likes and dislikes were mimicked by the little copycat. It went to the extent that Michelle often appeared to be a little clone of her senior of seven years. Eileen prayed on many nights that her little sister would one day find her own identity. This night was not one of them. This night found the girl asleep before her head had made a dent in her pillow.

Tiny sand particles bombarded the girl's bedroom window in the midst of a rainless storm. Protected by an army of stuffed animals, they slept, the little one tossing and turning while the big one lay motionless in a deep slumber. The only thing moving was her tiny eyeballs under her tightly shut lids. They darted side to side and up and down. Her sleeping eyes seemed to follow a movie, which only they were privy to witness.

In a large gathering room over a mile long, thousands of people congregated in hundreds of lines. At the head of each line, a gleaming neon sign screamed its companies' name, logo, and tagline. Beneath each sign and behind a four-foot counter scampered three or four identically dressed drones working as quickly as possible to assist the waiting masses.

She was standing in one of the many lines about twelve people back from one of the many counters. Thousands of voices at once bombarded her, creating a maddening buzz in her head similar to an enormous beehive. Enochlophobia grasped the child around her throat like a strong hand and preceded to tighten its grip. Never before had Eileen felt such fear just from being in a large crowd. On the verge of retreating into her inner sanctity, she suddenly felt a tug on her sweaty left hand. Pulling her a couple of steps forward and mumbling some indistinguishable garble stood a ginormous man.

Her tiny hand was engulfed in a gigantic brown vise grip attached to an arm that displayed great girth even under his fifty-eight-large electric-purple polyester leisure suit. She was being led by a six-foot-four, three-hundred-pound behemoth. Even with all his size and strength, this brown bear of a man handled her petite hand with the gentle care he would have surely shown his own cub.

Looking up at the giant, she was greeted with drips of warm sweat to her forehead and cheek. As she shook off his sweat, she noticed that pockets of perspiration had formed under his man breasts, creating smiley half circles staring down at her. His labored breathing and heavy sweating was more suitable for a YMCA, not standing in a line moving no more than twenty feet every five minutes.

"Who are you, and where are we going?" the teen shouted. Fighting to free herself, Eileen twisted her wrist and fell backward, wrenching her arm free and sending her body crashing to the floor.

Across the floor, she scampered on hands and knees dodging the multitudes of legs capped off with polished wing tips, comfortable penny loafers, and sporty leather tennis shoes. Slowly, the girl gathered her bearings and peeked around a huge column, looking for her would-be pursuer, only to catch a glimpse of what looked like a tea party in the midst of all the rushing people.

She couldn't be sure, but it looked like a round three-legged table complete with white sheet, teapot, cups, and saucers. There were four chairs. One held what appeared to be a duck-billed platypus whose bill looked to be hanging on by a thin hinge of corrugated muscle. In his dangling beak, a lit Camel flickered like a Christmas light. Next to the mammal sat a tattered old zebra. It looked so old that its black stripes appeared to be graying as she looked at it. The zebra's black nose was caked around the holes with a white powdery substance. It held one hoof up to its muzzle, attempting to catch the leaking milky substance and force it back into its hungry nostrils and mouth. Across from the zebra sat Raggedy Ann complete with a frilly white dress, ginger locks, freckles, and a black eye. Her happy, engaging smile was replaced with a gaping black hole that would have served any jack-o'-lantern proud. Her left hand was wrapped around the neck of a Jack Daniel's bottle, which was nearly empty. Her fragile luminescent right hand rested on a black Smith and Wesson .38 revolver sitting on the table. The final chair sat flipped over on its back with a dented can of creamed corn pouring out on to the tile floor. For a second, she sat mesmerized by the tea party scene. For some reason, the picture resonated somewhere deep within her. Abruptly, a dark cloud covered her, and the gentle giant leaned over the girl and verbalized more meaningless gibberish.

"Leave me alone! Get away from me! Get away from me!" she screamed.

The girl pushed and fought fiercely as bystanders walked by, oblivious to any wrongdoing.

"Eileen, wake up," Michelle said as she shook her big sister in attempt to wake her up from her dream. "Wake up! Eileen, you're having a nightmare!"

CHAPTER

6

It had been three years since the untimely passing of his grand-mother Lucy, and each year became progressively tougher financially for the Brown family. Virginia's hours had steadily declined over the last year. Failed attempts to find a good job left her upset and withdrawn from her family. To Virginia, her home had become a place of trial and tribulation. It had become an unhappy ending to a beautiful beginning. A loving upbringing filled with unlimited promise. Unfortunately, the vast potential was never realized. Her husband's insane jealousy had ruined her life and left her in a swooning downward spiral into drugs and the depths of depression.

Oliver's quick temper had gained him two assaults, one on a photographer and the other on her effeminate manager, Antonio. Suddenly *Maxine* had become a high-risk model, which no self-respecting manager or agent could permit. Mr. Brown's impulsive, violent behavior led to the premature ending of a flourishing runway modeling career, a failed marriage, five kids, and a job with little security and even less benefits. Now, her only concern was unloading her mother's house, packing her things up, and moving somewhere she could stretch out her wings.

Virginia had found an apartment in the big town of Montgomery. In reality, it wasn't very big at all. The majority of the town's population was students at the local college, West Virginia Tech. The actual population without the school would still be considered a small town at best.

Moving into the family's new place would have to wait because its lease wouldn't be ready for two to three weeks, and they were being forced out of their Kimberly home for failure to pay taxes. So, with little choice, Virginia agreed to stay with her longtime friend, Deloris Jackson. The Jacksons lived in Eagle. Eagle was so small that its name appeared on local maps without a dot beside it. It was located right smack in the middle of Kimberly and Montgomery, about three and a half miles from each town. Eagle housed some of the most incredible home locations comparable to anywhere in the world. Two-story colonial classics side by side with post-slavery shanty shacks riding thirty-foot cliffs, sandwiched between Route 60, the B and O Railroad tracks, and the Kanawha River.

Deloris bartended at the Top Hat, a hole-in-the-wall bar, which reserved the right to serve the town's pimps, pushers, prostitutes, derelicts, and other riffraff the town had to offer. She and Virginia had been friends since grade school. She was a single mother of three. The eldest was her daughter Cherry; in actuality, her real name was Sherry, but her youngest brother, Wabbie, was mentally challenged. He had a speech impediment and was unable to pronounce it correctly, so the mispronunciation stuck and everyone called her Cherry.

The middle child was Anthony. He was the same age as Andre but two grades behind after failing the second grade twice. At the age of ten, Anthony was already built like a grown man. He had a tiny head that sat on the shoulders of an Adonis, ten-inch biceps attached to arms that hung to his knees. His hands ended with fingers as thick as baby carrots. Anthony was born to be a bully! His mental sluggishness was more than made up for by his superior physicality, which he willed over his peers and dominated them with a pit bull-like tenacity.

Finally, there was Wabbie. He was an eight-year-old who suffered with severe Down syndrome and had an extreme dislike for clothing. From sunup to sunset, it was a never-ending battle for Deloris to keep Wabbie dressed. If she dressed him six times, he'd remove his clothes six times. His nakedness wasn't the problem; the problem was that anytime he had to urinate he would take off streaking through the house yelling, "Wabbie got to pee-pee! Wabbie got to pee-pee! Pee, Wabbie, pee!"

And he would, any and everywhere indiscriminately with reckless abandon. If you were in his path, there was a very good chance you may end up peed on.

Less than a week after they had moved in with the Jacksons, the first infant tremor had shaken the foundation of the Brown-Jackson family relationship. They swiftly grew. Virginia's other son, Eugene, arrived without notice from Ohio. A steamy relationship ensued between him and Cherry almost immediately. A straight right hand caught Wabbie on the chin as he made his way to the top of the stairs with his stream flowing high and wild like the first pee of the morning. Latice opened the bathroom door just in time to get a warm face full of piss. In a brutal retaliation, the girl lurched forward with a windmill of punches, causing the dullard to fall down a flight of stairs, landing him in the hospital and Latice on punishment for two months.

The fervor was then passed on to Anthony who thought he would even the score of his sister's deflowering and brother being hospitalized by kicking the snot out of little, defenseless Andre. He was sadly mistaken. Andre pulled a Mike Tyson even before Tyson's now-infamous assault on the ear of Evander Holifield. In the space of three days, there was more drama in Deloris's home than her acting group, the Daughters of Shakespeare, had produced in the past three years.

The dining room, much to both families' disgust, became the courtroom in which all quandaries were resolved and a holding cell until all punishments were handed out. All proceedings were centered around an old Brunswick pool table which often doubled as kitchen table, tripled as an ironing board, and had occasionally been confused with a bed a time or two. For the incoming youngsters, most of the first week was spent in this room. It was agreed by all involved parties that this was not how the two families were going to spend the next few weeks. Both families vowed to make an effort to get along for the remainder of the Brown family's stay. Tempers were still heated and feelings were still hurt; unfortunately, the size of the living quarters had not increased one square inch. To combat the volatile situation, family members with issues tried not to interact at all while other family members kept contact to a minimum.

Andre would never forget the last week spent with the Jackson family, but not because of anything that happened between the families in the old deteriorating house. It was a local event, which would leave a lifelong impression on the way that the boy would look at life from this point forward.

It was Friday, December 21, the last day of school before the Christmas break, and all the children in Mrs. Prop's class were required to bring one item in for show-and-tell. Most of the kids brought their favorite toys. Steven Boyd brought his Stretch Armstrong with dog bites through the stomach and chest, which leaked a red jellylike substance whenever he was pulled by his arms or legs. Tina Terry bought her Malibu Barbie with a hot pink corvette she had just received the day before at her tenth birthday party. Then, there was Charlie Waters.

Charlie was a quiet, reserved kid with a quirky personality. He didn't have very many friends, but everyone liked him. When called on by Mrs. Props to show his item, he looked nervous and hesitant to even stand and go to the front of the class. He shuffled from side to side like a little penguin as he walked to the blackboard carrying a green Samsonite overnight bag. Inside the case, he had a mason jar filled with a blue-green-colored liquid, which appeared to hold a badly mangled fetus of an unborn baby. He said that he got it from his brother, Marcus, who was studying to be a doctor at Georgetown University.

"I would like to introduce you all to baby Martin," he said.

His voice was low and scratchy as each word struggled to escape his mouth. He said baby Martin could communicate with you if you knew how to listen. Charlie placed the jar to his ear as if listening to something or someone. He said that baby Martin wanted to see the class. Then he began to rock the jar back and forth in a slow swaying motion, which caused the fetus's eyes to appear to open and close. Everyone sat speechless and unblinking, including Mrs. Props.

Charlie informed the class that we all carry our last name in life, into the womb with us until we are reborn and renamed. That's how he knew his name. The boy seemed to look at everyone at once as he held the class captive. He said that baby Martin was sad because he wanted to go to school and make friends because in his last life his parents needed his help on their farm, so he never had a chance to go to school. At this point, Mrs. Props stood and attempted to interrupt because she didn't like where this was heading. But as she did, young Charlie gave her an icy stare and told her that baby Martin remembered his breath being sucked out of him and the cold air which swooshed his mother's embryonic fluids back and forth. He recalled the hard steel that wrenched his newly forming ear right off his little head, the loud whoosh of air and the bitter cold, which was accompanied by blackness.

"Okay, everyone, let's have a big round of applause for Charlie," the overweight teacher said while quickly standing up.

All the kids sat silent and motionless, and a few even had tears running down their faces, except for Andre. He was the only one to actually clap. A ridiculous smile rolled up on Charlie's face as he walked back to his seat. He was pleased with himself and his accomplishment of leaving the entire class speechless. Somewhere in the back of his little mind, he thought that he may have a future in entertainment, but that would not be the case. In fact, little Charlie would have no future at all.

Later that evening around six o'clock, Marsha Waters called for her son to come home and eat. He was across the street playing with his friend, Billy Owens, when he heard her yelling for him. He told his friend bye and that he would try to come back after dinner. The youngster hurried out and ran up the driveway in haste. He ducked out into Route 60 as soon as the Mac truck passed him. Unfortunately, the boy did not see the 1969 Volkswagen Bug, which was right on its tail. It smashed into him, launching Charlie six feet into the air, ramming him headfirst into the unyielding pavement, from which he sustained a subdural hematoma, causing him to lapse into a coma. The roads of Eagle were even more treacherous and deadly than those of Kimberly.

Young Charlie's will to live was great; however, the injuries sustained were too much for him to overcome. The boy lay in a coma for four days until he ultimately succumbed to the great sleep on Christmas Day. Ironically, the boy's birthday was the same day, passing away on what would have been his tenth birthday.

The news spread quickly. The community had lost another member to the unsafe roads, which wandered through the unforgiving mountains of West Virginia. Many rumors surrounded the alleged driver of the Volkswagen. Some said that it was a kid from Deep Water with no license who had taken his father's car on a joyride. Others countered, saying it was his mother's first husband, George, whom she had left for Charlie's dad a few years earlier. However, in all actuality, the culprit was a man named Relondo Ferguson, a serial drunk driver. Ferg, as they called him, had twenty-two prior DUI charges in the past eight years. It was a tragedy that never should have happened as Ferg was driving on a permanently suspended license at the time of the horrific accident.

Charlie's wake was held at the Anderson-Harrison funeral home in Montgomery. Nearly his whole class attended the service. As Andre inched down the aisle to pay respect to his fallen pal, he remembered how Charlie snickered at the kids he had made cry just a few days before. He was dressed in a gray suit with a little black bow tie. Andre was sure that this was not his friend. This boy's head was the size of a large pumpkin with a thin mustache, an undeniable growth of peach fuzz on his chin; he also appeared to be two shades darker and much fatter than he remembered. It didn't even look like a kid. Andre thought to himself that this had to be a small man with a balloon head posing as Charlie.

That night, he spoke to his mom about death, about Charlie, and about baby Martin. He fired off questions like an assault rifle.

"Why do people get abortions?"

"Why does God allow kids to die?"

"Why did Charlie look so different?"

"What happens when you die?"

Suddenly, his questions were interrupted with sobs, sniffles, and finally a torrent of emotion flowing down his flushed cheeks.

That's when it happened! A fear of death took hold of the boy like a vise grip. Before his mother could even answer one question, Andre decided he would never sleep again because he had once heard that sleep is the cousin of death.

CHAPTER
7

In less than a year, the family's stay in Montgomery had run its course and Virginia's plans on moving back to the Golden State were once again on the table. Regrettably, the money necessary to make the trip to the West Coast was not on the table as well. Perhaps the trip to California was still a bit beyond her means, but she had saved enough money to move her family west even if it was just one state in that direction.

The move to the Bluegrass State came with a staggering loss to the family, one that had been a looming possibility since the passing of his grandmother. Due to Latice's and Virginia's inability to communicate without Lucy's mediation and wisdom, the daughter and mother grew further and further apart, leading to a predictable separation of ways. When the family moved west, Latice chose to move north to live with their great-aunt Mae, the sister of Grandmother Lucy, in Portchester, New York.

Although only a few hours away by car, Louisville, Kentucky, seemed to be light-years from Kimberly, West Virginia, to young Andre. In fact, this event, by far, eclipsed anything he had experienced in his short lifetime. He was but a child when he moved from Baltimore, still fresh from soiling his bedsheets and his little drawers. He had not made any long-term friends he would have to displace from his memory banks. After all, he was only four, for God's sake. Now, he was a year removed from his teens, and the past eight years had molded a sensitive, caring, polite young man who would have to reinvent himself. Andre refused to be preyed upon, eaten, and regurgitated back out a shell of his adolescent self by the city's public school system. His fertile fields of green had been replaced with gray concrete labyrinths. The caring family-oriented community they were raised on had been traded for a heartless city full of selfish individuals.

When the family arrived in Louisville, Andre had already begun to cut back the number of hours he was sleeping dramatically.

Days turned to weeks, weeks revolved into months, and months graduated to years. That's not to say that Andre did not sleep for years, but his actual sleep time on an average night varied from one to three hours. On a good night, he may have only lapsed into darkness for a mere thirty minutes. He maintained wakefulness, as he called it, through a variety of methods. The first order at hand was to stay one step ahead of his mother who was always telling him to turn out the light and go to bed.

The first method was saving his homework for bedtime. He would tell his mom that he had a little homework that he needed to finish. Once completed, he would study the upcoming chapters before they were even assigned to fight sleep. Unintentionally, he was becoming a very adept student.

Another tactic was reading his hundreds of Marvel and DC comics over and over again until he knew all the story lines by heart.

After reading the same books became redundant, he decided to create his own comics, both inking the story line and full illustrations. Over the past months, his drawing skills went from meager stick figures to well-defined sketches.

Sometimes, when he was confident that his mother was asleep, he would sneak to the living room and watch TV with the volume as low as he possibly could and sometimes with no sound at all. This turned out to be very risky because his mom had caught him several times already during her nightly trip to the bathroom.

Unbeknownst at the time to Andre, his nighttime activities were changing him. His personality was changing from an easygoing, happy-go-lucky kid to an irritable, easily annoyed pain in the ass. Nothing was ever done to his satisfaction. Gradually, he was becoming an anal-retentive pessimist without an eye for detail. His family noticed the changes, but no one knew where these personality disorders were stemming from. They assumed that the move combined with the leaving behind of his friends was somehow responsible for the dramatic character changes.

CHAPTER
8

Condensation stained the eggshell-colored walls near the ceilings of the old cottage. A constant war raged on in the Jokinen household. In attempt to battle the blazing Mohave heat, Richard had set his thermostat to a standing sixty degrees and had forbad anyone to touch it. Years of constant cool air colliding with warm air at the ceiling had created a kaleidoscope of random animal cookie-like shapes marching in all directions. However, upon closer inspection, the shapes were actually created by air bubbles under the paint and some spots where the paint had actually begun to peel.

One room that did not suffer the peeling paint eyesore was the girls' room. Why would it? All they had to fight off the intense summer's heat was an oscillating twelve-inch circular GE fan. Michelle sat with her nose pressed up against the GE emblem in the center with her hair blowing back like a black curtain in the wind.

Michelle spoke to her sister in a mechanically choppy fan-altered voice.

"It's so F'n hot," she said, avoiding using the actual curse word. "It's so F'n hot. It's so F'n hot. It's so F'n hot. It's so F'n hot. It's so F'n hot."

"Would you please shut up? You are being very annoying right now," her sister said frankly. "Believe me, if anyone knows that it is F'n hot right now, it's me!"

"Come on, Chelly," Eileen said. "We can handle the heat. It is either this or go out into the front room with Daddy and be forced to listen to country music while you slowly become a human popsicle. I know we can do this. It's not that hot in here. It's just mind over matter."

Eileen began telling her sister about a film she watched in her psychology class on the Shaolin monks of the Himalayan Mountains who have mastered many feats of mind over matter. Of all the scenes depicted, she recalled one in which a group of monks travelled from the monastery in the snow to the Indus River. When they arrived, they took off their robes and washed them in the river in below-zero temperatures wearing only their underwear. When they were finished washing their laundry, they put their wet robes back on, and their body temperature began drying them right on their backs.

"It was amazing," Eileen declared. "You could see the steam coming off of their bodies."

"Yeah, but they have nothing but time up there in the middle of nowhere," Michelle snickered.

"No, really, when they interviewed the monks they said they just visualized being in the desert during the hot season. All we have do is visualize being in Alaska or the Artic or somewhere cold," Eileen said with a faint smile.

"Come on, girl," she continued. "We can do it! What could it hurt to try?"

After a little more coaxing, Eileen had convinced Michelle to lie down on her bed. Then she told the younger sister to start breathing in deeply through her nose and exhaling through her mouth.

"Close your eyes and picture yourself in a blizzard in Alaska," Eileen said as she walked over and stretched out on her bed.

"Don't think about anything else, just the cold," she said in a calm, soothing voice.

Michelle attempted to listen to her sister, but inside she was just bored and sweaty. She could not maintain her focus for more than a couple of minutes at a time. Try as she might, her attention kept trailing back to Sal Agular, a boy in her third-period English class who kept passing her notes and asking her for her phone number.

Ooh, fifteen-below windchill factor, she thought. *Ooh, fifteen years old and almost old enough to drive. Oh, I give up,* she thought.

Maybe she could catch a quick nap and perhaps dream about snow because this visualization stuff was not working for her. Michelle sat up on her bed, looked over at her sister, and thought she really does look cool over there.

For some reason, focus came really easy for Eileen even when she was not trying. She had excelled at games of concentration since she was a little girl. Her dad had often praised her keen sense of observation and encouraged her to go into a field which would allow her to showcase her natural abilities.

"You would make a great detective!" he had told her on numerous occasions since she was a child. In fact, as a second grader, the girl was responsible for the capture of a man who robbed the local 7-Eleven convenience store. The man was entering the store as the girl and her mother were leaving. When questioned by the police, her mom barely remembered seeing the man. However, her daughter's detailed description led to the robber's subsequent arrest.

A bright, heatless sun reflected mercilessly off the white snow-covered mountains. Although blinding, its brilliance was no match for the cold's bitter bite. Eileen's twenty uncovered digits were quickly turning purple and growing numb. Why was she out here in the middle of winter in shorts, T-shirt, and no shoes? Something about the place was kind of familiar, but she could not remember why.

Fuzzy crooked lines swarmed the girl's empty memories as tiny icy spikes bombarded her physical senses.

I think I know this place, she thought.

The twisty unpredictable path led down the mountain to a river she could hear but not see. As she followed the path in awe of the countryside's natural beauty, she forgot the intense cold, her frosty feet, and the bone-chilling wind. In fact, she felt downright hot as if she was in a sauna. This winter wonderland began to feel like a mere illusion.

The thought of the warmth triggered her memory, causing her to recall that she was at home lying in her bed and sweating just a few feet away from her sister not long ago.

Smiling on the inside, she thought to herself that it must be the Himalayas. She began to ponder if this was an elaborate fantasy created by her imagination or merely a dream.

Perhaps, I am actually in the Himalayan Mountains, she thought to herself briefly.

But soon after, she answered her own question. Of course, she was not in the icy mountain, for she would surely be freezing to death. Nonetheless, everything around her seemed so real. She could feel the crunch of the snow beneath her feet, wind in her hair, and even detect the slight scent of a smoldering campfire.

Still attempting to get her head around the situation, the girl strayed from the trail only a couple of steps when her feet slid out from under her, and she plummeted down a steep embankment. Her body swooshed down the hill from left to right in an almost lazy S pattern like the waterslide at World of Waves Water Park. Panicked, she flailed her arms in hopes of slowing her descent. Eileen could hear the roaring crash of the river against the rocks getting closer as she slid down the hill. Finally, she was able to grab ahold of the trunk of what looked like the Charlie Brown Christmas tree complete with the one bulb at the top, causing it to lean over; it was capped off with the X shape nailed into the tree's trunk. Yet, it stopped her from plunging into the river below as if it had deep roots furrowed into the earth.

Eileen lay there wet and covered in mud while wondering just what sort of fantasy she was experiencing. Almost magically, an answer came from behind a snow-covered deciduous bush.

A strange voice spoke to the young girl who had yet to make it to her feet.

"It's the part where the damsel in distress gets rescued by the handsome prince."

Startled by the voice, Eileen rushed to her feet.

A white fox limped from behind the bush and approached Eileen at an exceptionally slow pace.

"Don't be fearful," the small animal said confidently. "I am a friend. Worry not of muddy water and cold. It only exists in your mind. Even as you look at yourself, you are as dry and snug as a baby in its mother's arms."

His words reverberated in her head with an echo. Looking at the fox, she realized it was not talking with its mouth. Instead, it was projecting the words into her mind and doing it with a megaphone, it seemed. Looking down at her clothes, she marveled that they were now unsoiled.

"You must learn that—" Before the fox could get out another word, he was interrupted by Eileen who was screaming at the top of her lungs.

"Why do you keep yelling into my head?" she hollered with her hands over her hears. "Don't you know how to talk like a normal person?"

"Normal is subjective!" the fox replied in a hostile tone. "However, I am sorry, didn't realize I was yelling as you so elegantly put it. Is this better?" he questioned as he lowered his voice significantly and lay down and cuddled up into a ball at Eileen's feet.

"Much," she said while bending over cautiously to stroke the fox's luscious white fur coat. "Who are you and where am I?"

"I am your guide, Oliver," the fox, who Eileen thought sounded quite intelligent for a wild animal, casually replied. "And you are in the Etheric Now. The difference between here and there is a thin line called consciousness. You have an incredible ability to focus your attention, and that is why you are here *now!*"

The amount of emphasis Oliver put on the word "now" was so powerful that the teen stumbled and fell off her feet once again.

"I don't understand," Eileen said, picking herself up.

"I know, but you will a lot sooner than most and infinitely faster than all of those who have lost touch with their imagination, for there lies the key to projecting one's consciousness," the fox said as he unrolled, stretched, and gathered himself.

"I am Oliver. Call for me when you have questions or in need of guidance. I will come," he said. "I am always near."

With that, the ashen canine limped back into the snow-covered bush and quickly vanished.

Beads of sweat rolled down the girl's face as the snow suddenly melted away and a bright-green forest with plush fields of grass took its place. Then, the heat in her bedroom blasted away the final constructs of her Etheric Now. The suffocating heat turned her focus into dust and her grassy fields into the bluish-green carpet covering the floor in their bedroom. Piles of snow just moments ago were now piles of dirty laundry splattered across the floor. The television, which sat on top of the nightstand, stood in the exact place where the fox spirit guide had vanished into the snowy bush. Her sleep-stricken fingers welcomed the prickly needles, which accompanied the transference of consciousness and the return to wakefulness.

The word "wakefulness" was such a strange word, she thought, as the word seemed to materialized in her head. However, after a second thought, she felt it was the perfect word.

Eileen lay on her bed wondering what she had just experienced. Oliver said it was transference of consciousness. Was there really an Oliver, or was he just a figment of her imagination? She might have thought it a dream, but deep down, she knew better. He also said it was a thin line between here and there. Eileen rolled over and looked at her sleeping sister and questioned what he meant by that. Her vision was a little blurry as she tried to focus on the red numbers on her tiny digital clock radio. She wished she had looked at the clock before they began the experiment. *No biggie*, she thought. She would make sure to do it next time.

Later that evening, the family sat down at the dining room table for what turned out to be a celebratory dinner for their dad's promotion. Margarita only had two rules at the dinner table. The first was that there was to be no talk of work or negative reflections from the day. And the second rule was to behave with the manners they were taught, which meant refraining from tasteless, off-color humor that they found to be the norm. The table was to be a place of reform and refinement even if the rest of their life didn't suggest it.

Margarita knew that her husband's good news had potential to turn sour really quickly when the kids realized that with their father's raise and promotion came with a change of address and, eventually, a change of schools. To counter a possible negative backlash from her children, she prepared her family's favorite meal. It was a traditional Colombian feast, bandeja paisa, which is a meal with servings so huge that it had to be served on a platter. The spread consisted of grilled mesquite steak, crunchy fried pork rinds, and spicy chorizo sausages on a bed of white rice with savory red beans and topped with a fried egg. A side of sliced avocado with sweet banana chips completed the feast. For dessert, she would serve arroz con coco, a chilled sweet rice pudding made with lemon zest and cinnamon sprinkles. Nervously, she wrapped, unwrapped, and rewrapped her index and middle fingers with her rosary beads and said a silent prayer that this dinner would pass without an incident.

From the outset, the omens proved to go against the chance of an uneventful evening. To start, Papa Richard was late getting in from work, and the kids were hungry and agitated. Tanya and Trevor volleyed insults across the table like a hot potato while innocent Michelle fanned the flames with gasoline to ensure the blaze kept going.

"So, what's the girl's name again who dumped Trevor in front of the whole class?" Michelle asked

"She didn't dump me! We both decided to break up," he said with an embarrassed look on his face.

"Then why were you writing notes begging her to take you back in fourth period?" laughed Tanya.

"Stop it! Stop it right now! Your papa will be home in minutes," Margarita said as her eyes repeatedly glanced from the door to her children. "I will not have nonsense at my table. Do you each understand me?" The rotund matriarch screamed, as she slammed a wooden spoon down on the table.

"Please, I beg of you, let us have a nice evening, nice conversation, and try to be happy for your papa tonight," she said as her voice lowered considerably.

Moments later, the familiar jiggle of Richard Jokinen's keys released the deadbolt lock separating him from his frosty living room.

After dinner, the family took their dessert, settled in the TV room, and watched the six o'clock *CBS Evening News with Dan Rather*. Richard kicked off his shoes, revealing a free-swinging big toe on his left foot. Spontaneously, the Frenchman seized his wife and pulled her into his loving arms. After bathing her face in a swarm of wet kisses, he happily shared the details of his new promotion and the perks that came with it, such as his company car and the new house in Lancaster they would be moving into at the end of the month. He said it had a huge backyard and the thing that made him happiest of all was that all his kids could have a room of their own.

"Well, Trevor would have the basement," he said. "But, hey, it's as big as an apartment down there with its own bathroom."

The mention of individual rooms seemed to seal the deal for the kids. After all, Lancaster was only twenty-six miles from Mohave, and they could still visit their friends on the weekends if they wished.

CHAPTER
9

Sleep deprivation is one of the oldest tortures known to man. However, the boy did not initially grasp the complexity of the issue. As far as dreaming was concerned, he hadn't dreamed since the Mary Terry incident. Or maybe, he simply hadn't remembered dreaming. Somehow, he understood that he wasn't allowing his dream cycle to complete its sequence. Andre thought he had figured it out; three thirty-minute blocks of sleep broke up throughout the night allowed him to feel rested enough the next day and dream free during his brief slumber, and that was just fine with him.

One night in mid-November, Andre was up editing his latest issue in the *Looks Like It's Over* series. These comics dared to cross the great divide, merging the mightiest heroes from both the Marvel and DC universes on a mission to save the earth. This book was the third installment in the line. This story chronicled the invading legions of Muldoor from the planet Zenia97x battling forces led by Superman.

His night was going well. It was already 2:00 a.m., and he had not faltered once. Wakefulness was under his control, but for some reason, he could not focus as he typically could on this particular night. Repeatedly, he drew and erased a scene of Superman flying through the cosmos toward Zenia97x seven or eight times until he had put a hole in the paper. This little mistake ruined the whole page, and now every block would have to be redrawn and inked. At least he knew how his next hour and half would be spent. He was right on with his approximation. Like clockwork, an hour and a half had passed, and again he was stuck on the same scene.

The paper grew fuzzy, and suddenly, his head felt like it had gained ten pounds, as he shortly nodded off. Quickly, he caught himself, shook his head repeatedly, and pinched the inside of his thigh to stay awake. These things were but a temporary solution to an inevitable conclusion. Andre's eyelids pulled themselves down as his eyelashes rooted into the soft tissue under his eyeballs. Seconds later, he suffered a full-frontal neck snap. He had lapsed. There was a split second when his neck started to fall forward that Andre consciously thought he could fight it and maintain wakefulness. He was wrong. Andre's eyes filled with white dots zooming past his head so fast that he thought he would hurl. The more he tried to focus, the more the beast rummaged through the pits of his abdomen, bubbling and churning upward. Finally, it burst up through his esophagus, spewing corrosive acids, burning his heart and lungs. Up his neck counterclockwise, the monster pushed, pulling the boy's chunky innards upward through the back of his throat.

Subconsciously, he prepared for the chunky payoff, but it never came. When he got that upchuck feeling and nothing came out, it triggered a hiccup. Andre had read a book on lucid dreaming and dream control by Dr. Harry Keith, in which the scholar said any trigger that makes you aware that you are dreaming is considered a hiccup, therefore, giving the dreamer the power to take control of their dream and do anything they desired in this stage.

As the youth's vision came into focus, he realized the dots were actually points of light, and he was in a vortex traveling at an extreme velocity. The tiny points of light grew depth, expanded, and vanished from his peripheral in fractions of seconds. Could this be what he thought it was? He squinted with all his might attempting to focus on the background of the dream. Slowly, his center of attention stabilized, and he realized the points of light where the stars that he had drawn of Superman flying through the galaxy.

Andre could not believe what was taking place. He was in his own comic book. He was flying through the cosmos himself. And with that conscious realization, his dream became lucid.

The stars shimmered, reflecting in a luminous assortment of colors; meteorites whizzed aimlessly like Fourth of July bullets in a galactic shooting gallery. A gassy oblong-shaped world wobbled on the outer regions of space. The planet was orbited by twin satellite moons, one-sixteenth of its size, one silver and one black. His speed continued to increase, and the planets and celestial bodies were flying by so fast that they started becoming distorted and indistinct. He had to be approaching what he thought was light speed because everything was turning into one continuous blur. It occurred to him that he was Superman, so he tried to look at himself. He didn't see anything at first glance, no body, just a ball of haziness or a light, wispy cloud. The longer he focused his attention, the hazy cloud began to take a shape very familiar to the youth—his own. Looking at himself in his dream created a real dilemma in his mind. He wondered if he was this wispy ball of consciousness, as well as a third party watching the dream from a distance. Then, it hit Andre: who was it back in his body? He felt the strange feeling of duality once again. As soon as that fleeting thought was released into the universe, he woke up at his desk with his neck as stiff as the pencil still lodged between his finger and thumb.

Andre sat there rubbing his inflexible neck, grasping for his fleeting dream memories. They lay parked on the outskirts of his memory like a word stuck on the tip of his tongue. Patiently he reached into his memory banks, attempting to withdraw any piece of information, which might help to release the wonderful dream that seemed so real. Frustrated with his failure to recollect his thoughts, the boy turned to the clock to see how long he had until his alarm went off for school. It was only 4:27 a.m., so he guessed he still had time to finish another page of his comic.

It was almost instantaneous. As soon as the lead touched the paper and he saw the star-filled background with a partially drawn man of steel, it triggered the memory of his dream. The recollection was so vivid and real that his whole being tingled to his core. Andre could not shake the feeling. He was positive his flight through space was genuine. He had never had a dream in which he was aware that he was dreaming. The brilliance of the stars, the cold void of space, and the unending speckled blackness all seemed so realistic.

In Andre's personal life, Louisville turned out to be not so bad after Andre got adjusted and made some new friends. The first was a kid from around the corner named Stevie Allen. He was only a few months older than Andre, but he looked significantly older. He already had a thin mustache and the patchy beginnings of a beard. Although they were about the same height, Steve's ten-inch Afro made him appear half a foot taller. The kid never stopped smiling, which was weird because even though he was thirteen, Steve appeared to still have all his baby teeth. Andre found this to be funny and dubbed his carefree, happy-go-lucky friend Smilin' Allen.

Steve was very mature for his age. In fact, he considered himself a young adult. He washed and ironed his own clothes, cooked his own meals, and was even capable of driving his dad's truck if necessary. He could even drink beer and smoke weed in the confines of his home. His mother told him and his brothers long ago that she would prefer they learned about these things at home instead of in the streets. Mrs. Allen also made it perfectly clear that she would not tolerate any of her boys getting in trouble of any sort with the police. If they ever were locked up for any reason, they were ass out, as she would say, and had better hope their father was willing to take time from his day to bail them out because she wasn't going to do it. It didn't take long for the Allen house to become a second home for young Andre.

Stevie's best friend was Kenneth Cooper, or KC for short. KC had a reputation for being a tough guy. Andre didn't know why because he didn't look very tough. And in all the time they hung out, he had never seen him beat anyone up. Nevertheless, everywhere they went, KC got the utmost respect from his peers as well as from the older kids.

Thursday night was teen night at World on Wheels Skating Rink on Twenty-Second and Broadway. This was the place to be for any kid who thought they were hot stuff. Everyone showed up, the best skaters, dancers, wannabe rappers, and those who just thought they were good-looking and cool. Stevie swore he was the best skater in the west end, while KC thought that he was the coolest at pretty much everything he attempted to do. It was an unusual day if KC didn't remind everyone that he was "all that" at least once or twice.

Andre, on the other hand, didn't fit in at the skating rink much at all. He felt out of place whenever he was there. He couldn't skate, dance, or rap. Andre struggled when it came to socializing in general.

While his friends were skating, Andre looked for a good place to post up and watch everything going on in the rink. He finally spotted a place right next to the speakers adjacent to the fire exit. From there, he could check out everything happening on the skate floor and throughout the entire building. Although rhythmically challenged, the youngster attempted to catch the beat of the George Clinton song banging through the giant speakers. Mentally, he counted the beats and attempted to nod his head on time. He chuckled under his breath as he pictured the silly look that must be on his face as he strained to look cool and on beat at the same time. While in his own world, he did not notice the two girls skating up beside him.

"What's so funny?" the shorter girl asked as she shifted her weight to one leg and put her right hand on the same side hip.

"What's up? I'm Lea, and this is my friend, Takisha."

For a second, Andre struggled to respond. Normally, he was not afraid of girls, but being caught off guard and out of his element left him momentarily speechless.

"Takisha thinks you're cute and wants to know if you want to skate with her on the next good song," the girl said with a faint smile on her face.

"I'm Dre," Andre replied slowly. "And can't Takisha talk for herself?"

"Yeah, I can," she answered, as she stepped up to the boy, crossed her arms, and rolled her neck around in a quick circle.

"Do you want to or what?"

"Yeah, I do, but I really can't skate that good," Andre said while looking down as if he was talking to the floor.

"That's okay, Kisha can't either," Lea said while fighting off a laugh.

Moments later, the group found themselves laughing as the three began to make small talk about why they had never met until now.

Suddenly, Takisha screamed out, "This is my jam!" as she bobbed her head back and forth to Vaughn Mason's "Rock, Skate, Roll, Bounce" that blasted through the huge Cerwin Vega speakers.

"Are you ready?" she asked Andre.

"Yeah, I guess, as ready as I'm going to get," he said as he turned around and began rolling, slowly, toward the rink's entrance.

He glanced back to make sure Takisha was following him when suddenly he was blindsided by three boys bent over skating in unison, one behind another like a Roller Derby team. The impact sent him flying sideways into the railing and end over end onto the roller rink floor. Andre shook his head, gained his bearings, and pushed himself up from the wooden deck when once again a group of boys smashed into him. This time the skaters didn't flee the scene. The three boys stood over him looking down upon Andre.

"What are you doing talking to my girl, punk?" asked the boy who appeared to be the leader of the small pack.

"You should kick his ass, Popeye!" one of the boys beside him shouted out.

"I said, what are you doing talking to my girlfriend?" he asked again since Andre never responded.

The kid leaning over him was so close that when he spoke, Andre's face was bombarded with thousands of tiny spit particles.

"I don't know what you are talking about. I don't even know your girlfriend," he replied as he fought to maintain his composure.

"Don't lie, you buster, that's her right there!" he said while he pointed to Lea. When Andre stood up, the boy flinched like he was going to punch him with his fist. From out the crowd someone screamed out, "I wish you would hit my roe dog!"

Pushing forward through the crowd, it was his friends. Popeye and his boys began whispering back and forth between one another when they saw KC and Stevie. Skaters were backed up like a logjam behind the would-be fight starters. Suddenly, the lights came on, the music stopped, and a troop of black jacketed whistle-blowing security on skates swarmed the area. KC rushed up to Popeye and said, "We can finish this outside if you want."

"Nah, it's cool," Popeye said. "We ain't got to do that! But this nigga was trying to pick up my girl! Am I supposed to just let that go?"

"I was trying to get with Takisha," Andre countered.

By this time, security was escorting the boys off the skate floor in different directions. Popeye and his friends were kicked out for trying to start a fight, while Andre and his friends went over to the rink's snack bar, ordered some fries, and made plans for what they were going to do next that night.

The night was frigid. KC's words fell from his mouth like sleet in the arctic air.

"Man, what's taking Stevie so long?"

Both he and Andre were standing outside in the World on Wheels parking lot while Smilin' Allen ran across the street to Little Kings Liquor Store. He had hoped to either be able to buy a gallon of Fall-City draft beer or maybe find someone who would buy it for him. Although only thirteen, he had purchased alcohol on several different occasions. Part of it was the boy did look older, maybe seventeen or so. Combine that with the fact that most inner-city liquor stores in the Ville would have taken the money from an infant if they could have made way into their establishment and provided the correct tender.

Finally, Stevie pushed the door open and dashed across the street with a brown grocery bag in his hands. The three met at the corner and began the trek to KC's house, which was about ten blocks away.

"Come on, let's get off of Broadway so we can crack this bitch open," Steve pleaded.

After passing the bag with the gallon inside it around a couple of times, the boys began to forget the icy weather. The more they drunk, the louder and more animated their conversation became. Two blocks into the trip, KC reached into his leather coat's inside pocket and pulled out what looked like the white stick off a Blow-Pop and stuck it in his mouth. With his right hand, he reached into his front pocket of his sharply creased Levi's 501s and came out with a brown Bic lighter. He promptly stopped, bent over, and attempted to shield off the persistent wind. Seconds later, coughing and laughing, he handed the skinny joint in Andre's direction.

"What's this?" he asked.

"That's that Acapulco gold, nigga. You better give it to Stevie if you can't handle it." Rolling on his words, KC nearly tripped over the sidewalk.

Andre had been around marijuana on numerous occasions in Kimberly. He had even seen his mom partake in a smoke from time to time with certain friends. How bad could it be, he thought, as he held the flimsy paper up to his lips and inhaled for his first time. The combination of the cold air and the hot smoke took the boy's breath away and sent him on a coughing attack, gasping for air. At the same time, a car drove by and placed Andre's first puff under a spotlight. In a panic and in the midst of his coughing, he threw the joint to the ground. Stevie immediately started cussing at him as he scrambled to catch their wind-blown joint down the sidewalk.

"Sorry, I thought that was the police!" he said as he fell down to the grown and busted up laughing.

"Let me get that brew, Kenneth. My throat is on fire."

Later on in the basement at KC's house, the trio laughed and joked nonstop about the look on Andre's face when Popeye pushed him down.

"You looked like you were going to cry! What were you going to do?" Stevie asked. Andre reclined back in the Lazy-Boy chair, took a second, and replied in his best James Cagney impersonation, "I was going to whack him, see, take his girl, and let him swim with the fishes!"

The boy laughed and took another swig of the beer, which was rapidly turning into backwash.

"Yeah, you should have taken his girl because your girl, Takisha, was a duck," KC said, and everyone began laughing uncontrollably.

While they waited for Andre's mom, Stevie reminisced on the fight he had last summer at Shawnee Park. From there, he jumped to the school bus incident. Legend had it that one morning last year on the way to school, a bunch of boys from the Beecher-Terrace Housing Projects got on the bus looking to start something with the first person who said something wrong. The gang of five boys rushed to the back of the bus and ordered everyone in the back four seats to get up and give them their seats. Everyone jumped up and moved except for one person. That person was KC.

He firmly told them he wasn't moving and that a couple of them were going to have to share a seat.

"You must be trying to get fucked up early this morning!" the fat boy with cornrows said as he took off his backpack and coat. His friends followed in suit. So, KC stood up and took off his coat. Suddenly, KC jumped up on his seat, and stepped over the backs of the next two rows of seats, stepping on and over the kids who were in them. He then turned around, jumped down, and socked the closest boy to him. In a rage, he threw a left hook, right uppercut, and a front snap kick all at the same time. More importantly, each blow reached its mark—the chubby boy with braids. The force of the impact sent the heavy boy flying backward, crashing into the emergency door exit, which came ajar and sent the big bully flying backward out of the moving bus and onto the hard pavement below.

"Now, what's up? Who else wants to take my seat?" Kenneth screamed, but none of the other boys dared to look at him or even say a word.

Stevie said the bus driver had to pull over on Muhammad Ali Boulevard and wait for an ambulance to make sure that the boy was okay. He said they ended up being over an hour late for school.

Andre jumped in and asked him how he knew all this stuff.

"Because I was there," Stevie said. "I sat there and watched it!"

"Well, why didn't you help him?" Andre asked.

"Shit, man, I didn't have time! By the time I jumped up from my seat and got to the back of the bus, it was over."

"That's why KC doesn't go to school with us at Zachery Taylor. The principal said that it would be safer for the other kids if KC went to school somewhere else."

The whole time during the story, Kenneth never said a word. He just sat there with the look of someone in deep concentration.

"Show me the move, man, show me the move!" Andre screamed. However, KC just sat there and smiled.

CHAPTER
10

The holidays had passed, as did the new year, and finally Andre had become comfortable once again, with his surroundings. Christmas had been very good to him this year. He had only received one gift, except for clothes, but it was a good one. It was a midnight blue twenty-six-inch Schwinn ten-speed racing bike. Unfortunately, he had not yet had the opportunity to ride it, and the calendar was quickly approaching March. News reporters were saying that this had been the most snow the tristate area had seen since the Great Fall of '49. All the boy knew was that he could not wait for the weather to break so that he could test out his new two-wheeled freedom.

In homeroom, Stevie and Andre made plans for a long bike ride the next day because the weatherman said the temperature would soar into the midsixties to low seventies, while making plans to ride from the west end down to the riverfront and loop back through Fourth Street to Broadway and back uptown to Shawnee Park. Crazy Chris Mack and Old Man Hands David Johnson overheard their plan and wanted in. What had started as a little ride between a couple of friends had quadrupled by lunch and turned into a regular Tour de Ville by the end of the school day. In all, there were eighteen cyclists by Steve's count. All day long, kids were approaching Steve and Andre to ask if they could ride along. The boys didn't care who went. They were just excited to finally be able to get outside, enjoy the weather, and ride their new bikes.

After school, Andre locked himself in his room and toiled over his pre-algebra textbook. He was preparing for a midterm, which would account for a third of his grade in the class. For the most part, Andre was a good student, but math was his weakness and his algebra book seemed to weigh a ton. He felt that studying variable expressions and equations was the equivalent of modern-day torture for kids. If given the choice, the boy would just as soon subject himself to a medieval torture like the rack or the infamous bamboo shoots under his fingernails rather than to spend hour upon hour laboring to understand how the ability to simplify variable expressions involving like terms and the distributive property would ever be useful in his life.

Systematically, he would do problem after problem and check his work against the odd answers in the back of the book. Occasionally, a light would come on in his little peanut head, and for a moment, he'd think that he was actually getting a grasp of it. However, as quickly as he would move to the next problem, the light would begin to dim.

Tired and frustrated, he decided to take a break, go downstairs, and see what his mother was cooking for dinner.

To his surprise, everyone was sitting at the dining room table, but no one was eating and he didn't smell anything cooking. His sister Keena sat at the head of the table bantering back and forth with their mom, while his brother Eugene slouched at his seat, appearing to ooze from his chair right onto the floor across from her.

"It's not right that we placed the Shah of Iran in power against their people's wishes. Now that the country is in turmoil with revolt, we blame them for taking our citizens hostage. What did our government think was going to happen when the Ayatollah Khomeini took power? They don't want us there, and they never will. They think of us as infidels!"

"That's not the point, Keena!" Virginia interjected. "Those people were innocent over there, just hardworking people trying to earn a living. They shouldn't be held captive based on their ideology or political beliefs, even worse someone else's radical views and extremist beliefs."

"Well, I think—" Keena attempted to say.

"Excuse my interruption," Andre interrupted. "But I do believe it's dinnertime, and I don't smell nothing cooking and I'm starving!"

"That's 'I don't smell *anything*,' and you can march your little butt into the kitchen and cook anything you like if I'm not doing it fast enough for you, young man," his mother replied sarcastically.

"Actually, I think we are going to go out to good ole Mickey D's tonight," she added. "Your mom's tired and doesn't feel like cooking."

"Yes, how did you know that's just what I wanted?" the older boy said, smacking his lips in anticipation.

"I need a Big Mac! In fact, I think I'm having a Big Mac attack! Why don't you let me drive to McDonald's, Ma?" Eugene asked.

"Because you don't have a license, that's why," she said, holding her palms up to the sky.

"I don't want McDonald's. It's garbage," Keena said. "It has no nutritional value, and it's disgusting! You mark my words, big corporations are going to ruin this country. You wait and see, either them or the corrupt banking institutions that they lie in bed with."

Once again, his sister was on one of her social reform tirades. Andre did not know where she got her feisty, revolutionary mind-set, but he loved watching her passionate exhibitions and listening to her well-formed arguments when she got on her soapbox.

"Well, you can find yourself something to eat in the kitchen if you like, but the boys and I are going to Ronald's to grab some of those tasty corporate burgers which you despise so much," Ms. Brown uttered. "Last chance, going once..."

"Okay, okay, bring me a fillet-a-fish with no tartar sauce and a Coke with easy ice, please," Keena said, looking like she had just made a deal with the devil.

"But I don't want any fries," she continued. "They are greasy sticks of death that clog your arteries and lead to congenital heart failure."

Twenty minutes later, the family returned carrying four medium-size white bags with golden arches in the center and dark greasy patches around the bottom. These bulging sacks of burgers looked primed to explode and disperse the food everywhere with every jarring step.

Soon, the arches were not the only thing that was golden, but silence was as well. Well, except for the crunching, smacking, and the chewing, which created a symphony of sounds drowning out the TV and John Davidson leading the studio audience into its trademark cry of "That's Incredible!"

After eating, Andre excused himself and made his way back to his room to get back to his studies. Feeling refreshed and determined, the youngster jumped back into his schoolwork with unwavering resolution. Before he knew it, he was hearing the singing of the birds outside his window. Not once did he fall asleep or even doze off for that matter, and it was nearly 6:00 a.m. The boy walked over to his window and pulled the curtain back, hoping to catch a glimpse of what he thought was a blue jay. Instead, he was greeted with an incredible pre-sunrise sight. From the horizon to the stars, the sky was a spectacular visual. Bruised purples faded into light gray puffs of dazzling yellowish marigolds exploding into an orange-ish red morning. For a second, he thought God must be a kid with a box of crayons. The notion made him smile, and he knew that for some reason today would be special.

Fifth period had come and gone. The lad's pretest jitters were no match for his deliberate focus. He may not have aced his midterm, but he was pretty sure he had not failed it. When the bell rang, Andre sprang from his seat and made a beeline for the nearest water fountain. When his thirst was sufficiently quenched, the boy exhaled and relaxed, allowing all the stress to flow out of his body and into the crowded hallways of Zachery Taylor Middle School. While bending over the fountain, he noticed numerous shadows moving up quickly behind him. When he turned, it was a mob of kids laughing and joking, headed by no other than Smilin' Allen. Stevie was smiling as usual, mouth wide open with his little teeth dyed green from the remnants of a sour green apple Now and Later.

"Aye, man, you are never going to guess how many people we've got rolling with us?"

"I give up, how many"? Andre asked.

"At last count, it was twenty-eight, not counting KC and his friends from Moore Middle School," Stevie said. "Shoot, I know it's a whole bunch of us. It's gonna be da shit, dog!"

The bell rang at 2:50 p.m., and chaos ensued thereafter as girls and boys exited doors in all directions, running to their lockers and then to their buses through the south exit. Those who walked home burst through the north exit doors in a race to see who could absorb the most of this beautiful spring day the quickest. Those who were being picked up by their parents took their time exiting through west doors into the parking lot, knowing that they would still be among the first to make it home on this incredible day.

A group of eight boys sat in the first four seats on bus 8332, eager to start planning. West Port Road was a twenty-five-minute ride to Louisville's west end, not including the stops once they got there. They had plenty of time to coordinate and put together a route that would allow them to see as many girls as possible while simultaneously taking them past as many stores and gas stations in case anyone got a flat or needed to stop for a drink. Everyone put in their two cents and congratulated one another on how dope of a plan they had come up with.

Andre leaned his back kitty-corner against the cold steel and the leather seat, so he could see all his friends as they spoke. The purr of the bus's engine combined with the caressing flow of warm air on the top of his head from the open window had a relaxing effect on the exhausted boy. Within a matter of minutes, the youth was feeling tranquil and unbound. He could hear the conversations but not clearly. In the distance, he could hear the bus driver telling some kids to sit down. He could see his friends, but it seemed to be cloudy or through a fog. He wanted to participate in the plans and the congratulations. Yet for some reason, he couldn't. His lips would not cooperate. The back of his head lay pressed against an open window, absorbing the shock of each bump sopped up by the tires. In his tranquil state, he felt sorrow for the bus's shocks because his head could identify with them all too well. He wanted to move his head to the leather seat, but he couldn't. It was only due to the fact he heard himself snoring that he realized he had lapsed. He did not know how, but he was watching and hearing everything in some form of sleep vision. However, as quickly as he thought it, he spontaneously awoke.

His mind snapped, and immediately, he felt a slight tug to his frontal lobe. It wasn't painful, but there was a definite discomfort. He tingled with delight as he thought back just minutes earlier. His friends were oblivious to his slumber. Now, their words were meaningless dialogue of no importance or concern. His every thought was an attempt to regain the momentary peace and freedom he had just experienced. Steve and David stood over Andre, blasting him with a cross fire of spittle as they yelled and laughed while gathering their things for their upcoming stop. Two stops later, Andre stood up, grabbed his book bag, and slid to the middle of the aisle, attempting to brace himself on the back of the seat as the Jefferson County School bus drew to a stop on Larkwood and Thirty-Ninth Street. He was sure they were telling him when and where the gang was going to meet, but at the time, he could not focus. No big deal, he thought. He'd just give Stevie a call when he got home.

The boy hauled his weary body up the steps and on to the porch, laboring as if he had just finished a marathon. He opened the door, looked up, and threw his bag down in disgust as he realized he still had two flights to go in order to reach his room. He called out to his brother and sister as he climbed the old staircase, but no one replied. He thought it was weird because they got home before him and were usually in a battle for the TV remote by the time he arrived. Their whereabouts were not his main concern; changing his school clothes and meeting his friends was his sole mission, so he continued his ascend the whiny steps. A squeaky bronze doorknob stood as an early warning sign for the darkness, which lurked on the other side of the door. Without fail, it would scamper up the stairs in haste when the door to the attic was opened. On the other side of the door, a squadron of nine calf-killing stairs stood guard at nearly ninety-degree attention.

The youngster pulled himself up the flight of stairs with the help of the banister one agonizing step at a time. When he reached the top, he threw his backpack down and unconsciously turned on the light at the head of the stairs. Slowly, he made his way to his bed, thinking that he would lie down for fifteen minutes or so, get up, call his boy, and see where they were meeting.

Andre collapsed down and sprawled out on his stomach across his full-size mattress, which sat on top of a worn box spring resting against the floor with neither frame nor slat. The boy's left hand hung lifeless between the head of the bed and the wall. The other arm dangled over the side of the bed, with his hand resting on the floor, fingers pressed against the dusty molding.

Mere moments had passed when the teen had regretted not leaving the light off when he entered his room, but over time, it had become a habit since the attic was naturally dark.

Loathing the thought of getting up to turn it off, the boy rolled over and reached out with his left hand in attempt to turn out the light switch over twenty feet away. To his amazement, his arm measured the distance and stretched deliberately toward the switch.

For some reason, which he did not understand, his fingers made no contact with the receptacle. They just passed through it each time he tried to turn it off.

At the sight of this, the adolescent's view changed without him moving an inch. This view seemed to be an overhead shot looking down from the ceiling. From this viewpoint, he was still lying down on his bed in the prone position, right arm resting on the floor, but his wrist and hand had vanished into the wall at the floorboard.

Stunned and in a state of disbelief, Andre put forth all his effort and focused solely on his right hand. His single-minded attention to his extremity had lent eyes to his fingers and nostrils to his hand, it seemed. At once, he sensed the cold darkness and could detect a faint stench of black water mold running up the side of a shabby two-by-four splintering out across the inner sheet rock.

Not to be outdone, his regular senses were still active as well. His fingers felt an electrical cord running down through the attic floor and what he thought was a gigantic hair ball or a dead mouse wedged between an inner floor joist and the drywall. The thought made by his floating self had a delayed reaction to the self on the bed with his wrist in the wall. It seemed like a three-second delay between the thought and him yanking his missing hand out of the wall.

It occurred to Andre that not only was he physically experiencing this event through some weird plastic body, but also, he was watching it as it happened from a floating third body, as his first body lay oblivious to the whole event. A jarring knock on his door sent him crashing to his bed, jolting him wide awake.

"Stevie Allen is on the phone for you again!" his sister, Keena, yelled through the door. "It's the third time, and I'm tired of answering it!"

Fifteen minutes later, the boy returned to his room dazed and still in a stupor from his conversation with his friend.

He could not believe that he missed the bike ride, two fistfights, the entire group's picture being taken by the *Louisville Gazette*, and KC and Stevie got the phone numbers of two good-looking girls from Ballard High School. On top of that, it was now almost ten o'clock, and he had not done his homework, ate dinner, or taken a bath, much less ride his bike. Where had the time gone? It seemed like mere minutes, an hour at the most. Looking back, he had definitely missed a great day with his friends, but the dream he had experienced still left him emotionally charged and hungry to repeat the episode. Andre could not believe what he was thinking, but he was looking forward to a good night's sleep for the first time in over two years.

CHAPTER
11

John Tucker stood out from other teachers at Zachery Taylor for a multitude of reasons, primarily because he was the only black teacher at the school. Also, he stood six foot three, weighing well over 300 pounds. When he was at playing weight, Mr. Tucker was a 275-pound quarterback assassin for the Los Angeles Rams. As a linebacker, the only lesson he taught was the penalty for holding on to the pigskin for longer than three and a half seconds was decapitation. Lastly, and perhaps most importantly, he was the only teacher who actually gave a damn about the welfare and education of the black students who nearly all were bussed from the inner city.

Mr. Tucker taught biology, but he wasn't just a teacher. He was an educator in the old sense of the word. He was a mentor, a coach, a father figure to some, and a champion for equal rights for all. He made it clear to the kids of color that in order to be successful in the real world, they would have to work twice as hard and be twice as good as their white counterparts. His class was tough for everyone; however, if you were a black student and male on top of that, it was nearly impossible to pass. This was not the case because he wanted to purposely hold them back, but rather because he wanted to challenge and elevate them intellectually. Mr. Tucker wanted to show them if they worked hard enough, they could achieve anything they dreamed.

When the bell rang, Mr. Tucker reminded the class to read chapter 30 from the textbook, sections 1 through 9, and be prepared for a possible quiz on osmosis.

"Oh yeah, pass in today's homework," he said to his class.

He reminded all exiting students that anyone failing to turn in the assignment would face the board of shame tomorrow. He ended the class with his patented, "Have a great day," followed by a "Let's get 'em, guys" with a strong hand clap as if they were breaking huddle.

Once all the students had exited his classroom, John walked over, pushed the door closed, and limped back to his desk. The NFL retiree suffered severe phantom pains three or four times a day all throughout his body, and one was coming on fast. It started in his knees and quickly spread up his hip and into his lower back. The former Ram opened his desk drawer and removed a brown medicine bottle. John pressed down and twisted the cap counterclockwise to open the lid. Then he threw his head back, popped two blue-and-white capsules into his mouth in one swift move, and washed it down with a dark liquid from a Cesar's Palace coffee cup. From 10:00 to 10:50 a.m. was John's planning period. He planned to put his feet up on his desk, close his eyes, and relax for the next forty-five minutes while his meds took effect.

No sooner than the professor had closed his eyes, he heard his classroom door open and click shut, followed by the soft fall of tennis shoes on the old wood floor. Before the middle-aged man could open his eyes, he heard the annoying screech of a desk being pulled toward his position. When he opened his eyes, he was greeted by the face of a child who looked to be filled with apprehension.

Young Andre had never personally confided in his biology teacher but had heard plenty of stories of students whom he had helped with personal as well as academic issues. The problem was the boy didn't know exactly what he wanted to say, where to start, or what questions to ask. He wanted to know if he was going crazy or if this was normal for kids his age. He thought that maybe he should get up and leave before Mr. Tucker asked him why he was there in the first place.

"What can I do for you, young Master Andre?" the teacher asked as he straightened up in his seat.

"I don't know, really," Andre said.

"Well, you must be here for a reason," Tucker countered.

The boy sat on his hands and squirmed as if he was being grilled under a spotlight.

"Time's money, son, and mine's wasting," Mr. Tucker said frankly. "Spit it out. What can I do for you? Aren't you supposed to be in class or on your way to class?"

The boy evaded the question and began.

"I don't know if you can help me," Andre said as he mustered up the courage to go on. "But I figured if anyone could, it would be you since you teach biology. I've been having these weird dreams. Really, they don't seem like dreams because I'm aware of everything going on around me."

"What do you mean you are aware of everything going on around you?" the teacher inquired.

The boy proceeded to tell his instructor about the incident on the bus and the dream he had in his bedroom with his hand and wrist passing through the wall.

Nearly twenty minutes had passed, and the youth was still talking. Words were flowing like an eruption from his mouth when the massive man finally interrupted him.

"Dre, I am very interested in what you are telling me. However, you do have get to class this period. I do have a couple suggestions for you to follow up on, on your own time."

Tucker leaned forward and removed his wallet from his back right pocket.

"This is a very good friend of mine," he said, plucking a card from his bulging leather receptacle.

Andre peered at the card, taking note of its smooth texture and uplifted lettering that even a blind person could read. "Dr. Eric Jacobson, PhD, University of Louisville, Dean of Psychology Department." Underneath his title, in half the size, almost as an afterthought in parenthesis, it read, "Specializing in Parapsychology."

"I think that maybe you had an OBE, Dre."

"A what?" the boy questioned.

"OBE, it stands for out-of-body experience," Mr. Tucker explained. "I think you should give Eric a call and tell him that you're one of my students, and tell him what you have told me."

"You said you had a couple suggestions," Andre rebutted. "What's the other one?"

"Well, your mother may not like this one too well," his teacher said with a faint laugh. "Ask your mother if you can cut a small hole in the wall where you think your hand was. This way you can see if what you thought you felt was actually there, simultaneously proving that it was or was not a dream." Andre literally screamed that it was a brilliant idea. Why hadn't he thought of it? The child was so excited, he nearly fell over as he leaped from his seat.

"Thank you, Mr. Tucker! Thank you!"

"Not a problem. Give Eric a call," Mr. Tucker replied. "I'm sure he will be a lot better suited to help with your situation than I am. Now get to class!"

The boy eagerly pushed the desk back into its position at the head of the row and sprinted from the classroom. Ten seconds later, the door burst opened as Andre stood panting and leaning over with his hands on his knees, pleading for a pass to class from his teacher.

Three days had passed since Andre had spoken with Dr. Jacobson over at the University of Louisville. The dean had sounded almost as excited as Andre had when they had spoken. Astral projection was what he had called it. After speaking for just a few minutes, it became clear to Andre that Dr. Jacobson was extremely passionate about this issue. The well-educated man spoke of the out-of-body experience with affection and an almost a religious fervor. The more they talked, the more excited he became. His enthusiasm was infectious, and it did not take long for it to spread to Andre.

Dr. J, as Andre had taken to calling him by the end of the conversation, had invited the boy and his mother to come out to the university to participate in a few sleep studies. He also gave him a list of authors and specific books that he found helpful in his journey to the other side. Dr. J told Andre to be sure that this was a journey he wanted to take because once he opened the doors, there was no turning back. To that, the boy assured the professor that the door had already been opened, and he had no choice in the matter.

Dr. J had been very helpful in the youngster's quest. The dean set up an Upward Bound university library card for the boy, presuming that his school would not have most of the suggested readings. He also provided him with firsthand knowledge about some of his personal experiences. Most importantly, he warned Andre of what steps to take if he ever felt he could not return to his body. Andre recalled the serious demeanor the professor had taken when he spoke on the matter.

"Pick a body part that has great significance to you. I always think of my nose because I have such a big honker, it's kind of hard not to notice," Dr. Jacobson said with a small chuckle. "Anyway, once you select a body part, always think of it when you want to return to your body. It will work just like a magnet drawing you back to your resting body. If you remember nothing we've talked about, remember that."

Dr. Jacobson moved closer to Andre and placed his hand on the boy's shoulder.

"Your mind may one day forget how to find your body," he continued. "But your astral body will always know where to find its physical counterpart."

Andre's conversations with Dr. Jacobson had propelled him forward on a mission to ingest as much information as his brain could hold. Andre searched the card catalogs for anything he could find on the subject. He read the classic work of Sylvan Muldoon, *The Projection of the Astral Body*, and he leaped right into Oliver Fox's *The Out of the Body Experience*. He then devoured Robert Monroe's *Journeys Out of the Body* and *Far Journeys*, but he still hungered for more. Next, he read *The Teachings of Don Juan* by Carlos Castandea, an anthropologist who supposedly studied with a Yaqui Indian shaman and learned the art of dreaming in the deserts of Northern Mexico.

Andre was learning so much in an extremely short amount of time. He had learned that OBEs could be triggered for numerous reasons, such as mental or physical fatigue, mental or physical trauma, dehydration, sensory deprivation, even psychedelic drugs. To Andre's surprise, people had been using these methods for thousands of years to induce OBEs. He was learning how to relax his body and induce the vibrations that preceded the OBE. Above all, he now had a mentor who was always available and willing to help him with the process. However, he could not shake the thought of the second option that Mr. Tucker had suggested. The thought had been lingering in his head, festering. The idea kept tumbling repeatedly in his subconscious, creating little bubbling manifestations to his conscious.

It will just be a little hole. No one will even notice it, he thought to himself.

He wanted to cut a hole in the wall and see if what he thought he felt was actually there. Despite his desire, Andre never asked his mom because he knew in advance that she would never go for it. He even knew what she would say.

"Hell no! You're not cutting a damn hole in the wall," he could imagine his mother's voice saying. "Are you out of your mind? Who's going to pay for it when we move out, so I can get my deposit back? Are you? I didn't think so!"

However, he still found the idea brilliant nearly a week later. A tug-of-war waged on in the boy's mind. Every time he came up with a point for cutting a hole in the wall, his fear of being caught would blast it with a counterpoint for why he should not attempt it.

Finally, the internal debate concluded. He would make a small incision into the wall, check his hypothesis, and discreetly move his bed a couple of inches to the right to cover up the crime. Now, his only question was what tool he would use for the job. Andre sat up, kicked back his covers, and grabbed a pair of dirty socks off the floor. He put the socks on and scampered over to his closet, bent over, and dug deep into the back of the closet looking for his Dingo cowboy boots he had worn only once since he received them two years ago for Christmas. The fit was snug and a little tight on his baby toes.

After adjusting to the fit, he ran downstairs and rummaged through the hall closet in hopes of finding a flashlight. The last time Andre ventured into the basement, the light bulb was burned out and there was over six inches of water covering the floor from a burst water pipe. This time, he was prepared for the worst.

Andre opened the door to the basement and clicked the light switch on, but to no surprise, the blown bulb still had not been replaced. To make matters worse, the light from the flashlight was so dim, he could barely see two feet in front of his face. At the bottom of the stairs on a steamer trunk sat a portrait of a clown that resembled Steven King's Penny Wise. The clown wore a crumpled green top hat cocked to the left side. His brown eyes glared from the painting and followed the viewers' every move. His nose was a ball as red and shiny as a candy apple. Then there was the mouth. His lips curled under in a frown of cynical disgust. The clown's pursuing eyes freaked the boy out, but the mouth's undeniable contempt for its viewers scared him and led him to remove it from his wall years ago before his eighth birthday. The boy set down the flashlight, winced, and turned the picture around so that its contemptuous stare was now facing the wall.

Andre remembered seeing an old toolbox by the water heater that had been there since they moved in. The problem was going to be trying to find it under all the junk they had piled up in the basement over the past couple of years. On top of that, there were spiderwebs from the floor to the ceiling. Nevertheless, he was on a mission, and he planned to see it through.

Twenty minutes had soon passed, and Andre began to consider abandoning his search. He had moved, rearranged, and stacked boxes to the ceiling, but there was still no sign of the old rusty toolbox. Before he could make up his mind to give up on the search, the flashlight made it up for him when the batteries died. Suddenly, he was in the dark, boxed in between the wall and boxes to the ceiling. At first, the boy calmly patted the head of the flashlight against the palm of his hand, hoping the batteries still had a little life left in them. After that failed, he attempted to move some boxes and make a path so he could get out. That is when he heard something. He was not certain, but it sounded like a chuckle. Then there it was again. This time, it sounded closer. A full-on panic took hold of the youth. He tried to tell himself it was all in his mind, but it was too late to be rational.

Fear now consumed him. In his mind's eye, he could see the clown and its contempt-filled smile waiting on the other side of the boxes. Unnerved, the boy lunged forward with all his might and pushed all the boxes down and scrambled for the stairs. In haste, he tripped over something in the darkness, causing him to barrel into one of the foundation poles face-first, giving him a bloody nose. Dazed and bleeding, Andre attempted to regain his bearings. Sprawled out on the cold concrete, he sat up, clinched his nose with his left hand, and attempted to push himself up with his right. As he did, he felt something sharp cutting into his fingers. It was a needle-nose saw, which had fallen from one of the overturned boxes.

A few minutes later after the bleeding had stopped, the boy was upstairs contemplating the upcoming job like a skilled carpenter. Andre measured and marked the top of his mattress with a small dot. This would mark where his arm had gone into the wall. Next, the boy slid his bed to the middle of his floor and grabbed the stainless steel Stanley tape measure. He then measured the distance from the dot to the floor. It was a total of eight inches. He divided the distance in half and added two inches up to give him clearance over the wood molding. He would bet his life that this was exactly where his wrist entered the wall. Unfortunately, he would be betting his life if his mother found out that he had put a hole in her wall and jeopardized her eight-hundred-dollar deposit.

Andre's initial attempt to penetrate the drywall was stopped by what he believed to be a stud, so he simply moved right a quarter of an inch and began with a sawing motion again until the needle-nose saw cut through the chalklike material. Slowly, he severed the wall. When he finished cutting it, he punched the centerpiece out, took a step back, and admired his work. The hole was about six inches in diameter with jagged chalky edges. Cautiously, the boy wiggled his hand through the drywall, feeling and anticipating with his fingers. Slowly, he edged his way down the side of the two-by-four until they made contact with a cold hard plastic electrical cord running down the back the stud. Carefully, Andre's fingers walked over a staple holding the cord to the lumber. Wary, he continued over the pointy wood until his fingers had reached the floor joist. It was then that

Andre realized there was an excruciating pain in his arm. The jagged edges around the incision were now cutting off the circulation into his bicep. Still, he focused on his fingers that much harder because this was probably as far as his arm could go with a hole this size. Here, the drywall felt slimy to the touch. The boy quickly moved his hand away from the nasty feeling, only to run into a furry surprise. What he initially thought was a dead mouse or a fur ball was merely a piece of Corning pink fiberglass insulation, which had somehow fell down between the drywall and the floor joist. A smile crossed the boy's face as he grasped the true complexity of his situation. He had proved that he was not imagining, dreaming, or just out of his freaking noggin. It was real. It all was real.

CHAPTER
12

It had been nearly two years since the hole-in-the-wall incident had gone by with no repercussions as far as Andre had known. His mom had gotten her deposit back from the house on Thirty-Ninth Street. That seemed like ages ago to the boy. Since then, his brother Eugene had signed up to become a United States Marine, leaving his mother shocked and in utter disbelief as he packed his bags for boot camp in Paris Island, South Carolina.

His sister Keena had carried a baby for seven months in total secrecy, going to school every day while acting as if everything was normal in her senior year of high school. Amazingly, she did not gain much weight or even suffered from morning sickness, frequent urination, or any of the other little delights of pregnancy. Almost as if by magic, the next day after finally telling her mother about her situation, she seemingly gained ten pounds and suffered from every ailment associated with a third-trimester pregnancy. In the scale of things, the two life events were rather miniscule in comparison to the biggest change the family had undergone: moving to the entertainment capital of the world, Los Angeles, California. Virginia Brown had finally made it back to Tinseltown.

For nearly two weeks, Andre sat inside their new apartment on Hillcrest and Santo Tomas, too afraid to go outside. The night before catching the Greyhound bus from Louisville, he watched an episode of the television show *20-20*. The theme of this particular episode was "Murder, Teenage Style." The theme music for the piece was "Another One Bites the Dust" by Queen. It depicted life in a neighborhood called the Jungle in South Central Los Angeles. In this neighborhood, or battle zone as Heraldo Rivera had taken to calling it, there had been thirteen murders in the month of June, and the summer was just getting started. Rivera blamed the outbreak of murders on a new drug called crack that had the city's Crips and Bloods battling over every square inch of the city's turf for the skyrocketing drug revenues.

The actual name of the neighborhood was Baldwin Hills. However, because of the clustering of apartments for thirty square blocks combined with a high density of palm trees, the moniker the Jungle seemed fitting, not to mention the wild animallike violence that occurred on a nearly every day basis. The gang that called the Jungle home was a Blood gang called the Black Pea Stones.

Everywhere you went in the Jungle, you would see the crimson letters BPS haphazardly tagged in the most curious places, such as on palm trees, street signs, apartment building roofs, freeway overpass signs, RTD buses, and anywhere you least expected to see gang-related graffiti. The Pea Stones were believed to be one of the more ruthless gangs in the entire city. One of its most ruthless solders was totally enamored with young Andre's older sister, Keena.

Marcel Edward Washington, or better known as Scooby around the neighborhood, was the first real gangster young Andre had ever met. Scooby stood 6 feet tall and about 165 pounds, not an ounce more. His light-skinned face wore the scars of a rough young life. These were not physical scars from the many fights he had been involved in. Instead, his face showed the damage that stemmed from his stressful lifestyle. Wrinkles, bags, and even a few early gray hairs mingled with the beads of coal on his head, which was usually covered by his red Neiman Marcus baseball cap. He wore black Levi 501s jeans that appeared to be three sizes too big, just the way he liked it. In his left back pocket, he carried a rather cheap-looking black handgun, or a Saturday night special as many called it. In Scooby's right back pocket, he religiously flew his red rag, which was always perfectly creased and ironed, hanging freely under a white Pro-Club T-shirt that was three sizes too big as well. At the ripe age of twenty,

Scooby had already been knighted OG by his peers for his willingness to put in work. At the age of eleven, he did his first drive-by on the Rolling Sixty Crips for murdering his older brother, Solomon.

Scooby considered himself to be a hustler first and a gangster second with lover running a close third in the race. As he explained it to young Andre, a hustler did whatever it took to get his money, period. Scooby's hustle was weed. He proclaimed himself the king of the dub sack. Being new to the street game and to its terminology, Andre had no idea what a dub sack was. For that matter, he had little idea what half the things Scooby said even meant. His ghetto vernacular was way beyond anything Andre had heard in Louisville.

"I get my money like Malcolm, by any means necessary," Scooby would say. "Bud is just easy. One time don't sweat you. And shit, everybody I know smokes mad weed!"

Scooby said when he couldn't get any bud to sell, he would resort to "jacking a mu'fucker" or "catching someone slipping and taking their shit."

"You mean robbing people?" Andre asked, showing his innocence.

"Yeah, a two-eleven nigga, a stickup," Scooby told him. "But you never want to jack people in your own hood 'cause that shit will come back to haunt a nigga every time. But you gotta be extra careful when you are in someone else's hood 'cause the wrong colors will get you killed, Blood," he continued. "That's the first thing your young dumb ass had better learn, Blood!"

The teen thought it was weird that every time Scooby finished a sentence he would say "Blood." Andre found Scooby to be rough around the edges but interesting, nonetheless. A few times when Andre had spoken with him, he noticed Scooby had seemed agitated or annoyed and would change every word starting with the letter *C* to a *B*. It took the boy a couple of times of listening to this lunacy to catch on to what he was doing. For instance, he might say, "I'm 'bout to bick back wit' some bhocolate bip bookies and a bup of boffee and bool-out, Blood." It made Andre scratch his head and wonder what on earth he was talking about.

CHAPTER
13

One day after school, Andre came home to find Scooby and his sister snuggled up on the couch watching *The Village of the Damned*. Immediately, Andre wanted to sit down and join in.

"I love this movie," he said. "Not as much as the first one, *The Children of the Damned*, but it's good too. Man, all we need is some popcorn."

When he squeezed in and tried to get comfortable, he noticed that neither his sister nor Scooby attempted to make room for him. He started getting the feeling that he was not welcome for their movie date. Before he could say anything, he turned around to two contempt-filled stares.

"Aye, yo, young Dre, popcorn would be good, but a chili burger would be way better," Scooby blurted out. "Why don't you run down to Hamburger City and get us some grub, Blood?"

"I don't have any money. What am I going to get it with, my looks?" Andre said sarcastically.

"Naw, Blood, we'll starve if we depend on your looks," he said, laughing. "Don't trip, I got us. But you got to go get it, okay?"

"No, I don't want him going all the way down there by his self!" Keena shrieked.

"He'll be all right," Scooby said nonchalantly. "Ain't nobody gonna mess wit' ya brother, so quit actin' all scary."

"I'll be okay," Andre said. "I'll see if Tony, Gary, and the guys want to roll down there with me. Give me some money, and what do you guys want?"

Before he knew it, he was across the street talking to his new friend T-Tone, who had been one of the first guys in the neighborhood to befriend him. T-Tone was kind of funny looking. He was about six foot three, but most of it was torso. His shoulders rolled over from bad posture sometimes, causing the illusion of a hump in his back. If that was not enough, he also had a chin that was so long it lent itself to every horse joke in the book. Regardless of his looks, Tone was still a cool, charismatic young brother with incredible dancing skills. He put the pop in pop lock.

Even though Tone was two years older than his sister Pixie, they were both going into their senior years at Dorsey High School. As of recently, the trio had been joined at the house by his much older sister, Lisa, who had recently lost her job at Lockheed for smoking crack in the parking lot on her lunch break. The girl's two boys, Ronnie and Tee-Tot, were also staying there. Although space could have easily been a problem for some families, the six took it in stride and thoroughly seemed to enjoy one another's company.

Fifteen minutes had passed, and Andre had somehow convinced G-Man, Ronnie Mac, and T-Tone to go with him to Hamburger City even though they were not getting anything to eat themselves. As the crew began walking down the hill, Tee-Tot screamed for the guys to wait for him. He had decided to go even though he despised anything that closely resembled exercise.

"Aye, Dre, you might want to change those pants before we go 'cause they kind of flamed up," Tee said, trying to catch his breath.

"Really?" Andre asked. "Do you guys think that I should change these pants?"

"They are kind of bright," Tone said. "But hell, we are in the Jungle, right?"

"Come on, y'all," Gary chimed in. "It's not that far, and we know everybody around here anyway. Let's just go and get back. I got some shit I need to do when we get back."

"I'd like to do your sister when we get back, but you don't see me rushing everybody," Ronnie joked.

"Does anyone around here go by their real names?" Andre asked only half jokingly. "What is it with all of the nicknames?"

Gary stepped up and said, "Friends give 'em to you. Some stick and some don't.

Gary explained, for instance, that Tone's was Horse Man, but people kept getting it confused and thought it was a reference to the size of his penis. In reality, his chin was the only thing that was hung, Gary told the group with a huge smile on his face.

"So, we ended up changing it to T-Tone," Gary continued. "But for reals, it protects a brother on the streets from people you don't want knowing your real name like your enemies and Johnny Law."

"No doubt, G," Tone added. "A nigga got to have an alias on these streets. We've got to come up with one for you, too, if you're going to kick it with us. How about Bob Hope? Don't he look like the black Bob Hope?"

From time to time, the youngest member of the click tried to stick Andre with the handle. Luckily, it never seemed to stick.

The five boys joked as they strolled leisurely down Hillcrest Street.

"Madea is so old that when God said, 'Let there be light,' she turned on the switch!" Gary said as he continued to bag on Tony.

"Well, your mom's hair is so nappy, she has to take a painkiller before she combs it!" Tone retaliated, patting himself on the back.

"Dawg, Ms. Brown so tall, she could dunk on Magic," Ronnie Mac said as he doubled over and fell on one of the many identical lawns to one of the many identical apartment buildings that ran for blocks and blocks.

"Boo! That ain't even funny," Andre replied. "What about your mom and her ashy-ass Sasquatch feet?"

Andre looked around at the guys to see if his response was funny. Apparently, it was because everyone was rolling except Tee-Tot, who looked quite upset.

"My mom doesn't have Sasquatch feet, you Bob Hope look-alike," he screamed.

"Easy, Pie Face, I am just joking around," Andre said as he hugged the chubby boy.

"Besides, her feet aren't Sasquatch feet," he continued. "They looked more like a combination of Bigfoot and Abominable Snowman foot busting out of those Vans she was wearing," Andre exclaimed as he took off, backpedaling away from the boy.

Tee-Tot began to chase Andre, and all eyes were fixated on the two as they slap boxed down the block.

Bloodshot eyes and dried salt lines down his cheeks gave away the hurt and pain that Rico "Squirrel" Johnson was going through. His heart felt like a shoestring was tied around it, constricting it to half beats only. Sandpapered eyelids polished his cried-out eyes between alternating rock hammer jolts to his temple. Most of the pain was from nonstop crying from the news he had received eight hours earlier. However, he realized some of the headache was a result of taking three Old English forty ounces back with nothing but a bowl of cornflakes on his stomach.

His best friend since birth, Eddie "Peanut" James, had been murdered by some Slobs in the jungle. Rico had promised himself and his homeys that someone would pay for the death of his boy before his casket dropped.

The black tricked-out 1972 Chevrolet Impala Glass House bent a right turn on the corner of Santo Tomas and Hillcrest, reeking of blunt smoke and spilled malt liquor. Inside the vehicle, locked and loaded, crouched four hardened thugs from the Five Deuce Hoover Crips on a mission behind enemy lines. The young men were looking for some payback—nothing less.

Squirrel rechecked the clip to his Mack 10 for the hundredth time. Systematically, he wrapped his blue rag around his hand and strap, making them one. Slowly, he sank back into his seat behind the wheel of his gray 280zx and followed closely behind his homeboys running decoy in the lowrider.

Silently, he contemplated over his next move. The stupid Bloods fall for it every time. They never see us coming, he thought. They were always mesmerized by the bells and whistles, intrigued by the switches and paint, and that's when Squirrel and his boys would creep up on them point-blank and *bang*! A smile moved across the killer's face as he thought about the simplicity of his plan.

"Yo, Loc, if you ain't gonna hit it, pass that shit! I need to get my smoke on so my aim is on point," he said as he inhaled a big cloud of smoke. "Then I can buck these bitches!"

"You wouldn't bust a grape at a food fight, cuz," joked his homey Man-Man as his eyes scanned the streets looking for victims.

"Watch me!" Squirrel shouted in a most serious tone. "Watch me put the first Slob niggas we see in a body bag, cuz! I put dat on my mama, cuz!"

Squirrel turned up the music, hit the blunt once more, and then set it in the ashtray. Without thinking, his right thumb pressed the button, releasing the clip into his lap. Then he banged the clip back in with the palm of his right hand as he steered the car with his knees.

The sparring match ended in a unanimous decision. Neither Andre nor Tee-Tot was going to be too much help in a fistfight. At least that was the conclusion drawn by both of the older boys, Gary and Tony.

"It's a good thing that you carry a golf club with you everywhere because you can't fight even a little bit," his uncle T-Tone jabbed.

"Man, it's farther than I thought to Santa Barbara Boulevard," Andre complained to an audience of dead ears.

Andre soon realized why no one was responding as he, too, noticed a customized black lowrider cruising past the boys, hitting the switches, lifting the front end of the car off the ground, then dropping it quickly and causing sparks to jump from the pavement.

"Man, that ride is tight," T-Tone blurted out.

"I know. I wonder if it has three-wheel motion?" Gary questioned.

"I like it when he drops it and the sparks fly out from underneath," Tee-Tot said. "It looks really cool."

"Damn, I bet I could pull all kinds of skeezers if I had that ride," Ronnie said as he placed his hand over his mouth, rocking back and forth in disbelief at what he was looking at.

"It's gonna take a ride like that for you to get a skeezer. You better get a toothbrush or a butter knife to scrape some of that cake off of your teeth first," Gary said playfully.

"Forget you. I ain't thinking 'bout you or your ole drippy Jheri curl," Ronnie said as he flipped G-Man the bird.

Meanwhile, Squirrel and his boys were getting ready for their next move.

"Yo, cuz, we got us some victims! You ready to lay these Slob niggas down?" Man-Man said as he pulled his blue bandanna up from his neck to cover his nose and mouth.

"Yeah, nigga, I was born ready! Let's kill these niggas for Peanut," Squirrel replied as he set his Mack 10 in his lap and grabbed his shades off the dash. "RIP, cuz."

"I love this shit, cuz," Squirrel continued. "I'm a predator, and these bitch ass Blood niggas is my prey! You feel me, cuz? Now, let's make da hood proud, Loc," the young assassin said, as he pulled his hoodie over his head to hide his identity.

"Slow down and turn the music down, cuz. You goin' too fast, and you're going to spook your prey," Man-Man instructed.

"Okay, grab the wheel, dog. I want to be the one that blast these punk muafuckers for Peanut."

As soon as the gangster grabbed the steering wheel, Squirrel placed his left hand on the roof of the 280zx and pulled himself up to a seated position in the window. He then leaned over the closed T-tops with the Mac in both hands and took aim at the five teens about to cross Santa Rosalia Boulevard.

Oblivious to the oncoming threat, T-Tone stepped off the curve, still admiring the lowrider as it cruised down the block.

"You know what? You're right, Ron. A brother could get some fine honeys in that ride. All the girls at Dorsey would be throwing that ass at m—"

Before he could finish his sentence, he was interrupted by the screeching tires of a gray 280zx whipping around the corner with a blue-hooded thug pointing a submachine pistol at them, point-blank.

"Yo, cuz, we bustin'!" the man screamed. In what seemed like an eternity, Andre's young life flashed before his eyes. In actuality, it was not his life that flashed before his brown puffy eyes. It was his deaths. Well, the deaths he had experienced in his young life. First, it was the caring matriarch who led her family with grace and dignity. It was his sweet grandmother Lucy. The next flash was his best friend to date. Even though she was a girl, Shawn seemed exuberant and full of life while waiting to play with her friend. Then there was a little man who transformed into a young boy before his eyes, showing him that the one was still the same regardless how he looked in death. No doubt in the boy's mind, it was his friend, Charlie. Then there was a man. He was an older gentleman standing slightly behind them. He looked familiar. Perhaps, he had seen him in old black-and-white photograph. To the boy, he looked like he was from another era, maybe the fifties or sixties. He was not sure, but there was something strangely familiar about him. For a second, Andre thought he was already dead and these four were to be his greeting party at the pearly gates.

"Pop dem niggas, cuz!" Man-Man yelled from inside the car. Ignoring his normal tendency to just spray into the most crowded area, Squirrel waited for a good shot. He wanted to smoke the young light-skinned Slob wearing the bright-red baggies and black Members Only jacket first. Then, he would blast whoever was left standing. Although he had done a couple of other drive-bys like this before, never out of a curve leaning over a polished roof. Balance was tricky enough without trying to aim. The seven pounds of steel bucked and reared in the killer's hand, and he had not even fired it yet. Slowly, he breathed in and held his breath as he locked in on his target.

"Move, move!" T-Tone yelled like a Marine drill sergeant to his troops who were all just a few feet away from the gunman. Andre and Tee-Tot where still on the curb with Ronnie Mac mere feet away from them. T-Tone, on the other hand, could have reached out and touched the sports car with no problem, not to mention, be an easy target if the shooter had decided to start with him. G-Man had fallen down trying to backpedal when the car first turned the corner. As Gary struggled to get up, he noticed Andre was running for cover while calling Tee-Tot to follow. Closely on their tail was Ronnie-Mac fleeing from the Crips, making a beeline to a parked pumpkin-or-ange Volkswagen Beetle.

Sensing that his main target was close to cover, Squirrel slowly released his breath, took aim, and steadied himself on the slick roof.

Steady, steady, and squeeze, he thought as he tried to calm his overly eager trigger finger.

"Yo, cuz, it ain't dem! It ain't dem! Stall dem out, cuz. That ain't dem," shouted one of the Crips from the Impala, which had pulled over a quarter of a block up the street from where they were.

"You lucky this time. You're gettin' a pass! But da next time, I'm-a smoke all y'all, even da baby Slobs, cuz," the boy pointing the gun said, as he slid back down to the driver's seat, handed his weapon to his homeboy, and sped off down Santa Rosalia in pursuit of more prey.

In disbelief, Tone still stood frozen in the middle of the boule-vard until an oncoming car honked their horn, warning him to get out of the street. Almost as an afterthought, the boy sprinted over to the VW as fast as he could.

"Let's get out of here before they decide to double the block," Tony said.

With that, the gang of boys took off running up the hill for home without a second thought of Hamburger City. Out of breath and in last place, Tee-Tot's little round body labored to catch up.

"I told you not to wear those pants, Bob Hope!" the youngest boy screamed at the pack as he realized he had no chance of catching up to the others until he had reached their apartment.

CHAPTER
14

Nearly a week had passed since the boys' close call on Santa Rosalia Boulevard. It was literally all they could talk about for days.

"The only reason they picked us was because Dre's pants," Tee-Tot said. "It was like wearing a big target on all our backs."

"If you live in the hood long enough, you will either see a drive-by, be a victim of a drive-by, or pull a drive-by, and that's just how it was," Ronnie Mac said frankly.

Andre did not care about the numbers or percentage of Los Angeles drive-bys. All he knew for sure was that he had only been in LA for a few months and was nearly a victim of one himself.

Smoked is what Tony had called it.

"We almost got smoked!" he repeatedly said.

Andre promised himself that from now on, he would stay aware of his surroundings. This place was like living in Beirut or some other war zone Harry Reasoner talked about every night on the six o'clock news. A number of times, Scooby had told the boy to stay on point when you're out there in the streets because someone was always looking to catch you slipping. Now, the gangster's words became as clear to the kid as glass. If that was how it had to be, then he would adjust. He had done it before, and he would do it again. Before, he had done it by choice, to fit in with others, and now it was a matter of survival.

Friday signified 168 hours of precious life lived since the encounter with the crazed gunman. Over the last week, Andre had limited his outside activities to going to and coming from school. For some reason, the boy felt that as of today enough time had been wasted worrying about the past and other things, which were beyond his control. If the gunman had started shooting, some of them may have been injured or perhaps killed, but he didn't for some reason, and they were all alive and well.

So "Give thanks and live life" resonated in the back of the boy's mind like Obi Wan Kenobi using the force on the Imperial Stormtroopers.

"Yeah, so give thanks and live life," Andre said almost in a reply but not to any specific individual.

Silently, he wondered where that thought came from, but he did not dwell on it for long.

The teen sprang from the couch to adjust the rabbit ears on the TV, hoping it would fix the crappy picture, when he noticed his friends in front of Tony's apartment with a couple of guys he had never met but had seen around the neighborhood. The boy just slightly pulled the curtain back and peeked through the crack. Glancing down, he noticed a dust-covered window seal with cob-web-filled corners. In between the window tracks, between the window and screen, rested a fly graveyard. It looked like hundreds of flies had somehow gotten stuck between the screen and window and was cooked by the sun. The baked flies were matted together like a melted box of Raisinets. The thought of matted flies in his box of Raisinets made him throw up a little bit in his mouth.

At first glance, he thought the boys were going golfing because each had a different type of club in their hand. Looking at the street-light, the boy thought it was too late for the sport, even if they were skilled golfers. The golf clubs were not the only thing that each boy had in common. Each of the guys were dressed in all black. With almost squadron-like efficiency, the group of boys filed ranks around the building and down the alley led by the smallest member of the group, Tee-Tot.

The youngster sat back down on the couch, kicked his feet up on the table, and made a mental note to clean that nasty screen or, better yet, trick Keena into doing it. Thinking of his sister, he realized he hardly spent any time with her since she had given birth to his niece, Chianni. She was always gone doing something with or for the baby. He laughed thinking that she was going to have her hands full with that little girl because she was only a year old and already had a bad disposition. Chi disliked everyone but her family. For some reason, she especially despised other little kids. Leaning back, Andre smiled and began to chant in unison with his static filled TV, "Jerry! Jerry! Jerry!"

"Come with me… Don't do it! Please come with me," the girl pleaded with the man standing on the steps.

Well, more like young Hispanic woman, he thought from the sound of her voice. But then she phased back into a girl and back into young woman again. Andre did not recognize her in either form. But hell, he did not recognize himself either. He appeared to have gained a hundred pounds and grown several inches. Nevertheless, he knew two things for sure: Number one, he was dreaming. And number two, his thoughts were coming out of an enormous fellow with a considerable perspiration problem.

Andre felt as if he were sliding around inside the great man's sweaty skin. His sweat-drenched brow squinted to hold his concentration on the girl. She was dark complexioned with stunning light brown eyes. Her flowing brown locks bucked and whipped wildly back and forth as the young woman struggled to lead the sweaty giant by a massive arm through multitudes of people and unending lines.

"What are you doing?" the big man uttered.

"I've got to make this flight or else," he told the girl, not knowing why. Despite her diminutive size, this girl / young woman possessed great strength in this dream world.

"I won't allow it!" she shouted. Stopping to catch her breath, she fell backward, nearly pulling the massive man on top of her.

While attempting to maintain his balance, Andre marveled at an old blue-haired lady walking a miniature red Doberman pinscher wearing a tiny top hat and tails with a rope for a leash in her left hand and the other hand pulling a shopping cart with thousands of dollars spilling over the sides onto the tile floor. With the skill of an

MMA fighter, the girl slid her hands from his arm to his wrist, bending it forward and twisting his thumb counterclockwise, sending the behemoth crashing to the ground like falling timber. With catlike quickness, she pounced on top of him.

"Please, please," she begged. Then she lowered her forehead to his chin and began whispering so softly that he could barely hear her.

In his concussed-like state, Andre the Giant battled to regain control of his bombarded senses. Overhead lights in the great room beamed like halogens on steroids, blinding him like a flash grenade. In the background, a blaring amplifier labored to spit clear messages through a suboperable speaker system, allowing only every other word to escape. Compile that with the claustrophobic feeling of swimming in another person's body was becoming too much for him to handle. He felt he had to wake up now or suffocate. He was no longer swimming in the gargantuan's frame; he was literally drowning in its sweat. In a panic, the boy tried with all his might to wake up. Then it hit him. He recalled his conversation with Dr. J.

"If you ever need to find your body, think of a body part," he heard Dr. J say in his head.

Andre was pretty sure this was not an out-of-body experience, but maybe it would work.

I am my big toe. I am my big toe, the teen thought in his dream. Seconds later, his eyes opened, and his thirsty lungs sucked up a healthy heaping of oxygen. Although his eyes were now open, and he was no longer short of breath, something still didn't feel right. When the boy attempted to rise up from off the couch, he instantly realized what was wrong. He was paralyzed! Once again, just like when he dreamed of Ms. Mary Terry. The last time it had eventually wore off, but he didn't remember how long it had taken. Andre contemplated what he would say if his mom or sister walked in and there he lay unable to move with a million tiny jabbing needles tingling his slowly waking body. Patiently he waited for his body to catch up with his consciousness, until fear began to set in. For an instant, he thought it was some kind of neurological disorder because his mind seemed to be working just fine, but the signals were not reaching his resting muscles.

Nearly ten minutes had passed before the feeling started return-ing to his extremities. His need to urinate was incredible. As soon as he felt confident that he could, Andre jumped up from the couch and ran to the bathroom to relieve his bladder, barely making it in time. Relived that he had not had an accident on the couch or some-where on the way to the restroom, Andre took a second to reflect on his waking up paralyzed while he concentrated on peeing in the toilet and not the floor. Silently, he wondered what really caused the inability to move. He wondered if Dr. J had experienced it or knew how to avoid it. Afterward, he bent over the sink, washed his hands, and began splashing cold water on his face.

Still drowsy and somewhat groggy, the boy was pretty confi-dent that he could induce an OBE in his current relaxed state. Andre contemplated where he should try to go. Slowly, he strolled back into the living room and cleaned up the mess he had made. Next, he checked the time, walked over to the front door to make sure that it was locked. He then took a final peek out the window. Just like he thought, not a soul in sight. No wonder he thought it was only ten forty-five on a Friday night; even his mother was still out. Why was he ready to go to bed so early? Then he answered his own thought aloud, "Because this is fun!"

To Andre, sleep was becoming a never-ending adventure. Now that he was learning how to wake up in his dreams, there were no limits to the things he could do. He could move really fast like the Flash, he could pass through solid objects, and he had incredible fighting skills. Although Andre had a plethora of his favorite hero's abilities at his disposal, his favorite thing to do was fly; he loved to fly. Whether he was soaring high above the tree lines of the forest or closely skimming across large bodies of water just inches above its surface, it didn't matter as long as he was flying.

Andre had once heard that if you fall in your dreams, you would die. He knew that this was not true. Andre had fallen hundreds of feet out of the air on numerous occasions. He would shake it off, take off running, and jump right back into the air with no fear. He now loved having the dreams that terrorized him as a kid because, now, whenever the bad man or monster was close to getting him, he could just fly away. Occasionally, there would be times in his dreams where his mobility would change, and he could barely run. It would be like running in quicksand or underwater where he could hardly move at all. However, as soon as he could, he would fly away, usually low enough to tease but high enough to evade any danger. He loved his new world, but he knew he still had a lot to learn.

Andre removed all his clothes with the exception of his white Fruit of the Loom T-shirt and his tighty-whities. Next, he loosened his sheet's hospital-corner tucks so that he would not feel restrained. Then he pulled back the top spread to the foot of his bed to prevent him from getting too hot. Now, he was ready. Lying on his back with his palms down, feet spread apart, and head facing magnetic north, Andre began breathing in slowly through his nose and exhaling through his mouth. Continuously, he repeated in his mind, *I am relaxed,* as he visualized himself growing as light as a feather until his astral body floated upward, rotating a half a clockwise barrel roll right out of his physical body. The trick was he had to allow his body to grow completely relaxed but maintain consciousness at the border of sleep. That was the tight rope because nine times out of ten, he would just fall asleep.

Hopefully, he could maintain consciousness until the vibrations started. That was the key because the vibrations created the slight separation between the physical and astral bodies, which permitted the soul to escape its daily confinement to travel freely at night.

"Come with me... Don't do it! Please come with me," the girl pleaded.

No longer changing from little girl to woman, she was now all woman with the temperament of a hungry grizzly bear. This time, he sensed a definite urgency, both in his determination to get through the endless terminal and by her unrelenting will to stop him. Once again, she led him by one arm, breaking through lines and knocking down cordoned-off sections, creating havoc in this once-orderly Grand Central-like station. Although aware that he was having the very same dream, he was totally incapable of stopping or changing it in any way.

CHAPTER
15

The next morning when Andre woke, he found his mom in the kitchen cooking breakfast.

"Hey, Ma, how was your night?" the boy asked as he opened the refrigerator and pulled out a carton of orange juice.

"It was okay, nothing special," his mother replied. "I went to the Pied Piper over on Crenshaw. They had a great little jazz band. I had a couple drinks and hung out with some friends. That's about it. How 'bout yours?"

"I didn't do anything, just watched some TV and went to bed. About what time did you get in?" he questioned.

"Hey, hey, who is the parent here?" his mother said, laughing.

"No, it's not like that. I was just wondering what time I fell asleep," he said.

"So, are you sure you're not going to put me on punishment if I tell you, right?" his mother said with a laugh.

"No, Ma, for real, what time was it?"

"I could hear you in your room snoring when I got home at about twelve fifteen," she said. "I pulled your door shut and went on about my business of getting ready for bed myself. Did you have any good dreams or anything last night?" she asked as she took a bite of her bacon and whimsically looked away.

"Are you making fun of me?" Andre asked her as he wiped the juice from around his lips with his paper napkin.

"No, not at all. I love you just the way you are."

Confused at her response, Andre interrupted his mother before she could continue.

"What does that mean?"

"Nothing. It just means I always knew that you were going to be special," she said as she stared at her son with loving eyes.

"Did I ever tell you the story about when you were just eighteen months old?"

"No, I don't think so," Andre said.

"Well, get comfortable and eat some of those grits with your bacon and eggs and check that toast under the broiler. It smells like it's burning. And while you're doing that, let me figure out where we were living when it happened."

She crossed her legs, took a deep breath, and lit a cigarette, which signaled to Andre that he was about to hear a rather long story.

"I'm pretty sure we were living on Balout Court because Bill had just gotten out of jail and promised me that he wasn't going to go back," she began. "And sure enough, the very next day, he got into a fight at the bar down the street. And what do you know, it's you and me, kid, alone in this huge three-bedroom house. I didn't like it there. It always seemed cold and damp, no matter how high I would turn the heat up. Anyway, I didn't like you sleeping in your room because I couldn't hear you," she continued as she realized she had gotten slightly off subject. "So, you slept in my bed with me most of the time."

"No wonder I have issues with girls," Andre said, smiling.

"Aw, be quiet and listen to the first time you freaked your dear mother out," she said as she flicked an ash into the glass ashtray.

"It was six a.m. on a Tuesday morning. I know this because I would always forget to turn off my alarm clock on Monday night 'cause I was off on Tuesdays. Anyway, the darn thing goes off bright and early, and I jump up thinking that I had to work. I am panicking and running around to get ready. And suddenly, it hits me that I don't have to work. So, I lay back down and get comfortable, but as soon as I close my eyes, I realize that you are not in the bed with me. I jump back up in utter terror, not knowing where you were. I searched every room in the house and then opened the front door to run over to the neighbors to use their phone, and there you were sitting on the steps with a little twig in your mouth. I remember it like it was yesterday. I asked you what you were doing, and you lifted your head up and looked me right in the eye and said, 'The same thing I've been doing for the past seventy years, getting my day started with a good smoke.'

"Your little voice seemed harsh and gritty, and your eyes were… I don't know, just different when you said it," his mother said, sounding concerned. "You really freaked me out at the time. I don't even know who you could have learned it from. No one was permitted to smoke around you. I wasn't even smoking cigarettes at the time, and Bill would not allow me to smoke weed in the same room with you. When I told Bill, he just laughed and said, 'I told you he was an old soul.'"

"So, what are saying?" Andre asked with a serious tone. "I was possessed?"

"No, not at all," she quickly replied. "Anyway, I don't think so…More like you remembered something from before, maybe. Whatever the case, I never saw anything else like that out of you as a small child. And believe me, I was looking."

Before Andre could ask another question, his mother finally changed the subject.

"Now, that's enough about the past," Virginia said to her son whose face showed a look of confusion and interest. "Let's talk about the future."

"The future?" the boy asked.

"Yeah, the future. How long in the future is it going to take for you to clean off this table and help your mother with these dishes?" his mother tried to say with a straight face but failed miserably.

"As far as your actual future is concerned, I don't worry about you very much," she carried on. "You're pretty well-grounded. I think that you will do just fine, but always remember that life is a choice. And you can do anything that you choose if you truly believe and set your mind to it. You are the one who creates your reality by your beliefs and the choices you make now. You would do good to remember that," she added.

"I don't think it's that simple," Andre said. "If it were, everyone would have everything they want."

"No, they wouldn't, Dre," his mother answered back quickly. "Most people have little faith, if any, in anything. That's what's wrong with this world now. People have no faith! All of the great books like the Bible, Koran, and even the Torah teach that belief is the key to a prosperous life. I'm not saying that I am the most religious person. However, I think belief is the key to everything."

Ms. Brown stood up, pushed her chair back from the table, and started walking out of the kitchen.

"I have something I want to give you," she said suddenly. "I was going to give it to you for your birthday, but that is a couple months away, and now seems more appropriate."

His mother walked into her room and returned moments later with a small book with a red jacket cover. It reminded him of a pocket Bible or *The Communist Manifesto*. She walked over and handed it to him. The title simply read *Quotes for Success*.

"I found this book at Goodwill," his mother said, looking at her son with a loving look. "And for some reason, it reminded me of you. After our little breakfast conversation, I think now is as good a time as any to give it to you."

Andre thanked his mother and gave her a hug. While he was unsure what to expect from the book, he could tell his mother's intentions were filled with love and care.

"Why did this book make you think of me?" he asked.

"I don't know," his mother said honestly. "It just did. You should read it. I believe it may be inspirational to you. Tell me what you think about it later," his mother said while heading back toward her bedroom. "I've got to get ready now. I'm going out to the Marina to meet with some friends about a play."

Andre strolled over to the couch, sat down, and kicked his feet up on the coffee table. After giving it some consideration, he thought he may as well see what this book had to say. The cover felt sticky to the touch like the last person reading it did so while eating a peanut-butter-and-jelly sandwich. Each page was bent back at the corners as if someone had marked it for future references, time and time again.

On top of that, the pages themselves were all tattered and starting to fade from having been handled so many times, the boy guessed. The first page of the book had one single quote: "Whether you think you can or you can't, either way, you are right"—Henry Ford.

The reading was very easy. Each page had about five or six quotes from famous or successful people. It seemed that his mom had been right on when she spoke to him earlier about choice and belief because nearly every quote spoke of the two in relation to future success.

The book provided a quote from Buddha, which resonated with young Andre: "All we are is the result of what we have thought."

The next quote underneath it was almost a direct paraphrase from Winston Churchill hundreds of years later: "You create your own universe as you go along."

The more he read, the more intrigued he became with the concept of belief.

The book also had a quote from Martin Luther King Jr., which Andre found to be quite inspirational: "Take the first step in faith. You don't have to see the whole staircase, just take the first step."

Almost three hours later and still in the same position, Andre understood why the book was in its current condition. He had scanned through it nearly three times, and the boy thought the book's author was trying to make an underlining point about belief. Several quotes kept coming back to him.

"Imagination is everything. It is a preview of life's coming attractions," a quote from Albert Einstein read.

Then there was what Robert Callier said: "All power is from within, and therefore, under our own control."

The final quote was from W. Clement Stone: "Whatever the mind of man can conceive, it can achieve."

The book ended like it began with one quote on the last page: "These then are my last words to you. Be not afraid of life. Believe that life is worth living and your beliefs will help create the fact"—William James.

Andre was pretty sure that the author was saying that we create our own reality through belief. Surely, life couldn't be that simple, could it? He sat up, placed the book on the table and his feet back on the floor. As he stood up and stretched his stiff legs, he heard his grandmother in his mind quoting her Bible as clear as if she were standing right in front of him. It was from Matthew 17:20, one of her favorite quotes.

"'You don't have enough faith,' Jesus had said. 'I assure you, even if you had faith as small as a mustard seed you could say to this mountain, "Move from here to there." And it would move. Nothing would be impossible.'"

The thought of her made him want to smile and cry at the same time. He thought she was telling him that it was just that simple. Still in disbelief, the teen struggled to accept that in life all you had to do was choose what you want and truly believe, and it would somehow be magically given to you. His grandmother's quote of Jesus was spot on. He did not have enough faith to believe it could really be that simple.

CHAPTER
16

At around 3:00 p.m., Andre heard a loud ruckus outside his apartment in the hallway. To him, it sounded like a full-fledged fight had broken out. Slowly, he approached his door to peek through the peephole when he thought he recognized some of the voices. Just to be sure, he peeked through anyway. To his surprise, it was the whole crew out in his stairwell wrestling and play fighting all the way up the stairs. He opened the door and jumped out into the hallway with his best karate stance and butt-kicking sound effects.

"Aa-taaa!" Andre yelled in his best attempt at sounding like a character from an old karate movie. "What's up, guys? What are you guys getting ready to do?"

"Yo, man, we getting ready to play some tackle football against Coco Street over in Baldwin Park," Gary said. "We wanted to see if you wanna play with us, bro."

"You can't be scared though," Ronnie blurted out. "No bitch shit! 'Cause somebody is probably gonna try and punk you, and we'll end up fighting. We always do."

"Don't trip though," T-Tone said confidently. "We're all cool. But some of them are Pea Stones, and when they trip, all their Blood brothers want to trip wit' 'em. Don't let these fools scare you. It's all in fun, but it will be some hard hitting," T-Tone said as he pushed his way past everyone and picked Andre up in a bear hug.

"I ain't no punk. Let's go," Andre replied, seeming to completely ignore the fact that his friend's arms were still wrapped around him from the bear hug.

"Hold up, let me throw on some sweats and change my shoes," Andre said. "Then I'll be good to go."

"All right, we're goin' to start over to da park," Tony said as he held his arm out and directed the rest of the crew out the door. "We'll see you in a minute."

Seconds later, the hallway echoed with laughter and loud squeaks from sticky tennis shoes.

After the game, all the boys gathered in front of Tony's apartment. It was a lot of fun even though they lost. Everyone was tired and all bruised up. And just as predicted, there was a fight. However, unlike the game, Andre and his friends did not lose.

"Dre, you were pretty nice out there," Tony said. "Did you play football back east before you came out here?"

"Just pickup games, not for my school or anything," Andre said. "I was too scared for all that. Besides, I'm more of a hoops guy. That's my game if you want to see skills for real," he added with a laugh.

"I think I'm gonna go out for Dorsey's team this year."

"Good luck on that 'cause they got some ballers, and I'm pretty sure they went to state last year," Gary exclaimed.

"Ay, man, I saw you guys last night dressed in all black and everyone had a golf club," Andre said as suddenly, remembering the odd scene. "It looked like something straight out of *The Warriors*. What were you guys going to do?"

"That's for us to know and you to find out, Bob Hope," Tee-Tot said, laughing.

"Man, shut up, Tee!" Andre said.

"Well, actually, Tee-Tot might be right on this one," Tony said as he looked down and scratched his horse chin. "I don't think Ms. Brown would appreciate us getting you into trouble, and you've barely been here a few months."

"What do you mean trouble?" Andre said curiously.

"Fuck that, be real with him!" Ronnie said frankly.

"The truth is we like you Dre, but you seem kind of soft," Tony said. "You may not be, but you seem that way. And if you got into trouble, you might tell on the rest of us."

"I'm not like that! I've never told on anyone in my whole life," Andre swore.

"Have you ever done anything that could get you locked up?" Gary asked.

"Yeah, kind of, well, maybe… Nothing really bad though," he said as he watched the boys' faces for disapproval.

"Dre, do you know the worst thing you could ever do to your homeboy?" T-Tone asked.

"What? Fuck his girl?" Andre asked with a confused look on his face.

"No, that's pretty low, but that's not it," the older boy said. "It's snitching on your boys. A crime that's punishable by death! Well, maybe not death, but you don't want to be labeled a snitch, believe me."

"I tell you what, go home for a while, and we will have a little meeting about our newest homeboy. Come back in about half an hour, and we will let you know what's up," Tony said, seeming to have become the unspoken leader of the group.

"Okay, cool. I'll see you guys in a few," Andre said as he looked for cars before he jogged across the street.

Before Andre could even grab the tarnished bronze doorknob to Building 4127, he heard the call. Well, actually, it was a whistle, but that was their call. The whistle sounded like a birdcall from the jungles of Brazil. He, himself, had not mastered it yet, but he was very close. Andre turned around, threw his arms up in the air, and shrugged his shoulders, like, what was the point of that. Covering his eyes from the glare of the sun, the boy headed back across Hillcrest Street. Blinded by the sun, he nearly walked right into the jaws of Colossus, the vicious pit bull of Curtis "The C" Collins.

Curtis was obsessed with the letter *C*. He drove a Celica, his girlfriend's name was Caroline, and he was a walking advertisement for Converse. He even called himself The C.

Colossus's low guttural growl warned the kid just in time to jump to his left. He was just inches away from getting bitten. Colossus snapped at the boy, sending dog spit all over Andre's bare leg. Curtis looked Andre right in the face, chuckled, and never said a word.

"Aye, did you guys see that? Curtis was just going to let his dog bite me," Andre said.

"Yeah, he's a dick! You wouldn't be the first," Gary said.

"So, what's up?" Andre asked to the group.

"We were going to let you kick it wit' us anyway, but we thought it be funny to let you sweat a li'l bit," Tony said as he offered his hand to Andre for some dap.

"We do have a little initiation planned for you though. Ask your mom if you can go to the Mardi Gras out at Westwood next weekend with us," Tony continued. "It's gonna be crazy."

The day was sweltering. Temperatures zoomed well above a hundred degrees even as the clock approached 6:00 p.m. It did not matter. The UCLA campus's annual Mardi Gras celebration was well on its way to being a smash as usual. Thousands of people packed the streets of Westwood Village. Sidewalks overflowed with a crayon box full of kids, resembling a Benetton advertisement.

The small town of Westwood sparkled with neon-like Vegas's little brother to the west. Palm trees lined perfectly manicured streets, as five-story parking garages towered over the rest of the town's buildings, old 1950s-style movie theaters and quaint, little eateries powered by high spirit-driven sales. Sprinkle in a few well-placed bars and dance clubs, throw in one of the largest, most diverse college campuses in the country, and you have the ideal location for wild, out-of-control young adult debauchery.

T-Tone piloted the blue 1976 Buick Regal off the 405 Freeway onto Wilshire Boulevard and turned left onto Gayley Avenue, just in time to catch a candy apple red 500SEL Mercedes Benz pulling out of a parking space right in front of the Westwood Village Arcade.

"Now, that's what you call front-door service," Tony smiled and said as he rubbed his elongated chin.

Laughter erupted throughout the car, and each and every boy knew that this was going be a night to remember. The five boys exited the Buick and viewed their surroundings like wild dogs crazed before the hunt. Never had Andre seen so many young people in one place. The night was electric! To his immediate left, four tipsy college girls stood in front of the arcade, making fun of every one as they entered.

"What's the plan? Are we gonna go into da arcade first and then go find some freaks or go walk around first?" Ronnie asked.

"I wanna go play some *Centipede* first," Tee-Tot said. "That's what I wanna do."

Mesmerized by the spectacle that was Westwood, Andre sat in wonder to endless scenery in every direction. A black 1974 Chevrolet Monte Carlo was being pulled over right in front of them by LAPD for bumping Grand Master Flash's "The Message" at what the village considered to be noise pollution levels.

"Let's see what's inside and then go from there," Gary said.

Young Tee-Tot led the troop into the building that echoed with a million sounds at once. High hats clanged, gunshots banged, and electrical buzzers, whistles, and bells reverberated back and forth between the four cushion-covered walls, which housed hundreds of video games, pinball machines, and a carnival gaming area.

Andre stood mesmerized by the sheer size of the arcade when a humongous shadow covered him, blocking out an entire section of blinking lights, creating a momentary eclipse upon the youth.

"Have you seen my son? Have you seen my kid, man?" asked a huge black male who resembled the NFL's single-season all-time rushing record holder. He questioned the boy as if he had known him and his son for years.

"No, Juice, I haven't seen him. Are you OJ Simpson?" the boy asked.

"In the flesh," responded the man who would one day racially divide a nation as the country held its collective breath awaiting the verdict of his murder trial.

Andre loved video games. His favorite were sports games like *Double Dribble*, *Techmo Bowl*, and *NBA Jams*, but he could pass time and quarters on any type of video game, be it *Dig-Dug*, *Contra*, or

Double Dragon. He loved them all. Right now, it seemed that all the games he wanted to play were occupied, so for now he was stuck playing two-player *Centipede* with Tee-Tot and losing badly.

An hour later, the group of boys met outside at the car.

"Here's the plan," T-Tone said. "It's about eight o'clock. The name of the game is Grab Ass. Everyone puts in five dollars, and the person who gets the most confirmed grabs at nine o'clock gets the pot. Here's the catch. Dre, you can't have the least amount of grabs because you're the new booty. If you do, you will be walking home, pal. Besides, if you let either Ronnie or Tee-Tot outgrab you, you suck and you need to walk home and reflect on how bad you suck," Tony said, laughing.

"You da one dat sucks. Your fat butt probably should walk home talking all that stuff, and you're the one who is probably gonna finish in last," Ronnie-Mac said as he popped his imaginary collar and brushed off the front of his black T shirt.

"What's up? What are we waiting for?" he asked.

"Let da games begin," G-Man laughed as he rushed into a crowd of people, waiting for the light to change.

The game was simple. Grab a girl's ass without being caught by her or anyone with her. The trick was to slide into the middle of a moving crowd and inconspicuously reach around someone else and squeeze an unsuspecting ass. It was a blast watching the girls try to figure out who just snatched their cakes, unless you got caught, and then it was try not to get smacked or worst.

Ronnie said, occasionally, you would grab someone's butt and that person would actually like it. However, on a night of over one hundred gluteus grippings, only one girl seemed unhampered by the event. In fact, she turned around and smiled in the direction of Tony and Gary, but neither would own up to their deed in fear that it was a trap to get them to tell on themselves. No girl was out of bounds. Just make sure she is of consenting age because anything less can get you thrown in the cage, as Tony so elegantly put it.

In the end, the contest was anything but that. It was not even close. T-Tone's Mr. Fantastic arms allowed him to pull off successful grabs from any number of nearly impossible positions. Ridiculous grabs around the interferer and between a second party, landing perfect pinpoint panty pops, capturing a night's best twenty-seven unwitting sets of buns. The next closest was G-Man with nineteen confirmed ass seizures. Not far behind tied for third set Andre and Ronnie-Mac with seventeen booty snatches each, which left little Tee-Tot in last place as usual.

The highlight of the evening for Andre was deciding to eat at the world-famous Fatburger. Perhaps, he could finally extinguish the mental picture burned into his mind by Fred G. Sanford's description of a fat burger.

From the moment he pushed the door open, his senses were kidnapped and taken on a voyage. The aroma pulled at the boy's nostrils, drawing his sense of smell away over the counter, through the swinging doors, and parked them over the grill close enough that the intoxicating smell from the simmering onions caused his mouth to water instantly. On top of that his eyes were hijacked every time a tray of food crossed his line of sight. His eyes darted left and right to chase head-size toasted golden buns, laced with garden green leaves, topped with huge ripe tomatoes toppling over on two cheese-covered quarter-pound beef patties so thick that they could choke a mule.

The sounds coming from the dining room were a symphony of resonance. New sandwiches being unwrapped and finished burgers' wrappers being crumbled up lay down the track. Fifty sets of teeth masticating in unison created a beat. The intermittent beep from the deep fryer proved to be a funky hook, accompanied by the occasional sound of sizzling flesh held the entire track together like a well-timed DJ's scratch.

The restaurant's vibe was laid-back and cool. The patrons behaved with an almost sedated kindness toward one another instead of their normal LA standoffish demeanor. At that moment, he wondered what his sister Keena would say about the people eating here. Probably something like there is a direct correlation to the sluggish behaviors displayed in this restaurant to the sedatives and tranquilizers like xylazine, which is often placed directly into the cattle's food source and passed onto the humans who eat it. Boy, she was rubbing off on him, he thought to himself.

Andre hoped that the burger's taste would finally put to rest the awful vision he had impaled in his memory as a kid. He visualized a Fatburger to be made totally of fat. All kinds of fats. He pictured the white fat off the back of baby back ribs layered across the bun. On top of that the greasy, soft fat which lined the edge of the T-bone steak. Top that with the slimy, buttery fat that hangs on the edge of pork chops. All this was held together by the stinky clumps of fatty membrane off dirty chitterlings. The Fatburger would be topped off with the crunchy and mushy fat skin of salt pork, sandwiched between two buns, which had become soggy from the greasy drippings. The picture had haunted his mind for years.

Andre had barely sat down and taken the first bite of his burger when Tee-Tot started pegging him for a couple of bucks so he could get something to drink. The new kid looked his round-faced antagonist up and down and then reached into his pocket and pulled out his last five-dollar bill and said, "Just a drink and bring me back all my change!"

"Okay, Dre, now it's time for the real test," T-Tone said as he stuffed his mouth with a handful of salty fries.

"This was just a warm-up. Everybody, finish up because we are headed to Leimert Park. Time to show this new booty what we really do for fun."

"Yeah, boy, I've been waiting for this all day!" screamed little Tee-Tot as he balled up his tiny fist and began punching his hand as he walked up to the counter.

Leimert Park was one block of green paradise in the middle of the Crenshaw Shopping District. Sandwiched between Crenshaw and South Leimert Boulevard on West Forty-Third Place set the community's own private patch of tree-covered serenity and relief from the hot summer days. However, the nights were a different story. Its location was conveniently located across from a notorious gay bar, the Cherrio. The park provided the perfect rendezvous spot either before the club opened or after it closed. Residents complained constantly about the homosexuals loitering in the park doing all sorts of ungodly things until all hours of the morning.

About twenty minutes later, the boys arrived back in South Central LA. They drove up Crenshaw Boulevard, turned right on Stocker, then proceeded one block and turned left on South Victoria Boulevard. There they drove three blocks and pulled over in a residential neighborhood.

"What's up? If you guys are tryin' to get me lost, it's working," Andre said.

"Don't trip, I know exactly where we're at," T-Tone said as he leaned over and opened up the glove compartment and pressed a white trunk release button.

"Okay, boys, you know the drill! It's time to make it all right."

"Make what right?" the boy asked, as he stepped around to the trunk with the others.

"Give me the black suede golf hat and the sand wedge!" G-Man ordered.

"I want the burgundy golf hat and the driver," Ronnie said, as he slid in front of T-Tone to grab them himself.

"Okay, I'm going to try and make this fast. Tee, get what you want, but don't fuck with my shit!" T-Tone commanded.

"Here's the deal. About two years ago, Ronnie was walking home from school at Adubon Middle when he was almost molested by two faggots as he was crossing the park." Tony never looked up as he handed his newest homey a black snapback Raiders cap and what appeared to be a six iron. "They attempted to push Ronnie into the men's room, but he kicked one in the nuts and took off running across Crenshaw Boulevard. Well, it's like this," he said, as he put on a gray suede golf hat and pulled out a Big Bertha Driver and closed the trunk. "Ever since then, we go golfing for punks in Leimert Park. Now pull your cap down as low over your eyes as you can, but make sure you can still see and listen up, and you might just get to tee off on a punk-ass fag tonight too."

"Okay, boys and girls, here's the plan. Huddle up, huddle up!" G-Man said, as he twirled his club through his fingers like a majorette with a baton. "Tony, you take the rookie with you, and I want you guys to lay low along the shrub fence on Forty-Third Place. I'm gonna take Tee with me, and we are going to post up directly across from your position behind the bathrooms. You give us the signal when they enter the bathroom. Ronnie, you know your job. You get to be the decoy with the boyish good looks hanging out on the benches right between both our locations. Everybody, got it! Good," said the dark-skinned boy with the long Jheri curl.

"Okay, Dre, this is mostly for you, because everyone else knows what to do if we get separated. If something goes wrong, meet back here. Don't wait at the car, hide somewhere close by, and if I'm not here in ten minutes. Take off for home! Do you know how to get home from here?" he asked.

"Yeah, it's up the hill over in that direction," he said, as he turned around and pointed north.

"Let's do it!" Ronnie Mac said as he took off at a good pace down the sidewalk.

The pace quickened, and before they knew it, the squadron of boys was making double time to the park. As they crossed Crenshaw, Andre contemplated what he was about to do. He had never been much for violence, nor was he a gay basher. In fact, one of his mom's best friends back home was as queer as a two-dollar bill, but he seemed to be a nice fella. Was he really going to hit someone with a golf club just to be accepted by his new friends? Even worse, was he going to beat someone up simply because of their sexual preference? He wasn't sure what he was going to do, but he would cross that bridge when he came to it.

It was about 11:00 p.m. when the first fly landed in their web. The brown-skinned man was short in stature, perhaps five feet six, with his hair permed out as fly as any woman fresh from the beauty salon. He wore a red leather suit with a black silk shirt unbuttoned far enough to reveal some chest hair. His pants were skintight to the point that they appeared to be cutting off his circulation. The figure-fitting pants bell-bottomed out at the ankle, revealing a pair of black leather disco boots with six-inch heels.

At first glance, the man could have been a body double for the pop star Prince. The pixie sauntered past Ronnie and threw him a smile. When Ronnie Mac returned the smile, the man turned around in his tracks and made a beeline to the boy sitting on the bench. The two passed the next couple of minutes talking when suddenly they got up and started walking toward the bathrooms.

"Okay, Dre, this it," Tony said as he stood up from his kneeled-down position and brushed the dirt from the knees of his Levi's. "Let's move in."

Slowly, the two boys closed the distance between their friend and themselves. Just before walking into the restroom, the gay man glanced back and caught a glimpse of the two boys approaching with golf clubs. It must have spooked their prey because, suddenly, he pushed Ronnie down, veered around, and took off running in Gary and Tee-Tot's direction.

T-Tone whistled a warning to let them know he was heading their way. The three boys rounded the corner of the building just in time to see their would-be victim pull a knife from his boot in mid stride without slowing down and attempt to cut G-Man's throat in one swift move. Luckily, Gary ducked in time.

"Get up, Gary, let's get his ass!" Tee-Tot shrieked. The five boys chased the leather-clad man south through the park toward Stocker Avenue, but it was hopeless. Even in a skintight suit and six-inch heels, the man still seemed to display world-class sprinter's speed. Not only did he leave the boys in his dust, he cleared the park's three-foot fence in stride like a hurdler in the Olympics.

"So, what now?" asked Andre.

"We reload the trap and try again," T-Tone said.

"What about him? What if he goes to the cops?" Andre asked, realizing the situation could end bad.

"Yeah, maybe we should get out of Dodge," Tee-Tot added.

"That punk ain't gonna do nothing... Come on, guys, fuck that," Tony said, trying to reassure the group. "Let's try one more before it gets too late."

"Okay, but I don't want to run decoy this time. Why don't you let Tee-Tot or Dre do it?" asked Ronnie.

"No, Tee looks too young, but Dre, yeah, I guess he could work. He's a pretty boy," G-Man interjected as he leaned over with his hands on his knees, struggling to catch his breath, as Jheri curl juice / sweat mixed combination ran down his face.

"Yeah, he thinks he's got that Shalamar thing going on." Tony laughed.

"So, are you down or what, Dre," Ronnie Mac asked as the five boys walked back over toward the benches.

"Yeah, I guess," he said as he wiped the sweat from his forehead. "What do I have to do?"

The night was still kind of balmy with a minimal breeze flowing in from the Pacific Ocean.

"You saw what I did. Just talk to them and try and get them to go into the bathroom with you, and we will do the rest," Ronnie Mac said.

"All right, but y'all had better get in there fast, 'cause I'm a kill that fool if he tries to touch or kiss me," Andre said as he crinkled up his forehead and made a sourpuss face, causing an instant belly-busting laugh from his friends.

Not even five minutes had passed, and already young Andre had a suitor. Roman Pace was a thirty-two-year-old insurance salesman who leaned more toward being a pedophile than a homosexual. Having a thing for young boys, Roman would often befriend local families with preteen males. He would do nice things for the family to get in their good graces, and then prey upon their unsuspecting children. At first, all appeared to be done in goodwill and as a community service by providing their boys with valuable mentorship from a pseudo-successful black male from within the neighborhood.

At a moment's notice, Roman would be available to the families for any number of reasons, including babysitting, transportation, or maybe to take them to the movie to get them out of their parents' hair for a couple of hours. It did not matter to Roman. He was always willing and ready to step up and help out. In reality, the only thing he wanted to help out was their genitals out of their pants, so he could suck on them like a Tootsie Roll pop. Eventually, he would be convicted for sex offenses against a minor and serve a minimal sentence in Folsom State Prison due to lack of DNA evidence. Upon Roman's release, he had been refining his approach to meeting young boys. Currently he was frequenting the local gay bar scene in hopes of finding an underage willing participant that he could bend to his will, both mentally and physically. Upon his first glance, he thought he may have found just what he was looking for.

Ever the cautious one, Roman walked pass the boy on the bench heading toward the Cherrio, never once glancing in Andre's direction. Abruptly, he turned and began walking back in the direction from which he had just come, searching his pockets and shoulder satchel as if he had forgotten something. As he walked by, the boy asked the man if he had a cigarette he could bum from him.

While he did not have a cigarette, he quickly told the boy he was willing to roll up a joint and smoke it with him if he wanted.

"What are you doing out here on a park bench," Roman inquired. "It's almost midnight."

"I needed to get away for a while," Andre said. "My mom be tripping, so I am trying to make some money to get down to my cousin's house in Long Beach."

"What are you trying to do to make some money?" Roman asked.

"I tell you what, let's go over to the restroom, roll one up, and we can come to some kind of agreement then. Is that cool?" Andre asked.

"Okay, let's go," said the prematurely balding man who held his arm out and pointed in the direction of the restroom like a maître d' might do at a fine dining establishment.

T-Tone and Ronnie Mac watched on with the pride of parents as their young protégé reeled in their quarry with the skills of a seasoned angler.

"Come on, Ronnie, let's move," Tony said to his nephew, pushing off the ground to stand up, only to drop right back down to the ground instantly, as he saw flashing blue lights traveling south on Crenshaw about to make a quick left into the Stocker Liquor Bank parking lot on the corner.

"Oh shit, it's the LAPD," Tony said.

"Do you think that they are over there about us?" the younger boy asked.

"I don't know, but they are too close for comfort and Dre needs us over there," Tony said as he slowly stood and peeked over the hedges toward the liquor store. "They just walked into the bathroom."

"Fuck, it's that Prince-lookin' ass fag over there talking to the police, and he's pointing in this direction," T-Tone said as he hunched over on all fours and began to crawl toward the bathroom.

"Give Gary and Tee the signal," Ronnie said as he took off across the grass after his uncle.

"We can't, da po-po might hear it too."

In the dark, on their hands and knees, the two boys made haste across the damp grass.

Inside the facility, Roman Pace held his nose with his left hand and fanned the air with his right.

"It's not that bad," Andre said even though the fumes from the stench was literally burning his eyes and causing his nose to run. Roman walked into the bathroom's stall bent over and began rolling toilet paper around his right hand. Over and over he wrapped it until his hand looked like it had a cast on it. He then turned around and began to wipe off the toilet seat.

Where in the hell are they? Andre wondered. He had been in here for over a minute already. Once the man felt comfortable that the seat was actually clean, he looked down and reexamined the cigarette-burn-covered seat then turned around and sat down.

"Have you done this before?" the man asked as he reached into his pants pocket and pulled out a sandwich bag full of marijuana.

Something was wrong, and Andre knew it. Maybe he should just leave now before this went any further.

"Done what before?" the boy asked as he covered his nose with the inside of his forearm to block out some of the disgusting odor emanating from within the filthy bathroom.

Feeling comfortable that the police could not see them from this distance, Tony stood up and began to run. He did not go into the restroom. He ran behind it and waved to G-Man and Tee-Tot to come over to him.

"The law is across the street talking to ole boy we just tried to jack, and Dre has a trick in the bathroom right now! We've got to get him and get the fuck out of here right now."

"Let's get out of Dodge! We got to get out of Dodge!" Tee-Tot kept saying over and over again, like a scratched record.

"Shut up, Tee. We are going to get out of Dodge. Ronnie, you and Tee break out, go back out across Leimert Boulevard, and double back to the car. We will meet you guys there," Tony said as he worked his way around the side of the building.

"No way, I want to help Dre!" Ronnie said as he attempted to push past his uncle who grabbed him by the arm and pulled him back against the wall just as the LAPD spotlight from squad car 304 shined on the front of the building from the park's entrance.

"You know damn well what I am talking about. This...coming into a bathroom with a grown-ass man in a public park in the middle of the night. What did you think I was talking about, Chinese checkers?" Roman said as he stood up and took a step toward the boy.

The predator was now close enough for Andre to smell the liquor on his breath.

"I thought you were going to roll us a joint," the boy said nervously, as he stepped away from the approaching man.

"So, now you want to play hard to get, huh?" Roman said as he reached out and attempted to grope the young man's genitals with one hand and placing the weed back in his pocket with his other hand.

"Let me see what you are working with boy," the man said, backing the teen into a corner. For a second, it was like a cha-cha. Roman would take one step forward, and Andre would take two steps back. Ultimately, he could go no further. Andre began to think that maybe this was the actual initiation. To see how he would handle himself if he had to. His friends or so-called friends were not coming to save him. He would have to do it himself. Andre began to size up the approaching man. He was a little taller than the pervert was, but he was probably outweighed by thirty pounds, easily.

"What is your name?" the man asked as he stepped even closer to the teen. "It really doesn't matter. You don't have to tell me if you don't want. I just want to make you feel good. It won't hurt, I promise. And then I will give you some money to get you to your cousin's house."

Meanwhile, the rest of the group were still struggling to make their next move.

"Any more bright ideas? Let's try one more before it gets too late," Gary said as he peeked around the corner to see what the cops were doing.

"I'm going in. Fuck it! If they see me, they see me. I've got to make sure Dre is all right," Tony said as he ducked down and attempted to get low as he possibly could. Just as the young man started forward, car 304 turned out its spotlight. Seconds later, two barely audible car doors could be heard closing and two tiny flashlight beams replaced the big one.

"Let's go, guys. We've only got a couple minutes before Johnny Law gets here. Hurry up, let's go," Tony ordered.

Inside the restroom, Roman leaned forward and violated not only the boy's personal space, but also he reached out and grabbed the boy's privates. Andre thought about trying his old friend KC's move, but there was not enough room. Without thinking, the adolescent shoved his provoker back at the shoulders with both hands simultaneously kicking his left shin with all his might, driving the pervert sliding backward on one leg across the wet concrete floor. Instinctively, Roman reached out to grab the boy, but his momentum sent him crashing to the floor on his right knee.

At that point, Tony rounded the corner with Ronnie close on his heels. The sound of people rushing into the restroom distracted Roman and caused him to turn and look back. That would be his last mistake tonight because when he returned his gaze to young Andre, he was greeted with a tennis shoe to the face, leaving him dazed, concussed, and bleeding on the bathroom floor. For a second, Tony looked shocked and forgot what he was going to say. Ronnie dashed past his uncle and landed a solid kick to the ribs of the man lying on the ground. He then leaned over him and snatched his wallet from his back pocket.

"The police are outside heading this way," Ronnie informed his friend who looked relieved to see them. "We have got to get out of here now!" The young gangster in training then bolted for the exit, pulling G-Man and Tee-Tot with him.

Smiling at his friend, T-Tone yanked him by his shirt and told him to run.

As the two boys darted for the exit, Andre turned around and ran back to the man still lying on the floor. He bent down, partially rolled the dazed man over, and reached into the man's right front pocket and removed the bag of weed.

"You promised me this anyway," Andre said before he stood up and sprinted for the door.

Running out the toilet, the youngster noticed two small beams of light shining in his direction. He was pretty sure that he heard someone in the distance faintly say, "Stop! Hold it right there."

His mother would kill him if he went to jail for any reason, especially if he had been arrested for assaulting a defenseless homosexual. Even if he was lucky enough to beat the case, she would be sending him to live with his stepdad, for sure. Andre followed his friends south and then west, exiting the park on McClung Drive and crossing Crenshaw Boulevard. The only person in the group he could see was T-Tone attempting to pass between a narrow passage between the Pied Piper and the Revolutionary Records shop. As soon as the boy ducked in behind his friend, he could hear the high-powered engine of an LAPD cruiser speeding down the boulevard with just its flashing lights on and no siren. It was a tight fit between the old two-story brick buildings. There was barely a foot and a half of space separating the two buildings. The narrow path grew tighter the closer he got to the alley. At last, he had broken free of the structure's snug grip just in time to catch a glimpse of what he thought was T-Tone's Nike going over the wall on the other side of the alley. Andre gathered himself to take the wall in one swift leap, but before he took off, he heard the chopping sound of air accompanied by a bright spotlight from above. It was the Ghetto Bird, the LAPD's paramilitary helicopter used especially for tracking high-speed automobile chases and finding suspects fleeing on foot. Realizing he would be seen going over the wall or hiding between the two buildings he decided to climb into the trash dumpster behind the Pied Piper and hang out there for a while and walk home in a couple of hours when things calmed down a little bit.

For the second time in one night, the youth's sense of smell was being bombarded. The stench of rotting flesh and dirty diapers hung around, like it dangled from one of those little tree-shaped air fresheners. Realizing that he had no choice in the matter, he tried to make himself comfortable. Patiently he rearranged and configured trash bags and attempted to make the best of a bad situation. Just as he challenged himself to relax, he heard the meaty rumble of a slow-moving V8 engine right outside the dumpster.

He could hear a static-filled radio beeping and cutting out with a monotone dispatcher in the background. His heart revved three thousand revolutions a minute in unison with the vehicle slowly inching its way down the glass-infested alley. Exhilarated and terrified at the same time, the boy sat motionless as a mannequin not knowing what the cops in the passing car were doing. Finally, the officers in the sedan seemed to grow tired of the alley and sped away with their spotlight trained on the residents' backyards.

Scared to peek out from his hiding place and totally exhausted from the day's activities, young Andre waited patiently, and time seemed to pass at a snail's pace. Unaware of how long he had been buried in trash, the kid began to lose wakefulness. Gradually blackness encompassed him, and the falling sensations were quick to follow. Down his body slowly sank through the trash bags, the dumpster, and the ground itself. Rising from the ground, Andre attempted to physically jump up into the air unsuccessfully. Realizing that he was no longer in the physical world, he thought to himself, *I can fly*, and he did.

He could taste a subtle hint of salt water in the Santa Anna wind blowing him toward his home on Hillcrest. It was like tasting with his whole body. Not only that, he could see in every direction at the same time, and the feeling made him sway with vertigo. Looking down on the hundreds of identical apartment rooftops left the boy feeling hopeless in finding his home. The world really looked different from this angle, he thought. *I wonder if my mom even knows I'm not home right now*, he questioned, and just like that, he was standing in the doorway to her room. There she was lying in her bed asleep with the light on and a novel on her chest floating up and down with every breath she took. Almost as an afterthought, he turned around and walked into his room, looked at his bed, saw that it was empty, and realized that he was still in the dumpster behind the Pied Piper. Seconds later the teen woke up, unburied himself, and slowly pushed open the black plastic lid, revealing the first glimpse of twilight. He climbed out, looked around, and hightailed it all the way home.

Fifteen minutes later, the teenager was sitting on his bed untying his shoes, wondering what happened to his friends. Taking off his right shoe, he noticed that his brand-new cream and baby-blue suede Puma Ecos were ruined. The entire toe of the shoe was covered in a hardened black substance. Probably blood, he thought, from the freak who had grabbed his genitals in the restroom. What a waste, he thought. That was the first time he had worn them. For a second, he thought it was Karma, but he dismissed that thought as soon as it came to him.

Getting into his bed, he rolled over, looked at the clock, and saw that it was 6:00 a.m., and he was just going to bed. He pulled his dingy white sheet up to his neck and placed his lumpy pillow over his face just in time as his mother looked in to check on him as she made her morning trip to the bathroom. Almost instantly, he felt the vibrations as soon as he closed his eyes and relaxed. He was exhausted. A light went on in his head, and he suddenly realized that the key to having a controlled OBE was being extremely tired. He would have to remember that when he came back, but now he focused and tried to manage his breathing and control his exit because his little flight earlier was but a tease and he wanted to soar the heavens. With his head to the magnetic north and his body vibrating like a person undergoing a massive seizure, he relaxed and let himself go.

When the vibrations stopped, Andre attempted to open his eyes. But he could not see anything. Open or closed, the view was the same total blackness. Once he adjusted to the darkness, he realized that his breathing was being restricted to quarter breaths. His locomotion was limited to a crawling position as if the gravity was now doubled. Try as he might, he could not stand. There was an invisible force holding him down.

The grown was smooth and cold to the touch like a metal, but it rolled and flowed like the earth within a cave. Even though he could not see anyone, he was sure that he was not alone. He had the eerie feeling that someone was right behind him staring down his neck. Even in total darkness, the boy felt hundreds of eyes bearing down on him. The thought was unnerving.

Petrified and fear stricken, Andre crawled around the murky cavern, recklessly plowing headfirst into wall after wall. With no true sense of direction, he crawled around again and again in what he was beginning to think was a circle. A couple of times he thought he had found an exit, only to hinge himself into a tiny pocket where turning around was nearly impossible. Even in those confined spots, he had a creepy feeling that other beings were jammed into the tight crevices with him.

Andre had learned many things about dreams since his early days. For instance, dream time could not be measured accurately during a dream. However, the OBE's time flow closely mirrored the real world's passage of time. He was not sure, but he believed he had been trapped in this hellish hole teeming with benign spirits for over an hour with no idea of how he was going to get out. Oxygen deprived and on the verge of a nervous breakdown, Andre attempted to focus on his physical body's big toe. At first nothing happened, and then he felt a strong suction yanking him upward, only to bounce him off the ceiling and back down to the ground, where he ricocheted around the cavern like a pinball. Not sure of what had just happened, the boy made a concerted effort to concentrate on his physical body once again, only to end with the same result. This time there was no doubt what had happened. He was being drawn back to his physical body, but the cave would not release him.

Exhausted and terrified that he had projected himself into an inescapable prison, the boy cowered into a corner and began to sob. As he sobbed, so did his invisible cellmates, amplifying his sobs a hundred times. On the verge of giving up, Andre attempted to stand once more, only to be forced back down by what felt like hundreds of invisible hands. Overwhelmed and frustrated, the boy sprawled out in defeat on the cold surface.

"Please tell me you are not giving up already... Is this to be your hellish resting place for eternity?"

"Who said that? Please help me, whoever you are!" the boy pleaded.

"You need no help. You only need to choose to be or not to be. Be here or be there, it's your choice," said the voice from within his head.

"I choose to be there," said his weak, trembling voice.

"Your words are but a conduit. Your belief is the actual vessel. I am your spirit guide Oliver, and I have been waiting for you."

"Why have you been waiting for me?" the boy asked curiously.

"Because if I hadn't, you would be stuck here until you figure it out, or not. Unfortunately, if you are trapped here, you may miss your chance to rejoin with her again," the voice replied.

"Who is her, where is here, and why is your voice coming from inside my head?" the teen asked as he attempted to push himself up to a sitting position.

"She is you and you are her. You are equal opposites. You may think of it like the yin and yang symbol, but in reality, you are a part of the same kindred spirit that divided itself millennia ago. In reality, you are but two of the many who separated yourself. I believe you humans call it soul mates. Here, this is your self-created purgatory. It seems that you are punishing yourself for some reason. As far as my voice is concerned, your mind is translating my thought pictures into words because there are so few words in your language to describe most of the things we need to discuss. Unfortunately, now is not a good time, for you have exhausted much of your needed energy creating this cavernous prison," the enigmatic voice said with remorse.

"What do you mean creating?" Andre asked.

"Just as I said before, you created it with your thoughts," Oliver said.

"So how do I get out of here?" the boy asked, as he braced himself to try to stand again.

"It is simple. Choose not to be here and forgive yourself for what you have done. Next, feel for your physical body and focus your single-minded attention on it and allow your body's magnetic attraction to draw you back to it."

"Forgive myself for what?" the boy interrupted.

"That is a question you must ask yourself." Oliver's voice faded out with one last utterance. "I am usually available. You need but call."

CHAPTER
17

Lancaster, California, is located sixty-nine miles north of Los Angeles, a region known for its scorching days and its frosty nights. This high desert town is famous for two things: one of the most respected actors of her time, Judy Garland, and a hotbed of UFO activity to rival the likes of Roswell, New Mexico. Records going back to the early 1800s show Piute Indian drawings displaying what they termed as sun disk in the sky high above the Northwestern Mohave Desert. That area is now the home of Edwards Air Force Base. The government quickly aligned itself with local company, Lockheed Martin's Shunkworks Department, specializing in aerospace technology. Many believe that its 1947 opening was a direct response by the government to deal with the overwhelming number of sightings in that area.

Unbelievably, in the first year of its inception, magnificent inventions came on the heels of alleged UFO-crash-site cover-ups. It became the birthplace of the United States' first jet engine, supersonic engine, and top secret planes like the Bell XP-59A in the base's early days, not to mention the dynamic stealth technology, which would magically appear out of nowhere in the late 1980s.

The transition from Rosamond to Lancaster proved to be no challenge at all for the Jokinen family. Richard had felt that the family had all come together like a team, handled the move, and became a closer unit since. He noticed that most of the bickering, pettiness, and jealousy had disappeared given that the kids now had their own rooms. He, himself, had found privacy to be overrated. Growing up with eight brothers and four sisters in a three-room cottage, he knew not the meaning of the word. The bond between his brothers and sisters was tighter than connected five-thousand-by-five-thousand chain links. Their closeness was a contrived plan by their father, Louis, who had experienced family disloyalty firsthand from his gutless brother Antoine.

Antoine sold out both his family and country to the Nazis in hopes of gaining political favor and replacing Marshal Pétain as premier of France. He provided the Germans with crucial information leading up to France's defeat in the Battle of France and their subsequent surrender in July 1940.

Swallowing as if his teeth were just for decoration, choking down his breakfast, and scanning the morning paper with a blank stare, Richard Jokinen imagined this house empty, the echo of silence ringing throughout, with all his kids grown, self-sufficient, with families of their own. The house in this case was not a house, but a huge nest surrounded by four walls and no roof, exposing a beautiful cloudless blue sky. In the middle of the nest on a bed comprised of matted grass, hay, assorted twigs, and enough lint to start a massive dry fire. He lay with his beautifully matured wife of fifty years. Every day, he prayed he would be able to keep his cherished wife despite her discontent. One day, he would make this the private love nest they never had when they were young.

The dream, to his dismay, was way off in the future. His baby girl was only twelve years old, and at the rate Trevor was going, he would probably still be living with them long after Michelle had graduated from college.

Snatched back into reality by the sound of a glass shattering on the linoleum floor, Richard reached for his chest, held his breath, and whirled around to see what was happening. It was Eileen balancing too many items in her tiny two hands. The glass of orange juice was the first to find the floor. Like a rookie juggler, she found the handle on her book bag but bobbled the tube containing her favorite Claude Monet prints and her October copy of the *Smithsonian*. Like Bounty, the quicker picker upper, her magazine began to absorb the glassy orange substance from off the floor before she could reach down to pick it up.

Reaching down to the floor, bending at the knee, Eileen looked up and began speaking to her father.

"My class is going to the MOAH today in downtown Lancaster," she said. "Could you give me ten dollars, please."

"The what? Every time I turn around, you girls need money for something or another," her father complained.

"The Museum of Art History. Remember, I told both you and mom last week," the girl said from one knee as she shook the glass free of her soaked magazine.

"Okay, okay. Come over here and give your ole poppy a hug," Richard said, smiling as he pulled his chair out from the table.

Smiling back at her dad, Eileen placed her right hand down on the ground to push up and screamed instantly.

"Ouch! I got glass in my finger."

Once again, the girl dropped the book. Again, it landed in the spilled juice, on its back this time, wide open just in time to catch some of the girl's free-falling blood droplets.

Ten minutes later, Eileen rushed back into the kitchen with a Band-Aid on her right index finger, rushing in jeopardy of missing her bus. To her surprise, her mom was mopping the kitchen floor and had already cleaned up her mess, placed her book bag on the broken chair by the basement door and the tube containing her prints on the counter.

"Mom!" Eileen panicked. "What did you do with my magazine?"

"I threw it in the garbage. It was soaking wet, ruined. What else would I have done?" Martha questioned.

The teenager removed the lid from the trash can, held her breath, and frowned as she gingerly stuck her left hand into the kitchen receptacle and felt around for the book. Pulling it out, she realized that her mom was right; it was ruined, and she hadn't even read it yet.

On its back now, the book trickled juice down the sink's drain. Eileen leaned over the sink, carefully separating the pages. She hoped that the Monet articles where savable. Her little fingers peeled softly into the corners of the soggy pages to undo them, only to find that her prayers had been answered. The middle of the publication was still as dry as a bone in the center, except for her blood, which had spilled onto the picture of *Claude Monet Painting in the Garden*.

The stainless steel scissors shimmered, reflecting the light from the window as the girl attempted to cut the dry pages free of those already swollen and consumed by the liquid.

Eileen was ecstatic for the chance to save the article, not only because she loved Monet's work, but also because she hoped to learn more about this founding member of the Impressionism movement of 1874. She wondered why they had gone away from the traditional style of a crisp outline of the subject matter for the more unblended patterns that emphasized the light and shadows of a scene

Art was her life. She dreamed of one day working in a successful commercial art firm, retiring from it, and one day opening a gallery of her own, do private shows featuring local artists and some of her own work.

As the girl placed the pages into her art folder, she began to close it, then Eileen reopened it and closely examined the page she had bled on. Amazingly her droplets had formed a nearly perfect red daisy in Monet's completely purple garden just above the L in his first name Claude. For a second she marveled at it, then slid it back into the slot, closed the folder, and placed it in her book bag.

Realizing she had wasted far too much time to make it to the bus stop before her bus left, she decided to try to catch a ride with her dad on his way to work. In the back of her mind, she already had known that she would be riding with her father since she had first seen him sitting at the table having breakfast.

Even though Eileen's school was fifteen minutes out of his way, not to mention during peak morning traffic, there was nothing Richard would not do for his firstborn. Nowadays, it was not about the spoiling. Old Rich simply wished to spend a little more time with his little Leeny Leeny Jelly Beanie, as he referred to her as. She was no longer his little girl; she was growing into a beautiful young woman. And very soon, he would have to compete for her attention with thousands of horny young men with but one intention—deflowering his little Leeny.

Words between the two had always been at a minimum; their relationship was a tight one nonetheless. Their bond was a subliminal borderline psychic connection he often suspected. This morning was no different. Just as his daughter fixed her mouth to ask him for the money once again, Richard lifted his butt slightly, removed his wallet from his khaki Dockers, and handed her a twenty-dollar bill.

"Thanks, Dad, but I don't need this much," the girl said as she leaned over to give her dad a little kiss on the cheek.

"Don't worry about it. Take it, just don't tell Tanya. I swear, if I paid a monkey a dollar to get off of my back, I'd have to give your sister one as well," he said, laughing, as he put on his left-turn signal and merged into the turning lane.

Eileen leaned her head back on the top of the seat, closed her eyes, and began to visualize the route her father was taking to her school. The air in the car was stuffy, and the girl could swear she was starting to smell her dad's false-teeth-induced bad breath. It was horrible, a combination of buttermilk, coffee, and nicotine from cigarettes he secretly smoked in the backyard. The girl cracked her window slightly, inconspicuously inhaled all the fresh air her lungs could hold, kicked her feet up on the dashboard, and slowly dozed into a quick nap for a couple of minutes.

As she dozed, she began to visualize the route in her mine's eye. It was a blurry nondescript view of Avenue J heading west. Like bad sonar, she could draw a contour image of vehicles fleeting by her father's doo-doo brown 1978 Ford F150, but nothing clear enough to identify their make or model. *Concentrate. Bypass the distraction,* she thought. *I can go farther. Focus, focus, focus...,* she repeated to herself.

When her vision cleared, she was in art class sitting on the teacher's desk, surrounded by her friends and classmates. Eileen attempted to wipe her disbelieving eyes with her sleeve.

Monet's Painting in the Garden hung on the teacher's blackboard, eager to be witnessed. Frolicking purples rolled across the canvas unhampered as the viewers marveled the magnificent work of the iconic Impressionist.

"Purple is my favorite color," Patty said, pulling her yellowish green gum out of her mouth and twisting it around her finger over and over again, then untwisting it and placing it back in her mouth.

"I don't like it. It's too purple. Everything is purple," Karen said, turning her head like a cat viewing an object from every angle.

"What do you think, Eileen?" the bleached blonde with the bronze surfer-girl tan asked.

"Yeah, Ms. Art Critic, what do you think," asked Patty, Eileen's best friend since Mr. Morgan's second-grade class.

Eileen attempted to answer her friend's question but was distracted by the distinct twang of a country music song she recognized playing in the back of her head. She was surprised and uneased by the Conway Twitty tune she knew all too well from riding with her father. "Gotta find my way back to my baby," he sang ironically.

"I love the touch of the single red daisy in the midst of all the purple orchids," the girl said as she climbed down from the desk, walked over, and pointed up at the board.

Glorifying in her ability to bring the unnoticed to the table, she twirled around to face her, no doubt, astonished friends, but instead she found only the white fox Oliver sitting on her teacher's desk, staring at her attentively.

"In the universe, in galaxies both near and far, there are a minuscule number of events that occur out of coincidence," the vulpine said as it leaped from the desk and slowly floated toward the girl in defiance of gravity.

"Always double-check your work. Even your keen eye can be deceived by the obvious," he said as he vanished and reappeared behind her.

"Your sight is not enough. Trust the words whispered by your soul, for they will never lead you wrong."

"What is this all about?" Eileen questioned as she spun around to face her new friend.

"You will know when the time comes you have placed yourself on the path."

Still the haunting melody being emitted pulled at her eardrums.

"Come back, darling. I'll be waitin' for you," Conway Twitty sang in the background.

"Wake up, Leeny. Wake up, we're here." The girl's father shook her by the shoulder and said, "Have fun at the museum and try not to miss your bus home from school this afternoon, okay." Still slightly groggy, the girl pulled her hair away from her face, checked for sleep in her eyes, opened the door, and tested her sleepy legs on the sidewalk below.

"Okay, Dad, I will, and thanks for the ride. See you this evening," she said as she closed the door, turned, and walked away from the rumbling pickup truck.

In her homeroom, a delicious variety of conversations flowed between Eileen and her two friends Patty and Karen. The main course was boys with a little gossip thrown in and a side dish of who was going to the prom with whom.

"Excuse me for interrupting you, ladies, but some of us would like to finish taking roll before the always exciting morning announcements start, if you don't mind," Mrs. Alwiss said. She then turned her attention to the game of twenty-one in the back of the room.

"Patrick, you get rid of that gum in your mouth and bring that deck of cards up here to my desk right now!" the teacher instructed.

Just as the bony freckle-covered adolescent placed the deck of Bicycle cards on his teacher's desk, the intercom buzzed then whistled with feedback, introducing the most uninteresting person on the planet. Principal Willard spoke with an overly exaggerated East Coast Bostonian accent. He tended to extend a word's pronunciation to the point that you forgot what the word was by the time he finished saying it. Both faculty and students alike despised the morning announcements in which Principal Willard always found a way to pay homage to his beloved East Coast and bash the Golden State in which he lived. Headlining the events of the day, the administrator's mind-numbing voice droned on about the weather or lack of weather and who needed a weatherman in Sothern California anyway. His request for all students attending the field trip to the MOAH to meet at the bus loading dock after homeroom even came across boring and uninteresting, causing those who were excited about the trip to question their reason for wanting to go to the museum.

The first half of the day flew by, and the girls were now finishing up their lunches across the street at Carl's Junior. Totally excited about the Monet exhibit they were about to view, Eileen rushed her besties to get back to the museum.

In the lobby of the MOAH, the trio reconnected with the rest of the class. Mr. Steel took roll and addressed the group, a mixture of his art students ranging from the ninth to the twelfth grade. He took a second to inform them that he would be monitoring their behaviors and he hoped that the day would finish without incident.

"I'm proud of you guys' behavior up until this point," Mr. Steel said one moment too soon as one of the boys ducked down in the crowd and declared, "Yeah, I'm proud, too, of these *nuts!*" inspiring a loud burst of laughter from the boys in the group. After the roar died down, the teacher turned around, dissected the crowd, and said, "Mark Jones, I'd know that raspy, cracker-stuck-in-your-throat, billy goat gruff voice from a mile away. Unless you would like to spend the rest of the day glued to my side, I'd suggest that you get your act together and pipe down. Is that clear?"

After a second of silence he repeated himself, "I said is that clear?"

"Yes," the embarrassed adolescent uttered under his breath.

"Good, now that we have an understanding, let's proceed to the Impressionist exhibit," said the dapper thirtysomething instructor with a flair for the dramatic.

The northwest corner of the museum housed the Imperfect Perception Exhibit. This showcase featured paintings from nineteenth-century trendsetters mostly from Paris like Eugene Boudin, Mary Cassatt, Paul Cezanne, and Edgar Degas, who fueled the fire for change in the period from the traditional not only in art, but in popular culture and politics as well.

In a semicircle, about twelve feet from the classic *Monet Painting in the Garden*, she stood in a group of twenty or so students listening to the curator spout fact after fact about the life of the accomplished artist.

Like a hawk she observed.

To her right, Patty sneezed uncontrollably as if the flowers on the picture produced actual pollen.

The portrait glistened with life. Eileen quietly absorbed its contents and blocked out the curator's dialogue, Patty's sneezing, Karen's excessive perfume, and Mike Williams behind her bragging to his friends about his supposed threesome last night with two cheerleaders from Palmdale High.

Something was missing. The painting was somehow incomplete. Top to bottom, left to right, and a diagonal corner-to-corner scan left the girl feeling confounded, nauseous, and more determined to put her finger on the glitch. Even after the assembly moved on, she stood stuck.

"Hey, girl, are you coming, or what?" Karen asked as she fanned herself with the museum's brochure.

Just as Eileen turned to look at her friend Karen, it caught her eye, better yet, didn't catch her eye at all. Deliberately, the girl stepped as close to the painting as she could get without crossing the black velvet rope. It's not there, she thought. Zooming in on the bottom center right of the picture just inches above the frame, there was no trace of the single red daisy in the sea of purple orchids.

The girl crossed her arms, closed her eyes, and attempted to picture the page she cut out of the *Smithsonian* earlier that morning. Oblivious to everything going on around her, she focused. Unaware that her two friends were now standing beside her, Patty on the right waving her left hand up and down in front of her girlfriend's face to get her attention and Karen beside her rolling her right index finger in a circular motion to the side of her head.

"That's my chick, but I swear, she's not all there sometimes," Karen said. Still, the girl concentrated. In her mind's eye, Eileen pictured the red daisy located just above Monet's signature.

Trembling in frustration, she bit down on her bottom lip until it began to bleed. The taste of the blood stung her like a nine-volt battery, subsequently triggering her memory. Oliver said there are no coincidences. Double-check your work, he said. Like the taste in her mouth, the blood was hers, and the red daisy was not real; it was created by her blood. The signature, that's what's wrong, she thought. Just below where the red daisy would have appeared on the painting stood the L in his name Claude, it stood straight up and down with no signature loop at its top.

Now with her eyes wide open and the faint taste of blood in her mouth, the teen scanned the room. She shook her head in disbelief and ran her fingers through her tangled hair. Without acknowledging her friends, Eileen located the curator, jogged over to her, bent over, and whispered something in her ear. The tiny Asian woman turned to the girl, looked up, and said, "What do you mean a fake?"

"You know, an imitation, counterfeit, a replica with a bad signature," the girl said.

"You don't know what you're talking about. This is an authentic Monet," the woman said as she walked away. Remembering the curator's name from her introduction she said, "Look, Mrs. Sekino, I know that you think that I am just some kid from Antelope Valley High, which I am, however, Monet is my favorite artist. I have studied all of his work, and I know that the signature on this painting is not right. I would suggest that you get the museum security, the Lancaster police department, LA County sheriff's office, or someone in here immediately, unless you are responsible for this bogus misrepresentation of a masterpiece." She screamed at the fleeing woman, causing nearly everyone in the great room to turn and look.

Within the hour, the museum was crawling with both uniformed and plainclothes officers. Everyone in the MOAH was detained and questioned. The finding from the investigation concluded several days later, acknowledging that seven historic works of art had, in fact, been compromised prior to their visit to the Lancaster museum, artworks valuing well over forty-two million dollars. Investigators concluded that the actual heist was believed to have taken place at or between 1:00 and 1:45 a.m. on Sunday morning from the San Bernardino Museum of Natural History. The perpetrators were yet to be determined, but early indicators suggested that it was an inside job.

Twice in her short life, Eileen had been recognized for her civic loyalty. This time, she was being acknowledged by both the mayor and the district attorney's office. In salute to her keen attention to detail, she was awarded the Joe A. Callaway Award for Civic Justice.

With the insight of blind Lady Justice herself, DA Harvin saw the girl's unlimited potential and offered her a two-year scholarship to any Cal State school upon the completion of a two-year degree at Antelope Valley Junior College. The lawyer also promised the young girl a part-time job at the district attorney's office when she graduated high school, hoping he could steer her toward a career in law.

CHAPTER
18

Nearly three months had passed since the Leimert Park incident. Both T-Tone and Tee-Tot had been picked up by police on the night of the jackings. Luckily, neither Tony nor Todd had been identified by either of the two victims. Rom P thought that the older boy looked familiar, but in his concussed state, he could not be totally certain.

The self-inflicted punishment was becoming a distant memory as well. Until he thought about it, then he would mentally revisit the traumatic experience, leaving him anxiety filled and oxygen deprived like a claustrophobe in an elevator.

Over the summer, Andre had actively participated in nine unprovoked assaults across the Los Angeles County area, no longer focusing solely on the local homosexuals who were often broke and penniless. Andre suggested that the boys target those with the most to lose.

"If we can go to jail for this, it may as well be worth it," Andre would tell his crew.

He suggested that they hit the target close to tourist areas with easy access to freeways. After kicking the pros and cons back and forth, the guys agreed unanimously.

Their locations and tactics varied, but the results were always the same. A strong-arm robbery with two options for their victims, "Kick it in" or "Get beat down!" Usually, targets gave up their belongings without a fight, but there were a few hero types who wanted to save face. They should have just kicked it in and saved their face, but they chose option two, the beatdown.

Andre stormed out of the apartment after an argument with his mom about the hours he had been keeping as of late. At the curb, Tony waited for the last member of the crew. Andre hopped in the car and immediately slammed his palm into the blue leather dashboard of the aging Buick Regal as the boys headed out on a mission.

"What's wrong with you, fool? Don't you ever put your hands on Betsy again. This is my baby! You are just a passenger. Your ass will be walkin' or catching the bus back to the hood," T-Tone said as he examined the dash like a concerned lover.

"My bad," the boy confessed as he tried to wipe the earlier blow away like dust.

"I've got stuff on my mind. I think my mom is going to try and send me back to live with my stepdad in Ohio or my sister, Lanessa, and her sorry-ass husband in Louisville," he told his friends.

No one spoke a word. No reason to respond to the boy and speculate about what Ms. Brown would or would not do. So, the other three boys sat focused on their mission, finding a mark in the Marina Dell Rey's Marriott parking lot.

Sweating profusely and sparring with bouts of dizziness, the advanced-in-his-age jet-setter navigated around the marina looking for Ocean Drive in a panic. Still distraught by the call from the front desk interrupting his showing at the Yacht Exchange, the esteemed philanthropist felt an urge to pull over and throw up his stomach's content.

Just a couple of hours ago, he was having poached eggs, dry wheat toast, and grapefruit juice with his wife Lorain on their hotel room's balcony overlooking the Pacific Ocean. Lorain complained of a lack of an appetite and a severe migraine. He assumed that his junior of more than thirty-five years was not interested in accompanying her husband to admire his latest investment, A brand-new top-of-the-line fifty-foot Ocean Alexander Mark II, four cabins, two baths, wall-to-wall luxury, a fiberglass cruiser complete with twin Detroit Diesel engines. He had hoped that the two would pilot the vessel down the coast around the Gulf of California and then cut through the Panama Canal. From there they would swing due north across the Caribbean Sea, up to the Gulf of Mexico and, who knows, maybe stop in the Bahamas for a couple of days, before continuing on to their home in South Beach.

With the reckless demeanor of a driver at a Saturday night demolition derby, Malone Sacchino barreled into the hotel parking lot with all four wheels of the silver Phantom Rolls Royce locking up, burning rubber, and grinding to a halt, sending tiny pebbles flying. Not the least bit concerned about the exiting airport shuttle van he nearly sideswiped, the geriatric driver leaped from the vehicle with the dexterity of a much younger man and made an all-out dash for the lobby.

His graying temples had nearly conquered his entire scalp, leaving but remnants of his once brunet roots. Thin as a whip, with the wit of one as well, Malone stayed one step ahead of his competition by staying both mentally and physically fit.

"Aye, yo, man, did you see that Double R that just pulled into the parking lot? That shit was bad!" G-Man said as he began to rock back and forth faster and faster in the back seat, like an epileptic on the verge of a fit.

"I know, right?" T-Tone added. "I bet that old fool got loot."

"Yep, and I bet he's coming right back out too," Andre said.

"Why do you say that?" T-Tone asked as he turned around and stared at the boy in the passenger seat. Andre laughed, looking at his long-chin friend, thinking of the joke, a horse walks into a bar. He wiped the smile off his face and said, "Because look how he parked. He's barely in his space, and if the driver of the Camry comes out first, chances are he will open his driver side door and hit the Rolls. Not only that, but he left the top down on one of the most expensive cars in the world, and I didn't see him running with the keys in his hand. He probably left them in the ignition," grasping to catch his breath.

"Damn, ain't you a observant nigga," Ronnie Mac said as he opened his door to stretch his legs.

"So what's up, is that our vic?" Ronnie asked as he pulled a zip-lock sandwich bag half full of a light green marijuana and a pack of Zig-Zags out of his pants pocket.

"What do you think, young Dre?" Tony asked. "You seem to have all the answers over there."

"Yeah, I think we can get him," the boy said as he leaned over, smirked, and gave his big homey some dap.

Once within the hotel, Malone took a direct line to the concierge's desk. Drenched in sweat, he noticed the pain spreading from his chest to tightness in his chin, but nevertheless he continued to look for the hotel's most accommodating employee. Unaware of why he was feeling so tired, he finally spotted the person he was looking for. It was Maurice, the hotel's concierge.

"Mr. Sacchino, are you okay? You're looking a little peaked," he said as he walked around the counter and assumed his position.

"Yes, I am fine. Are they still in the room?" the elderly man asked the boy in matching burgundy vest and slacks.

"Yes, as far as I know, no one has left the room," he said as he stuck his left hand out, palm to the mirror-covered ceiling in anticipation of a tip.

In the hallway, staring down at the intricate carpet designs, burgundy paisley patterns outlined with power blue squares, swimming in waves of cream, with his key in hand, Malone stood in contemplation outside room A-1723. It had been almost six months since; he had hired a private detective to keep tabs on his overly busy wife. What had he expected? Of course, eventually she would want the company of someone a little closer to her own age, but he would never have expected it to happen this soon, still newlyweds in the second year of their marriage.

The senior took his time, composed himself, and inserted the door key into the lock, turned the knob, and stepped into his suite. The parched throat and the peculiar delayed beat in his ticker made the old-timer think for a second that perhaps he was feeling a bit more than nerves. Every step wreaked havoc with his erratic heartbeat. Stepping down into the sunken living room caused the elder's sketchy heart to slow and skip a beat. At a snail's pace, he rounded the corner and opened the door to the master bedroom. Although Malone braced himself for what he was about to see, it still hit him like a cattle prong to his chest, when he witnessed his darling Lorain duck out from underneath the sheets near the foot of the bed with her naked boobs clapping like an audience responding to an applause sign, followed by a balding age-spot-covered geezer who appeared to be ten years his senior slowly inching his way out from underneath the comforter at the head of the bed.

The sight of his lovely wife with another man sent the old fellow reeling backward into the hallway wall. Devastated with a heavy heart and disbelieving eyes, the senior regained his composure, shook his head in disgust, then bolted for the door without a word. Now that his beliefs had been completely confirmed by his own eyes, Malone had wished his private investigator's firsthand account and pictures had satisfied his profound need to know.

Exiting the front door of the Marriott, the old chap grimaced as he realized there was an electric twinge shooting up his left elbow. He heard a flock of gulls crying in the distance as he struggled to locate his car in the crowded parking lot. Sooner than expected, he spied it and made a labored approach to a vehicle that seemed to move farther away with each toiling step he took toward it. Like a mirage, the Phantom shimmered in the distance.

Finally, at the Rolls, Malone wondered what his next move would be. He had planned to take Lorain out on the Mark II and sail up the coast to Santa Barbara for a test run to see how she handled. Not now, perhaps never, he thought, as he crawled into the cockpit of the machine and slid the key into the ignition.

Hunched over his steering wheel, leaning forward, struggling to make a left turn against the oncoming traffic, the driver suspected the migrating pain in his left arm combined with the countless other symptoms he'd suffered this morning could only mean one thing. His next stop would be the Marina Del Rey Hospital emergency room. Attempting to recall the location of the hospital, the senior never noticed the blue Buick Regal following directly behind his vehicle.

Lying down on the floor of the back seat, Andre held his breath in fear of warning ole white top before he was ready. What was he thinking? Did he have to volunteer just because he came up with the plan? Not having anticipated what would come next, the boy took a second to marvel at how plush and fresh smelling the carpet was. Even riding on the floor this car was far smoother than any other vehicle the boy had ever ridden in without question, he thought.

Keeping time in his head Andre guessed that almost three minutes had passed since leaving the Marriott. He told the guys to hang back and wait for the signal.

"I'll make him pull over and then y'all can rush him!" he said like an excited eight-year-old kid on Christmas Eve.

"Okay, but what's the signal?" Ronnie asked, puzzled as if he had missed the major part of the plan.

"When he pulls over, duh…," Andre said, looking at his friend like he was stupid.

"I guess what I am asking you is how are you going to make him pull his old ass over?"

"You know, that's a good question," the boy said with a laugh.

"Just leave that to me to figure out."

Suddenly the old man plunged his shoulders back into the seat as if he had just been rear-ended, Malone clutched his chest with his right hand, temporarily losing control of the Rolls, sending it flying out of its lane and up onto the sidewalk. Andre jumped up, leaned forward, and saw the old man looking barely conscious. With one eye closed, the other half open, and his left hand barely gripping the bottom of the steering wheel.

Noticing movement from his peripheral vision, the driver lurched left, yanking his car off the sidewalk across his lane and into oncoming traffic. At that moment, the teen reacted, grabbing the wheel, pulling the vehicle back into their lane.

"Who are you, and what the fuck are you doing in my car?" the man choked out, gasping for air, fighting to maintain consciousness.

"I'm the person who just saved your life," the boy said, speaking too soon as Malone passed out, causing his foot to smash the gas pedal to the floor. Within seconds, the luxury car was just inches away from running into the back of a red Ford Taurus. The Rolls plummeted down the boulevard at seventy miles an hour with their speed increasing rapidly. Andre attempted to steer the car with his left hand and pull the failing old man over to the passenger's seat with his right. He couldn't do it. The man was too heavy, and they were mere inches away from the crimson taillights. The boy released Malone and yanked the wheel left, passing the car just seconds before colliding. Realizing that he could not move the man and drive at the same time, Andre smacked the man nearly as hard as he could. When the ancient one did not respond, he smacked him again, even harder!

"Wake up! What's wrong with you? Wake up!" Andre screamed at the man who removed his foot from the gas, fighting to maintain consciousness.

"Help me…I think I'm having a heart attack. Will you drive me to the hospital?" Malone pleaded.

"I can't do anything with you laying in the driver's seat. Can you slide over?" the boy asked as he tussled to lift the elderly man across the soft leather armrest with one hand and steer with the other. Slowly, Malone inched his way across the cream-colored bucket seat divider with the help of the boy tugging at his two-hundred-dollar Armani shirt. Although Andre had never driven before, he jumped over the armrest and slid down into the seat like he had done it a thousand times before. He had seen others do it at least that many times. How hard could it be, he thought. As soon as he felt comfortable, he was back to business.

"Why would I do that? So you can have the police arrest me when we get there," the boy asked the old man.

"I wouldn't do that. I would just as soon kill you myself than turn in to the cops. Where I come from, we handle our own problems, son," the incapacitated man said as he forced himself forward and leaned against the dashboard.

"And how you gonna do that? You look in bad shape over there, old man," the cocky boy said as he glanced over at the man's wrinkled fingers fiddling at the glove compartment latch.

Before he knew it, with uncanny quickness the man had opened the glove compartment, stuck his hand in the box, pulled out a black Magnum .357, and pointed it at his head.

"This is the same gun that Dirty Harry used to blow the head off of numerous bad guys. I figured if it's good enough for Clint, it's good enough for me," the old guy said as he leaned back against the passenger-side car door and aimed his weapon at the would-be robber.

"Make a left at the next light. Don't try anything stupid and listen to me for a second," Malone said, as his weak arms trembled to hold up the massive revolver.

"I am usually a good judge of character, and even as I am sitting here having a heart attack, I can tell you this...," the man said and dozed out for a second with the gun dropping into his lap. A few blocks back, a siren's wail could be heard approaching fast. "You watch the road, not me. The hospital is up here somewhere. Just follow the ambulance about to pass us in a minute or two. I should pop you one just to teach you a lesson about what stealin' gets ya. Take my advice. Robbing people is not for you, ya too soft. You should find a different line of work," said the man who was now sounding more like an old fifties gangster than a retired businessman. In the rearview mirror, Andre noticed a procession of cars behind him pulling over to the right, so he did so in turn. The emergency vehicle bypassed a mile of traffic via the turning lane blaring a banshee's scream and a yellow trail from the recently painted center-lane boundary lines.

"Now you get over in that center lane and you follow that fucking thing like your life depended on it, because it does!" Malone said, clutching his chest with his right hand and bracing the pistol on his left thigh.

"I'm gonna do you a favor, son." Placing the hand cannon on the floor, he reached into his back pocket. "I don't know why I am doing this, but like I said before, I am a pretty good judge of character, and my gut tells me you're a good kid. If crime is what you want to do, then so be it, but find something you're more suited. What you're doing here will get you killed. Take this," Malone said as he removed a handful of one-hundred-dollar bills from his billfold and handed them to the boy driving his prize automobile.

"If I were you, I would put half of that money in my back pocket and keep it for myself and share the rest with your friends trailing us in the blue Buick. Now start blowing that horn until you get the attention of some of those nurses over there helping the ambulance."

Several white-scrub-clad nurses swarmed the Rolls Royce, screaming at the vehicle's driver.

"Tell your boys what you will, but thanks for getting me here in one piece," Malone Sacchino said as he threw his hands up as if he was surrendering to Elliot Ness and his untouchables.

"Over here, over here, I'm having a heart attack," he shouted as he closed his eyes, crossed his heart, and said three quick Hail Marys.

As the nurse was pushing Malone away in the wheelchair, he asked her to stop, and he gestured for her to roll him around to the driver's side. In his debilitated state, the onetime gangster turned philanthropist said two things to the boy before being rolled away.

Making his hand into a gun with his index finger pointing directly at the boy, he said, "The next time you may not be so lucky," as he pulled his thumb down as if he had just fired the gun.

"And give me my damn keys before you get some crazy idea!"

Andre watched as the old man vanished into the building. As Andre opened the car door, he glanced around in search of the Regal, and realized the Magnum was still lying on the floor beside him. Without a second thought, he picked it up and attempted to place the huge weapon in his waistband, but the barrel was too long. He quickly considered a couple of other options, but neither worked. That's when he heard the old man's voice in his head saying, "What you're doing here will get you killed!" With that thought, Andre took a long look at the black .357, opened up the glove compartment, and shoved the weapon back to from which it came.

CHAPTER
19

By the end of summer, Andre's intuition proved to be right. Virginia Brown had made arrangements for her youngest child to be sent back to live in Kentucky with his oldest sister, Lanessa. Once again, the young boy would be relocating from friends and everything else he had grown so accustomed to.

After finding a huge wad of cash in the boy's sock drawer, Virginia suspected that her son was on the wrong path; unless she was hoping for jail or early death for him, she knew she had to do something quickly.

Never the dictator, his mother gave him a chance to explain what he and his friends had been doing to get the money. Unwilling to tell on his friends, or how he had acquired the money, the two agreed that leaving Los Angeles might be in his best interest.

Initially, Andre fought the notion of leaving Southern California; already he loved it there. The endless beaches, the ridiculous selection of hot women, and the gorgeous weather year-round, but he knew if he stayed, he was heading for trouble. In the end, it was the words of Malone Sacchino that made up his mind for him.

"The next time you may not be so lucky" echoed and bounced around inside his head like an electron. Perhaps it was not the words so much as the memory of him pointing the Magnum .357 at his face. Whatever the case, the decision had been made.

Lanessa and her husband Barry Gunderson had been living in their west end home on Forty-First and Market with their sons

Marcus and Derrick for almost three years before Andre moved in with them. She was a sensitive, caring sister, in many ways more attentive than his own mother. Her affectionate, sincere nature was only exceeded by her insightful ability to say the right thing at the right time, regardless of whom she was speaking. Had the urge ever struck her, she could have been a great diplomat on the world's political stage.

Lanessa was thrilled to have her baby brother come and live with her family; Barry, on the other hand, saw it a little bit different. As a foreman for K&I railroad, he had worked hard for everything he had in life, and it was his opinion that his family was struggling enough without having to worry about another mouth to feed, especially some teenage knucklehead whom his mother could not handle in the first place. The only good Barry saw in their new resident was that they now had an in-house babysitter for those nights when they wanted to go out clubbing.

Her boys were polar opposites. Marcus was the oldest, separated by four years; he watched over his younger sibling like he was Derrick's guardian angel. Cursed with astigmatism at birth, young Marcus was wearing thick corrective bifocal lenses with little brown horn-rimmed frames bolted tightly to his head by a black elastic band at the tender age of one. The thick glasses gave the perception that the child was extremely intelligent. In reality it was not perception; the boy had knowledge of things that no normal eight-year-old should know. His knowledge of current events would lead one to believe the boy spent all his time watching *Headline News*. He was an enigma! His unbound curious nature gave way to a "chicken or the egg" scenario. Was his extreme intelligence the result of his inquisitiveness or his inquisitiveness the true reason for his intelligence?

Derrick, on the other hand, was a physical specimen in every way. At first sight, his Hershey-like complexion melding into a strong jawline, perfectly spaced eyes, and a million-dollar smile combined to create a subliminal illusion of trustworthiness to the onlooker. Unlike Marcus, Derrick cared about nothing but himself. His self-centered, narcissistic attitude was only overshadowed by his stubborn will to have things his way.

Every night, the boy would display his unrelenting resolve in reaction to his eight o'clock bedtime. From the time his mother tucked him in, kissed him on the cheek, and turned off the lights, he would scream at the top of his lungs for thirty to forty minutes on end. Any Olympic swimmer would have killed for lungs like his. The Gundersons tried nearly every punishment in the book to change his behavior, but nothing worked. Nothing, not beatings, restrictions, chastising, or reprimanding, and they even attempted to rebuke Satan out of the little hellion. Still, he demonstrated his resolution each and every weeknight at bedtime. No tears, no sobs, or weeping, just a megaphone-quality squeal which often lasted for hours until the boy was totally drained and passed out from sheer exhaustion.

Andre's arrival probably inconvenienced the boys more than anyone, because the two of them now had a roommate and were being forced to share a bed and give the other to their uncle. Derrick wasted no time introducing his uncle to his impressive set of vocal cords. On his first night back in the Ville, Derrick went for his all-time record of four hours of continuous howling broken up by mere moments of catching his breath.

Fatigued from the three-day bus ride and worn out from trying to tune out his four-year-old nephew's temper tantrum, Andre rolled over on his back in his tiny twin bed and prayed to God that this was not what he had to look forward to for the next two years.

Desperately wishing for sleep to take him, Andre attempted to turn down all random thoughts and chatter inside his head. He attempted to remove every inkling of internal noise, control his breathing, and internally force his heartbeat to slow down. Finally, he could feel his entire body begin to relax. His wish was about to be granted as darkness engulfed him, quickly followed by the sinking sensation just as assuredly as lightning is followed by thunder.

He felt the lumpy mattress under his butt melt away to thin air, and fleeting thoughts slowed and became three-dimensionally clear as day. A momentary sense of cosmic understanding was swiftly dislodged by violent vibrations moving throughout the boy's body like a crushing wave from a tsunami. The quickening vibratory state increased the boy's heart rate by five times its normal pace.

Mentally prepared and spiritually thirsty, Andre released all his inhibitions, pushed his fears to the outskirts of his consciousness, and allowed the out-of-body experience to take its natural course. Unhinged from the vibrations and free to ascend his astral body's detachment from the physical world was suddenly halted by a loud house shaking, *kaboom*! Terrified and trembling, the boy jumped up to a seated position in fear that the hot water heater had just exploded and blew up half of his sister's home.

To his surprise, in the darkness, everything appeared to be normal. Six feet away his nephews slept soundless. A tiny crack in the door revealed a faint light emanating from the bathroom, the same room that housed the hot water heater. Still shaking from the perceived blast, the boy crawled out of bed hesitantly and took a measured walk through the house. Astonishingly the house still stood in its entirety with no signs of a blast.

The first thing the next day, Andre gave his old friend Dr. Jacobson a call, only to get his annoying answering machine message with the doctor's voice over the Village People song "YMCA." Instead of the chorus singing, "Y-M-C-A," Dr. J was singing, "Leave a message today," offbeat and out of tune. At the beep, he did what was asked of him. What started as a brief message ended up being a race to get everything in before the beep sounded. Nevertheless, he thought that he got the most important things in the explosion and his urgent need to talk to him.

Going back to school in Louisville was one of the things Andre was actually looking forward to doing. He had hoped to go back to Ballard High School with his old classmates, pick up where he had left off with his old girlfriend, and hopefully earn a starting spot on the varsity basketball team; unfortunately, he no longer lived in the correct neighborhood. No problem, he would just use one of his friend's addresses that lived in the proper district. He had done it before to go to Moore Middle School with Steve and KC. At first, everything seemed to be going great with both his ex-girlfriend Nordria and the hoop squad, but that did not last long.

It was one week before the season opener against Trinity Catholic. By the window, Andre sat in a cluster of eleventh-grade boys joking about their teacher Mr. Sutherland's toupee. Homeroom was usually boring, but this morning his boy Adam was on a roll. He was killing their biology teacher's hairpiece, wardrobe, thick glasses, and his incredible case of halitosis. They were laughing so hard that Mr. Sutherland had to tell them to settle down several times. Just as Adam started cracking on him again, calling him Professor Yuck Mouth, a soft knock at door 217 calmed down their ruckus.

Through the door walked a skinny pale-skinned freckle-faced red-haired girl wearing a burgundy-and-gold Bruins basketball T-shirt, blue jeans, and a pair of untied white-and-burgundy high-top Adidas Top Tens. At six feet four, her arms dangled low like willow branches, and her thin, delicate hands held a yellow slip of paper gripped tightly in her bony, pale fingers. With an awkward gracefulness, she snaked her way through the lab stations and up to their teacher's desk at the front of the class. Like a ballerina, she handed him the note, curtsied, pliéd, and pirouetted herself right out the door at the front of the classroom.

The whole class held its collective breath as they waited to see whose name was on the note for the principal's office.

"Mr. Brown, looks like you're the lucky candidate for an early morning date with Principal Hamstead. I take it you know your way to his office," Mr. Sutherland said as he extended his arm, holding out the yellow slip for the boy to come and get.

In a hard orange plastic chair between a chunky blond kid holding a bag of ice over his left eye and some Gothic dweeb blacked out from head to toe including eye makeup and fingernail polish, Andre patiently waited his turn to speak with the school's commander in chief.

A three-foot pine counter extended from one end of the office to the other with only one swinging door in the middle, allowing the mingling of students and the office's staff. White walls outlined with burgundy-and-gold trim converged at the center of the north wall with the school's crest dominating the majority of the wall. Above the windows looking out at Westport Road hung pictures of the president of the United States, Ronald Reagan; state governor, John Y. Brown; and the secretary of education, William Bennett. To the left of the pictures, in the corner on a gold flagpole to the ceiling Old Glory proudly blew in the breeze of the central air-conditioning.

George Hamstead was a bony man with a pencil neck. His size 15 shirt collar swallowed his little neck like a spaghetti noodle sticking out of the thumbhole of a bowling ball. His head appeared to bobble on its tiny support. His lips were as thin as a line, surrounded by thick smile lines from years of kissing ass. His small beady eyes twinkled with contempt and sparkled with condescension. George reveled in passing judgment on other's choices but suffered from analysis paralysis when making the minutest decisions of his own.

His broad pug nose housed two tiny pig nostrils, which were not the cause of his asthma but probably did not help his situation either. He thought that his ears were his best feature. Perfect in both shape and size, they had but one problem. Since the age of eighteen, the hair in them seemed to grow faster than he could cut it. Within three days of going without a trim, his ears looked like baby black Afros were sprouting out of them. Cursed with looks even a mother could have trouble loving led him down the lonely road of isolationism and predetermined conclusions about people solely based on their outer appearance. In Principal Hamstead's office, being attractive, self-assured, and having a strong sense of self-worth was an immediate path to detention, suspension, or possibly even expulsion.

Principal Hamstead poked his head out of his office door, read Andre's name off a clipboard, and told the boy to come in and have a seat. Across his desk, he observed how the boy carried himself, his quiet confidences, his subtle good looks, and his smug disposition. Although he did not know this child, he knew deep down he did not like him.

"Do you know why you are here this morning?" the principal asked, as he picked up his coffee cup, examined its contents, and proceeded to sip the steamy liquid.

"If I had to guess, I would say that someone at this school does not like you being here very much," the man said as he set his cup down.

"Why do you say that?" Andre asked with a look of total confusion plastered on his face.

"It has been brought to the board of education's attention and subsequently to mine that you do not actually live in our district. I have taken the liberty of removing all of your possessions from both your hall locker and the basketball locker room. If you have any more belongings on this campus, I'd suggest that you grab them quickly because the next TARC heading back to the west end will be arriving in approximately ten minutes, according to the bus schedule. I'm not sure where you are supposed to be attending high school, but I suggest that you get there and get enrolled immediately. Do you understand me?" the man with the undersize neck asked.

"Yes, sir," the boy replied as he rose up from his chair, walked over to pick up his belongings, and said, "I think that shirt is way too big for you. You should try the husky boy's department at Sears," with a smile as he opened the door and walked out.

That was just the beginning of a one-year four-high school debacle. Pleasure Ridge Park, or PRP as it was known, was the actual school the boy was supposed to attend; however, after a mere month, the youth decided that it was not for him, so without as much as a word to his sister, he unenrolled there and reenrolled at Eastern High School, the home of the eagles.

He liked it there because he knew a lot of kids that had gone to Westport with him before it was dissolved. After Westport closed, its students were dispersed between Eastern, Ballard, and Wagner.

Aside from the fact that he had no chance to play basketball there, he was content. The Eagles were the reigning conference champs two years in a row behind six-foot-seven all-state junior power forward Herbert Cooley and six-foot-three all-city shooting guard, sophomore sensation Dee-Jay Franklin. Basketball would become a spectator sport for Andre. Nevertheless, school was becoming fun to him once again.

Without basketball, the enterprising young man had too much time on his hands and not enough money. He needed a contingency plan. Something he could do after school once he finished his classwork, a hustle on the side to line his pockets with some of the rich county kids' money.

Because drugs were not his thing, and jacking was not an option, Andre had no choice but to be creative. Imaginative thoughts soared just above his reach as his stomach competed with his brain for the remaining sustenance fueling his body.

Walking through the lunch serving line, smells danced and aromas boogied, tantalizing the boy's sensory glands, causing his stomach to shudder and rumble furiously at the lunch lady serving lasagna. His hunger was making it hard to inspire original thought. Perhaps he would have to put it on hold till after lunch.

Herbert Cooley's favorite class next to gym was lunch with his upperclassman twin brothers Andrew and Allen. They made the fourth-period lunchroom an insult battlefield. If you did not know how to bag or play the dozens, you did not want to be forced to eat in the cafeteria with them because if they did not like you, you would get no peace.

Stretched out with his ankles crossed, exposing gray-and-blue argyle socks inside size 18 docksiders, Herbert sat behind an empty tan lunch tray with remnants of red sauce, a little fruit cocktail juice, and two empty chocolate milk cartons, spinning a worn leather Wilson basketball on his fingertip, laughing at his brother Al bagging on some kid at the next table's worn-out tennis shoes.

"Aye, Dre, yo, Dre!" Herbert screamed across the cafeteria and motioned for his old friend to come over and have lunch with his brothers, Chris Mack, Zeb Meyers, and a couple of other boys he did not know.

As he approached carrying his lunch tray, the six-foot-seven post player stood up and fired the Wilson like a bullet across the room at Andre. While carrying his tray in his right hand, the boy snatched the pass out of midair with his left and started dribbling toward the table without missing a beat.

The proverbial light bulb is said to go on in a flash and leave traces of innovative residue. And so it did, and within the two seconds it took the boy to track and catch the ball, he had an incredible idea on how he could make money, and he was dribbling it with his left hand. Oblivious to the passer, his right hand would author his payday.

Drawing near to the table, the boy pump faked a hard chest pass with his left hand on the down dribble and handed the young giant the ball on the up bounce.

"Hey, man, how was Cali, and why are you back so soon? I heard that you were over at Ballard, but I thought they were just talking. Are you going to come out for the team or what?" The youngest Cooley in the clan's mouth ran fast just like his metabolism. The lean, fat-free 185-pound boy spat question after question, trying to learn about how life was in Los Angeles in their first five minutes of talking.

Five days and three conversations later, Andre had convinced his friend that the two of them could use a few more zeros in their nonexistent bank accounts. He explained his plan to the D-1 prospect, and broke down the economics of the agreement. The idea was to get as many basketballs as they could, have Herbert sign them, and he would sell them to the Eastern students or any other kids who knew of his stardom. His spiel was simple.

"This little investment of $50 to $100 will be worth thousands 20 years down the line after Cooley's pro career was over." The price of the ball was determined by its quality. Bottom-of-the-line ball, an orange outdoor ball was $50. Middle-of-the-line ball, an indoor-outdoor ball was $75. Top-of-the-line ball, a leather indoor ball was $100. The balls came in all conditions, and some of them were new, still in the box, some slightly used, some played ragged, ready for retirement, and on a couple of occasions, the ball belonged to the kid and they still paid regular price for the autograph. The two agreed upon a flat $25 per signature, and Andre would cover the cost to provide the balls.

Time grew wings, and so did the basketballs. Within less than a 2-month period, the young entrepreneur had sold in excess of 160 balls. Unfortunately, one of the collectibles went to the son of the University of Louisville's athletic director, who promptly contacted Eastern's Principal Simmons and chastised the school's leader for allowing such gross negligence to occur right under his nose. In the back of his mind, Director Martin prayed that this little incident would not jeopardize the all-state forward's collegiate eligibility because U of L was recruiting his talents as hard as every other college in the nation.

Needless to say, once again, this time after only a fifty-five-day stay, Andre found himself sitting in the principal's office, awaiting the wrath of a different principal with a totally different agenda, but a completely good reason for wanting him passed on, not in the biblical sense, but literally gone from his school grounds as quickly as possible.

In the interest of their star athlete, Eastern High School's administrative department chose to take no action in the matter of the autographed basketball fiasco. In the end, the policy-making body decided to handle it like a referee's call. No harm, no foul. No one was wronged, and all parties involved were happy and satisfied. The only punishment handed down was the expulsion of the mastermind behind the incident, as a consolation prize for his playing and not speaking with anyone about the episode; he was allowed to keep all his profits from his entrepreneurial endeavor.

With only four months left in the school year, Andre was desperate to find a school so he would have enough credits to go to the twelfth grade in the fall.

His options were few; either be forced to attend one of the inner-city public schools, Shawnee, or Central and suffer all the problems associated with the urban public educational system.

The conditions were deplorable within the old asbestos-filled walls of the early-twentieth-century buildings. Chances were he would probably end up a statistic in a decade riddled with student victims of phenomenally high dropout rates. The rates in neighboring counties were 39 percent lower. Any board of education member with a half of a brain should have seen this as a red flag.

These same schools were notorious for graduating ill-prepared citizens into the workforce. In some cases, their students were functionally literate at best. Children expected to compete without the basic necessities to build a foundation. Top to bottom, the inequities were innumerable. The most obvious were trying to teach current curriculum from outdated textbooks. Combine that with underqualified teachers running some classrooms more closely resembling day care centers than dwellings of intellectual stimulation.

His only other option was to try to get a hardship transfer to Wagner High School, which he lived only one street east of their school zone. After a lot of praying, some string pulling by Dr. J to fellow alumni Principal Malcolm Hollingshead, and a little good old-fashioned fingers crossed, four-leaf clover, lucky rabbit's foot fortune, Andre's hardship request was accepted.

The following four months blew by like a breeze. Andre's inability to follow Barry's rules led to his spending his senior year in Ohio with his stepdad, attending North Gallia, a small 1-A rural school where 4-H was more popular than basketball. Life in the country moved at a snail's pace, and so did the year.

Without incident, graduation came and went like a summer carnival, and so did Andre. In the end, the boy had gone to an astonishing fifteen different schools in a twelve-year period. Within a month of the cap and gown ceremony, he had purchased a Greyhound bus ticket back to California with money he had made at his first real job, cooking breakfast at the original Bob Evan's restaurant. To his surprise, his mother told him to get the ticket to Lancaster, California, because she had recently moved to the high desert in hopes of getting away from the crime in inner-city Los Angeles.

CHAPTER
20

For the second time in as many years, Andre was about to take the cross-country trip by bus. This journey would span 2 1/2 days across 2,234 miles traversing the continent all alone. However, this time, he was a lot better prepared.

Before leaving Gallipolis, Ohio, the boy went to visit his friend, Little Smitty, on Buck Ridge to grab a small bag of smoke for his journey. He bought a dime bag and rolled up ten joints. He then rolled them up tightly in a sandwich baggie and stuck the bag into a pair of white tube socks and rolled them up. He placed the socks in his book bag, along with another pair of socks, a pair of boxers, a pair of Levi's, his black Double-X hooded sweatshirt with a red "Just Do It!" Nike T-shirt. Also, within the bag, he packed a Speed Stick deodorant roll-on, toothbrush, tube of toothpaste, bottle of Polo cologne, and his trusty wave brush. The biggest difference between this trip and his last trip lay tucked away in the front compartment of the bag, his new Sony Walkman portable music machine and his small collection of hip-hop tapes.

Andre boarded his bus in the little college town of Athens, Ohio, at 7:00 p.m. His first stop would be at 12:00 a.m. in the city of Dayton, Ohio, and there he would find something to eat and smoke the first of his doobies.

Later that night, buzzed from the weed, Andre sat staring out into the black night with his head bobbing from side to side as he listened to EPMD's "You Gots to Chill" on his Walkman. Relaxed to the max and mesmerized by the star-filled sky, Andre sat, lost in his own world, until he was jarred back into reality when the Play button clicked up, signifying the end of the tape. The boy removed his earphones, allowing them to hang around his neck, slid his butt across to the open outer seat, stood up, and removed his backpack from the overhead compartment to grab another tape from it when he accidentally hit the passenger in the forward seat, knocking his book out of his hand in the process. Apologizing, he placed his bag on his seat and bent over to pick up the man's book which had settled under the adjacent aisle seat. As he dusted off the small book, he realized it was *Quotes for Success*, the same book his mom had given him a few years ago. Handing it back to the elderly gentleman, Andre observed, to no surprise, that the man's book was in the same run-down condition as the one he owned.

"I love this book. I have read it over fifty times," the boy exclaimed as he sat down and began rummaging through the bag's front pocket in search of another tape to listen to.

Settling down and gazing out the window again, the boy began to ponder if the teachings of the book and all the other esoteric knowledge he had consumed over the past six years had any real value, or perhaps it was just a bunch of occult mumbo jumbo.

He had not thought of the book in quite a while, but he still remembered it well. It taught that the key to having anything you want in life was to choose it. Speak it, accept it as if it has already happened, and be thankful for that which had been given, as if you had already received it.

"What's the purpose of having knowledge if you don't use it?" a little voice whispered in the back of his mind.

I might as well try it. What could it hurt? he thought.

"I choose wealth," the boy said aloud, a lot louder than he thought because of the music blasting through his headphones, causing numerous passengers to turn around and look back at him, including the man directly in front of him and the fidgety woman sitting across from him with a small toddler cuddled up next to her, fast asleep with her thumb in her mouth.

I am a multimillion-dollar lottery winner, the boy thought to himself. *I have an abundance of wealth and prosperity*, he added.

He promised himself that from this day forward, he would make these affirmations to himself morning, noon, and night until they came to pass.

A little before 4:30 a.m. found the teen delirious with an insatiable need to urinate. Probably the repercussions of the 7-Eleven Super Big Gulp forty-ounce around the world he mixed up and sucked down at the stop in Indianapolis. The boy's bladder was pounding like he had a second heart in his underwear. In a sleep-induced stupor, Andre staggered to the back of the moving vehicle, cracked the door to the restroom, and both his open mouth and nose were immediately violated by a powerful overwhelming stench of urine and feces that sent him staggering backward like an actual punch. Quickly he pushed the door closed with one hand and grabbed his eager-to-leak penis with his other. About three seconds passed, and the boy realized he had two choices: either man up and take the smell for a couple of minutes, or piss his pants. It was that simple.

Moments later, the boy returned to his seat fully relieved and none the worse except maybe some singed nose hairs, perhaps a little nasal membrane damage, and an unsettling notion that now he knew what shit sandwich tasted like. Viewing the bus's passengers, Andre guessed that he and the driver were the only two people awake on the Greyhound, and from the looks of the empty freeway, he guessed possibly in the entire state. Sliding his back up against the wall and stretching his legs out across the empty seat, the boy attempted to get as comfortable as his surroundings would allow. Nothing seemed to work; there were irritants in every possible position. The tweed fabric seat covers pulled at his hair each time he turned his head and clung to his socks whenever he moved his legs. When he leaned his head back against the window, the cold air from the air conditioner froze the back of his neck, sending chills down his spine. Resting his head beneath the window, the boy found only hard steel on the back of his head and an inflexible armrest lodged in the small of his back. Searching for a more comfortable position, Andre noticed that the three seats in the back beside the restroom were open. Sitting up straight, he contemplated. Surely that was enough space for him to lie down comfortably. He began to stand then realized why they were open. The smell back there must have been unbearable if there was no one willing to stretch out in the most spacious spot on the bus. Now standing, the boy reached into the overhead compartment, grabbed his bag, and removed his Grim Reaper hoodie, rolled it up like a pillow, placed it between his head and the window, then extended both legs freely into the aisle.

The bus's slow shimmy from side to side had the relaxing effect of a mother rocking her baby's crib, allowing young Andre to fall into a drowsy state. Before he knew it, he had fallen into a semi-conscious state. While he still lay focused, the boy made a conscious effort to project from a moving vehicle for the first time. He visualized a counterclockwise mini dust devil spinning around his legs, rapidly making its way up to his waist, and engulfing his midsection before swallowing up his shoulders and head. With all his concentration, Andre willed his astral double out of his physical body by sheer focus alone. As he felt liftoff and the beginning of separation, he heard something. At first, it was but a whisper and barely audible. With each body part separation, the sound repeated a little louder and more clearly. When his left astral arm was freed from his physical body, the sound came through distinctly; it was a cold, metallic laugh, one that set his hair on ends and sent chills down his spine. A primal fear struck deep, flushing tears of terror through the closed eyelids of the boy sleeping on the Greyhound. Like a butterfly from its cocoon, the boy's shoulders and neck dislodged from its physical counterpart coincided with a ghastly, horrific laugh that nearly caused the boy's bowels to break. Fear stricken and shaking, Andre leaped upward into an upright sitting position, yelping like a puppy that had been stepped on. The disturbance caused dozens of eyes to instantly open and overhead lights to be turned on in unison all throughout the bus.

CHAPTER
21

Eileen had always enjoyed a challenge, and that is precisely what District Attorney Harvin issued to his entire staff. She had hoped that life in the DA's office would be a lot more exciting, but with her second year of college at Antelope Valley only a week away, she found the only thing it provided her with was a ton of paperwork to go along with more homework than she could handle.

With everyone present, Skip Harvin offered a one-week Maui vacation, complete with airfare and hotel accommodations for two, to anyone with information leading to the identification of the alleged valley drug kingpin, Donnie Dollar. Up until now, he had merely been a myth, no more tangible than the Loch Ness Monster or the great Northwest Sasquatch. Supposedly, he was responsible for the outbreak of the crack infestation that was flooding the streets and quickly reaching epidemic proportions in the small desert town.

Time after time, confidential informants, busted low-level drug dealers, and dope fiends alike would spew the name Donnie Dollar like Christians at a holiness revival scream in the name of Jesus. Still, no evidence could be produced to link him to the drugs or prove his actual existence.

Eileen had not been this excited about her job since she had taken it almost a year ago today. Finally, she had an opportunity to do some investigating on her own and show everyone that she could actually make a difference in the department. It was perfect;

she already had a built-in cover as a student at the biggest party juco in the nation.

That night, in Eileen's room, Trevor joked with his sister about her crazy ass plan. She sat on the edge of her bed, clicking her shoeless heels together like a fidgety kid staring at her idol.

"Trevor, I was wondering...Since you have way more friends that like to party than I do, do you think I could hang out with you and your friends this weekend so I could do a little snooping? Well, so to speak." A cinnamon and apple blossoms incense burned on the top of her cherrywood bookcase, producing a deliciously appealing smell. On the shelf right below, her trusty old clock radio struggled to maintain its signal in a losing fight to static. He scratched his head, stuck his hands in his pockets, and began to pace back and forth.

"Naw, I don't think so," he said, frowning. "All of my friends like you as it is. If you go out with us, no one will pay any attention to me."

"Aw, come on," she said. "If you do, I will hook you up with Karen. I see how you look at her. You want her bad and you know it!" After minutes of contemplating and continually wearing a path in her carpet, the boy finally replied, "Okay, okay, but only if you bring both Karen and Patty to the Quartz Hill's desert party this weekend. You do that, and we have a deal," as he walked out of her room with a sheepish smile on his face.

Andre stepped off the bus into what seemed like an oven. The heat was nearly unbearable. The sweltering 103-degree temperature drew an instant sweat bead on the boy's brow. Looking around for his mother, he realized he was in a ghost town, for not a being walked the sole-melting streets. The only signs of movement were the heat waves bouncing off the scorched concrete in the distance. The hum of industrial-strength air conditioners from the surrounding buildings provided the only proof of some semblance of civilization.

Patiently, Andre sat perched on his suitcase. Partially shaded by the bus stop sign, he awaited his ride and rescue from the blazing heat. Once again, he thought that she had forgotten him and left him to fend for himself. Smearing the streaking pearls of perspiration from his forehead with his dirty fingers, the boy's face began to sour as he contemplated how easily she had sent him away for the past two years without as much as an occasional call except for his birthday and major holidays when she was obligated to perform her motherly duties. Irritated and saddened, Andre tried not to care if he was or was not an important part of her preoccupied life.

As quiet as a cat, a sky blue Buick Bonneville inched up to the curb behind the boy lost deep in his thoughts. The screeching of the opening passenger's door, the whoosh of refrigerated air, and the smooth crooning of Marvin Gay's "Let's Get It On" could not do what one small whiff of his mother's L'air Du Temps did in mere seconds, bringing him back from his inner depths like ammonia reviving a knocked-out fighter. Instantly at Virginia's appearance and her soft caressing touch of his cheek with her loving hand, all animosity toward her was lost. Although no longer a child, he longed for his mother to pick him up and hold him tightly, erasing all the hurt and heartache with her never-failing mother's love.

Standing directly behind her loomed the black Doc Savage. Even without looking directly at him, Andre could tell by his reflection in the car's window that he was a massive man strapped with forearms that popped with veins and biceps that rippled from hours of tedious workouts. His black hair glistened in the sunlight with activator-triggering mountains of rolling curls ending in lamb chop sideburns. His broad face hid behind a pair of gold aviator sunglasses with mirror lenses, while his cool, gentle smile made him seem impervious to the blistering heat. His mother lifted the boy's chin up then turned and pointed to the man to her rear and identified him as Jessie, her fiancé. Immediately he realized that once again he would be playing second fiddle for the affection he felt she had owed him.

The car's air-conditioning was a beast. It subtracted the external three-digit temperature to sixty-five degrees within the time it took to close the door. Vanilla aroma twirled throughout the inner cabin and clung to its upholstery almost to the point of being breathtaking, and not in the good way. It was a quick ride from the bus station on Lancaster Boulevard to their apartment located in a cul-de-sac on Raysack Avenue. As they pulled into the horseshoe-shaped driveway, Andre noticed a liquor store just across the street with a huge three-feet-by-three-feet poster in their window with a block-shaped L, signifying the California Lottery was sold there. The boy smiled and took it as if it were a personal sign from God.

Exiting the vehicle, the boy realized that all the apartment buildings were exactly the same, with exception to their color. Each building housed a quad-plex of apartments. The door was in the center leading into a hallway with two doors flanking stairs at the bottom and two doors at the top. Grabbing his bags from the trunk, he noticed two girls and a guy directly across the extremely wide street watching his every move. His mother gave him the keys and pointed to the bottom apartment on the right, telling him that she would be in, in a couple of minutes. Andre dropped his suitcases off in the living room and stood amazed as the entire room teemed with life. Plant life flourished everywhere. Foliage blossomed into leaves of emerald, creating a miniature rain forest in the sitting room. The boy walked back out on the building's porch, sat down on the steps just in time to see his mother thanking and kissing Jesse goodbye. Instead of happiness for his mother's newfound love, his blood boiled and his heart raged with jealousy. Even with his brother and sisters out of the way, he would still be forced to play second fiddle and accept what he thought was secondhand, leftover love to which he had become accustomed. As she passed Andre, she asked him if he was hungry because she was going to make some lunch.

Looking over the neighborhood, he thought this place did not look too bad. He had definitely lived in worse places. The area was very clean with sporadic palm trees popping up between some build-ings. The entire cul-de-sac was lined with huge receptacles just inches from the curb. The majority were black. However, there were blue ones and green ones mixed in as well. He figured that it must have been trash day, but he was not sure what the color distinctions indi-cated. The air even smelled clean on the high desert. There was quite a difference in the air quality between here and Los Angeles. As he was scanning the block, he realized that his neighbors from across the way were now heading in his direction.

Both girls were very attractive. The dude was nice but seemed a little off-kilter or something. The cute brown-skinned girl said her name was Dina and Ted was her brother. She said they lived right across the street in Building 4202 with their mother and sister, Stephanie.

The other girl was her best friend, Torri. She was light skinned with dazzling green eyes. Her hair was pulled back into one long black ponytail. Her body had curves on top of curves, and her clothes barely covered them. She was the definition of an exotic beauty. Torri said that her mom was Piute Indian and her father was black. The girl's aggressive nature made Andre somewhat uncomfortable. She stood so close to him when she spoke that he could feel her breath on his cheek. He was not sure, but he thought that he had also felt her cone-shaped breasts against his arm a couple of times. She told him he should come see her some time at the Pink Penguin, a local strip club. He smiled at the invite but did not reply. He had never been to one and was unsure if he wanted to be what Scooby had called a trick. Just as quickly as they had come and introduced themselves, they were leaving and walking back across the street when suddenly Ted turned around and shouted, "We are going to a desert party tonight out in Quartz Hill. If you want to roll with us, there's plenty of room." Andre said okay, he would let them know later, then he took one final look at his new neighborhood and retreated into the cool apartment to see what his mom was making for lunch.

Before eating, he explored the apartment a little more thoroughly. He liked the setup; his room was close to the front door, while his mother's room was at the far end of the hallway, in case he ever had to sneak in or better yet sneak someone out, he thought to himself and smiled. After washing his hands, he stepped into what would be his room. The furniture looked like it was passed down from an episode of the *Brady Bunch*. It was a light pine with scratches and scuffs from previous owners that could be seen upon closer examination but hardly noticeable from a distance. A huge throw rug held down the middle of the floor; it rang out with black pride whether intended or not. The rug's outer rings were black, and inside it were spheres of red surrounding its green center. The room's walls were eggshell like the rest of the dwelling but somewhat stained not in the paint's color, more in its aura. Something about the room made him feel kind of sick to his stomach.

Eileen was a ghost, pale and cold. She sat on the hood of her Nissan Pulsar NX, uncomfortable with the social gathering, while her brother and friends raged out of control. Pelts of dust attacked her bare ankles. The crackling bonfire spat tiny sparkles of flame in every direction, while the rustling wind propelled the sulfur-flavored fragments on high with tendrils of white smoke. In the distance, Karen and Patty danced their way toward their friend as they dodged a renegade tumbleweed scampering across the wasteland in search of anything to smash into.

"Girl, my toes are jacked walking around in this dirt field. If I was thinking, I would have worn shoes," Karen said, as she leaned against her friend's car and attempted to refasten the heel strap on her brown Birkenstocks.

"Yeah, they are. They look like little burnt pigs in a blanket." Eileen laughed.

"Well, yours would, too, if you got your butt off of your car and started mingling. Besides, aren't you supposed to be working under-cover?" Karen whispered as she struggled to remove the cap from her peach Bartels and James wine cooler.

"Yeah, you're right. Let's go and see if we can find out who has sum crack," Eileen said with an uneasy smile as she slid her butt off the warm car's hood.

In the moment it took to reach the dusty ground, the girl began to question everything about her being at the party. Were her black skintight biker shorts and low-cut V-necked tie-dyed T-shirt too sexy and revealing? Her friends implored her to show more cleavage. After all, they always said her bosom was her best feature. If her mom had seen her before she left the house, she would have told her she looked like a slut or a common streetwalker. Was she really cut out to be a private investigator? Could she release her social anxiety and pretend to fit in, or was the huge neon question mark flashing on her forehead noticeable to any and everyone who glanced upon her? Above all, she wondered would she ever be able to do away with the enormous wall surrounding her, blocking out the opposite sex like a solar eclipse blocks out the sun. Now, more than ever, she wished she had been blessed with social dexterity like her little sister, Michelle.

"Come on, girl, loosen up. Here, bitch, drink one of these berry Seagram's coolers. It will relax you," Patty said, removing the top and reaching her arm in her direction.

Hours and several coolers later found Eileen having a relatively good time in comparison to past parties, yet her insecurities still screamed violently inside her head. Together in her subgroup, the young woman danced with her friends and a couple of guys that Patty had met and introduced to them.

Gust of wind blew in from the west, bringing ominous veils of gray upon the darkened sky. The bonfire flames flickered rhythmically as they danced with the zigzagging wind.

"Looks like it's gonna storm!" one of the boys said as he moved in closer, attempting to make Eileen his dance partner instead of just dancing randomly. Stepping back and creating a barrier between the boy and herself, Eileen questioned arbitrarily, "Has anyone seen Trevor?" After a moment and no response, the girl raised her voice and asked again, "I said, has anyone seen my brother?" This time one girl shrugged and the other said, "Not in quite some time."

Instantly the girl's motherly instincts kicked in, triggering a look of concern on her face. Without another word, she left her friends in search of her younger sibling.

"Hey, don't trip, he's probably somewhere making out with one of his little girlfriends," Karen yelled from the distance. Still she continued on her quest to find her brother. Sometime later after nearly covering the entire parameter of the desert party, she recognized what could only be her brother's slim silhouette in the vague moonlit distance sitting with his back against a lonely two-branch Joshua tree.

A baby jackrabbit scampered across her path as the sky rumbled like a huge empty stomach. The arid breeze carried a flatulent-odored passenger.

"Trevor...Trevor, what's wrong? What are you doing over here all by yourself?" Eileen asked as she held out her hand and looked up toward the sky, realizing that a fat raindrop had just crashed into her forehead and was now running down her cheek.

"Are you okay?" she asked as she bent over and kneeled down beside her brother.

"I was so worried about you. Please tell me. You can talk to me." The boy looked up with tears in his eyes and met his sister's sincere gaze with an empty stare.

"I don't...can't...not good at," he stuttered, throwing both hands up and covering his reddened face. She put one hand on his knee and attempted to comfort his obvious pain.

"I don't know how. I mean, I can't..." His voice faded out like lights in a theater.

"I'm not good at keeping them."

"Keeping what?"

"Girls!" he replied.

"They always like me at first, but...they, they always get bored with me or something and quit me," the boy said laboring to push the words from his mouth.

"I...I'm tired of this. It...it hurts so bad every time," he said as he snapped his neck back, whipping his deep brown hair from his eyes.

"Sometimes I wish I...I wish I was dea—" But before he could finish his sentence, his sister placed one hand over his mouth, the other around his neck, pulled him close, hugged him tightly, and together the two began to sob.

On this Saturday evening, Virginia Brown sat across the couch from her number two son, for the first time in two plus years, and still their conversation seemed sterile and cold. Most of their dialogue flowed in what was a predictable circle to Andre. She would ask her son what he planned to do now that he was out of school. If she did not like his answer, she would pat him on the leg, smile, and say, "No, really, what do you plan on doing now that you are an adult?" Andre knew what she wanted to hear, but he tried his best to keep a straight face and continue the ruse by acting oblivious to what she was wanting to hear.

"If you are going to live here, under my roof, you must go to college." Virginia stopped beating around the bush and questioned his desires, his plans, and ultimately, goals for the future. Tired of being badgered, he said, "I am going to win the lottery."

"No, really, what are you going to do?" his mother asked.

"I told you, Ma, I am going to win the lottery! You told me anything the mind can conceive, it can achieve. I believe if I choose to be a multimillion-dollar winner, I will be."

"I'm not sure it works like that, honey," she said, smiling. "Okay, I tell you what...If you hit the lottery, you can do whatever you want to do, but until then, you are going to find a job and get your behind enrolled in school! It's free, so there is no reason for you not to go. Besides, it's a great way for you to start meeting people." At least that was one thing the two could agree upon.

Andre's room was directly across from the dining room right beside the bathroom, and at the end of the hall stood his mother's bedroom. The boy rearranged all the furniture in the room so that the head of his bed could be facing north. That night he got down on his knees and said a prayer, asking God to look over his family and to bless this room because it made him feel slightly sick to his stomach every time he entered it.

On the threshold of sleep, Andre drifted aimlessly, awake enough to know that he had not fallen completely asleep, yet sleepy enough to realize that he was close to losing any chance of regaining wakefulness.

Millions of tiny needles pierced his body repeatedly all over but never in the same place twice. Small dust devils began to whip around his toes, slowly migrating toward his heels. Widening its spin effortlessly, they churned around his lower calves, whisking over the back of his legs and above his upper thighs.

As the vibrations picked up their pace, Andre tried to slow down his breathing and focus on a controlled projection. He would try to go visit his sexy neighbor from across the street, Dina, and her comical brother Ted. Maybe she was still awake and he could tell her about what he saw and ask if it was accurate. No, that might be weird, he thought, especially for someone he had just met. She might think that he was some kind of Peeping Tom or something.

His thoughts were everywhere; one moment, he planned to ask Oliver for Friday's winning lotto numbers, then it was gone, a memory lost. As many would be as his hyper senses engaged eight separate thoughts simultaneously, the vibrations were agitating around his midsection, closing in on his shoulders and neck quickly. The whooshing air sucked all sound from the room as it swallowed his head.

With absolute attention, Andre thought about a point directly above his head, then visualized it, shrinking to the size of a pinhead where he simply snatched it from the air and placed it just above the bridge of his nose right above his eyes parallel to his pineal gland. Like a wedge, the boy slid his imaginary little finger down into the corner of the orifice and slowly pushed it open until he could see through the other side. The normally boring beige walls were now bathed in a milky undercoat of vibrant pink, yellow, and green pastels, breathing new life into the otherwise listless room.

First, he slid his entire hand through the tiny hole all the way up to his shoulder as if he was putting on a T-shirt. He contorted and wedged his wispy forehead through, the tiny opening already occupied by his left arm and thorax. The tiny space pushed his face back ninety degrees, with a sticky friction pushing and pulling his plastic face until it finally burst free of the hole, spinning his neck, right shoulder, and the rest of his body through like a whirling derby.

The room sparkled with little points of light blinking through pasty watercolors. Unseen waves crashed against the walls with rhythmic fluency. Slowly he swirled counterclockwise in the room like a satellite in zero gravity. Attempting to regain control of his blurry site, the nerves up the back of his neck jittered like ant feet on a paper plate. Blinded by wild instinct, the boy was ready to leap back into his body at the first sign of trouble. Again, he sensed someone or something very close to him. He could hear it, smell it, feel its presence, tickling the tiny hairs at the nape of his neck like hot breath creeping purposefully upward, sending instant goose bumps across his shadowy fleshless form. The spine-chilling sensation was accompanied by what sounded like a haunting series of low guttural gulps of air. Still struggling to adjust his sight, the panic-filled young man fought to control his growing fear. Slowly the shimmery, soft-colored world began to rematerialize as his stereoscopic view came back into focus. Although he could see no threat, his other senses still stood on high alert. Slightly woozy from the gradual rotation, the boy attempted to stabilize himself and concentrate on journeying across the cul-de-sac to his new neighbor's home. When the rotary motion finally stopped, he found himself with both face and toes pointing toward the ceiling. Once more the balmy, wretched breeze made its presence known, accompanied by a recurring snort and a barely audible whistle.

Terrified and on the verge of scrubbing his partly successful projection, he decided to turn and view the astral entity which threatened his etheric form before diving back into his physical body. With but a thought, his eyes now peered down from the stucco ceiling and trained with trepidation on what beast he would find behind him. To his surprise, the beast was no beast at all, merely his partially covered sprawled-out form lying in his bed with his mouth wide open, snoring to the high heavens.

The next morning Andre awoke, cleaned himself up, got dressed, and made his way downtown in hopes of finding a job to satisfy his overly concerned mother. Six hours and five applications later, Andre decided to grab some lunch at the home of the creepy clown who bared the golden arches. Although he had never intended to apply at any fast-food restaurants, a sign and a cute Mexican girl working the counter changed his pliable mind. The girl said, "May I take your order please?" Andre noticed a sign on the front of the counter asking in big bold letters, WOULD YOU LIKE TO BE A CREW MEMBER ON OUR TEAM? He said an emphatic yes to both.

Within one week of being in Lancaster, he had placed his mom's mind at ease by both finding a job and attending open registration at the AVC registrar for the fall enrollment.

The insistent heat of the high desert never wavered as August turned to September; if anything, it doubled down, sending temperatures soaring into low triple digits the first two weeks of its calendar. Still new to the area, the boy thought that this weather was more suitable for the beginning of beach season, rather than the first day of school.

It did not take the young freshman long to realize that eight o'clock classes were for the birds. Fortunately, his first and last 8:00 a.m. class was one that he really loved, basketball 101, which was taught by John Murphy, the head coach at the college.

Andre held his breath as he changed his clothes for class. Pee-splashed urinals battled the reeking blend of stiff sweat socks and deodorant-less armpits for funk supremacy in the aging locker room. Unable to withstand the powerful stench any longer, Andre found himself nearly running to the door to escape the nose-clearing fumes.

Like a lobster diver submerged until his lungs burned on the verge of exploding, the boy burst through the door to the gym, fell to his knees, threw his hands up in the air, and inhaled as much fresh air as his young lungs could handle. The flat smack of multiple basketballs bouncing off the hardwood floor was only overshadowed by the echo of screeching tennis shoes cutting left and right across the freshly waxed court.

At the end of the class, Coach Murphy called Andre and two other boys over to the bleachers where he sat and asked them if they would like to try out for the men's basketball team. He informed them that practice was held at four o'clock sharp, Monday through Friday.

Leo Braun stood six feet five. His curly blond hair rolled in waves upon the youth's wide brow. Liquid blue eyes trained on each word as it left the mouth of the Antelope Valley coach. Without a second thought, the kid from Lone Pine, California, turned down his offer. He said that his studies and pursuit of an acting career would not allow him time for more than one hour a day of hoops. He confessed that he was flattered for the consideration but respectfully declined the offer and scampered off toward the stinky locker room.

Andre and the other boy eagerly jumped at the offer.

Rufus "Corn" Walker was a 6-foot, 180-pound brown-skinned white boy trapped in the body of a brother. His short black hair was beady and curled tightly to his scalp. His eyebrows were thin and neat as if waxed weekly, accenting two shifty dark marbles that seemed to watch everything at once. His lips were thick and dry, housing yellow-stained food-filled choppers, which produced a smell that greeted the listener before his words did. Corn was an Army brat who had migrated from Anchorage, Alaska, by way of Louisville, Kentucky. Once Andre learned that he was from the Ville, they bonded and instantly began to build a tight friendship.

The two learned that they had lived mere blocks away from each other when he lived with his sister on Forty-First and Duncan.

Corn lived on Thirty-Ninth and Duncan with his parents while his dad was stationed at Fort Knox. In fact, Corn had attended PRP where he was an all-county shooting guard when Andre was supposed to have attended school there as well. It turned out that the two boys had numerous things in common as well as mutual friends from the old neighborhood.

After a quick change, the two boys exited the horrible-smelling locker room where Andre asked Corn, "What do you think the odds are of us living in the same neighborhood and never meeting until we moved 2,700 miles across the country?"

"Man, it really is a small world," Corn replied. The new friends laughed, exchanged numbers, and rushed off in different directions, hoping not to be late on the first day for their nine o'clock classes.

Andre's hasty exit from Marauder's Pavilion had been delayed by an unexpected collision. With his head down and his undivided attention on the campus map attempting to locate Jansen Hall, the young man smashed headfirst into a young woman attempting to enter the pavilion as he was exiting.

Eileen crumbled backward with her books going one way and bag carrying her workout gear going the other. Barely avoiding a nasty spill off the two-step entryway onto the hard concrete below, the girl shuffled her feet and gracefully flung both arms back behind her falling frame just in time to soften her landing.

"What are you doing, jerk! Why don't you watch where you're going?" the girl screamed from a sitting position where she examined her hands for bruises.

"I...I'm sorry. I didn't see you coming," the boy replied as he rushed over to pick up her suede gray bag with all of its contents strewn across the sidewalk. Recklessly, without thought, Andre began shoving the girl's things back into the bag.

"Damn, I just got my nails done yesterday," the girl whimpered. "Thanks a lot, asshole. Now, they look like crap!"

She gently rubbed her hands together and then lifted herself from the pavement. Bending over to pick up her notebook, she looked at the boy for the first time. She paused, and for a second, she thought she knew him. There was something so eerily familiar about him that she broke out in goose bumps.

Bowing to grab the last of the girl's garments, Andre glanced up at the belligerent beauty. Like a statue, he momentarily froze with the article of clothing in his clutching hands.

"What are you planning on doing, taking that home and trying it on or something?"

"Trying what on?" the boy questioned as he looked down and realized he was holding a green spandex leotard.

"No…no, not at all. It's not my color," the boy said sheepishly as his light brown skin tone faded to crimson.

"Do I know you…I mean, have we met?" the boy asked with a look of bewilderment on his face.

"No, I don't think so, but there is something strangely familiar about you. But one thing I do know is that you should pay closer attention to where you are going before you hurt someone," the girl said, as she snatched her belongings from the boy's hands and sashayed off into the building.

Later that day, Andre arrived fifteen minutes before basketball practice to find that Corn was already there shooting around in the gym with some other guys who were trying out for the team. A couple of the kids were from Denver, Colorado, while the other two were from Los Angeles. One of the young men from LA was a little bit older than the other boys. His name was Donnie. The entire time he was on the court he never shut up. All he did was brag and talk shit. He claimed that he was going to be the best ballplayer produced in the history of Antelope Valley. After watching him play, Andre acknowledged to Corn that Donnie was a talented ballplayer, but he recognized right away that he was a selfish hot dog who would always put his personal achievements over the interest of the team.

Not to be outdone, Corn challenged Donnie word for word with gamesmanship of his own. After several verbal altercations and a couple of near skirmishes through the course of the practice, it became clear to all who witnessed that the two young men had a mutual disdain for each other.

At the end of the practice, Coach Murphy called all the boys over to the center of the court and made it clear that he would not tolerate any of this ghetto trash talk foolishness. He also made it clear that any physical altercations would lead to immediate dismissal from the team.

That evening Andre basked in the excitement of his first day of college. The campus was incredible, smooth postmodern architecture surrounded by colorful, blossoming flowers and plush green grass sprouting everywhere, the complete opposite of the rest of the thirsty, colorless desert town. He actually thought that he might enjoy studying the classes he had selected. His professors seemed somewhat interesting in their first-day lectures, especially his black history class with Dr. Ron Mc Dowel, who told the class to call him Dr. Mac. On top of all this, the head basketball coach had seen him as being talented enough to try out for the college's team. Then there was the girl. She was as feisty as she was gorgeous. He was sure he had seen her somewhere before, and the way she looked at him, he was positive that she had felt the same way; in fact, she, herself, said there was something familiar about him. If only he had thought to ask her name resonated in his mind to the point that he became haunted by the question. Finally, he concluded that the campus was not that large and he was bound to see her again sooner or later.

CHAPTER
22

Donald Pickens AKA Donnie Dollar was born in East Saint Louis but was relocated to the beautifully manicured lawns, which accompanied the ugly, mean streets of Lynwood, California, by his sixth birthday with his mother and two brothers.

This cross-country relocation was mired in struggle from day one. The three boys were constantly harassed and bullied by the neighborhood gang the Cross Atlantic Bloods. No guardian angel would come down from the heavens to protect them, just as none had in the ghettos of Saint Louis.

Donnie was an intense, fiery, hot-tempered boy who refused to be disrespected; even after coming home on numerous occasions with black eyes and bloody lips, he promised himself that he would never bow down, or be intimidated by anyone regardless of what set they claimed.

Bullies learned quick as did most of the older established gangsters that this ill-tempered adolescent would be a force to be reckoned with. The word on the street was that young Donnie was Loony Tunes, willing to ride on anyone without a second thought and crazy enough to challenge any G indiscriminately without fear of consequences. In a dare from his younger brother Thomas, Donnie stole his mother's .22-caliber Ruger from her underwear drawer and ended up shooting and killing Antione Miller, a seventeen-year-old boy from the hood who kept beating up and robbing his older brother, Robert, on his way home from school.

In Lynwood, California, by the age of eighteen, most residents spoke of Donald Pickens with either reverence or fear. He lived for the now, with no expectations or false hopes of what tomorrow might bring. For those he considered his friends, he would share all his ill-begotten gains whether they participated in his criminal exploits or not. He regularly displayed selfless acts in his community for homeless derelicts and the well-to-do middle class alike. His personality was both magnetic and repugnant, and those whom he labeled foes had the life expectancy of a common housefly, but being the awkward spider he was, he often clumsily snipped his own webs before the trap was completely woven, allowing some enemies the opportunity to flee into obscurity.

Just one day after his eighteenth birthday, Donnie was picked up by two LAPD detectives regarding the homicide of East Coast Crip Michael "Crayon" Reese. Although no charges were filed and no physical evidence could be brought forth linking him to the murder, Detective George Diaz assured the boy that they knew in fact that he was a party to the homicide. His partner Detective William Brumbly told the boy that a personal informant from his set was telling it all, who, what, when, and where. Rest assured, he said, they would be keeping close tabs on him and building a case against him for the future when he screwed up again.

"And of course, you will screw up again. You aren't that smart, Pickens," Officer Brumbly said, just before opening the door to the stale, breezeless interrogation room to release him.

The early morning combination of dew and fog refreshed and revived the weary murder suspect. Four pay phones greeted the newly released inmates as they exited the cavernous dungeon. In his lifetime, this was probably young Donnie's first true experience with freedom. Until now after his short fourteen-hour stay at the vaunted LA County jail, freedom was just a word that held little truth on the inner-city streets. Because the way he saw things everyone he knew was a slave or prisoner to something. Be it their drug habit, religious beliefs, political affiliation, job or career, gangbanging preference, Blood, Crip, La Famila, Triad, or Skinhead, they were all captive to something. Some sucker-ass brothers he knew were even slaves to love, willing to do anything, and occasionally anyone they feared coming between them and their prize possession.

His uncle Johnny sat in a semiconscious state with his head on tilt, ready to bob at any second. The yellow foam under the cracking hard leather seats caught lingering slobbers from the center of his brown lips. The sunny yellow Dodge Dart crowded the curb and ignored the parking meter, kissing its right front quarter fender. Waiting to pick up his sister Edna's middle boy from the lockup found Johnny on this side of the equation for the first time. Usually it had been him wandering out in the wee hours of the morn, desperately hoping for a ride.

Donnie jumped in the car and immediately turned his nose up and frowned. His car reeked of smoked cigarettes and BO. Looking down, he noticed the ashtray was full of half-smoked butts with ashes running over the side, spilling onto the floor. Donnie had always looked up to his uncle, who returned from Vietnam a decorated war hero. Over the past three years, he seemed to be slowly deteriorating both physically and mentally. He served as an Army Ranger force recon. He told stories to Donnie as a kid that both inspired pride and terror of his uncle. He told young Donnie how the US government would send his battalion in to buy tons of heroin from Vietcong villages and then order them to return the same night and kill everyone, including women and children, leaving the tribe leader's heads on a stick as a warning to neighboring villages.

He also made it clear to the youth that, that same heroin was being dispersed into inner cities across the country in attempt to destroy the urban communities' family base. Time after time, he would tell his nephew that the military was no place for a black man, but this was not one of them.

"Donnie, I'ma get right to the point! You're fucking up, son, and me and yo mama are worried that at the rate you're going, you ain't gonna make it to see twenty-one. Boy, don't you know if something happened to you, it would break ya mama's heart?" the boy's uncle said as he turned the key in the ignition and put the car in gear. Looking over at his favorite nephew, he said, "I know, I told you many times that Uncle Sam ain't no uncle of yours and the military was no place for a black man, but I feel that it might be the only way to save yo life. Well, at least get you on the right track. Besides, there ain't no wars going on, and it will teach you some discipline, let you see the world and make a man of you."

"I am a man!" the boy said as he rolled down his window and allowed his hand to flow with the wave in the cool breeze.

"Look, boy, I ain't gonna lecture you on what's right and wrong, 'cause God knows I've done more than my share of wrong. I just want you to realize that there is a lot more to this world than these fucked-up Compton streets. These streets are a trap, son, and these devil-ass crackers don't want you to escape 'em. All I ask is that you consider talkin' to a recruiter because you got more God-given leadership skills than any man I've ever known. Don't waste it, boy!" he said, as he reached under his seat, pulled a small bottle of Night Train out, removed the cap, turned it up, took a big swig, then placed it back, lit a cigarette, and never said another word until he pulled in front of the house to drop him off.

"Tell ya mama I'll call her later today."

Looking back, Donnie did not know why he did it. Whether it was the heartfelt words given by his uncle, the tireless looking over his shoulder, or maybe it was the smug look on Detective Brumbly's face when he guaranteed he would be back. The cop said he wasn't that smart. Perhaps it was just the instinctive feeling that the hangman's noose was slowly tightening around his neck.

Several days later on a Thursday morning, the brightest smog-free day he had remembered in Los Angeles in quite some time, a desperate, misguided thug marched recklessly into the Army recruiting office on Long Beach Boulevard and Sanborn Avenue with hopes of changing his life. Within one hour of speaking with Staff Sergeant Williams, Donnie had signed the dotted line, promising four years of his life; within twenty-four hours, he was pledging his allegiance to Uncle Sam with fifteen strangers he had never seen before, and within seven days of the previous Thursday, he was on a bus destined for Fort Leonard Wood, Missouri, where he would undergo boot camp.

According to his uncle, it was the most challenging test of endurance he had experienced in his young life. He claimed that boot camp was far tougher than the Nam physically, but not mentally. He said the sergeant's main job was to try to break him and expose his every weakness, test his guile, measure his desire, and extract every drip of fortitude from his poor soul for the duration of the camp. All in the name of building a better soldier, but in reality, that was bullshit, he said. Their true goal was to break you down to the very last compound, then rebuild you in a mode that they could reprogram and control mind, body, and soul.

From the first morning of basic training, it was clear that whatever Johnny had seen in his nephew was very apparent to his platoon sergeant, Mavis Hartsgrove, as well. Hartsgrove watched in disbelief as E2 Pickens destroyed the standing record for the eight-mile morning run by three and a half minutes with a sixty-seven-pound pack and his twenty-seven-pound weapon. Any physical challenge assigned by the sergeant, Pickens took it personal and refused to be outshined by any of his peers.

Perhaps it was the toughest thing Johnny had ever done, but for Donnie, it was a breeze, so much so that by the last week of boot camp, each of his sergeants and commanding officers urged him to "get the go!"

"Get the tab, son" became the greeting he received from every officer he passed in the course of a day. Donnie was not sure that he wanted to be an Army Ranger up until this point; he was just going through the motions. He figured he would do his four years, take advantage of the GI Bill, get a loan, and be back on the streets, and it would be business as usual. However, this time he would model his business after the corporate world. As CFO, he would be the orchestrator, touch nothing, simply find a few willing soldiers and a couple of capable sales managers with established teams, and he could watch his paper grow from a distance.

He had heard horror stories about the sixty-one days of hell. Actually, the first three days were hell, the assessment phase; the rest was just a really bad nightmare. Anyway, that's what Staff Sergeant Miller had called it.

"It was worth it, the most gratifying thing I ever accomplished," he would tell him every day. Lieutenant Colonel Teflon Tolliver told him that he had it in him, and it was his duty to "live up to the honor and prestige of the Ranger Corps. Son, you can be a part of the top 1 percent in God's military, but you have got to want it as much as you want to breathe!"

The night before graduation at lights out, his bunkie, Tyler Pagliaci, from Boise, Idaho, asked him what drove him to be the best.

"I don't know what drives me to work so hard, but I can tell you this. On the streets if someone pushes you, you have to push back. I'm used to pushing back harder than anyone else. I see every order given to me by my COs as them pushing me, and that motivates me, knowing that no matter how hard they push they can't beat me, not even at their own game," he said.

The next day Donnie graduated at the top of his platoon with honors. He had ten days' leave, so he caught a jump on a C-4 Galaxy back to Los Angeles, spent the Fourth of July holiday weekend with his family where he told his mother and Uncle Johnny that he would be leaving on the tenth of the month for Ranger training at Fort Bennings, Georgia. His uncle grimaced like he had been hit with an unexpected gut punch.

"Are you sure about that?" his father figure questioned.

"As sure as I know I'm gonna have the itis after I finish eatin' this big plate of ribs, greens, and macaroni and cheese," he laughed.

"Not to discourage you, young buck, but you know that only one in every three will complete the training, don't you?" Johnny asked.

"Yes, I know, but that's okay, because I intend on being the one of the three," Donnie said assuredly.

"I know, that's right, nephew. You can do anything you want. I sho 'nuff got confidence in ya, boy," the man said as he grabbed his sister, picked her up, and kissed her on the cheek. Both were wearing pride-filled smiles as wide as all outside.

On July 10, PFC First Class Pickens reported for duty at Ranger Training Brigade, Fort Bennings. Master Sergeant Robinson Ramirez stood no taller than five feet eight and a quarter inch in his boots, but he carried himself like a giant. His stride appeared elongated, for a man of his height, and even his stance seemed to widen, bringing his diminutive size even closer to the spotless floor. Ramirez's exaggerated arm motions made it look like he was about to take off running at any second when he walked. His hands were small sporting digits the length of Vienna sausages. Regardless of all that, Donnie realized that even a pocket-size Ranger was a razor-sharp weapon capable of doing a considerable amount of damage in a short period of time. The sergeant checked him in, directed him to his housing, suggested that he get unpacked, then locate the mess hall, and then get some shut-eye because "revelry is early, and you have a long day ahead of you, Private."

The blare of the revelry horn from the factory-grade speakers rang flat and muffled, adding insult to the agony. Could it really be four forty-five already, he thought, as he pulled his pillow from under his head and placed it over his face, just as the lights came on and Staff Sergeant Dryer reminded the dorm that they were not at the Holiday Inn and they had five minutes to make their racks and be ready for chow.

Within eight minutes, he and forty-nine other men were walking into a spacious mess hall with over three hundred men already sitting down, eating. There was something eerily familiar about this picture, he thought, the click-clack of forks on plastic trays. There were hundreds of isolated conversations blending into goulash. Everyone wearing the same stressed face, everyone wearing the same bad-fitting uniforms probably mass-produced for pennies on the dollar. He was sure he had been here before. The smell of food triggered his saliva glands and made his mouth water, reminiscent to the way his mother's homemade biscuits had when he was young. That thought quickly eroded as he glanced down at the food on his tray. There were two burned shriveled-up links compressed in a greasy cellophane foreskin, a small cup-size bowl of what appeared to be dry, lumpy oatmeal with possible rat droppings on it, and in the corner straddled between two sections resting on white toast partially falling off the tray were powdered scrambled eggs with so much saltpeter in them that they were nearly florescent. Donnie guessed that this meal wouldn't satisfy the middle school version of him. Hearing the idle grumbles from the desperate, anxious men suddenly reminded him of where he had known this place. The cutlery was steel, not plastic, and the participation was by choice, not forced; however, everything else about this place reeked of LA County jail all over again.

After a quick breakfast, day one of the assessment phase was underway. There were no ceremonial procedures or elaborate build-ups, just a few simple words from the base commander, Colonel Taylor.

"Men, those of you who complete these 8 1/2 weeks of training will ensure that this country's fighting force will remain number one in the world. This is, with no doubt, the hardest thing you will ever do in your life. Be prepared to go to hell and back. Compared to this, combat will seem like a walk in the park on a Sunday afternoon. We produce the best of the best, the cream of the crop, the most elite fighting force, and most effective leaders on God's green earth. Godspeed and good luck," he said, then he saluted the group of 340 men and proceeded down the walkway toward his office.

Within seconds of Colonel Taylor's departure, Staff Sergeant Dryer stepped up and ordered the men into two lines. He instructed the soldiers that from now on the man across from you is your Ranger buddy and you were responsible for his well-being. He told them that if your battle buddy fails, you fail. He then informed them of the Ranger's secret pledge

"A Ranger never leaves a Ranger behind. Remember that, live by that, and die by that," he said followed by, "After me, now let's make double time."

Donnie's Ranger buddy was Private First Class Alfonso Hildebrandt from Austin, Texas. Alfonso was a hulk of a man. He stood 6 feet 7 and weighed in at close to 315 pounds of what looked like solid muscle. His stabbing gray eyes sat propped up high by pow-erful cheekbones. His nose twisted and turned as if it were the victim of multiple bad breaks. His chin was strong and valiant, sporting a deep clef in its center. At first glance, he appeared to be wearing shoulder pads under his uniform. Amazingly, his gigantic frame did not slow him down a bit, not that he was fleet-footed, but he had no trouble keeping pace with men half his size.

After a 5-minute run, the platoon stopped at a sandy beach area, where the Ranger buddies were matched up in aggressive hand-to-hand combat, pit fighting style. Each match lasted 10 minutes, followed by the combatants being forced to carry their competitor around the pit in a symbol of brotherhood. This was followed by a 100-yard bear crawl in cold mud under 2-foot-high strands of barbed wire. After completed, the whole procedure started all over again for 9 hours straight.

Although outweighed by 115 pounds, Private Pickens made a heroic effort to compete with the much larger man, taking him in 19 of 25 bouts, and even more impressive was his ability to tote Hildebrandt's gigantic frame around the 100-yard course.

Twenty hours in with only a breakfast fit for a child in his stomach, Donnie realized that the only thing he could count on in this day was maximum perspiration, total exhaustion, and the endless shouting of orders from a squadron of sergeants to "do it right or do it again!" The closest thing to nourishment that he and his fellow soldiers were going to receive in this never-ending day would be the inflexible cake of dried mud on their fatigued faces. On the brink of collapse numerous times, Donnie clung to the words he told his mother and uncle.

"I will be one of the one in three that completes the training," he repeated to himself over and over again, until the words barely made any sense at all.

With his body on the verge of shutting down and his mind unable to prevent the inevitable, the private prepared to submit to defeat when from a bullhorn he heard the voice of Staff Sergeant Dryer ordering the men to collect their Ranger buddies and head back to their barracks.

Not to his surprise, but a testimony to his unwavering commitment to not being pushed, he had survived day one of the assessment phase. By the time he had reached his bunk, it was the best he could do to remove his combat boots, and in that moment he was thankful that his bed was the bottom bunk as he lay back and passed out.

The deafening silence of a dead man's sleep hid the failures of his comrades. With what seemed like only a couple of winks, revelry came in just three short hours of his body's collapse into darkness. To his surprise, over fifteen bunks in his dorm were now free of bedding and missing the soldiers who had occupied them just hours ago. In all, forty-one of his peers had washed out in the first day and quietly quit in the night.

Still dead tired and groggy, Donnie tried to gain control of his sleepwalking body. After a quick shower and a breakfast smaller than the day before, the young solider began to recognize this for what it was. It was orchestrated torture and psychological warfare for the domination and control of his person and soul. Just as his Uncle Johnny warned him it would be.

Day two was water survival, drills designed to test the men's comfort level with both water and heights. Donnie's heart sank with the news of what the day would cover. The young man did not know how he would fare against either obstacle. As a boy, he had learned to swim but only in the community swimming pool, which was sad, he thought, because growing up in Lynwood he was only three miles from Long Beach and the Pacific Ocean. Now heights, that was a different animal, he thought. He was terrified of flying but had no true fear of heights. Instinctively, his real fear was of falling, which was a true possibility in the drills he was about to perform.

Donnie watched as rolling gust of wind battered his colleagues standing on a fifty-foot platform attached to a twelve-inch beam, which they were expected to walk across normally without fear. At the end of the beam, there were three steps to climb, and then they were expected to traverse twenty foot of rope, high-five a Ranger sign, release, and fall into the frigid water below where they had to swim twenty yards to the finish line.

Biting his lip and compartmentalizing his fear as best he could, Donnie closed his eyes and began to ascend the lofty pole, despite a bone-shaking tremble rattling his body from head to toe. Once at the top, he swiftly ran across the beam into the whisking wind, leaving his fear nipping at his heels, racing to catch up. In haste, he tripped and fell over the top step but somehow managed to grab the rope line on the way down. After locking his grip tight, the soldier began to slowly rock back in forth, gathering momentum until he could kick his legs up over the line, where he then locked them in heel over ankle and promptly began crossing. With only the thought of beating the best time, he smacked the Ranger sign, grabbed his nose, and held his breath in anticipation of the cold water below. Donnie exited the icy water to what he thought was unanimous rumbles of approval from both his peers and superiors alike. However, upon closer inspection, he realized that the rumbles were not about him but his Ranger buddy whom all eyes were focused on, frozen in fear atop the platform, refusing to move forward or retreat back down the towering pole.

"Move forward or quit, Ranger," echoed upward from a sergeant standing directly below the tower.

"You're wasting my time, soldier. Move forward or get off my fucking pole. That's an order, Hildebrandt!" Still immobilized, too scared to move, Alfonzo stood at the edge of the platform. First Sergeant Mulligan dashed from his position to the edge of the water, unholstered his .45-caliber Colt, aimed it up at the private, and said, "Either start moving forward or get your ass back down that pole now, or I will shoot you down where you stand. Do I make myself clear, Ranger?" the first sergeant questioned.

It was then that Pickens sprang into action. Still cold and dripping wet, the private first class sprinted to the ladder, pushed the waiting soldier out of the way, and began to climb the pole with unbridled determination.

"Get your ass off of my pole, Pickens," shouted Sergeant Mulligan. Deaf to the commander's words, he proceeded. At the top of the platform, the wind had picked up and was now exerting its will. His loose clothing fluttered in its persistent grip. His ears whistled as the baby gales attempted to blow him backward.

"Listen, Alfonzo, you can do this. It's not that hard. Yesterday was ten times harder than this. Do you want to go home a failure?" Donnie asked.

"No, sir, I don't," he replied.

"Get your fucking head out of your ass! I'm not a sir, I'm your Ranger buddy. You can do this. Let's go. I am right behind you." Over the angry wind they could barely hear the irate orders still being barked from below.

"Do you have a girlfriend back in Austin?"

"Yes."

"What's her name?"

"It's Maria," he choked out.

"Imagine that this beam is only one foot off the ground and your girlfriend Maria is waiting on the other end of those steps in nothing but a bra and panties, ready to give you the best sex you have ever had. Would you still be standing here?" his new friend asked.

"No, I wouldn't," the enormous man answered.

"Then go get her. She's waiting for you to come and fuck her brains out. What are you waiting—" Before Donnie could finish his sentence, young Alonzo Hildebrandt was off and moving across the beam even faster than Donnie, himself, had gone.

After Donnie had pulled himself from the water for the second time, he was approached by the first sergeant who pulled him to the side and told him that what he did was exemplary leadership; however, if he ever disobeyed another direct order from him, he would throw his butt in the sling and have him court-marshaled.

The would-be Rangers' next challenge was the cold water swim test, which was conducted in a forty-five-degree pool in which the soldiers were expected to swim twenty-five yards in sixty pounds of gear.

Anxiously awaiting his turn, Donnie rushed and plunged himself boot first into the pool as soon as his name was called. He sunk like an anvil. Thrashing about violently, the weight of his gear pulled him toward the lonely bottom below. Instantly there was a vehement knock in his bones from the cold. His ears rang with pain the closer he got to the pool's floor. Tiny bubbles raced to the surface as he watched them rise in slow motion. Numbness clinched his extremities and burned his numb skin. The young man kicked his feet feverishly and smashed downward with his hands for what seemed like minutes before he finally started to climb toward the distant surface.

With aggression, his head burst through the freezing water, and his greedy lungs gobbled up all the air they could hold. His stiffing limbs thrashed about pointlessly, making little forward progress. Several times his head sank beneath the icy water, taking his breath away. Desperate, his mind bypassed the fear that he might fail this test and jumped ahead to the thought that he may actually drown. At the point of panic, his adrenaline kicked in, reenlisting the services of his frozen limbs. Realizing that thrashing about wildly was getting him nowhere but exhausted, he made a conscious effort to relax and try a different approach. Instead of fighting the water, he decided to let his buoyancy do most of the work, and he began to use the breast-stroke for the distance of the course. In the end, he was just thankful that there was no time limit on the obstacle.

Hunger pains cried to be acknowledged sixteen hours in, but they were ignored. From the pool, the men embarked on a five-mile run to the legendary Army Rand Obstacle Course. Ten monster challenges that begged the soldiers to quit at each new hurdle.

Battling exhaustion and mental fatigue, the Rangers were bombarded with verbal assaults each step of the way.

"Don't quit on me, soldier! Get back up and do it again, Ranger! Do you want to quit? Are you going to quit?" A nonstop barrage of negative verbiage with very little motivational encouragement as if the sergeant's ultimate goal was to see you fail. One by one, it became clear that only 100 percent commitment would be acceptable. At this point, the men's biggest enemy became self-doubt.

Twelve midnight rolled around, and the surviving men were ordered to load up in full combat gear. Private Pickens hunkered over beside his Ranger buddy Hildebrandt, gasping for air as the men were instructed in the rules of the forced march. Unlike every other drill designed to instill teamwork and leadership, this fifteen-mile hike was a personal challenge of endurance. The rules were simple. Keep pace or you're out. In this event, trying to help your fellow Ranger could cost you everything you had worked for up until this point.

Within the first two miles, the flat muddy road started giving way to a slow, steady incline as the Georgia hills began to consume the once-even roadway, which slowly disintegrated into a bumpy narrowing path. The clearing vanished into a dense tree-filled rise flowing in vibrant vegetation.

Halfway through, Donnie's thighs trembled with each mounting step. The joints in his knees hobbled to his straining calves, but his sore, throbbing feet took in the brunt of the torment from the steepening mountainside.

At least the cool night air was refreshing, he thought, as he glanced up at the star-packed sky. Looking behind him he no longer saw Alfonzo, and for a second, he wondered how far he had drifted back into the pack. Without a second thought, his mind drifted forward in time to a place where leisure was the order of the day and his main concern was collecting his money and watching it stack to the ceiling. Of course, nice cars and beautiful women would follow, but respect and power were the driving forces that fueled his desires. He would show them; he would show them all. If he could complete Ranger school, there would be nothing that he couldn't accomplish.

The break of dawn was welcomed by the gentle sprinkling of the morning dew and the joyful song of a robin giving praise for surviving another dark, dangerous night. Unlike the robin, survival for PFC Pickens was not quite a certainty yet. His weary body now lacked the energy to negotiate the rugged terrain mainly due to severe muscle cramps; however, that was simply one of his ailments. The others included difficulty catching his breath, memory loss, inability to focus, irrational depression, intense irritability, and acute anxiety fluctuations. In short, extreme fatigue now dictated his every step.

For moments at a time he would become bewildered and confused about his surroundings and whereabouts. Totally discombobulated, he lost his balance and fell tumbling end over end twenty yards until his descent was abruptly stopped by the ungiving trunk of a mighty scarlet oak. His ribs instantly shrieked in agony. Consumed with exhaustion, he felt like a fighter whose corner was telling him to stay down after being caught with a massive uppercut, sending him to the canvas. While his mind pleaded with his body to quit, his heart would not allow it. Staggered and dazed, the soldier regained his feet and rejoined the ranks of his fellow Rangers.

By ones and twos, the dejected group of would-be Rangers limped underneath the ivy-covered wooden sign, indicating that they had made it to Camp Darby. For fifty hours straight, the men had endured with barely enough calories to motor their soon-to-be killing machines.

Hardly cognizant of his surrounding but mindful enough to remember his pledge he had accepted to be his brother's keeper, Donnie held back at the entry as dozens of tired, weary men passed, awaiting his Ranger buddy. He never came.

In direct contrast to the men he had led, still spry and agile as if ready to march fifteen more miles, Staff Sergeant Diaz hurdled a bench and leaped upon a table that stood in front of it and addressed his exhausted men.

"Rangers, the assessment phase of this training is over. It has been a success. Those who are no longer with us were either weak or unprepared, and they have been weeded out. Of the 340 soldiers we started with, less than two-thirds of you remain. It is now that your true quest begins. Men, it is my honor to welcome you to the wooded wonderland of the Darby Queen and your first day of Ranger school." The sergeant saluted the surviving men with pride and stepped down from the table.

At Camp Darby, Rangers were forced to suffer two weeks of nonstop weapons training stuffed with taxing 20-hour days of combat drills. It was here that men would actually fall asleep in standing positions, which happened so often that the sergeants had a name for it they call it droning. In hopes of surviving the physically grueling days, the men took to all sorts of extremes like burning themselves with lighters, sticking themselves with pins to something as simple as chewing on coffee beans for that extra boost of energy needed to complete their daily task. In the first 20 days, another 90 men were forced out due to their inability to tolerate and withstand the vigorous expectations and requirements set for them by their trainers.

The next phase took the remaining soldiers to Camp Merl, the remote mountains of Georgia where they would be subjected to punishing mountain combat training, like rappelling down wet and rocky 100-foot cliffs with fellow Rangers toting their line in a controlled 50-foot descent where each man was expected to walk backward down the mountain face with no hands, having absolute confidence in their Ranger buddy.

From there it was on to swamp training combined with combat operations over the last 10 days. During this time, each Ranger was expected to take the lead as commander on a given mission. Each mission was graded go or no go. If a Ranger received to many no gos, he was out of Ranger school. Many of the men who would wash out would recycle and try it all again. By this point, each and every man was worn out, mentally stressed, and getting by on pure adrenaline alone. In the end, only 105 men had endured the challenge, and as he said he would, PFC Pickens stood to the test and walked away 20 pounds lighter but 100 percent more confident and immeasurably prouder than he had thought possible. Just as he knew he would, he had beat the odds and ascended to the summit. The one percentile of the most elite fighting force on the planet, simply by refusing to be pushed and always pushing back a little harder.

After Ranger school, PFC Pickens planned to see the world and do it on Uncle Sam's dime, so he requested to be stationed somewhere in Europe.

Judging by the reaction time to his request and the effectiveness to which his orders were carried out, it was obvious that his government had wanted him overseas as well. In a matter of two weeks, he was stationed at USAG Ansbach. The isolated base was located on the northern outskirts of Bavaria, a couple of hours from the Alps and about forty kilometers from Nuremberg. Although the base had never been in as much as a skirmish since its inception following World War II, the base's motto was "To be part of the fight!" Even though a trained killer by definition, Donnie silently hoped that the fight would be at least another thirty-two years incoming; that way, he would be long gone.

Donnie considered himself to be a hooper since his earlier days back at Dominguez High School. He loved to show off his incredible skills in front of crowds, and as fate would have it, with just the hopes of getting in a couple of quick games to remind him of home, he chanced in during the annual tryout for the USAG basketball team.

Within the first two games played in open-gym format, both coaches agreed unanimously that PFC Pickens deserved a position on this year's team. Lieutenant Colonel Morgan showed immediate concern that he was too flashy and not a team player, yet he loved the fact that he was a Ranger. Master Sergeant Firestone was equally impressed by that fact, but more impressed with his killer instincts on the court. The sergeant countered that Pickens would add some spunk to their passionless team and give them the lethal scorer which they so desperately needed.

Just like that, with but a couple of words from Colonel Morgan to his commanding officer, his job description changed, and he was no longer PFC Pickens, short-range logistics coordinator; he was PFC Pickens, long-range bomber. His real job was shooting baskets for the Ansbach Travelling Team, and it was a full-time job. His team would leave for months at a time travelling all throughout Europe. On a couple of occasions, they had played in tournaments in both Africa and Australia. He loved it. This was his dream. He was a professional athlete paid to travel and play ball. Maybe he was not getting paid like a player in the NBA, but he was confident that within six months of his discharge from the Army, he would be.

Four years, three months, and twenty-two days after signing up for the Army, Donnie Pickens walked by Staff Sergeant Williams's recruiting office on Long Beach Boulevard and Sanborn Avenue and never glanced in its direction. With his seabag strapped to his back, wearing fatigues and black combat boots, his mind-set matched his wardrobe. Not that war was what he wanted, but he was not above it, especially now that he was officially certified war ready by his great Uncle Sam.

The filthy streets of Lynwood housed a vast assortment of trash. Donnie crossed the busy boulevard and hurdled a convention of beer bottles littered across the sidewalk and spilling over into the grass. A few steps away, he dodged a stinky white Pampers oozing a brownish green substance with two skinny pigeons tugging at it with their wings flapping and feathers scattering baby feces in all directions. For a minute, he thought of the unspoiled streets of Germany, then he realized that the dirty, grimy, low-down conditions that they were subject to made the Compton / Long Beach area ripe for criminal enterprises, especially drugs, to help escape their crappy reality. The vet looked down and noticed an orange-tipped syringe balanced on the curb needle up, waiting for an unsuspecting shoe to make its acquaintance. Ever aware of his surroundings, Donnie looked at the trap and smiled as his long legs avoided the obstacle and devoured the intersection at Beachwood Avenue in four quick strides.

Instead of turning right on Beachwood and heading home, he made a left and a quick right onto San Vicente Avenue and headed over to his best friend COD's house. Since kids, Christopher Oliver Dempsy was always the hustler. Donnie remembered in the fifth grade he would buy five-cent Blow Pops before school and sell them at lunch for fifty cents. When they went to junior high, he moved up to five-dollar joints, and now since he had been away, he was the man said to have a direct connect to the Mexican Mafia and access to some of the purest white girl available this side of the Rocky Mountains.

COD was the only person that Donnie had told he was on his way home. His plan was to use the GI Bill to get a small business loan and start a couple of businesses to wash the dirty money he was about to start making. The ex-soldier looked both ways, discreetly crossed the street, walked around to the side of the house, and knocked on the door which led to the basement. Since kids, the basement had always been COD's domain. His parents rarely ever bothered him down there.

Moments later, a tall thin dark-complexioned young man opened the door. His eyes were huge. The white area of the eyeball dominated his iris, like a drip of chocolate syrup in a glass of milk.

"You look like you put on a few pounds since the last time I seen you," the man said as he opened the door, and gave his friend a bear hug, lifting him off the ground before letting him in. The two men descended into the smoky, dark basement, exchanged pleasantries, and immediately got down to business.

"Let me show you something, Blood. I ain't shown dis to nobody," he said, as he bent over and pushed the trunk at the foot of his bed to the side. His bad knee cracked as he kneeled down and pulled back a brown throw rug, revealing a hidden compartment in the floor.

"I'm glad you're back, Blood! Because I need some help with all dis shit, man," he said, as he slid his fingernails under the tiny space in the cracks between the two-by-six boards composing the floor. Donnie's eyes widened to match his friend COD's when he saw the pile of bricks stashed under the floorboard.

"Damn, G!" Donnie screamed. "How many do you have there?" Donnie asked.

"I don't know for sure, but I think it's about fourteen left. Shit, my boy Juan brings dem bitches to me by the duffel bag. He don't even be trippin' over the money because he gets way more den he can handle anyway. He just ask me to pay for like two a week. He brings 'em faster than I can get rid of 'em," Chris said with a crooked smile.

"Well damn, how much are they goin' for, my brother?" Donnie asked with a stone face. "Sixteen thousand dollars apiece, Blood, but I'll hook you up for 15,500. So how many do you need, my nigga?" COD asked. The Ranger walked over to his seabag, turned it upside down, and began dumping its contents to the floor until a Phillies cigar box spilled out onto a pile of mismatched socks and dingy T-shirts. Donnie bent over, grabbed it, pried the lid up, and removed a thick stack of hundred-dollar bills held together by four thick rubber bands, one on each end with two in the middle.

"This is every dime I saved from the Army. I've got 24,000 dollars right here. Give me one and a half, and I'll give you 23,250, leaving me with a little change until I can get it rolling," Donnie said to his boy.

"Fuck dat! I'm not breakin' down shit. I'll give you two, and you owe me the difference. What's dat?" COD asked as he cracked the knuckles on his left hand.

"That's 7,750 dollars."

"Well, dat's what you owe me, homey," Chris said, as he threw his friend two bricks from the hidden compartment in the floor.

In no time at all, Donnie's ragtag team was making five times what he was making before. Within two months, his three-man crew was breaking down and chunking up three kilos a week. Thanks to

COD's incredible connection, Donnie's business gained traction fast. It didn't take long for the word to get out that Donnie was back and better than ever. Good news travels fast, but hate travels even faster. Already, Donnie's jealous competitors were leaking information to the neighborhood narcs.

Over the past couple of weeks Donnie had noticed an increase of unmarked cars around the hood. The final straw was when he saw one parked directly across the street from his mother's house. It made no sense; his entire team took painstaking efforts to ensure that their discreet activities remained discreet. The realization began to set in that no matter how good his plan was or the precision to which it was carried out, you cannot predict the degrees to which the crab-in-a-bucket mentality permeates the inner-city communities all through the country. With the words of Detective Brumbly still fresh in his mind, "You aren't that smart, Pickens," playing over in his head like a scratched forty-five record, he decided to call his crew together for an emergency meeting.

Donnie sat on the hood of a 1972 brown Nova, slowly rocking his head back in forth to the beat in the family's old dusty garage. Repeatedly he looked at his wristwatch, wondering where his crew was. It had been over an hour since he had paged them. Donnie sat, shaking his head with disgust when he heard a tremor of bass from down the block. When his brother Boom pulled into the driveway, his music was bumping so hard that Donnie could see the trunk of the car vibrating.

Boom, Donnie's youngest brother, was the best salesman of the group; on average, he was able to move a bird and a half a week by himself. Benjamin Thomas Pickens was four years younger than his brother. He was given his nickname because he loved to use a Mossberg twelve-gauge pump whenever he did his dirt. It didn't matter what it was, drive-by, a robbery, or as a holiday noisemaker, any occasion for shooting, a shotgun was what Boom was using.

Ten minutes after Boom arrived, a white 1976 Cutlass Classic forced its way into the tiny one-car driveway. In unison, both doors opened, and Jesus and Monté spilled out. Best friends since kids, the two did nearly everything together. When Jesus decided to stop going to school and sell drugs, Monté was right there with him. Not to be outdone in a true showing of loyalty, Jesus pleaded guilty to an assault charge that he was not even involved in to make sure that his buddy did not have to go to the juvenile detention center alone.

Jesus was Mexican, but all his friends were black, and even his girlfriend was a petite chocolate delight. Monté would tease him, saying he was Hispanically challenged. Ever since a Border Brother had murdered his father, the only Latinos he associated with were his immediate family and Father Francisco Luis at Our Lady of Grace Catholic Church, who had been helping him to deal with his demons and self-hatred for the past nine years.

Monté was a mulatto, with reddish-brown sunbaked skin. Tight ebony waves sprouted from his head. He wore a neatly trimmed goatee. His build was tall and linkee.

The dirty garage's rafters housed an assortment of unique connecting spiderwebs, allowing cannibal arachnids to dine on their unsuspecting neighbors. The multitude of webs bounced and vibrated with the bass of the boom box, leaning against a makeshift shelf above a broken dusty white Kenmore washing machine.

Donnie slid down from the hood of the Nova, and slipped around to the rear of the car and reached up and grabbed a filthy rope attached to the garage door, which he swiftly pulled down. Brushing his hands off, he walked over to the portable stereo and turned down the volume. Donnie clapped his hands together and began to rub them in a washing motion.

"Do any of you guys know why I called you here? Anybody? Anybody?" he questioned as he stared into the faces of the three men. He waited about ten seconds, and then he kicked a gas can sitting on the ground, sending it flying in the direction of Boom, who barely moved clear of it before it smashed into the wall. "See, that's the shit I'm talking about! That shit right there...You guys are walking around all willy-nilly in a daze and shit, oblivious to all of these fuckin' undercovers riding through our hood, watching everything.

"We have to be smarter. Starting right now, we have to change it up. The first thing that we are going to change is where we do business. From now on, Lynwood belongs to Boom. He makes the most money here, so, the rest of us have got to find a new area to set up shop. That means every connect that you have here, give it to Boom. I'm giving him mine too. It's too much heat here for all of us to continue moving the kind of weight we've been doing over the last few months. Shit, I personally know ten people dealing something in a five-block radius of here, not to mention those that I don't know," Donnie said, as he walked over to Monté and Jesus.

"I think that you two should go back down to Riverside where you're from and get it cracking out there. I am heading north to Lancaster where my baby mama lives. Think about it. We have access to way more shit than the four of us could ever hope to move. What we have to do is spread out and build a network of hustlers who are as hungry as we are and take this shit nationwide. I don't know about y'all, but I don't see no mutherfuckin' reason why we can't be filthy rich in the next five to six years!" he said as he smiled and began to bob his head back and forth slowly as if the music was turned up full blast.

CHAPTER
23

Headlights lit up the night street, but darkness covered everything with the exception of the yellow line down the middle of the two-way road. With no sound, the roofless vehicle embraced every curve and devoured steep uphill stretches like a straightaway. In the distance, a timber owl questioned the night as it perched in a large oak tree under the black star-filled sky.

Andre lay back and took in the magnificent view of the heavens. Clustering specks of light winked down at the young man from a time long past. Almost as an afterthought, Andre realized that the vehicle he was riding in was piloting itself. What he had once believed to be a car had morphed into a solo cockpit aircraft minus the roof. His stomach dropped when he glanced down, noticing that the floor was gone as well. He now soared over trees, which were giants to him mere moments ago, and they now appeared as tiny as twigs.

Finally grasping the fact that he was dreaming, Andre let go, the illusion of the aircraft disappeared, and he was flying among the clouds unaided. With no obstacle but the horizon, the boy pressed forward, faster and faster until his dream eyes began to burn and blur. With but a thought, he torpedoed forward, increasing his speed until he felt a snap, followed by a slight tug, pulling his head backward, hurling him end over end in the direction of huge redwoods populating much of the earth below.

Spiraling out of control toward the massive trees, the boy was struck by a fleeting thought that he was not really a body, more of a mist, and the physics of this world should not affect him. It's all mental, the thought whispered, but the words could not change the fact that he was just seconds away from crashing into the biggest tree he had ever seen in his life headfirst. The long branch reached out and smacked him right out of the sky, tossing his frame sideways to its neighboring limb, which immediately thrust his doll-like body down, corkscrewing it into the trunk of another tree wide enough to drive a Mac truck through. Off the hard dark bark, the boy's head banked, sending him plummeting twelve feet straight down to the leaf-covered ground below. Moments later, Andre rolled over and patted his arms and legs to make sure that he was still all in one piece. Getting up, he groaned like an old man although he felt no pain. Slowly he began to run, swiftly picking up speed to leap for the sky, when he realized he had a strong urge to urinate. For a second, the boy forgot that he was dreaming, stopped running, and walked over to a tree, unzipped his imaginary pants, and eagerly began to pee behind one of the huge redwoods. It only took a second for the streaming gush of warm piss to cross the border between sleep and wakefulness, propelling the boy from his slumber into a mad dash for a bathroom.

Andre sat with his head leaning against the window of the Antelope Valley Transit Authority bus, taking in the desolate beauty of the desert. One lone business held down the entire block of Avenue I and Twenty-Fifth Street West. Black and orange plastic flags hanging low from a string around the top of the building accompanied by a multitude of carved jack-o'-lanterns littering the windows served as a reminder that he had already been in Lancaster for nearly three months and the start of the basketball season was fast approaching. Without looking, Andre reached out with his left hand, grabbed his trusty backpack, and set it on the floor between his legs as a crowd of passengers patiently waited for the doors of the AVTA bus to open. Andre watched as some people deposited coins and others flashed plastic-covered bus passes. The next two stops filled the bus nearly to its capacity, and one by one the morning travelers quickly devoured the seats and consumed nearly every inch of standing room.

Andre sat on the edge of his seat, with his face pointed at the window. No longer for the view, now he did so to protect himself against the putrid smell emanating from the partially open mouth of the middle-aged businessman sitting beside him. Every time he exhaled a sour mixture of what Andre assumed to be morning breath, cigarettes and coffee oozed out, corrupting all the breathable air in their crowded section. The young man was on the verge of getting up and surrendering his seat to the man with bad oral hygiene, when the man himself stood up and pulled the cord, signaling his stop on the corner of Thirtieth Street West and Avenue K.

Of the fifteen kids that got off the bus in front of Antelope Valley Junior College, Andre was the last to exit. The folded back doors of the bus flashed the young man back to the dream he had last night. The vehicle he was riding in had doors, which folded out and disappeared, he remembered. Virtually sleepwalking, Andre stepped into the student parking lot en route to the gym when a badgering horn blared at him, awaking him from his impeded state.

Eileen yelled from her car half joking and half irritated, "Don't you ever watch where you are going?" She giggled.

Without thinking or looking, he responded, "What are you talking about? I had the right a way!"

"Dang, you are way too uptight," the girl laughed.

Looking up, he stood dumbfounded. He wasn't sure at first, but behind the sunglasses and the business clothes, it was her. The girl he had stayed up late thinking about since the first day of school.

"I don't mean to sound corny, but I could swear I know you from somewhere," Andre said as he walked around to the side of the girl's car.

"I'm Andre," he finally said.

"Wasn't me, unless you moved out here from Mohave. I doubt that we've ever met before the other day," the girl replied as she turned the steering wheel of her NSX guiding it into a parking space directly across from where the boy was standing.

Andre was mesmerized by the girl's natural beauty. Eileen gracefully exited the car. Her legs were tan and shapely. Covered slightly above the knee she wore a tight black skirt, a sheer white blouse, and a formfitting, bus-accentuating black suit jacket. She bent over and pressed a button on the side of her seat, causing it to fold forward. She then leaned in and came out with a checkered brown and tan bag, which looked like it could be substituted for a checkerboard. She looked so professional that for a second the boy questioned if the young woman was a student or a professor here at the college.

She closed the door, turned around, looked up at the guy who had just introduced himself as Andre and had an instant case of déjà vu, causing her to pause for a second.

"Hi, I am Eileen," she said as she stuck out her hand.

"Ya know, there is something kind of familiar about you too. You're not on the most wanted list, are you? Maybe I seen you on the wall at the post office or something," she laughed.

"Just kidding, well, I've got be in class in five minutes, but it's nice running into you again, I think," she said.

"Hey, do you want to get together and do something sometime?" he asked.

"I don't know. I don't have too much time between school and work, so it's kinda hard. Besides, I don't even know you," she said as she backpedaled off in the direction of Lindley Hall.

"Come on, trust your gut. You know I'm a good guy," he said, trying to make the most innocent face that he could muster.

"I'll see you around, and maybe next time we can hang out and talk for a while, okay…," she said with a smile that made the young man think that he might actually have a chance.

Later that day around lunchtime, Andre found himself sitting in the student center eating a toasted club sandwich talking with Corn about his sister Latice, who was coming in from New York tonight. Andre shared some of his crazy stories about his sister, like how she almost put his eye out as a kid while playing Cowboys and Indians with a real bow and arrow. Then he explained that it had been nearly ten years since he had last seen her. When Corn asked why, Andre set down his sandwich, placed his right hand on his chin, breathed in deeply as if about to give the boy sitting across from him a long explanation. Corn was listening intently when he thought he heard their names being called out in the distance. The two boys turned in unison and glanced across the center to where they thought the sound was coming. Once Andre realized who it was, he pointed across the room to the lunch line.

"Hey, isn't that ya boy Donnie over there screaming at us."

All the way in the back of the lunch line, more than forty yards away, Corn and Andre could hear Donnie yelling across the student center telling the two boys not to go anywhere. The flamboyant Los Angeleano pimped over, placed his tray on the table, sat down, and began talking smack. It never stopped with Donnie.

"So, what were you marks over here talking about?" Donnie joked.

"Ya boy, Dre, just told me his sister is coming to town tonight," Corn said.

When Andre was not looking, Corn smiled, shook his head up and down, and waved his hands in the shape of a Coke bottle to Donnie.

"So, is she fine or tore up?" Donnie asked.

"Fool, she's my sister. What do you think?" Andre questioned.

"Well, she must be tore up, cause yo ass is tore up from the floor up," the ex-Ranger said.

He and Corn both laughed ridiculously while Andre sat across from them with a serious look on his face.

"No, for real, man, my sister is coming into LAX tonight, and I don't know how I am going to pick her up. I don't have a car, and neither does my mom," Andre said.

"What time is she coming in?" Donnie asked.

"At six thirty on United. What's up? You gonna take me?"

"I don't know. You gonna hook me up wit' her?"

"Hell nah, man! But, if you take me down to pick her up, you will be the first one she meets, so if you've got any game, you won't need me to hook you up with her," Andre said.

"Shoot, I want to go too. I ain't got nothing to do," Corn added, as he threw a handful of chips in his mouth and washed it down with a long gulping drink of Gatorade.

"Okay, I'll tell you what… If you guys bring some girls to my party this weekend, I'll drive you down there tonight, but if we are going I have to take a quick trip to my Mama's house to grab some stuff after we pick her up, okay," Donnie said.

"Thanks, man, I appreciate it. What time do you want to go?" Andre asked.

"We'll have to leave right after practice if we want to make it down there by six thirty. It's gonna be close 'cause if we get caught up in that 405 rush-hour traffic, we ain't never gonna make it down there on time. Meet me in the south parking lot right after practice and be ready to roll," Donnie said, as he popped the top on a can of Coke.

"Okay, cool." Andre agreed.

The late evening's sun had grown even stronger during the day. Andre walked out of the Marauder's Pavilion into ninety-eight-de-gree temperatures and began to sweat instantly. A couple of seconds later, Corn exited the side door of the gymnasium behind his friend. The Alaskan transplant seemed impervious to the subtropical tem-peratures, spinning and dancing across the sidewalk, celebrating the fact that he was finally going to see the city of Los Angeles. He could still hear his dad's voice.

"It's just outside of LA. You will be able to go to the beaches, explore the city, rub elbows with the stars, and get an education all at the same time."

He wondered at the time if his dad had actually known that the college was more than an hour and a half from the city.

"Yo, Dre, where's that fool Donnie?"

"I just saw him go out this door a couple minutes ago when you were in there running those week ass lines on Tracy and her yuck mouth friend Misty," said Andre.

"Do you know what he drives?" Corn asked, trying to moon-walk across the concrete.

"I don't know, but from the sound of it, this might be him pulling up right now," Andre said, as he shaded his eyes so he could see what kind of car it was with the boom from the bass he could feel standing five feet away on the curb. The glare from the sun on the black paint and the limo-tinted windows echoed back a blinding reflection to whoever looked directly upon the vehicle. As the shiny car pulled up, the tinted window slowly went down, revealing a familiar voice.

"Y'all gonna get in, or just stand there gawking like you've never seen a Coup DeVille before?" the Ranger asked.

"Damn, man, this is a bad-ass ride. Is it new?"

"This bitch is clean. How can you afford a brand-new Caddy and go to school? Do you have a job or something that we don't know about?" Corn asked.

"Man, kill all those damn questions? You writing a story for the school paper or what?" the older man asked.

"Nah, man, I need a car myself. Shit, I'm tired of riding the bus," Corn explained.

It was a quick trip from the college to the 14 Freeway. Andre kicked back in the passenger seat, wondering what Donnie's hustle was. The crimson leather seats of the Cadillac worked like sedatives on the tired boys after the hard practice. The copilot sat in a semi-conscious state, reflecting on the side-busting sprints the team was forced to run every time someone made a mistake. For a second, he relived his shortness of breath suffered earlier as he stood bent over in two, attempting to catch his breath. Fading out of the thought and back into the present, Andre promised himself that he would have a one-on-one with Donnie one day in the near future when it was just the two of them.

Nearly one hour and a half later, the sleek vehicle pulled up to the arrival gate for United Airlines to find Latice at the sidewalk's edge with a four-piece matching set of Louis Vuitton luggage. She leaned against the largest suitcase with the look of total disgust plastered across her face.

"Aye, man, pull over. That's her right there. She's the one that looks totally pissed off. Believe me, you do not want to get on her bad side," Andre said, pointing at a girl in a gray fox hat and a black leather jacket with a matching fox collar.

Andre jumped out, ran up to his sister, and gave her a huge bear hug.

"What's been up, sis, it's been a long time. I'm glad you finally decided to bring your skinny butt out here to the West Coast with the rest of the family. Sorry, it took us a little longer than we thought. I hope you haven't been waiting for too long. I'm really surprised you came. I thought you hated the West Coast," Andre said as he grabbed the biggest of her four bags and struggled to position it by the trunk.

"Something came up, and I needed to get away," Latice said as she averted her eyes from her brother's.

"Yo, Donnie, pop the trunk. Aye, can I get a hand from somebody?" the young man yelled to his friends in the car.

Before he could finish his sentence, Corn had bounced out of the back seat, ran up, grabbed the next largest bag, and asked Latice in a dry English accent.

"May I take your bag, madam?"

Latice took a double take at the young man speaking. For a second, she was suspended in disbelief when she saw whom the British accent was coming from. The surprise coaxed the first smile out of the young woman since they had arrived.

Once all of her luggage was squeezed into the trunk, Andre introduced Latice to his friends. The young woman talked as if she had been starved for conversation. Andre tried to remember if she had always talked endlessly. He also marveled at how well-rounded she had grown. Latice engaged all three men seamlessly at the same time.

"I love your car, Donnie. It's rear-wheel drive with the 350 engine in it, right? Is it the 5.0- or the 5.7-liter model?" she asked.

"Shit, I don't know. I just put gas in it and keep the oil changed, that's all I know," Donnie replied.

The woman leaned forward, placed her left hand on the back of the driver's seat, and said, "I'd love to drive it sometime. Maybe you could show me around Lancaster?"

Donnie smiled and replied, "I think that could be arranged."

When Donald Pickens finally reached his mother's house, it was early evening. The clock on the car's dashboard announced the time as seven fourteen.

A cool breeze fluttered through the open windows, carrying the undeniable aroma of barbecued ribs. On cue, someone's stomach growled as if in response to the lingering smell.

"Man, do y'all smell that? Bro, please hurry up, I'm starvin'!" Corn said, as Donnie exited the car, leaving them sitting there in front of the house.

"I'm kind of hungry too. I haven't ate since noon eastern time," the caramel-complexioned woman said.

"What do you want to eat, Corn? That's a funny name. That's not your real name, is it?" The girl poked.

"No, it's a nickname. Supposedly, that's the first word I ever spoke. Not Mama or Dada. It was corn. Anyway, that's what my mother says, and they have called me Corn ever since. My real name is Calvin, Calvin Rufus Walker, but a woman as fine as you can call me anything you like," he said timidly.

"Really, that's sweet, you're sweet," Latice responded, flashing him a quick smile.

"Please, you guys are making me want to puke up here," Andre said, laughing.

"Oh, shut up, boy, you're just jealous," Latice said, returning a laugh of her own.

Nearly fifteen minutes had passed, and Donnie was still in the house without a word to his passengers waiting on his return.

"Maybe I should go knock on the door and see what's taking so long," Andre suggested. Just as he reached for the door handle, Latice lurched forward, grabbing him by the shoulder, and said, "Did you guys hear that? Turn down the radio." It was barely audible, but there was definitely arguing coming from inside the house. The three sat on edge, staring at the house, when a full-blown ruckus shook the walls inside the home on South Street.

Just as Andre opened the door and stepped out of the car, the front screen door was blasted off the hinges by Boom's flying body. Headfirst he crashed onto the solid concrete. With catlike agility, Donnie pounced from the door, landing square on Boom's midsection with his knees knocking the remaining air from his brother's lungs.

Boom lay stretched out concussed, struggling to catch his breath, looking up at his sibling's hands around his neck smashing his head repeatedly into the walkway.

"Wha-what did I do?" Boom struggled to get out as black and red dots exploded from the inside of his eyelids. Dazed on the verge of losing consciousness, he tried to understand the words Donnie was screaming down at him.

Andre stood in shock as Latice screamed from inside the car.

"Do something! Stop him. He's going to kill him!" she shrieked.

The girl's cry sent Andre flying into action. Around the car, he ran full speed toward the two men fighting and launched himself, arms extended, toward Donnie, who was pounding his unconscious brother's head into the ground. He struck Donnie around the shoulders and neck, knocking the man sideways into the grass. The trained combatant rolled backward with the hit, flipping his attacker over the top of him, landing Andre flat on his back.

Donnie stood up, limped over to Andre, bent down, pointed his finger in his face, and told him to stay the fuck out of his business if he valued his life. Donnie brushed the dirt and grass stains off his pants and told Andre to get back in the car because they were leaving. Andre got up and asked, "What's up? What are you guys fighting for?"

"Just get in the car and don't worry about it," Donnie responded.

"Oh yeah, I almost forgot what I came for," the man said as he turned around and slowly walked back in the house.

Boom staggered to his feet, just as his brother was exiting the house. When Donnie exited the house, he was carrying a gray and white backpack. He walked right by his sibling without as much as a look. That's when Boom reached into his back pocket, pulled out a chrome .380 pistol, pointed it at Donnie, and screamed at the top of his lungs, "If you ever put your fucking hands on me again, I will blow your fucking brains out! I promise you…You will be sorry. I promise you." He repeated as tears streamed down his ashy cheeks.

With that, Donnie turned around, walked directly up to his brother's extended arm, pressed his chest against the barrel, and said, "What are you waiting for? I'm here right now, so handle your business. If you ever steal from me again, you're gonna wish that you had shot me when you had the chance. I mean that," as he gingerly walked over, unlocked the trunk, threw the bag in it, then opened the driver side door and got into his car and drove away.

The silence was blaring on the trip back to Lancaster. Even the powerful lyrics of Public Enemy's "Chuck D." could not inspire more than a couple of words from any of the car's passengers.

The next morning, Andre called Donnie and thanked him for the ride to LAX. During their conversation, the boy asked his friend if he could pick him up and give him a ride to school because he had a couple of things that he wanted to talk to him about. The veteran agreed as long as he did not ask him a bunch of questions about why he and his brother were fighting.

Andre was in the kitchen pouring a glass of juice still in disbelief that skinny little Latice could snore so loudly. Even over the hum of the Amana refrigerator, he could hear the young woman's erratic breathing patterns emanating from the sofa bed in the living room. It was 10:40 a.m. when Donnie Dollar pulled up in front of Andre's apartment. He heard the Cadillac's flat obnoxious horn outside his home, which inspired him to chug his juice and run through a mental checklist to ensure he had everything he would need for the course of the day.

The morning was brisk. The timid sun radiated just enough heat to evaporate the frosty tips of the grass leaflets. The distinct smell of eucalyptus hung on the chilly wind.

A trail of hot smoke fell off Andre's words as he hollered "What's up" to his neighbor Ted across the way getting into his 1974 Ford Capri.

Donnie sat distracted, staring into the face of his beeping pager when Andre got in the car. The young man's pleasantries were ignored by the driver as he threw his car into gear and rapidly pulled away from the curve.

"Where's the closest pay phone around here?" Dollar asked as he kept his attention divided between the road and the handheld device, which he scrolled through number after number.

"There's one right over there," Andre said, pointing across Avenue I to the Screaming "J" Liquor store.

Moments later, Donnie stood hunkered over the phone with his back to the vehicle, noticeably trying to keep his conversation private.

Inside the car, Andre sat on the verge of a torrential sweat until he leaned forward and turned down the blasting heat. Without the ragging heater, the interior of the car fell silent. He could barely hear through the closed window. He wasn't sure, but he thought he could hear a definite sense of agitation in his friend's voice.

"Is everything okay?" Andre asked as Donnie got back into the car. Although his voice said things were fine, the look on his face said something totally different. The look worried Andre, and he wondered if now was a good time for him to pry into what Donnie actually did to get his money. Just as the car started to pull off, Andre asked Donnie to hold on for a second while he ran in the store and bought a lottery ticket.

The two men were talking about their upcoming scrimmage game against College of the Canyons when Andre just came out of nowhere and said, "I can help you, ya know."

"Help me what?" Donnie questioned.

"Help you make more money," he said. "I've been hustling since I was fourteen, and I know you didn't get all that extra loot that you're always flaunting from the Army. I'm not sure what you are doing, but I can tell you're doing something. Come on, man, hook me up! I promise you, I'm not a snitch, plus I'm a quick study. You only have to show me something once," Andre said as he double-checked his lottery ticket numbers and stuffed the piece of paper deep into his front pocket. Donnie took his eyes off the road for a second and stared into the eyes of his teammate and said, "I tell you what, let me think about it for a minute, and I'll let you know something in a couple days, okay."

"Okay, that sounds fair enough," Andre agreed.

Donnie Dollar could be taken a number of different ways, but literally wasn't usually one of them. In this case, when he told Andre that he would let him know something in a couple of days, he did just that.

It was Thursday night at 11:15 p.m. Andre was just ending his shift at McDonald's, walking across the parking lot to the bus stop when he thought he heard someone calling out his name. He turned around and looked, but saw no one. Slightly freaked out, he continued on his way when he heard it again. This time, it came from much closer; in fact, it sounded like it had come from one of the vehicles he had just passed. He turned and looked but still stood baffled. In the parking space directly to his rear sat an old, beat-up Ford Pinto hatchback with limo-tinted windows. He thought the vehicle was empty when he walked by it. Slowly he walked up to the driver's side door and paused, poised to knock on the window, when the door suddenly flew open, releasing a huge cloud of smoke and a rambunctious roar of laughter. To his surprise, it was Donnie and Corn. Their faces carried bright, shiny smiles, while their eyes were so tight that both looked like black Chinese.

"Come on, get in," Donnie said.

"What's up? Where we goin'?" Andre asked.

"I'ma have you take a ride with me and Corn real quick. You down, or what?" Dollar replied.

"Okay, let's roll. Corn, get in the back," Andre said.

"Hell naw! You get in the back!" Corn laughed.

"All right, all right," Andre said as he pushed the seat up, squeezed through the tiny space behind the boy holding a piece of a joint, and nearly hung himself on the synthetic seat belt attached to the bucket seat.

"Damn, Corn! Would it kill you to try and sit up a little bit?" Andre asked.

Within two minutes of driving down Avenue I, Donnie looked around, scrunched up his face, turned up his nose, and said to Andre, "Man, you smell like fried shit!"

"I know, it's the grease from the quarter-pounder patties. It pops all over me when I'm flipping them. Usually the first thing I do is go home and take a shower."

"I don't know, D. I think he may have smelled worse some days right after practice," Corn joked.

From the back seat, Andre peered into the rearview mirror, wondering where the three men were headed. Adrift in the thought that he would no longer have to work in the fast-food industry, he inadvertently began to stare into Donnie's eyes. Unaware of Andre's intrusion, he turned on his blinker and made a right turn onto Beech Street. Like a black hole, Andre was drawn in deeper and forced into a tailspin. For a second, he felt vertigo like the first time he mixed beer and marijuana and tried to lie down on his bed. The intense spinning forced the young man backward against the awaiting seat. Moments later, the car began to slow down, and Donnie made another right, followed by a quick left into an alley. About three houses in, the driver pulled up to a garage, flipped down his sun visor, and pressed a white button on a black remote attached to it, which caused the garage door to open. The springs on the tattered door cracked with agony as the door lifted in almost cryptic slow motion. Finally, Andre began to break from the dizziness spell. As he shook it off, he wondered what had caused it. There was nothing unusual about Donnie. Andre had never thought of himself as a psychic, but normally he would get some type of a vibe from a person he had been around a few times, but not Donnie. For a second, he thought that he had seen something, then it was gone. That's when he was sucked into the emptiness. Never before had he experienced such a vacuum of nothingness. After the car stopped and the dizziness passed, Andre chalked the incident up to motion sickness.

The tiny weathered garage barely had enough room for the two-door compact to open its two doors. Cobwebs gathered in the rafters, and resilient weeds freed themselves through cracks in the crumbling concrete.

The two men exited the car and followed Donnie through a door, which led into a backyard. An eight-foot pressure-treated wood fence protected the yard that raised two Lisbon lemon trees which littered the ground with overripe fruit. There was no walkway, just a worn dirt path through the grass leading up to a covered patio. Just before entering the back door, he told the guys to hold tight for a minute while he put his dog Red up. Red was a traditionally marked tall elegant Doberman pinscher, more like a cat than a dog.

The hound followed her master to a back bedroom with the stealth of a ninja. When Donnie closed the door, there was neither a bark nor whimper. Seconds later, Donnie returned to the door and told the guys to come in and lock the door behind them.

"Damn, man, is your dog always that quiet? That's kind of spooky, a big dog like that not making a sound," Corn said as he walked up to the kitchen table, pulled out a chair, and took a seat. It only took the boy a second to realize that the room reeked of urine. Glancing down at the hardwood floor, he noticed that his brand-new Nike Legends were resting in a puddle of piss.

"That's right, and she's sneaky too… She will creep up on you and bite you right in your ass if you're ever around here nosing around when I'm not here," Donnie said with a crooked smile.

"The reason I brought you here is because both of you told me that you wanted to make some extra money. So, I got a little business proposition for you," Donnie said, as he walked out of the room, momentarily disappearing into a back room from which he emerged with the same gray and white backpack from his mother's house.

"Y'all come in here to the living room but wipe your shoes off on that filthy ass towel on the floor as you walk into the hallway. Red has that kitchen all pissed up. I don't know why, but if I don't get here to let her outside in time, she always goes straight under the kitchen table and squats right there."

Corn and Andre rounded the corner to find Donnie sitting on a plush burgundy couch with the backpack sitting on the coffee table in front of him.

"Have a seat and let me tell y'all the rules of this here," Donnie said as he took hold of the backpack, pulled it to his lap, and unzipped its gray zipper. He reached into the bag and pulled out a quart-size ziplock freezer bag two-thirds of the way full of a white substance.

"Do you know what this is?" he said, looking at his two guests.

"Yeah, it looks like a lot of coke to me," Andre said, leaning forward in his seat.

"Yes, sir! It's 252 grams of A-1 Peruvian Flake, to be exact. Nine ounces of the best coke you're going to find anywhere around here, and that's a promise." He looked at Andre and threw the package over to him. Donnie then reached into the backpack once again, pulling out an identical bag also containing nine ounces, and tossed it over to Corn.

"Okay, gents, here's the deal. If you take this package, you owe me $6,300 bucks. No ands, butts, or ors, and no bullshit. I want my money! That's 700 dollars a zip. For you new booties, zip means ounce," he said, laughing.

"I'm hooking you up. You can make over $1,400 profit on each zip and more if you want me to teach you how to cook it up into rock cocaine. Crack is a different animal, though. If you start serving that shit, you're gonna have fiends coming to your house at all hours of the day. I don't think you boys are ready for that yet. Just turn on your little white friends at the college or your job and see who likes it. Keep a low profile and watch who you fuck with. You will be surprised the people you know who already messes with it."

"How much time do we have to get rid of all of this? This is a lot of stuff. It's not like I've got clientele lined up waiting blowing my phone off of the hook," Andre said with a nervous smile on his face.

"I'll give you plenty of time. Don't worry about it. I already know that when people try it, they're gonna tell their friends and want more and more of it, because it's that good. Just wait, you'll see. You boys are about to get paid. This is a perfect setup. Andre is over on the east side, my boy Corn is right off campus, and I'm up on the hill. We can have this whole town sewn up," Donnie said, laughing hysterically like he had just heard the funniest joke of all time.

The digital quartz clock displayed one forty-five when Andre exited the car in front of his house. The dope in his underwear shifted when he took his first step, threatening to escape down the boy's black greasy pants leg. Quickly, he adjusted the package by shoving his left hand into his pants pocket. The wind's chilly bite reminded him of the cool fall evenings he remembered from West Virginia as a youngster.

The gray Nissan Pulsar pulled into the Antelope Valley Jr. College parking lot behind a slow-moving procession of what seemed like fifty cars to Eileen. Normally very patient and adept to playing the cards she was dealt, this morning found her anxious and internally charged about what the day held for her. She could feel it. Some might call it intuition, which for many originates in their guts, but not for her. Her telltale signs came like the lightest buzzing of a mosquito just inches from her ear. Every couple of seconds, the girl would wave her hand by her ear as if to shoo away an invisible pest. Today she would receive a lead on the Dollar case. Either that or she was just plain nervous about the grade she received on her midterm in Dr. Marrow's biology class.

The young woman adjusted her hair when she noticed it in the door's shaded reflection. As she reached for the door's handle, the door pulled open before she even touched it. Pleasantly surprised by the occurrence, she stepped through the door to find Andre there opening it for her. Immediately he threw her a smile and a cheery morning greeting.

"Good morning, Ms. Dang…you look like you should be going to a business office, not a classroom," he said.

"That's because I go to a business office right after my ten o'clock class," she said, walking past the elevator and heading for the stairs.

"Really? And what kind of business office do you work in?" he asked as he followed her up the stairs.

"I work at the DA's office for DA Harvin," Eileen said with a jabbing smile.

Andre stood silent for a second before he could gather a response.

"Well, look at you, already off and running towards your career. I wish I knew what I was going to do with my life," he said, laughing as he took the last two steps in one stretch.

"I don't want to work in law. I would prefer to work in the commercial art field when I graduate. This job, I guess, just kind of found me."

"It must be nice to have good jobs just find you. You don't want to know where I work. Anyway, that's another story. Speaking of another story, what are you doing tomorrow night? A friend of mine on the basketball team is having a party, and you should come and bring a couple of your fine-ass friends with you."

"I don't think so. I'm not much for parties," she said as she played with the bangs of her thick auburn locks. Eileen stopped just short of her classroom, turned around, and gave the boy a little smile and a goodbye wave.

"Come on, it's going to be fun. Good music, friends, plenty of alcohol, and best of all, I'll be there," he said.

"Maybe next time, I really need to study this weekend," Eileen said, making a sad face to her new friend.

"Okay, well, you can't say I didn't invite you when you hear about it from all of your friends on Monday talking about how live it was," Andre said as he turned around and slowly started walking away, occasionally glancing back over his shoulder, hoping that she would stop him. Just as Eileen turned to walk into her classroom, the girl's right arm involuntarily began to swat at her right ear. That's when her inner voice said, "Thought you were supposed to be on the lookout for a lead on the Dollar case." With that, she turned around, walked out of the class, and called to Andre to come back.

"I can't promise you, but maybe me and a couple of my girl-friends will stop by if I finish studying in time. Where is it going to be?" she asked.

Andre walked out of Lindley Hall with mixed emotions. Part of him tingled with excitement at the thought that Eileen might show up to Donnie's party, while the rest of him shuddered in dread, wondering if he should have just invited the DA's assistant to his drug dealer friend's party.

Friday night came quick. Andre had asked his neighbor Ted if he wanted to go to the party with him, hoping that he would drive. He agreed after Andre assured him that there would be plenty of college girls there for him to meet. To that, Ted bashfully replied that he just wanted to look at them and he didn't care if he talked to one all night.

The next stop for the two was at the Sunset Apartments where Corn lived. Before the pair could start up the stairs, Corn had stepped out onto the porch where he greeted the two young men.

"I saw you pulling up. Love the ride. It looks fast. By the way, I'm Corn," he said as he extended his hand to Ted. "Yo, I'm ready to go, but I've got to get something to eat. Is it okay if we walk across the street to the Taco Grande to grab a quick bite?" Corn asked.

From there, they would try to buy some beer and then head to the party in Quartz Hill.

The car ride to Donnie's was as dry and boring as the scenery taken in during the drive. Ted's stereo hissed with the static cries of a busted speaker caused by a self-installed Pyle Driver Amplifier, forcing the driver to turn off the radio, rather than listen to his beloved hip-hop all muffled and distorted. Each of the young men stared off into the darkness, lost in their own thoughts. No words had been uttered since they left the liquor store. The only sound was that of an intermittent popping of the tops of Milwaukee's Best beer cans. Lonely Joshua trees stood isolated in the darkness, kept company by only sand, and sporadic cactus pups. The first three miles were a mirror image of the last three miles as K and Forty-Fifth Street West turned into L and Forty-Fifth Street West. The desert's solitude was finally interrupted by a billboard introducing passersby to "Quartz Hill, the Diamond in the Desert." Several moments later, the primer-coated coupe whipped into the Emerald Estates housing track.

It only took moments to see that there was something big going on, because the sidewalks stood covered with cars for blocks and blocks. Slowly, Ted navigated the crowded streets, dodging packs of kids walking. Andre patiently searched house addresses looking for 44237 Newport Way, but realized that an address was not going to be necessary as the car eased past a gigantic Winnebago blocking half the street. Donnie's entire front yard was covered with what looked like over five hundred kids to Andre.

"Say, Ted, blow your horn and make those kids in the driveway move! This is our boy's house, and we are special guests, so keep blowing it until they move and we can park there. This way we can keep a close eye on your car and get out of here in a hurry if we need to," Andre suggested.

After exiting the vehicle, the three boys plotted a course around the masses on the lawn and plowed straight through the crowd of people standing in line, causing tempers to flair, and bad blood to rise. A couple of Mexican kids started talking shit, but the boys didn't want to ruin Donnie's party before they even talked to its host. To their surprise, there was Latice's skinny frame blocking the threshold with the door at her back, holding a metal bucket with a sign on it reading five dollars for guys and two dollars for gals written in red magic marker.

"What are you doing here?" Andre asked Latice.

"What do you mean? Shoot! It's boring at the house. I'm glad that De came and rescued me. If it wasn't for him, I'd probably be sitting at home right now. He's a pretty cool dude, and he's straight up. He told me about his girl and son, and we are both just looking to have a little fun. Besides, I was waiting for a certain someone to call me, but he never did," she said as she looked past Andre and directly at Corn.

"How did you end up on the door?" her brother asked.

"Oh, De told me I could make some extra money if I wanted, so I found this bucket, made a sign, and I've been here ever since. It's been a really good night so far," she said with a sly smile.

"From the looks of things, it's only gonna get better," Corn said, pointing out to the mob of thugs loitering in the streets, the swarm of skaters hanging out on the lawn, and the monster snake of a line coiling back from the front door, slithering down the littered driveway, and curling out into the jam-packed street.

"I think I had better stay with you and protect you and all of your money and stuff," Corn said to Latice as he pivoted in front of her, looked her up and down, then gave her a sly smile of his own. Andre walked over to Corn and whispered in his ear, "Be careful what you say to Latice, because she's not to be played with."

"Okay, if that's what you want to do. I'm going to see if I can find my friend Ted a girl and congratulate your boy on the ridiculous turnout at his party." He gave Corn some dap, pushed the door open, and walked into the house.

A black light bulb in a lamp sitting on a table by the door created an array of bouncing shadows dancing on the walls of the hallway leading to the living room. When they stepped into the opening, the temperature climbed ten degrees as a multitude of bodies linked like a human chain throughout the giant room. Bonded, none quite the same, yet all connected by two or more intermingled body parts. Andre dreaded the thought of trying to pass through the living barrier blocking his path to the sliding door opening up to a gated back-yard. The packed crowd was being funneled into the kitchen where it ended in a bottleneck of individuals jousting for position to be next at one of the two pony kegs of Stroh's beer jutting out of the twin ice-filled stainless steel sinks. Little beads of sweat popped through the tiny pores in the boy's forehead as he pushed through the meld-ing mass of bodies. Like a wave, a sudden lurch on the left side of the room moved gradually across the swarm in sections, till the kids next to the boys were pushing them back in the direction from which they came. When he finally reached the door, he slid it open, turned around, and looked back to Ted who had been assimilated into the crowd dancing with some chick to Run DMC's "Run's House."

The brisk autumn air quickly revitalized the young man as he stood on the patio scanning the groups of people scattered across the backyard. As he studied the scenery, he hoped to see the sexy silhou-ette of his new friend from the DA's office, but she was not there. It did not take long for him to spy Donnie standing with several other members of the basketball team huddled around an in-ground bar-becue pit set ablaze.

"What's up, fellas? You guys ready for our scrimmage Tuesday against College of the Canyons?" Andre asked as he walked around the pit and shook each individual's hand.

"I'm ready, but I don't know about your boy Don, 'cause you know he gonna shoot every time he touch the rock, or till Coach Murphy pulls him." Big Ice laughed.

"You ain't got to worry about me. You know I'ma get my shot off every chance I get," Donnie said as he joined in, laughing. To Donnie's right stood Ray Wilkins, a towering seven-foot-one fresh-man with the coordination of a baby doe. His wilting posture reduced him to a mere six-feet-eight man-child.

"What about you, Andre? Are you ready? You think you gonna get sum run?" Donnie asked.

"Hell yeah! I better. Besides, everybody is going to play. That's why they call it a scrimmage, man," Andre said with a big smile.

"Yo, I thought you were going to bring some girls?" Donnie said, staring right at Andre.

"Man, look around. Don't you see all these girls out here and in the house? Who do you think invited them? Me, that's who," Andre said, with his best Tony Montana impression, a huge smile, and his two thumbs pointing back at his chest.

High above the party brittle leaves clashed in a sudden death match where the losers are plummeted to the ground and subjugated to mulch.

"How did you get here?" Donnie asked.

"My boy Ted brought me and Corn," Andre replied.

"Is that right? Where is ole nappy head Corn?"

"He's out front with Latice. Aye, that reminds me, where is your baby's mama?" Andre asked.

"What, why you ask me that because your sister is here? Nigga, please. Stacy hates it here and be tryin' to get out of the desert every chance she gets. She goes to her mama's house down in LA damn near every weekend," Donnie said as he scratched his head and silently wondered if there was another reason why she left every weekend.

"Damn, man, there's no need to get all defensive. I was just asking. I need to go grab me another beer," Andre said as he turned his can up and drained the last few drops from it.

"Me, too, I'll walk in with you. Did you see the two kegs in the sink?" Donnie asked as he walked over to Andre and put his arm around his shoulder.

As the two young men walked over to the patio door, Dollar asked his young protégé how things were going and if he had dumped any of the dope he had given him. Before he could answer, he turned the conversation to Corn.

"Did you know that he has already gotten rid of half of his stuff and he has some friends coming in from Vegas tomorrow to buy the rest?" Dollar asked just before he opened the sliding door.

"Nope, he didn't say anything to me about it," Andre replied.

"Well, you need to get busy… If this was a game of one-on-one, you would be getting your ass kicked." Donnie laughed but somehow maintained a straight face while doing so. The look eerily reminded Andre of the look the heart attack-stricken old gangster had given him as he held the Magnum .357 in his face.

The duo was accosted with a balmy junglelike atmosphere as soon as he closed the door behind them. The sliding door wore a steamy coat that covered its entire surface, fogged up from top to bottom, except for a little note that someone had written on the window with his finger, "Help me! I can't breathe." Andre tapped Donnie on the shoulder, pointed to the note, and said, "Maybe you should open a door or something."

"Fuck 'em! Let 'em sweat," Donnie said with a chuckle. Andre just shook his head and dove into the pack. The youngster appeared to be performing hand-to-hand combat as he cut through the thick of the woven crowd. Through the dense mass, Andre could see Ted's head bobbing from side to side as he did the wop. He tried to call out to him a couple of times but realized it was practicing senselessness to try to compete with the deafening bass being pounded through the fifteen-inch woofers.

Voice strained and unable to grab Ted's attention, Andre pressed onward, closely followed by Donnie. As he began to ease through a tight spot, he felt a slight tug just above his left wrist. Turning around expecting to see Donnie's chiseled mug, he was surprised to find Eileen with two cute blondes in tow.

"Really, are you just going to walk right by me and not speak when you are the one who invited me in the first place?" she asked as she released his sleeve, took a step back, and crossed her arms.

"I'm sorry, I really didn't see you. Do you think I would try and ignore you after all the begging I did to get you here?" he said, smiling. He then turned and motioned for Donnie to come over to him. As soon as he was close enough, he grabbed him, pulled him closer, and asked him if he had somewhere quiet where they could talk. Donnie shook his head and began to work his way through the crowd.

"Hi, I'm Andre!" the boy screamed awkwardly to the two girls standing behind Eileen.

"Follow me. We are going to go somewhere a little less noisy," he said as he grabbed her hand and began to pull her behind him as he ducked in between posers and steered around partiers dancing in the large room. Donnie looked back to make sure his homey and the girls were still in trail as he made a right turn down a hallway just past the dining room, where there was a small line of people waiting to use the restroom. He stopped just beyond the line at the next door waiting for Andre and the girls.

He opened the door and said, "Look over the mess. I put most of my living room furniture in here, but least it's plenty of places to sit down."

"You ain't never lying," Andre said as he tried to step inside the room. It was a clusterfuck. There was a beige couch blocking the entrance which everyone had to climb over, and across from it sat a similar-colored love seat standing vertical on its arm to make room for two brown La-Z-Boy recliners bunched up against a gray couch with matching love seat and chair lodged between a coffee table and two end tables stacked one on top of the other beside a huge fifty-two-inch Sanyo television buried in the corner.

Just as everyone started getting comfortable, Donnie jumped up and said, "I've got a better idea. Any of you ladies thirsty? I've got something I want everyone to see anyway."

Once again, they were on the move. Andre trailed the group, battling to stay within nose distance of the wonderful smell being emitted from Eileen's hair. He was not sure, but he believed the swarm had grown thicker just since they had gone into the room filled with furniture. He thought that maybe Latice was letting too many people in and should lock the door and only let people in when some of these people left. It was not his party, so he would wait for the host to make that decision.

The pace was slow, but steadily Donnie dissected the multitude of people mashed in the living room and merged into the less packed hallway leading toward the front door. Just a few feet from the entrance, Donnie ducked into a brown door on the right side of the hallway leading to the garage. He stepped down, turned the light on, and said, "Watch your step." At first, there was silence, and no one said a word as the florescent light gained brightness.

"Wow! That's impressive. Did you stack all of those like that?" Karen asked as she stepped off the step onto the smooth concrete floor.

"That's pretty cool… Do you mind if I grab one?" Patty said when she stepped into the garage.

"No. Help yourself. Sorry, they're not cold. By the way, since my rude-ass friend isn't going to introduce anybody, I'm De," Donnie said.

"Well, De, I'm Eileen. The bubbly little one is Karen, and the feisty tall one is Patty. Now do you mind if I ask? How does a man come by a mountain of wine coolers that reaches the ceiling?" the young woman asked with a cynical look on her face.

"No, I don't mind. That's a good question. I made a bet with a good friend of mine a couple weeks ago that the Lakers would beat the Clippers. This is how he paid me. We always give each other shit that the other doesn't want. The last time the Clippers won, I gave him a brand-new set of rims and tires. The problem was they were made specifically for a Volkswagen." He laughed.

In the center of the garage floor on a two-by-two wood pallet stood an almost Christmas-tree-like stack of wine coolers reaching to the rafters. The bottom layer was covered with an assortment of Bartels and James Wine Coolers climbing three stacks high. On top of the B and Js with just a thin sheet of cardboard separating them stood a mixture of Seagram's Wild Berry Coolers. The packaging for their product bloomed like bulbs on a Christmas tree, bright-red raspberries frolicking with deep purple grapes surrounding the most radiant oranges, giving life to the thirty-six four-packs of libation.

The next layer consisted of the clear beverage designed for those with a more sophisticated taste in wine coolers. Its bright blue label and unique transparent liquid implied that Zima would be crisp and refreshing. The reality was it made you thirstier with each taste bud-obliterating sip. Zima stood in the minority; there were only two layers of the see-through liquid in the tree.

California Wine Coolers graced the top four layers. Each new stack was smaller than the one underneath its bottom with the top tier supporting just one four-pack centered in the middle, creating a peak that extended beyond the rafters.

Karen twisted the cap off a grape Seagram's cooler, walked up to Donnie, smiled, and said that she loved his house and he was just a swimming pool away from having a new roommate. He laughed and told her that he would have a pool if it were not for his three-year-old son Tyreek. Maybe when he gets a little older, he told her.

Still standing on the step, Eileen stood eye to eye with Andre, wondering why this person seemed so familiar to her when she was positive that she had never met him.

"Are you sure you never visited Rosemond or Mohave?" Eileen asked.

"Yes, I'm sure. I've never been to either of those places. I know what you mean though. There is something strangely familiar about you too. Do you want a drink?" the boy asked as he walked over to the wine cooler monument just a few feet away. Andre grabbed an orange California Cooler, turned around, about to hand it to Eileen, when out of the blue he thought to ask Donnie who was watching his house. Right on cue as if rehearsed, a loud crashing sound echoed from the house through to the garage.

"What the fuck was that?" Donnie yelled as he broke into a full-speed run for the door with Andre right behind him. As soon as they reached the hallway, a tidal wave of bodies from the living room were being pushed back toward the front door. Like swimming against the current, the two fought the living surf and made their way to the kitchen where the ruckus was coming from. When they finally reached the kitchen, Donnie could not believe what he was looking at with his two eyes. Locked in mortal combat on his linoleum floor, five bodies tussled like the main event at a WWE cage match. He wasn't so surprised that people were fighting in his kitchen, but he was surprised at who it was destroying his custom kitchen cabinets. It was Jesus and Monté battling three Hispanic guys he had never seen before. Earlier in the week, he had invited them to come up for the party, but he didn't really expect them to make the long drive from Riverside.

Donnie leaped upon the counter, crawled over to the sink, turned on the cold water, and pulled the black plastic hose out as far as he could and began spraying water on the men kicking and punching one another on the floor. When the water did not deter them, he lifted the pony keg from the left side of the sink and slammed it onto the back of the closest Mexican to him.

"Enough with the bullshit! I'm going to start shooting mutha-fuckers in a minute. Now get up off my floor and get the fuck out while you still can!" Donnie shouted and leaped down from the counter.

"Ay, Don, I'm sorry, man. But these peachy Vatos need to be taught some fucking manners," Jesus said as he threw his bruised hand up to the counter and pulled himself up.

"Shit, I was talking to you too. You and Monté. Since you can't respect my house, get the fuck out! Come back when you got some-thing for me. Now kick rocks," he screamed.

"In fact, the party is over! Everybody, get their shit and get the fuck out!" Donnie pushed through the crowd, shouting.

"Party over! Everybody, out!"

"Yo, Dre, tell your girl, her friends, and any other chicks that want to stay, they don't have to leave. I'll tell the fellas from the team the same thing, and we will have our own little shindig," Donnie said as he pushed people toward the front door.

Within ten minutes of the homeowner's first utterance for everyone to disperse, his house was cleared, except for those he had asked to stay. Twenty minutes later, even the stragglers were gone from the block, leaving only the remnants from an alcohol-laden parade which had passed through.

The raging bash had been dismantled in favor of a smaller, more sociable group of about twenty-five partiers hanging out in the huge living room, dining room area. Off in the corner, Eileen and Andre attempted to get to know each other a little better.

"This is more of what I had pictured when Donnie told me he was going to have a party. Not that insane monster crowd he had jammed up in here." Andre laughed.

"I know, it was crazy, right? Why did you call him Donnie just now? I thought his name was De?" Eileen asked as she leaned against the wall and took a drink from her bottle.

"Well, you know De is short for Donnie, right? I think he is more likely to introduce himself as De to females and Donnie to males." As the words left his lips, it had occurred to him what Gary from the Jungle had told him just a few years back. He said that the alias was a protection from those that you did not know that well, and perhaps he should have referred to him as De as well.

Other than the stumble, Andre thought that their conversation flowed freely without pause. Interestingly they shared common beliefs like pro-life, spirituality, and strong family values. When Andre talked, Eileen studied him carefully. Closely, she observed his mannerisms. With the eye of a seasoned gambler, she watched for tells, and without being too intrusive, she scanned his features. There was no question these were eyes that she knew.

"I don't mean to be rude, but were you ever fat? Maybe you were big boned as a kid," she said bashfully.

"No, why do you ask?"

"For some reason, when I look at your face, it reminds me of someone. Except that person was huge, much larger than you." The wooden legs of the tan sofa scraped the wall as Ice and Ray carried it from the hallway into the living room where they promptly found a place and set it down. Close behind them followed Corn and Ted carrying the other couch, led by Donnie giving orders as if he were the acting foreman on the job.

"Dre, you need to get your lazy butt up and help out," Donnie said as he instructed Corn where to place the couch.

"I don't see you doing anything except running your mouth. Come on, man, why don't you help me carry one of the love seats in here so Eileen and I can have somewhere to sit," Dre said as he walked up, grabbed him by his baggy white T-shirt, and began pulling him toward the room filled with furniture.

The two sat and talked, oblivious of everyone else in the room until around three o'clock when Patty staggered over to Eileen and told her she had to go because she had to work in the morning at eight. Eileen knew right away after looking at Patty's cockeyed smile that she was hammered.

"Okay, give me a minute," Eileen said, as she leaned in and asked Andre if he would like to come over for dinner at her house tomorrow because her mom was going to cook a big dinner.

"Sure, what time do you want me to be there?" he replied without a second thought.

"I'm not sure. Here, take my number and call me around three," she said as she reached in her purse and pulled out a pen and paper to write it down. When she stood up, Andre stood up, too, and thought to try to kiss her but chickened out at the last second.

"Okay," she said with a smile as she turned and moved to collect her other friend who was sitting on the couch, talking with the handful of partiers who were left about why men cheat. Eileen stepped in and said, "Yeah, yeah, we know you did everything for him. Anytime, anywhere, you were always down for whatever. Let it go, girl. He was a jerk. Move on, grab your stuff, and let's go."

"Yeah, girl…moo-move on, forget about, forget about that asshole, and grab one of these cuties," Patty slurred as she pointed to the couch with Donnie and Ted sitting on it.

Donnie tapped Ted on his knee with the back of his hand and said, "Man you better get that girl's number boy!" Ted generated a huge smile but didn't say anything.

"No, I had better get your number, boy," Karen said with a smirk and the raising of her eyebrows as they marched off toward the door.

Just glancing around the room, Donnie realized that two of his guests were missing. He did not see either Latice or Corn. Abruptly, he bounced up from the sofa without a word and began to walk through his house room by room in search of the couple. With each step, his forehead grew wrinkles, pulling his eyes to a squint. His jaws clinched tight, allowing his tongue no movement. Once again, Corn was standing in his way, he thought. The first day of school, the two had clashed on the court and nearly come to blows. Their every encounter pitted the two type A personalities in a verbal chess match. For the Ranger, it was a deeper dislike. Donnie despised Corn's well-mannered, goody-two-shoes, middle-class family upbringing. The word *Oreo* came to mind when he thought of him. Looking back, Donnie realized that Andre was the conduit, which made it possible for the two to get along without the endless combativeness. None of that mattered now; the only thing that mattered was finding them because he was sure that old Corn was well into his Mr. Nice Guy routine with Latice. With each door, he found himself more anxious to what position he might find them. After checking every room, Donnie walked back into the living room in the act of sitting down when he popped right back up and darted for the garage.

"What are you doing? You're making me dizzy," Andre said, as he leaned back on the love seat.

Opening the door to the garage, Donnie found Latice sitting on the step in front of the door and Corn sitting cross-legged across from her next to the wine cooler tree.

"Yo, Cornie, get your ass up. I think your ride is about to leave," Donnie said as he released hold of the doorknob in his right hand, turned, and walked back toward the living room.

"I'm gonna call it a night," Donnie said as he ushered his remaining guests to the front door. As the group dispersed, Andre turned and asked his sister if she needed a ride home, and she replied, "I'm just going stay here tonight. De is going to take me shopping at the Palmdale Mall tomorrow."

"Okay, whatever, just thought I'd ask," he said as he screamed out, "Shotgun," to Corn, who was just about to open the passenger door of the Capri.

CHAPTER
24

With sleep still in his eyes and the sky not quite blue, Andre rolled out of his bed and went in search of the cordless phone. To his surprise, it was on the charger. He gathered his thoughts then shuffled off to his room and called Corn. The phone rang seven times, and Andre was just about to hang it up when a groggy "Hello" echoed from the headset. After apologizing for calling so early, he let his buddy know that he could use some help moving his packs, and he was wondering if his friends coming in from out of town needed any more yae. Corn told his teammate that he would check, but he was pretty sure that they did because they had asked him if he had a whole bird. Thirty minutes later, Corn called Andre back and assured him that they would be able to take any amount they had to offer. He had known Little Moe as kids in Anchorage. Moe claimed that all the white girl out in Las Vegas was worthless garbage, stepped on so many times that cooking it up was not even an option. Plain and simple, he was looking for a good, trustworthy connect. Corn informed Andre that they would be in town around three, so he should come over before they got there so he could watch his back during the transaction.

In the time leading up to the three o'clock meeting, Andre's emotions would have made an amazing line graph. When he thought of dinner with Eileen, his endorphins shot to the ceiling, leaving him high on puppy love. Conversely, thoughts of the drug deal with unknown variables slammed him back to the ground instantly. The thought of the quick cash rocketed him back up nearly to the heights

232

from which he had just fallen. However, his position at the summit was short-lived in fear that her parents may dislike him. The alternating peaks and valleys left Andre exhausted. On top of that, he did not feel comfortable about the upcoming meeting. Maybe it was just normal to feel apprehensive about a drug deal with someone you have never met, he thought. Suddenly his thoughts were interrupted by Jessie calling him from the living room letting him know that he was about to leave and if he still wanted a ride he had better come on.

"Okay, I'm coming!" he yelled as he grabbed his book bag full of narcotics.

Andre got into the car and almost instantly broke out into a cold sweat even though Jessie's high-powered air-conditioning unit was blowing full blast. His conscience was suffocating him. Andre knew that it was wrong to be in his mother's fiancé's car with enough dope to get them both ten years in the state penitentiary.

"Are you okay, Dre? You don't look so good," Jessie said as he adjusted the radio station.

"Not really. I'm feeling a little motion sickness, I think," he said as he doubled over and contemplated his actions. He could hear Jessie talking, but it may as well have been Russian. He recalled being told once that robbery was not his bag. Well, maybe drug dealing was not his bag either, he considered. He hoped the guilt he felt in his heart was not apparent to Mr. Nelson each time he turned his eyes from the road to speak to him.

"Dre...Andre! What street did you say Corn lived?" Jessie asked.

"Fifteenth and J-10. It's the apartments across from the movie theater," Andre said as he sat up and leaned back into the plush blueberry seats. As the Bonneville pulled into the Sunset Apartments, Jessie turned to Andre and said, "If you ever want to talk, feel free to give me a call," he said as he pulled down his sun visor, dropping several business cards onto his lap.

"It's the first building on the right," the young man said, pointing out the window. The driver stopped and handed his passenger one of his cards and told Andre to call him if he needed a ride later.

"Thanks, Jess," he said as he jumped out of the car and started running up the steps, only to hear Jessie screaming for him to come back. When he looked back, he could see his mom's boyfriend through the half-open window holding up his book bag. Immediately, he ran back down the stairs to the vehicle, opened the door, and took the bag.

"You can't do any studying without these. Man, you must have a lot of books in here. This thing weighs a ton," the gentleman said with a smile.

"Yeah, lots," Andre said as he closed the door for a second time.

Eileen leaned over the old wood chopping block setting on the Formica countertop cutting up onions and green peppers for her mother's enchiladas. Beside her to her right, sister Tanya stood chopping chicken breast up on a cutting board of her own as she questioned her elder of two years about her dinner date.

"You have never brought anyone to dinner. What makes this boy so special?" Tanya asked, then looked over at her mother whose back was turned, and slipped a tiny piece of chicken into her hungry mouth.

"Yeah, what's so special about this dork?" Michelle said as she stood in front of the sink churning lemon slices on a white juicer into a clear glass pitcher.

"Who said there was anything special about him? He's just really nice, and something is very familiar about him," Eileen said with a wondering smile on her face.

"Ooh…you like this boy, I can tell. It's just like Henrique all over again." Tanya laughed.

"I don't remember any Henrique," Michelle said.

"That's because you were just a little meha. Leeny was in the fourth grade, and I was just in the second. I remember she would always have that same silly smile on her face when she would talk about him or write his name on her notebook." Tanya smiled and asked her sister if she had kissed him yet. To the left of Michelle stood Margarita mixing masa and salt together in a large mixing bowl. Silently she listened to her daughter's conversation until the kiss question came up.

"Less talk, and more cooking, girls. Maybe less talk after you answer the question, Leeny. Did you kiss him?" Margarita said as she poured in a cup of water and began the mixing process again.

"No, ma'am. I would have if he had tried to kiss me, but he didn't," Eileen said as her cheeks began to turn crimson.

"You must really like this boy," her mother said as she dumped out the ingredients onto a lightly floured board and began kneading the dough while she waited for a response from her eldest daughter.

"It's…it's something about him. It's almost like we already know each other or something. It's weird, I can't explain it," she said as her words fell off into silence.

"If you say so. You kids nowadays, but I cannot say you have bring home boys a lot. Actually, I do not think that you have bring home any," Margarita said.

A delicious aroma filled the kitchen as two medium-size pots simmered on the Amana range's top.

"You girls have done good. I finish. Go do fun thing. Watch your music TV, talk on phone, draw your art," Margarita said as she began to flatten out the tortillas.

Andre paced back and forth across Corn's living room floor.

"Bro, would you please stop walking in front of the TV. Don't you see me playing John Madden?" Corn said as he frantically pushed the buttons and maneuvered the joystick, whipping his hands back and forth, nearly pulling the cord out of his Sega Genesis console.

"Yo, where are they at? It's three thirty, and they haven't called or anything. It don't feel right. I know he's your old friend, but how well do you know him now? Do you trust him?" Andre asked.

"Yeah…I think so."

"What do you mean you think so?" Andre barked back.

"He's my boy. We talk every so often," Corn said without looking up from the television.

"I hope you're right. Man, I'm supposed to be over at Eileen's house at five. I wish they would hurry up. I have to walk up to Avenue K and catch the bus," said Andre.

"It's cool, don't worry about it. If they aren't here in the next thirty minutes or so…you can leave and I'll handle it with Lil Moe by myself," Corn said as he continued to play without looking up.

"Why don't I call Donnie and have him come over to watch your back? I'm sure he'd be cool with that," Andre said as he continued to pace back and forth, this time between the kitchen and dining room.

"I've got this. I trust Moe. You need to just chill and let me handle it," the military brat said as he paused the game, set down his controller, stood up, walked over to his friend, and tried to assure him that everything would be all right.

"Why don't you just take off now. It's a quarter to four, and who knows what time the next bus is gonna run on Sunday," Corn said with a smile as he patted his new best friend on the shoulder.

Moments later, Andre rejoiced in the beauty of the day as he walked north toward Avenue K. In an almost dreamlike state, he experienced what he thought was meant by living in the moment.

Time had seemingly stopped. The stress of waiting on Little Moe was gone, and the fear of meeting Eileen's parents had vanished as well. He felt liberated, free of thought, effortlessly gliding across the sidewalk toward his destination when he noticed that the passing cars were silent and only the faint song of a lovestruck blue jay danced on the wind. He felt at one with the world as he glanced up at the brilliant blue sky, which held but a few wispy clouds fleeing the distant sun.

As quickly as the timeless event began, it was over, and he was grounded back into reality by a capital L across the street in the window of the AM/PM convenience store. Momentarily, he wondered if he had time to run in and grab a lottery ticket before the next bus came. Without a second thought, he dashed across the street, into the store, and purchased a ticket for the Wednesday drawing. Normally he played the same six digits, but since he was fearful of missing the bus, he asked the clerk for a quick pick instead. As he exited the store, he saw his bus coming to a stop on the other side of the street.

Corn jumped up, startled, when he heard the knock on the door. Still consumed and somewhat distracted by the video game, the young man strolled over to the door and began opening it without looking through the peephole. As soon as the door cracked open, someone on the other side of the door kicked it with a tremendous amount of force. The door smashed open, crashing into the unsuspecting face of Corn, sending him flying back into the mirror on the hallway wall. Quickly three masked men rushed through the door. The one in front carried a pistol, which he quickly began to bash the butt into the stunned boy's face repeatedly until he crumbled to the floor. When the pistol whipping stopped, the two men in the back stepped in like a well-practiced drill. The first man stepped up, kicked the boy in the ribs, then pulled him up by his collar as the second man removed a roll of duct tape from his jacket, ripped off a piece, and covered the boy's mouth with it. The two men then each grabbed an arm and began dragging him through the apartment, looking for the bathroom. Once in the restroom the man with the gun told Corn to bend over, hug the bowl of the toilet, interlock his hands and fingers together like he was praying. The man with the tape then kneeled down beside him and began taping his hands together. Once he was sure that their victim was taped securely, the masked man stood up and backed away from the man taped to the toilet. The man with the gun then stepped forward, pulled the tape off Corn's mouth, placed his gun in the boy's face, and said, "If you scream, I will blow your motherfucking head off! I'm just going to ask you one time. If you lie to me, I will come back in here and put one in the back of your head. Do you understand me?" The man holding the gun asked with a gruff utterance of words that sounded choked up. Corn shook his head up and down, indicating that he did.

"Where is the coke?" he asked as he stood over him, pressing the barrel of the pistol against the back of his head. With tears streaming down his face and barely able to complete a sentence for stuttering, Corn nodded his head to the right and uttered the words "My bedroom closet in the gray backpack."

"You had better hope I don't come back in here," the man said as he nodded to his henchmen to go check the bedroom.

After a couple of minutes of searching, one of the men yelled back to the bathroom.

"Yep, we've got it!"

"Well, youngster, it's been nice doing business with you. Now, you stay right there and don't go nowhere, you hear," the hoarse man said, laughing as he walked out of the bathroom.

Slumped over the toilet, near the point of hyperventilation, Corn struggled to catch his breath. Bleeding and battered, he could hear the men whispering in the next room. Consumed with fear, he expected the gunman to return to the bathroom and make good on his promise at any second. The next thing he heard was the rush of feet over broken glass, followed by a slam of the door. Momentarily, the boy listened for any sound, not sure if the jackers had actually left or just closed the door with them on the inside. Several minutes passed before Corn actively began to try to free himself.

Fifteen minutes later, Corn still could not free himself. The person who had bound his hands together had done an incredible job. The angle at which he had been taped prevented him from getting any leverage to try to stand up and lift the bowl off the seal. He was positive that the man who tapped his wrist was not Lil Moe, nor did he think the guy with the gun was him either. He had only seen them momentarily from a standing position but had surmised that the three men were all about the same height. Each man was taller than Little Moe, he was pretty sure, because at last check Moe was no taller than five feet four on his best day. He may not have been there, but he damn sure set him up. He would bet his life on it. He had been stupid. What was he going to tell Donnie? He had just been robbed for a half a kilo. What was he going to tell Dre?

Reflecting mere minutes ago he guessed that the trio was not in the apartment for more than five minutes. Corn understood the severity of the situation. Every second that he spent facedown in this putrid toilet bowl harboring thick brownish rows of calcification intersecting fresh bumpy designer skid marks trailing off into the water, Moe and his boys were that many more seconds closer to being home free with fading visions of Lancaster in their rearview mirror.

Andre stepped off the AVTA bus on K and Tenth Street East and looked around in attempt to gain his bearings. Moments later, he was standing on the sidewalk in front of a house comparing the address on the scrap piece of paper Eileen had given him at the party to the number stenciled on the curb. Quickly he was swept away by the smell of the girl's perfume on the paper. He shook it off, pulled himself together, sprinted up the steps, and rang the doorbell. To Andre's surprise, the girl that opened the door looked just like a miniature version of Eileen. The boy stood with his mouth agape, stunned.

"Hi, is Eileen here?" he finally forced from his mouth.

"I didn't think you could talk for a second. Yeah, she's here, come in. Eileeeen!" Michelle screamed then turned and pointed toward the couch and told him to have a seat.

"Man, you two look just alike," Dre said with a disbelieving shake of his head.

"Yeah, I get that a lot. I'll go get her," the young girl said with a smile as she walked away.

The young man found himself shivering as he sat patiently waiting. As thousands of goose bumps popped up on his arms, he found himself wondering if it were colder in the house or outside. The amazing aroma emanating from the kitchen made the juices in his stomach talk, overruling his weak flesh to sit and bear the chilly room in wait of the delicacies to come.

A 6-foot-3, 250-pound man with graying temples and a mature receding hairline entered the room, moseyed over, and plopped down on the cushion right next to Dre. He looked at the young man, leaned forward, grabbed the remote control, turned on the television, and said, "Do you like basketball? Because the Lakers game is about to come on in a minute. By the way, I'm Mr. Jokinen, and you can call me Mr. Jokinen." The tone at which he delivered his words made Andre think he was about to hear a high hat in the background. His words came across very casual and friendly until he introduced himself as Eileen's dinner guest. Dre noticed his entire demeanor change. There was no steam shooting from his nostrils or horns sprouting from his head, but he did bare his teeth when he informed the young

239

man that he would be okay with him as long as he respected his daughter. If not, he would have a problem with her father. He then smiled and offered the young man something to drink.

"Michelle, bring me a beer!" he yelled. "You're not old enough to drink, are you?" he questioned the boy.

"No…no, sir," he spouted.

Michelle ran into the room with a red can in each hand and slid in her sock feet right up to the coffee table in front of the couch.

"Here, Dre, I bought you a Coke if that's okay," she said as she handed her dad a frosty can of Budweiser.

"So, are you a Lakers fan?" Richard asked the young man to his left.

"Oh yeah, I love Showtime. Magic is the man, well, next to Jordan, of course," young Andre said without making full eye contact. The talk of basketball bridged the generation gap and allowed the two men an equal ground to build their relationship.

"Eileen told me that you are on the basketball team out at the college. Do you think you will get any playtime this year?"

Before Dre could answer the question, Trevor walked into the room and barged into their conversation, saying that "Coach Murphy is an asshole. He kicked me out of upward bound for the whole summer last year."

"Watch your mouth, son. This is Andre. Your sister Eileen invited him over to dinner, so watch your manners," Richard said as he turned up the volume on the remote.

"Yeah, I've seen you around up at the college, but I kind of stay to myself," Trevor said as he examined the hardwood floor, not making any eye contact when he spoke.

"You should come out to a game. I hear it's a great time when we win. Plenty of people socializing, having fun. It's a good way to meet people," Andre said with an inviting smile.

"Do you think I need an invitation from you to go to a game out at the college and have a good time?" Trevor scowled.

"No…I was just saying now that we know each other, we could hang out together sometime if you like," Dre countered.

Inside, he was praying that Eileen would come and save him from this awkward conversation. Andre had almost forgotten how cold it was in the house until he felt a dribble of snot draining down on his lip. Quickly, he wiped it away with his sleeve, and when he saw his watch, he realized it was nearly five thirty and he still had not seen the person he had come to see. Suddenly it occurred to him that he needed to call Corn and find out how things had gone with Little Moe.

"Well, I hope you're not one of those people who gets out in public and act like you don't know me 'cause that will really piss me off. And I can guarantee Eileen wouldn't like it very much either," Trevor said as he continued to talk on about the matter under his breath but barely audible to anyone but himself.

Dre found himself in a conversation that was spiraling downhill very quickly. He had hoped that Mr. Jokinen would step in and say something; anything would do. Looking at Eileen's dad, he realized that no help would come from him. Richard's eyes had glazed over, the wrinkles on his forehead had tightened, and his ears had perked forward with his shoulders slumped under, in total submission to his thirty-six-inch Sony television. He was no longer just watching; he was in the game free of all external distraction.

"Okay, boys, dinner is ready. Everyone, come into the dining room," Eileen said as she walked over to Andre and held out her hand for him to take it.

"Would you like to wash up?" she asked as she led him to a small restroom off the kitchen across from a laundry room. When he exited the bathroom, Eileen grabbed his hand, quickly pulling him into the laundry room, and closed the door. Andre was about to say something, then it occurred to him to just be quiet and see what she had in mind. The tiny laundry room left the two pressed in close quarters against the washing machine. The young woman grabbed him by his waist, pulled him in close, rose up on her tiptoes, and planted a long wet kiss on Andre's mouth, leaving him stunned.

"Now, was that so hard? Why didn't you just do that at the party so we could get it out of the way? Now let's go have dinner. My mama is a really good cook." Once again, she grabbed his hand

and led him, this time into the dining room where she sat him at the table between herself and Michelle. Richard sat perched at the table's head. Down at the other end of the table sat his wife Margarita, only seven feet away from him, yet the two could not have been farther away if he had been in France and she in Columbia. To the right of his mother sat Trevor beside his twin, Tanya.

Eileen was pretty surprised at how well the night had gone. Her entire family was actually well-behaved in front of her guest. Her dad refrained from lecturing, Tanya was not a total bitch to one of her friends for once, and Trevor did not spaz out about his recent breakup, except for one outburst that none of his family loved him because he was not a girl when Mama told him that he could not have a fourth enchilada.

After dinner, Margarita asked Eileen to help her remove the dishes from the table. When the two walked into the kitchen, Margarita set down the plates on the counter, grasped her eldest daughter's hand, and told her that she thought Andre was a very well-mannered handsome young man. When the two finished cleaning all the dishes from the table, Eileen informed her mom that she was going to give Dre a ride home and she had planned not to be out too late. When Eileen walked into the front room, she found Dre leaning against the wall in the hallway with the telephone pressed to the side of his head.

"I was trying to call Corn, but the phone just rang," Dre said as he hung up the telephone.

"Maybe he's out with one of his girlfriends," Eileen said with a smile.

"Yeah, maybe," he responded.

"Are you ready to go? I think it's only fair that I know where you live, since you know where I live," the girl said as she dangled her keys from side to side.

"Okay, I'm ready, just let me go tell your mom bye, and thank her for the terrific dinner," Andre said as he walked off into the kitchen.

Donnie sat on a stool in the kitchen looking mad at the phone just before he slammed it down on the hook.

"Fuck! This is the fifth time I have tried to call Corn today, and it's starting to piss me off. Latice, get your shit. We've got to get out of here. Laurie will be home at any time."

"I don't want to go back over there. It's too small for the three of us. I wish I had somewhere else to stay," Latice whined as she wandered off into the other room to get her things.

Without full thought of what he was saying, Donnie belted out.

"I may have a solution for your problem. Are you scared of dogs?" he shouted from the kitchen. Moments later in the car the two discussed Latice staying at his stash house. He warned her that he kept his dope there, and other than him stopping by a couple of times a day it was empty except for his dog Red. She did not care that this character Donnie Dollar was some kind of big-time drug dealer, nor did she care about the fact that the house had dope in it. She was a big girl, but she was concerned that her naive little brother was getting involved with him.

"I'll tell you what. We will go by there, and you can look at the place and decide for yourself, but first I need to run by Corn's pad real quick," Donnie informed Latice as he made a left turn onto Fifteenth Street West. Seconds later, the two were pulling into the Sunset Apartments parking lot where he edged up beside a beat-up gray Toyota Celica, threw the car into park, and turned off the ignition.

"Open up the glove compartment and hand me that strap," Dollar said as his face turned stern as stone.

"What are you talking about, strap? All I see is a gun and a bunch of papers," Latice assured the driver.

"I'm talking about the gun. Hand it to me," Donnie instructed her, and he then leaned forward, tucked it into the small of his back, and got out of the car.

"What do you need the gun for?" Latice questioned him as he started walking away.

Donnie did not reply. Instead, he adjusted his shirt to make sure his weapon was concealed and then made his way toward the steps that led up to apartment E-208. When he reached the landing to Corn's apartment he noticed the door was cracked.

"Corn...Aye, Corn, you in here!" Donnie yelled as he pushed the door open and observed broken glass stretched across the carpet leading up to a smashed mirror from which it came. Slowly he stepped into the apartment and removed the .38 Smith and Wesson he had tucked in his pants. The worst thoughts imaginable rushed through his mind as small shards of glass crumbled beneath his feet.

"Corn, Dre," Donnie shouted, as he systematically cleared the apartment room by room as he was taught in Ranger school. He stopped in his tracks when he thought that he heard something. Once again, there it was, a muffled yelp coming from the next room over. With weapon extended, he slowly pushed the door open to find Corn duct-taped to the base of the toilet. Donnie tucked his pistol back in his pants and removed a pocketknife from his front pocket, bent over, and carefully sliced through the tape holding Corn's hands together. Corn attempted to stand but only fell back to the floor in anguish after having been bent over for the last four hours in that torturing position. Once again, Donnie stooped down beside his friend, this time helping him to a sitting position. Donnie told him to prepare himself because he was about to pull the tape from his mouth.

After explaining to Donnie what happened and whom he thought was responsible, Donnie was furious, incensed that he had just lost nearly a half of a kilo, with no way to get it back.

"Where the fuck was Dre? Why wasn't he here when you were conducting business for both of you?" Donnie screamed, spitting little particles across the room. Dollar's rampaging tirade was interrupted by the closing of the door followed by the sound of footsteps over the broken glass, causing Donnie to draw his gun again.

"Hey, what's up? Where are you, guys?" Latice almost whispered from the living room, inspiring Donnie to help a limping Corn from the bathroom and into the living room. As soon as Latice saw Corn, she shuddered, ran over to him, gave him a hug, helped him to the couch, and asked if he was all right. Donnie watched from a distance Latice's concern-stricken face in the sight of Corn's condition. He also observed the tender way in which she cared for him, displaying passion she had yet to show him even after spending the night with him. Subconsciously, he knew that she would choose him in the end just as he knew that Coach Murphy would choose Corn as well as the starting shooting guard, because he was a safer pick.

As he watched, disdain bubbled in his gut and his hatred fumed. He knew what must happen next. It wasn't the thought of the two being together, nor was it the money he had just lost. It was the competition. In his mind, all competition was bad. Just like his corporate mentors, he not only desired a monopoly, but an uneven playing field to ensure his success as well.

While Latice cleaned the cut on Corn's forehead, he gave Donnie a full account as to why he had told Dre to leave even after Dre had made it clear that he didn't trust Little Moe. He willingly accepted the blame, explaining that as kids, he and Moe had always claimed that they would take a bullet for each other.

The digital clock on Eileen's dashboard read eight fifteen when her gray Pulsar pulled onto Rayden Street. The two were so distracted, laughing and talking about her family at dinner, that Eileen had to swerve to miss a toddler playing in the street. As soon the vehicle came to a stop, Andre jumped out of the car and grabbed the child wearing just a T-shirt and Pampers in the cold October night.

"Oh my gosh! Where did that baby come from?" Eileen screamed to Andre who was now carrying the baby toward the curb, when he turned around and walked back toward the car.

"Just park right there," he said as he pointed toward the next building just ahead on the right.

"I think this baby belongs to the lady two buildings down, but I'm not sure which apartment she lives in," Dre said as he took off down the block carrying the runaway baby.

As soon as he entered the building, he knew right away from which apartment the baby had escaped. The door to the apartment downstairs on the left was wide open. The stench of urine reeked from the apartment, polluting the entire stairwell. Andre held his breath as he knocked on the open door. After knocking numerous times with no response, he decided to enter the dwelling. The television volume was deafening. Dirty clothes, toys, and trash littered the food-infested carpet.

"Hello…is anybody home?" he yelled several times as he walked through the putrid-smelling home holding the little girl in his arms. Walking into the dining room, he answered his own question. Passed out on a tan love seat with her arms and legs pointing in all directions lay Wanda Fleming. Her plump frame covered nearly every inch of the flattened chair. Her thick neck hung back over the arm of the chair with her long blond hair resting on the floor. The inside of her stout arms and legs were besieged with track marks.

"Hello…hello!" he screamed at the unconscious woman to no avail. Finally, at his limit, totally sickened by the sight and the whole situation, he kicked the woman's fat leg and screamed, "Get up! Get up!"

Finally, Wanda squinted her eyes open, wiped the dried spit from the corner of her mouth, and attempted to focus on the person standing over her. When she realized he was holding her baby girl, she instantly popped up to a sitting position.

"What are you doing with my Libby?" she squealed, lunging forward, reaching out for her daughter.

"I'm not doing anything. The question is what are you doing? I just found her out playing in the street while your ass is in here passed out. I should call children services on you," the boy scolded as he handed the little girl over to her mother.

Suddenly the obese woman jumped up and screamed, almost as an afterthought, "Oh my God, where's Becky?" Panicked, the suddenly concerned parent lumbered off to the girl's bedroom where she found her five-year-old daughter curled up asleep at the foot of her twin bed. After seeing the second daughter asleep, Dre turned and headed toward the door. As he exited the door, Wanda waddled up with Libby in one arm, and she reached out to the door with the other and slowly began to shut it, but before she did, she stuck her head out the door and told Andre, "Thank you for bringing back my Libby. If you ever need anything, regardless of what it is, just let me know. I may not have much, but I have my word." Her words reverberated in his head as he jogged over to Eileen who was now standing by her parked car.

Words were few as the black sedan rushed north across Division Street, perfectly timing nearly every traffic light on its way as Donnie made double time taking Latice home.

"Will you take me to your stash house tonight? Please, I really could use a little time to myself," Latice pleaded as she rolled down her window to get some fresh air.

"Why don't we just do it tomorrow? I've got some shit I need to do."

"Please, De, I'll make it up to you, I promise. I just don't feel like dealing with my mother tonight. Do you know what I mean?" Donnie nodded.

"Okay, I'll take you over and introduce you to Red, but tomorrow I want you to clean the place up for me. It's a mess."

"All right, you have a deal," the girl said as she attempted to give him a half a hug as he drove.

The introduction was brief, consisting of a couple of sniffs to the back of the hand followed by a subtle lick of Latice's knuckles and a retaliatory petting of the head, followed by a brisk scratching behind the ears of Red, and the deal was sealed.

As soon as he felt positive that the two females could comfortably coexist, he grabbed his keys, jumped in his car, started it, then he turned the ignition off and walked back in the house.

"I don't think you will need it, but if someone ever tries to break in while you're here. I keep a 9-millimeter pistol in the living room, in a holster Velcro'd to the underside of the coffee table," he said as he walked over and showed her its location.

"Sleep tight, I'll talk to you tomorrow," he said as he exited the house for a second time. Once in the car he began making plans on how he would deal with Corn as he made tracks back to Quartz Hill.

Andre Brown unlocked the door, turned on the hall light, and made his way to the living room with Eileen right behind him. He had intended on picking up the phone and calling Corn when he saw a note on the coffee table on the back of an electric bill envelope from his mom. Twelve years later, his mother's favorite way to communicate with her son was still a simple note left behind for him to find. Her message was short and sweet.

"Hey hon, I decided to stay over Jessie's tonight. There is a pan of lasagna in the oven, enjoy. Call Jessie's if you need me. Love, Ma."

"Looks like we have the place to ourselves. I'm not sure where Latice is, probably still over Donnie's, I'm guessing," Dre said, as he turned on the television and invited Eileen to have a seat.

For the two, conversation came with ease. There was no uncomfortable silence or forced dialogue. In many cases, they found themselves finishing each other's sentences. Everything was great until Eileen asked Dre.

"What is your favorite thing to do?"

"Sleep," he replied, and everything changed. She was totally repulsed by his answer.

"What do you want from life, to be some kind of bum or something?" she questioned as she stood up and backed away from the table.

"Please tell me that you're not one of those lazy no-good-for-nothings that expects us hardworking taxpayers to foot the bill while you lay around and sleep."

"Wait a minute. Hold up...hold up, slow down. I'm not a lazy bum. That's not what I'm saying. When I say sleep, I really mean dreaming. I love dreaming, well, lucid dreaming, to be exact. Have you ever heard of it?" he asked, as he patted the cushion next to him and invited her to sit back down.

"I'm not sure. What is lucid dreaming?" the girl asked as she sat back down. The moment he started explaining it, an image flashed in her mind. It was a face, kind of familiar but not. The impression popped in and out so quickly that only a melting purple outline remained. He wanted to tell her about the OBEs, but he thought it might be too soon. As if reading his thoughts, Eileen informed Dre that she frequently practiced visualization, but was not sure if that was anything like lucid dreaming.

What the heck, he thought.

"No, visualization is more like an out-of-the-body experience," Andre said, sliding closer to her position.

"Now I've heard of that," she said proudly with a big smile as she leaned in closer as well. Like a magnet, the two were drawn together with their lips meeting in the middle. This time when their lips met, voltage sparked, and the two were separated by a static electricity pop, causing Eileen's bangs to stand on end, pointing straight up in the air.

"That was weird," she said as she tried to lay her hair back down with her hand.

"No, sparks usually fly when I kiss a girl." Andre laughed as he slid back away from where she was sitting.

"Tell me more about one of your visualization experiences," Dre said, pretending that he had pulled out a pad and pen, ready to take notes.

"Okay, let me think. Once, I visualized that I was in the Himalayan Mountains in the freezing cold."

"Hold up, go back to the start. Are you asleep or awake when you do this?"

"I'm awake, silly, just in a meditative state. Are you going to listen or just keep interrupting me?" she said, giving him the stare from hell.

"Okay, I'll shut up."

"I could literally feel the bite of the icy wind on my face and cheeks. At one point, I fell down, and my clothes were all wet. My feet and hands burned like the beginning stages of frostbite. It was miserable, and then I was warm and dry again."

"Just like that, you were back and warm?" Dre questioned.

"No, I was still there, but I was dry and warm. Actually, I visualized a friend…This is gonna sound weird, but I visualized a friend, and he told me to believe I was dry and I would be. He was a white wolf, well, fox, actually," she said as she stared at the ceiling, trying to recall.

When she said white fox, the hair on the back of his neck stood up and started tingling more violently than he had ever experienced. Although Dre had never seen the owner of the voice, it would make sense that his animal personification would be a fox.

"Was his name Oliver?" the boy interrupted.

"What did you say… How could you possibly know that?" Eileen asked in a state of disbelief.

Suddenly he was taken back to the night Oliver had rescued him from the cave. His words now echoed clearly in his mind: "I am here so that you might have a chance to meet with her again. She is you and you are her. You are both equal opposites, soul mates."

"I know that because you did not visualize Oliver. Oliver is real. He is our spirit guide. I believe that's just part of the reason why we feel as if we know each other," Andre said, contorting his face to match Eileen's stunned look of disbelief.

Hours buzzed by, and the night was quickly being devoured by the pair's insatiable desire to bridge the links which somehow connected them. It seemed that with every change of topic, so did their position on the couch.

The stroke of one found the two lying together with their heads at the north end of the couch and their midsections perfectly matching up like spoons. Their words had grown too few, and their breathing had thickened. Andre found himself gazing at the ceiling with Eileen in his arms, and by the rise and fall of her breast, he was pretty sure that she was already sleeping. With each passing minute, Dre could feel himself grow more relaxed. Tiny vibrations massaged his skin as the subtle signs of an oncoming OBE approached his stress-free body. Prickling sensations enveloped his frame. Briefly he wondered if Eileen could feel them as well in her early sleep state. He had decided quickly that he would barrel roll out of his body as soon as the vibrations grew strong enough. He could tell it would not be long because the speed at which the vibrations caused his muscles to twitch was twice as fast as normal. One moment he was looking at the ceiling; the next he was looking at the floor. He was floating two feet above the matted beige carpet that ran wall to wall throughout the apartment. It happened so quickly that he didn't even feel his body rotate.

Slowly he began to regain his bearing. Controlling his astral form was still a challenge. No longer was he flesh and blood. He was a mist at best. Sometimes he saw his body as he had remembered it, only to watch it dissolve into a floating ball of vapor. Mentally, he commanded himself to stand. Although he never saw his form change physically, his point of view now peered from six-foot center of attention.

In this state, it was hard to concentrate and maintain a train of thought. Usually he would create a plan of action prior to his leaving the body. Once out, his astral body would function on auto-pilot. When he awoke out of the body without a plan, he found that his astral body functioned like a remote-controlled car with a dying battery. It only received some of the signals, and when it did finally respond, its movements were herky-jerky.

He planned to exit through the front door, float outside, locate the moon, and attempt to fly up to it. The process was slow, but he compelled himself to the locked front door. Before it, he stood, unable to pass. Normally without a thought he would just pass right through walls, ceilings, and doors. For reasons unknown, an invisible barrier blocked his exit from the room.

Eileen awoke, standing in an unfamiliar room. She felt funny. Her equilibrium was off, and her vision was all blurry. She wasn't sure, but for a second, she thought she was seeing in every direction all at once. The room seemed familiar, but her mind was in a fog. She thought to explore her surroundings, and with the speed of the thought, she had completely viewed the tiny apartment. She suddenly realized that she was still at Dre's house, but there was no sign of him. As she headed toward the front door to leave, Eileen became infuriated. How dare he just leave her here without saying a word, she thought. She could not explain the irrational fury raging inside her. As she tried to grab the doorknob, her hand just passed right through it. It was then that she noticed her hand was transparent. When she looked down for her legs, they were there for an instant then faded into a wispy mist with a pinkish tint hovering slightly above the ground. It took her a minute, but she was finally beginning to understand what was going on. She had done it. To her, it felt like a dream, but somehow she knew that she had projected out of her body.

The freedom she experienced was liberating. Never before had she felt so unbound. Eileen's sense of clarity was elevated to limits far beyond anything she had achieved through visualization. Everything seemed to sparkle, and the colors of the world were more vivid than she had ever remembered. She couldn't believe it; just minutes ago she was talking about OBEs with Dre, and now she was pretty sure that she was having one.

Still in front of the door, she stood, unable to move forward. For the first time since the projection had begun, she wondered where her body was resting. The thought of her physical body triggered a tugging reaction to the back of her forehead, drawing her instantly backward, spinning her around, hovering directly over her body. On one hand, Eileen felt perplexed in her duality, while on the other hand she reveled in the knowledge that she was more than just a physical being. An inner calmness set in, and Eileen felt her astral body lower into her physical where the girl found herself submerged in a familiar dream arguing with a gigantic man in a purple suit.

Andre extended his pseudo arm into the dark pinewood panel door. Determined not to be denied again, he continued to press until finally the door's integrity gave way, accepting him, fully sucking him through it, completely shooting him out the other side of the door and into the still night air. Once outside, he grasped to recall what he had planned to do once he freed himself from the apartment. Set afloat on the easterly wind, the young man studied his surroundings. The night was silent, holding its breath, when he heard a violent coughing attack coming from somewhere in the immediate area. Gliding out toward the road, he heard it again and noticed it was coming from a couple of buildings down. Sitting on her stoop, smoking a cigarette sat Wanda Fleming in just a flannel nightgown, hacking with each smoke-filled breath she inhaled. While observing his neighbor, Dre noticed that he was experiencing an excruciating pain coming from his left arm. When he looked to his arm, there was nothing there, yet the throbbing persisted. He did not want to return to his body, but he knew that he had to. With but a thought of returning, Dre's eyes opened, facing the back of Eileen's auburn locks. He was lying on his side with his left arm trapped under his new girlfriend's waist. The limb was totally numb and all tingly.

"Eileen…Eileen, lift up, my arm is asleep," the boy said as he shook her with his right hand. The girl looked back and smiled as she slowly pushed herself up to a seated position.

"I'm glad you woke me because I was having this stupid dream again. I used to have it all the time. Now I just have it every once in a while."

"What's the dream about?" Andre asked as he attempted to sit up as well.

"I'm in this huge room with a lot of people moving in every direction. Anyway, I'm always arguing with this really big guy wearing a purr—" But before she could finish her sentence, she stopped and began to stare deeply into Andre's eyes, as if hoping to find an answer there. Moments passed, and she turned away and said, "I think I may have had an out-of-the-body experience, before I even had the stupid dream."

"Why do you think that?" Dre asked, as he reached his left hand back and began massaging his own stiff shoulder.

"Because it was crazy! I saw my body melt away, then seconds later, I saw my physical body asleep on the couch. I feel like I just crossed the boundaries of limitless freedom. If I learn how to control it, there is nowhere I can't visit. I'm so excited."

"So what happened? Start from the beginning of what you remember," Dre said, matching Eileen's excitement.

"Is it okay if I tell you about it tomorrow? I am really tired. I'd better go home."

"You don't have to go home. You can stay here. Don't worry, I'm not a creeper. You can sleep in my room, or we can sleep in my room. I'll be good," Dre said with a hand gesture, instructing Eileen to follow him.

"How do you know I want you to be good?" the girl said with a partial giggle.

Within minutes, the two long-lost friends were both asleep again. This time, they slumbered lying back to back, Dre with his mouth open slightly, snorting occasionally, and Eileen quietly with her arms crossed, appearing to give herself a hug.

CHAPTER
25

The silence of the early morning was corrupted by the unapologetic blaring ring of the telephone. On the first ring Andre barely blinked, still in denial, unwilling to accept that he was not dreaming. On the second ring, he was forced to face the facts when Eileen jumped out of the bed to a standing position and screamed, "Oh, shit! I've got an eight o'clock class, and work at nine."

"Relax, it's barely six thirty," Dre said as he forced himself to a sitting position and pointed to the red glowing digits on his clock radio.

"Who in the world is calling this early?" the young man said as he shuffled his sock feet across the floor and out the door to answer the phone. On the fifth ring, he picked up the receiver and said hello to an empty line. Internally, he promised himself that he would not cuss. With malice, he slammed the headset, turned face, and headed back to the bedroom. The moment he set foot down in his room the phone rang again.

"My God! Really...is this really happening this morning?" Andre said as he about-faced and made double time back to the telephone.

Dre's cheery hello was met with a dismal, gloom-stricken response from Corn.

"Where have you been, man? Fuck! I've been trying to call you since last night!" To Dre, his friend sounded frantic on the verge of a breakdown.

"What happened? Tell me what happened?" Andre pleaded.

"I got jacked yesterday, right after you left."

"What? What do you mean?" Andre countered.

"I fucking got robbed by Lil Moe, or his boys. I don't know. They were wearing ski mask."

"What did they get?" After a couple of seconds without a response, Andre repeated. "What did they get?"

"They got it all," Corn said as his voice fell quiet.

"Dude, you need to come over here so we can talk. Please, get over here as soon as you can," he said then hung up the phone.

"Is everything okay?" Eileen walked into the room and asked.

"No, Corn got jumped by some guys who were supposed to be his friends. Do you think you can give me a ride over there?" Dre asked as he walked into the bedroom and removed his sweatpants and grabbed a pair of jeans out of his dresser drawer.

"You aren't going over there so you guys can retaliate, are you?" Eileen questioned as she stood in his doorway with disapproving eyes.

The heat of the early October morning reminded Donnie how much he missed the mild temperatures of Lynwood. Often, he wished that he had remained there and sent Boom to this awful desert.

Driving to his stash house, he reveled in the solace of the early morning as he contemplated how he would take care of Corn. In many ways, he was happy that Corn would no longer be around, because since they had met the two had been at odds. Dre was a different story. There was something about him which he could relate. He smiled to himself as he concocted a plot that would eliminate Corn and hold Dre accountable for their loss. His internal smile grew into a full-blown guttural laugh as he thought that he might get some more use out of his fat-man suit after all.

Donnie Dollar turned down the volume on his new NWA cassette tape as he pulled up in front of his house on Beech Street. For a couple of moments, he sat in his car, surveying his neighborhood, when a black Ford Freemont drove by, slowly triggering a memory from just two days before. Donnie had pulled into his driveway to find Detective Brumbly and his partner Detective Diaz waiting in a black Ford Freemont. The two officers quickly stepped out of their vehicle and greeted Donnie as he exited his. Detective Brumbly's words were few, but he assured his suspect that he was still on their radar and they were well aware of the activities he was conducting on the high desert. Brumbly mumbled something about keeping one's nose clean as he disappeared into the car. The Freemont started down the driveway and abruptly stopped and began to back up toward the front door, which Donnie was about to enter. The passenger-side window began to roll down, and Detective Diaz stuck his head out the window and said, "Oh, by the way, the grand jury will be meeting next week to discuss reopening the Crayon Reese case. I just thought you might want to know," and began to laugh uncontrollably as he rolled his window back up. Walking up his walkway, he kept a lazy eye on a bum rummaging through the blue receptacles placed out on the curb on the opposite side of the street.

Opening the door, he was greeted with a quick reminder that he needed to have his carpets cleaned. Red's presence was a necessity and nuisance at the same time. The time on his wristwatch was 5:45 a.m. when Donnie picked up the phone and dialed Jesus Jimenez. Pickens's military background dictated his early hours, but being an asshole was something he pleasured in from time to time. The empty silence from the headset resting against the side of his face gave way to a recoiling ring and a disgruntled "Hullo" from the other end.

"Wake your punk ass up, SA. it's almost six o'clock! You gonna sleep all fucking day?" Donnie said with malice in his voice.

"Come on, man, it's too early. Call me back in a couple hours," Jesus pleaded.

"Fuck that, get up. You owe me one, and I've got a job for you. Do you remember that Oreo, Corn?" Donnie paused and pulled the receiver down as Red began to bark at a fevered pitch. I'm gonna call you back in an hour. Be up and be ready," Pickens commanded as he slammed down the receiver.

The click of Red's nails tapped a Morse code warning on the hardwood floor as she paced back in forth, agitated because she was enclosed in the bedroom with the girl. The low purr of the engine outside had alerted her. Red's clipped ears perked up when she heard the jingling of keys. She ran to the window then to the side of the bed and issued a low guttural whimper to the girl lying on the bed. Irritated at the girl's lack of response, she began to tap the edge of the mattress inches away from Latice's face with her paw, hoping to get the flowery-smelling female to open her eyes.

The girl's fluttering eyes opened to a hazy black knob resting inches from her face. As her vision became focused, she realized it was Red's big black nose with her moist nostrils breathing directly in her face. The deep voice coming from the other room had startled her at first until she realized it was De. Latice rolled over to the edge of the bed and picked up her jeans, slid them on, then tiptoed over to the bedroom door, and pressed her head lightly against it.

As she listened, her eyes grew as large as fifty-cent pieces as her ears tuned in to De's one-sided conversation. She thought she heard Corn's name and some kind of job. As Latice's excitement grew, so did Red's. The girl's anxious tension was being transferred to the dog, who instinctively began to bark uncontrollably.

Stunned, she stood, face to the wall, until the sneaky dog began to bark at her repeatedly. Alarmed that the incessant barking might bring Donnie in the room, she ran and dove into the bed and got under the cover.

Andre arrived at Corn's apartment to find the door cracked with smoke and the smell of bacon escaping from the kitchen. Through the crack in the door, he could see Eileen's friend Karen standing in front of the stove wearing just a white T-shirt with a large fork in her hand. Andre opened the door, walked in, and called out to Corn to let him know that he was there. Corn emerged from the master bedroom wearing a golf ball-size lump on the left side of his forehead and a matching swollen black eye, which had begun to turn purple and gray below his bloodshot eyeball.

"*Damn, homey!* Are you all right, man?" Dre cringed as he asked his friend about his well-being.

"Yeah, I'll live, but I'm more concerned with how we are going to..." Corn stopped and pulled Dre close and whispered, "Pay Donnie his money." Corn's brown skin became pale as he expressed his concern to his friend.

"I've heard stories about how ruthless he can be from people."

"What people?" Dre asked.

"Just people, a couple guys on the football team are from LA that I know, but I believe them," he said as he walked into the kitchen, put his hand around Karen's waist, pulled her in, and kissed her.

"I take it you remember Karen? I would invite you to stay and have some breakfast, but there's a good chance that me and my little boo bear might have to put breakfast on hold, as fine as she's looking right now," Corn said then kissed the girl again.

"So why did you tell me to come as soon as possible?" Dre questioned with an uncompromising glare.

"Oh, I just wanted you to see who I hooked up with last night."

"Are you fucking serious! You could have told me that over the phone. We've got some serious business we need to take care of immediately. Meet me in the student center around lunchtime."

"You're crazy if you think that I'm coming up to the school looking like this. Call me and we can meet somewhere."

"Whatever, man," Andre said as he walked out the door and pulled it closed behind him.

Donnie opened the door to the bedroom, and Red sprinted out of the room, down the hall across the dining room, stopping in the kitchen at the back door, where she began pacing back and forth. He glanced over at the girl covered from head to toe in the bed, turned, closed the door, and made haste to the back door to let Red outside before her patience outlasted her bladder.

Donnie sat on the couch staring from the phone to the clock and back to the phone. Screw this, he thought, as he looked up at the clock one last time and lifted the phone's headset from its base.

"Come on, homey—" the voice from the receiver said before he was rudely cut off.

"Fuck that! Save it, get your ass up if you're not already. You've got work to do," Donnie screamed into the phone.

"Come on, De, it ain't even been thirty minutes yet," Jesus pleaded to his OG homeboy.

"Look, man, I want your ass up here in the next hour and a half, no later. Do you fuckin' hear me? I said do you fuckin' hear me, stupid?" Donnie barked into the phone.

"Yeah, I hear you," Jesus sniveled back.

"Well, hurry up! I want you to go fix that bitch-ass nigga Corn today," Donnie exclaimed and slammed down the phone.

On the other side of the wall, Latice stood, shaking her head in disbelief, wondering if he had just said what she thought he said.

Dollar was sitting on the patio watching Red, who appeared to be tracking a mystery scent near the rear fence, when he finally heard a knock at the front door.

When Donnie opened the door, there was no greeting or small talk. He simply turned, nodded his head in a direction, and his legs took off on that course. The two men walked through the house and had seats on the patio.

Never one to consider herself a snoop, Latice felt compelled to know if Donnie had really intended to have Corn murdered. In all actuality, she would have chosen Corn over Donnie if he had been interested. She got a vibe from him that his female preference was more of the pigmentally challenged, smaller-lipped variety. Nevertheless, she would have given him a chance had he tried. The young woman looked both ways as if crossing the street before she slipped into the bathroom and closed the door. For a second, she paused and looked around, then stepped into the tub, cracked the window slightly, then crouched with her back to the wall, in hopes of hearing Donnie's conversation.

Jesus reached into his pocket, pulled out a pack of Newport menthol cigarettes, removed one, and tossed the pack on the table. He then began to fiddle around in his pocket, looking for his lighter, when Dollar smashed his hand down on the table and screamed, "Are you fucking listening to me?"

"Yeah, go 'head, I'm following you, homes. But shit, I've got a habit, and when it calls, I've got to smoke," the Hispanic man said as he sparked his lighter, inhaled deeply, and sat back in his chair.

"Okay, let's try this one more time. It's really simple. This kid is as addicted to arcades and video games as you are to those damn cancer sticks. He goes to the one across the street from his apartment on Fifteenth Street West every day right after practice. You know the one. It's in the plaza with the Del Taco and Jay's liquor store.

We went there a few times. Do you know where I'm talking about?" Dollar asked.

"Yeah, I know where you're talking about. There is a Heavenly Donuts in the plaza, right?" Jesus questioned to confirm he knew exactly where his friend was speaking.

"We get out of practice at four o'clock. He will be there at about four thirty. I'm not sure how long he will stay, so I suggest you pack a lunch and just be ready to kick it there for a while. Go get a G ride and park it in the plaza, keep your eyes open, and when you see him, do a drive-by on him and anybody with him. You know how we do it. Oh yeah, I've got a special toy for you to bury his ass with," Donnie said as he shook his head up and down with a broad smile on his face.

"All right, I got you, but after I do this, all debts are settled. Agreed?" Jesus said as he extended his hand to Dollar.

Latice slid down to a sitting position in the tub, with her two tiny hands covering both of her eyes and most of her nose. Silently she sobbed for a boy she barely knew. Mired in disbelief, she questioned whether she should try to contact Dre and have him warn Corn or should she just mind her own business and allow this bumpy road to take her wherever it led. With that thought, her sobs dried up and her teary eyes began to twinkle as she stepped from the tub and pulled the curtain back. Latice stood in front of the mirror, wiped away the remnants of her smudged mascara, and mustered up a partial smile, which immediately reminded her of the psychotic clown picture that Andre had hanging over his bed as a kid.

The temperature was flirting with ninety degrees inside the Marauder's Pavilion when practice came to an end. Coach Murphy kept practice light, knowing that they would be scrimmaging Canyon Country tomorrow for at least three hours or longer, depending on how much good work the two coaches could get out of their teams. Coach Murphy called everyone in at the center of the court and told his team to be in the gym by 2:30 p.m. because the bus would be leaving at 2:45 p.m. sharp. He ended the practice by telling everyone to try to get some rest tonight because tomorrow was going to be a long day. Almost as an afterthought while walking toward his office, the coach turned and told Corn to grab some ice for that huge knot on his head and stop by his office before he left, because he needed to speak with him.

Dre and Corn lagged behind the rest of the team, walking into the dressing room as they discussed what the coach had wanted to talk to him about. Just before opening the door to the locker room, Andre reached out, grabbed Corn by the shoulder, and told him to skip the arcade tonight and get a ride over to his pad because he had some ideas on how they might be able to get Donnie his money.

"I can't, Karen is going to meet me over there when she gets off from work. Then she's going to take me out to dinner," Corn said with a big smile as he attempted to open the door. As he did, Andre extended his leg and pushed the door back closed with his burgundy and white size ten and a half Converse Weapon tennis shoe.

"You really need to take this shit serious. You're the one who got robbed by his so-called friend. You're the one who said Donnie has a rep on the streets of LA, but you're more concerned about this chick than trying to figuring out how to fix our situation. You should have her drop you off over at my house after dinner, or…at least call me later," Dre said as he removed his foot from in front of the door, opened it, and walked into the locker room.

The six-foot-two athlete stood hunkered over the brightly colored green and white arcade machine. His hands were a blur as he rapidly pressed the lateral movement buttons with his left and the torpedo fire button with his right. His concentration was at its peak, with two spaceships interlocked, letting off rapid-fire photons at the incoming legion of alien ships. Of all the video games he played regularly, Galaga was by far his favorite. Corn loved the arcade as a kid because he could go there, immerse himself in games, and forget all his family problems. Once there, all the arguing and fighting which happened at home was locked away in the back of his mind until his father got drunk and jumped on his mother again.

Absorbed with clearing the board on level 13, Corn failed to notice his date slide up behind him and wrap her arm around his waist, causing him to startle and jump away from her grasp.

"Sorry, babe, I didn't see you walk up. I guess I'm still a little bit jumpy," Corn said as he tried to return his hands to the control buttons right on time to see both of his two remaining ships blown up by a cluster of falling missiles.

"I'm sorry, hon, I didn't mean to mess you up," Karen said as she stepped into him, looked up, fluttered her eyelashes, and puckered up her little lips for him to kiss.

"It's okay, babe. I was about finished anyway. Are you ready to go, because I'm starving. I haven't ate since your yummy breakfast this morning," Corn said just before he leaned down and kissed the most beautiful girl he had ever slept with. Corn bent over, picked up his backpack, threw it over his left shoulder, and placed his right arm around Karen as the couple dodged a squadron of kids dashing from game to game as they headed for the exit.

The reluctant hit man's eyelids grew weary as they focused on the front door of Aladdin's Arcade as they had for the past two and a half hours waiting for his victim to leave. Just moments ago, he had seen his first familiar face entering the arcade. It was the short curvy blond girl from Donnie's party a few days ago.

Jesus eyed the Heavenly Donuts shop, which he had parked directly across the lot from. Quietly, he wondered if he had time to run over and grab a quick cup of coffee, but then he thought better of it. Jesus leaned back in the bucket seat, extended his arm between the seats to the blanket on the car floor, covering the fully automatic AK-47, or new toy as Dollar had called it. While his eyes spotlighted the door, his fingers surveyed the supreme craftsmanship of this Russian killing machine. The union of the wood stock and the steel barrel was as true as any marriage between a faithful husband and a loving wife.

Fingering the weapon, the killer realized he had a real dilemma. The AK was too big for him to shoot and drive at the same time. Had he known the job in advance, he could have brought Monté or someone else to handle the wheel. Jesus looked around the parking lot then slowly pulled the blanket-covered gun to his lap. After he was sure no one was watching, he placed his hand under the cover, wrapped his finger around the trigger, and lifted the weapon up and rested its barrel on the edge of the passenger's side window as a brace, and with his other hand, he held the steering wheel. After holding the position for a few seconds, he was confident he could do it; however, he had never fired an AK-47 before and wasn't sure how much recoil to expect, and how much it would throw his aim off. For a second, he considered doing him right here in the parking lot when he walked past his position, but then he would be shooting directly into the business, endangering innocent people. Jesus set the weapon on the floor, leaned over, and pulled up the latch, then he slid the barrel between the latch and the window frame, and to his surprise, the latch held the gun barrel in place like a vise. Somewhat astounded by his own cleverness, he almost failed to notice Corn and Karen walking out of Aladdin's arm in arm.

Immediately he set the weapon down on the seat and started up the engine. Jesus drove south through the parking lot and made a right turn on J-7 street. He then made another right on Fifteenth Street West, picked up the weapon by the stock, placed his finger behind the trigger, steadied the barrel of the AK between the latch and the window frame, and slowly drove up the block, trying to time the couple's arrival at the crosswalk so he could unload on them before they crossed the street, then he could quickly drive six blocks to the freeway and be on his way out of town before the police or paramedics ever reached the scene.

Corn held Karen's hand as the two walked past Heavenly Donuts. He walked slightly ahead of her, urging her to walk faster as he spouted off some drivel about how he was a hungry growing boy who had to eat every four hours or he would lose 0.05 pounds of muscle mass. She laughed and told him he was full of shit, but not to worry because Don Cucco's Mexican Restaurant was just a few minutes away.

For a moment, Corn stopped in front of Jay's liquor and contemplated going in to grab a pack of gum, but then thought twice about it and figured it could wait till later.

"What are you doing? I thought you were hungry," Karen said as she gave his hand a slight tug.

"Ow, just thought I'd grab some…Ah, forget it," he said as the two continued up the sidewalk and edged up to the corner where a red light stood, halting their progress. The two paused at the corner, swinging their enclasped hands back and forth, smiling at each other, waiting for the light to change.

Corn turned from Karen, observed the approaching blue Oldsmobile Delta 88, and smiled, thinking how beautiful life was and how good things were going for him. Suddenly he was on top of the world. He had just learned that he would be the starting shooting guard in the scrimmage tomorrow, and on top of that, his new girl-friend was not only one of the hottest girls on the campus, but she was probably one of the freakiest, too, he thought.

Jesus observed the happy pair as they came to a stop, just mere feet away from his quickly approaching vehicle. His eyes narrowed, and his heart rate increased as he tightened his grip on the hair trigger. The AK bucked like an untamed bronco when the assassin squeezed the trigger. A rapid succession of spent shell casings flew from the gun, ricocheting off the ceiling, banking into the passenger-side rear win-dow, piling up on the back seat and car floor. The spit-firing rat-a-tat of the machine gun lasted only seven seconds before it belched an empty click, accompanied by the squealing of rubber as the driver/triggerman punched the gas and made a hasty departure from the crime scene.

The smile on the boy's face turned into an opened black hole of surprise when his eyes recognized the familiar sick sadistic smile from behind the steering wheel and the barrel of a gun protruding from the passenger-side window. He tried to scream and push Karen away, but as he did his eyes captured a white burst of flame from his peripheral vision, which coincided with hot pellets of lead tearing into his chest, shoulders, and ripping huge gaping holes into his neck, propelling his body backward toward the ground. Looking up at the blue sky, gasping for air, he tried to turn his limp neck toward Karen, but nothing happened. As the last twinkle of life fled his annihilated body, the boy whispered a brief prayer and thought of his mother.

Andre sat at the kitchen table working on his essay for Mr. Glass's English 101 class, accomplishing very little as he stressed out about the call he had yet to receive from Corn. The odor of fried salmon cakes from dinner flooded the apartment, still lingering in the air nearly three hours later. During his short time of knowing Corn, Dre considered him to be rash and immature, but never dumb or stupid. Ignoring their responsibility to Donnie was both. Andre pushed his composition book aside, lifted both of his hands to his head, and began pulling his hair in frustration. Agitation had driven him to the verge of picking up the phone and calling his friend, but he decided to be patient and continue to wait for his call.

When the phone finally did ring, Dre screamed out to his mother to let her know that he would get it because he was expecting a call.

Andre answered the phone with a rushed "Hello." On the other end, his greeting was answered with silence.

"Hello, who is this?" the young man asked. When the stillness finally broke, a faint choked-up voice said, "Have…have you heard?"

"Heard what, who is this?" Dre asked.

"It's me…Eileen," the barely audible voice forced out.

"Karen and Corn were shot. I'm…I'm sorry, but your friend didn't make it. I'm here at the hospital with Karen's family. She is still in the OR in critical condition," she said as tears streamed down her face.

"What, when, where…" was followed by an elapsed time of his own silence.

"Dre, I need to ask you a few questions about your friend De, Donnie, or whatever his name is…Andre, are you there?" Eileen asked again and again before the young man found his voice.

"Yeah, I'm here. Is it okay if I call you back, or maybe you could call me when you get home and let me know how Karen is doing?" Dre said, as he hung up the phone without waiting for her response.

Andre closed his eyes and felt the rush of sadness clutch his fractured heart. The pressure of warm tears forced their way through his closed eyelids, inspiring an echo of sobs. The young man rested his head on the table and was nearly startled to the floor when the telephone rang again. This time, both he and his mother answered the phone in unison.

"Hello."

"Hi, can I speak to Dre?" the voice from the other end responded dryly.

"I've got it, Ma, hang up," the boy said quickly.

"Dre, my man, I take it you heard about what happened to ya boy Corn. It's a shame. Shot down in his prime. You got to be careful out here in these streets. You never know what's coming around that next corner. You know what I mean, Dre?" Donnie said with a remorseless chuckle.

"So, what's up? Are you calling to threaten me?" Dre asked.

"Not exactly, but you do owe me quite a bit of money, you know. I've got an idea I want to run by you on how you might be able to pay me back and make five or six thousand for yourself. Be outside in fifteen minutes. Don't make me have to blow my horn," Donnie said then hung up the phone immediately.

Dre stood out on the curb in front of his apartment, watching the smoke from his exhaled breath disappear in the night sky. Two buildings down, he observed Wanda Fleming's kids playing in front of their building with neither coats nor shoes in this chilly October weather. The longer he watched, the angrier he became. He really wanted to go grab little Libby and Becky, take them inside, kick the crap out of their mom, and give her a piece of his mind, but now was not the time. He didn't know why the scene irritated him so, but he guessed it was the accumulation of everything over the last couple of days threatening to explode.

In the distance, he could see a vehicle missing one of its headlights bearing his way. The driver seemed to be deliberately taking his time poking down the street. For a second, Dre wondered if he should be nervous, and his instincts told him to be prepared to dive behind the Chevy truck just a few feet away if necessary. As the car whipped around in front of his position, he recognized the beat-up tinted-out Ford Pinto that Dollar was driving.

Moments later, the Pinto pulled up in front of the Dollars' Beech Street home. When the two men walked through the door, they found Latice sitting on the couch, stroking Red's beautiful coat, and watching television. The boy and his sister exchanged pleasantries, and Donnie told Dre to follow him into the bedroom because he had something he needed to show him.

The second bedroom was damp and reeked of mildew. Donnie opened the closet door, and nearly his whole body disappeared as he contorted to reach something that seemed to be buried just beyond his reach somewhere in the left corner of the closet. Finally, he straightened up and backed out of the closet, carrying a large black suitcase. Donnie turned around and plopped the luggage on the twin bed, reached over, unlatched the lock, and opened up the case.

"Step over here. I want you to get a good look at this. Come closer, it's not going to bite you," Donnie said as he began pulling a light brown fat bodysuit from the container. Upon Andre's closer inspection, he noticed that the suit both looked and felt like real human skin.

"Okay, so what's up with this?" Andre asked as he continued to inspect the suit.

"I think it will fit you. You and Monté are about the same size and skin complexion. Yeah, I think it will work," Donnie said under his breath.

"You think what will work?" Dre asked.

"Put the suit on."

"What?" Dre asked.

"I said, put on the fat-man suit!" Donnie insisted. He reached out his arm and handed the synthetic skin to Dre. He tried to dial it back a little, saying, "I told you I have a plan. First, we need to see if you can fit the suit. Okay?"

"All right, I'll try it on, but at least tell me what you've got in mind, man," Dre said as he began shedding his clothes.

"Here's the deal. I have some people in Columbus, Ohio, who wants five birds and the fat-man suit is how we are going to get them there. It will carry eight kilos comfortably, no problem." Donnie said, as he grabbed Dre by both hips and pulled the midsection up so he could slide in his arms.

"My boy Monté wore it a few times last year, with no problem at all."

"Then why don't you have him do it?" Andre asked.

"Because Monté don't owe me shit! You do," Donnie said, trying to maintain control of his temper.

A light knock on the door was corresponded by Latice asking if everything was okay in the bedroom, in which Donnie was quick to respond that the two were just handling some business and discussing a few things.

Dre twisted his arms and contorted his body to adjust into the tight formfitting suit. It was a challenge to get the inner fat lining to lie properly after being stored away in the suitcase for the extended period of time. The suit's butt padding had slipped down into the upper thigh region, which had pushed the lower thigh down, mashing the knees of the suit below his actual shins. It took nearly fifteen minutes to tweak the padding so that all of the suit's body parts were aligned anatomically correct with his body.

"So how does it feel?" Donnie asked.

"It's actually not as bad as I thought it would be."

"Check this out," Donnie said as he told him to pull his right arm out of the sleeve. When Andre did, he showed him the slits built in to the upper bicep area designed to hold a formfitting kilogram of coke around the arm. There were additional slits cut into both buttocks, both thighs, and calves as well.

"That's pretty cool, but what about ID? It's not like I can use mine when I'm gonna weigh an extra 100 pounds with the suit," Dre said as he looked at himself in the mirror.

"Don't worry about it. I've got someone taking care of that too," Donnie said with a huge smile as he walked back over to the closet and pulled out a huge purple suit with tiny black pinstripes.

"I've even got clothes for you," he said, still smiling, showing every tooth in his mouth like a great white shark.

"Really, where's the pimp hat that goes with it?" Dre asked, shaking his head in disgust.

"Aye, it is what it is. It was one of the only suits I could find in that size. Now get rid of the shitty attitude and be ready to go come this Friday. I'm going to have my girl book you a flight tomorrow, and as soon as you take off the millionaire maker, I'm going to take a picture of your mug so my guy can get your ID ready as soon as possible." Donnie paused for a second then hollered out for Latice to bring him a couple of cold beers out of the refrigerator.

26

Detective Bill Brumbly was sitting at his desk nursing an awful cup of coffee courtesy of Lancaster's finest break room vending machine. Apparently, his bifocal prescription was no longer working because no matter how he held the Sheppard case file, he could not read the fourth number in the suspect's last known phone number. What he initially thought was a three was suddenly looking more like an eight. No sooner had he accepted it as an eight than it morphed into a six. Frustrated, Bill removed his glasses, extended his arm, holding the paper as far away from his face as he could. He then closed his right eye and began squinting out of the left, attempting to read the number, when he heard a voice from behind, asking if he needed to borrow an eye.

To the twenty-three-year officer's surprise, it was Donald Pickens leaning against his lunching partner's desk.

"Well, if it isn't the Devil's nephew. To what do I owe this visit?" Detective Brumbly asked as he set the file down and picked up his glasses from his desk.

"Well, I had to be in court this morning for a paternity suit, and I just happen to have a piece of information that you and Detective Diaz might be able to use to your advantage. All I ask for is a little consideration when and if the Crayon Reese case resurfaces in the near future," Pickens said.

"And what exactly do you deem a little consideration?" Brumbly questioned as he crossed his stubby arms and leaned his fat fatherly face to a forty-five-degree angle.

"All I ask is that you remember I threw you guys a bone. I know it's not a homicide, but I'm sure you will get an I-owe-you-one from the department you decide to share this information with," Donnie said as he stuck a piece of Wrigley's Spearmint gum in his mouth, balled up the wrapper, and threw it into a wastebasket nearly twenty feet across the room.

"Okay, so what do you got, Pickens? Why don't you come over here and have a seat at my desk and we can talk about it," Brumbly said as he pointed to a chair, then walked around his cluttered desk and dropped his stout 210-pound frame into his plush hemorrhoid-friendly Oxford office chair with a blown-up donut in the center of it.

Several days had gone by since the day of Corn's murder. The whole event seemed surreal; he heard about the shooting, and then he was gone. Although he never said it, Andre was crushed by his friend's death. On top of that, he would never be allowed the opportunity to say goodbye to his friend, because his family had flown his body home to Anchorage, where his funeral would be held. It all had been a blur, and Andre could barely remember the scrimmage they had lost badly just a couple of days ago at Canyon Country. With everything going on, basketball was the least of his concerns.

Andre sat in the living room looking at the television, totally oblivious to what he was watching. It had been three days since he had last attended a class. Virginia Brown sat to her son's right on the couch, rubbing his hand, chatting with him about maybe taking some time off from school, but all Andre heard was a *womp womp, womp womp womp* sound like he was living in the *Peanuts* cartoon. When the front door opened, Dre jumped up from the couch with alarm, ran to the doorway to see who was letting themselves into the house. To his relief, it was Latice carrying a huge Army duffel bag.

"What's up, li'l bro? You doing okay? I'm really sorry about your friend. I liked him. He was a nice guy. Unlike your other friend, I may sound like a hypocrite, because I am staying over his place, but you shouldn't trust him," Latice said as she squeezed past him in the hallway.

"Then why are you staying with him?" Dre asked as he followed her into his bedroom where she kept most of her things.

"Because, I need my own space. It's barely enough room here for you and Ma. He's never really there. Besides, I'm just going to stay there until I can afford to get my own place," she said as she began stuffing some of her things in the huge green bag.

"I do need to talk to you about De," the girl started saying, then paused, stood up, walked over, and closed the door to the bedroom.

"De had his boy Jesus kill Corn."

"What? How do you know that?" Dre asked.

"I heard him give Jesus the order. I was using the bathroom when I heard them out on the patio talking," Latice said.

"Damn, that's messed up! I don't want to believe it. I kind of suspected it, but I wasn't 100 percent sure," he said, then looked down at the floor and shook his head back and forth slowly.

"I don't know what the two of you were discussing the other night, but I wouldn't trust him, if I were you. I met people just like him when I was in—" Latice stopped midsentence, then picked up her bag, gave her brother a kiss on the cheek, and gracefully walked into the living room where she sat down next to her mom. The two proceeded to chitchat about what was happening on their favorite soap *All My Children.*

The day before his flight, the entire Antelope Valley basin was flooded with a strange autumn fog, which flourished, holding morning traffic prisoner. The westerlies finally freed the afternoon, and a serene red sky tanned evening rooftops.

Andre sat on his bed, glaring out at the night sky, struggling internally whether to confirm the district attorney's intern's suspicion that De was indeed the Donnie Dollar who was flooding the valley with cocaine. Mentally confounded, he wondered the legal ramifications if he broke down and told Eileen everything from the beginning. Being honest with himself, he was more fearful that the beautiful career-oriented young woman would no longer have any interest in him, if she learned that he was a common street hustler.

The weight of everything all at once had left Andre intellectually disabled and emotionally distraught, realizing that all the fruits he had sown in his young life had undoubtedly led him down this sketchy one-way street.

In the end, Eileen was neither judgmental nor endorsing of his actions. However, she made it clear to him that her biggest concern was for his safety. Over and over again, Eileen pleaded with Dre to change his mind about taking the trip. Salty tears streamed down her face as she warned him that if things went bad, she would be powerless in keeping him from going to jail. Angrily, she pelted the boy with awkwardly thrown blows in attempt to convey her displeasure with his decision.

"Are you just going to ignore the dream?" she screamed as she reached out and grabbed her friend. Regardless of Eileen's position, Andre trusted her implicitly. He must because he had just given an employee of the Los Angeles County DA's office the blueprint on how he intended to smuggle five kilos of dope, the destination, date, and flight number all wrapped up with a pretty little bow on it. Instinct told him that it was the right thing to do because chances were good that he was going to need her help in the near future. If he were lucky, he would make the trip, handle the delivery, and be back in a couple of days. Then he could pay his debts and cut all ties with Dollar. He promised Eileen that after his return, he would do everything in his power to help her put Donnie away for Corn's murder.

It was Eileen's presence by Andre's side which kept the young man anchored in the faith that his plan had a good chance to actually work.

Across the room dangling in the open closet, on a thick bamboo hanger was one triple X rotund gender-neutral synthetic skin bodysuit. To its right hung the size 58 large electric-purple pin-striped Pierre Cardin suit. Under his bed in a briefcase lay five individually wrapped kilos of A-1 Peruvian Flake. Dollar had fulfilled his end of the bargain; he had even acquired the fake ID. The name below his picture on his new California identification card was Milo Webster. It listed him as being a six-foot-one, 275-pound resident of Valencia, California. Andre was super impressed by how real the card looked;

he could not see any difference between his real ID and the fake one when he compared the two.

Eileen walked over to the closet door, pulled it completely open, and said to Andre, "This is it! This is the dream, Andre. I know you know it. I knew the moment when you started telling me your plan. I can't believe it. It was you in my dream all the time. And…and when I saw this." With her forearm, she wiped away her tears, then reached out and touched its arm, grimaced, then shrank away in disgust.

"Yes, I know, but it's gonna be okay. We can use the dream to our advantage. We have a good plan. I promise you, it's gonna be okay." With three healthy strides, he was on top of the girl, attempting to comfort her as he slid the closet door closed with his left hand.

"It's getting late, and I've got to make sure I make it down to LAX on time."

"Would you like for me to give you a ride in the morning?" Eileen asked.

"No, I couldn't do that to you. The last thing I want is for you to get into any trouble, but thanks," Dre said with a big smile.

"Well, is it okay if I spend the night?" Eileen asked, blushing as she sat down on his bed and began to unbutton her blouse.

The night had grown late when Andre was awakened by the sound of a bouncing basketball. Within seconds of stepping out of his bed and touching the cold floor, the young man realized that the filthy matted carpet in his room had been replaced by hardwood flooring. The surface felt smooth yet sticky to the touch of his bare toes. In his sightless state, the room seemed boundless, but even in the darkness he sensed familiarity with the distinct smell the room kept company. From the shadows, the silence was interrupted by a *swish* sound, which quietly reverberated through the vast area. When he looked up, he was blinded by a huge spotlight, which illuminated the room like daytime.

Ten feet above the ground, suspended on a bright orange rim, with a flowing white net attached to nothing sat Oliver the fox. His white fur coat reflected the shimmers of the florescent light like the colors seen through a snowflake. His long thin snout curled back into a frightening smile, revealing his razor-sharp canines. Oliver stood up and began to make his way down to Andre's height by way of an invisible circular stairway.

"Do you remember the quest we vowed when we chose to return to the physical reality?"

"What do you mean we vowed?" the young man questioned.

"Concentrate, focus your intent. You must choose to remember," the voice said directly into his head.

"Remember me, I am not what you see before you now. You choose to see me this way. Perhaps it's because of your early fascination with a certain author."

In a stupor, under his breath, almost like a question, Andre said, "We are the same. We are the same. We are the same!"

"Yes, we are the same. We are all the same. Why do you think that nearly every ancient religion teaches do unto others as you would have them do unto you?" Oliver asked with his eyes twinkling like diamonds. With that, he began to float upward and fade away into the bright lights. The intense massive lights then shrank down to a miniscule glow of a firefly. Just before its radiance was snuffed, it squeaked.

"You must remember our vow."

In the darkness, Andre found himself lying on his back in his full-size bed with Eileen curled up to his right side, still locked in her cuddle position.

The shrill buzz of the alarm drew a quick slap from Andre's left hand. Rolling over, he attempted to focus on the fuzzy red numbers on the clock. He was not sure, but he thought it read 3:30 a.m. That was when reality kicked in; that was the time he had set it for, and he had several things he needed to do in order to get ready for his 6:00 a.m. flight.

The suit itself was very simple to put on; however, it took him nearly fifteen minutes to adjust and align its flab accordingly. Initially, he thought it would be a challenge to put on the Pierre Cardin suit over the mounds of rubbery skin, but it proved to be no task at all. After dressing, Andre walked outside to gather his nerves and breathe in some fresh air. Once he had regained control of his faculties, Andre strolled into the living room, sat on the couch, and began to count the money Dollar had given him for trip necessities, like the hour-and-a-half cab ride down the mountain to Los Angeles International Airport. It was just after four o'clock when Andre heard the dull honk of the horn from the Checkered Cab, which had just pulled up in front of his apartment.

As the cab drove away from his apartment, the young man wished that he had thanked and kissed Eileen before he left, and subconsciously he grasped that he still might have that chance.

The sky was still dark when the taxicab arrived at the departure zone for South West Airlines. In the back seat, Andre had begun to sweat torrents into his underwear. As he slid his butt over to exit the cab, he could feel his butt pads roll over to his hip. Promptly, he adjusted the bunched-up area then labored to lift himself out of the vehicle. Functioning in the fat suit was more of a challenge than he thought it would have been. If he had it to do again, he would have worn it around a little to try to get used to it. Even something as simple as reaching his gigantic forearm through the passenger-side window to pay the driver was a challenge.

After retrieving his arm from the window, Andre attempted to turn and run toward the automatic sliding doors, only to be forced to stop and set down his suitcase after only a couple of steps. With both hands, the young man grabbed his lower back, pulled up, and jumped at the same time in hopes of adjusting the fit of the suit. He then set forth at a medium pace through the door with his eyes in search of the ticket counter for South West Airlines.

The line was minimal to reach the blond woman with an outdated seventies bouffant hairdo. Once in front of her, her words floated by his ears like music notes to the dead. His consciousness teetered between sedated and out of the body. Somehow, he mindfully responded to her inquiries. She had asked him if he had been in possession of his bags prior to his arriving at the ticket gate or something along those lines when he shook his head and responded yes. As soon as she handed him his ticket and boarding pass, he smiled, nodded his head, and took off in search of boarding Gate C-22.

Already feeling the extra weight of his situation, as well as the suit, Andre winced when he saw the "out of order" sign for the escalator going up. He waited for a second as impatient travelers buzzed around him like he was moving in slow motion. Once the path cleared, he made his way to the outer banister and began his accent up the two flights of stairs with the assistance of his right hand and the attached handrail. Silently the young man wondered how he would be able to wear this synthetic sweatbox for the next eight hours when his every pore was on the verge of suffocating. As he reached the second step of the first landing, Andre could finally see the preboarding checkpoint. Almost in concert, he noticed the squishy sound emerging from his shoe with each step. The confluence of his sweat had been draining into the soul of his shoes and now producing an annoying squeaking sound with each step.

With but two steps to go to reach the top, the purple behemoth was halted by a strong tug to the back of his suit jacket. Just like in the dream, there she was behind him, Eileen looking tattered with bloodshot eyes and runny mascara. With a silent mouth and pleading eyes, she led her first lover back down to the two flights of stairs.

"Please don't do this," the young woman pleaded.

"It's going to be okay. I've taken care of everything. I promise," Andre said as he wrenched his wrist free of his girlfriend's vise grip. Her tiny fingers left pea-size imprints in his malleable skin.

"Have faith, I've got this. Take a deep breath and trust in my plan. Now go home. I'll call you after I've landed in Columbus," Andre said as he bent over and gave Eileen a soft kiss on her lips.

This time the two flights of steps went a little easier; however, his adrenaline had kicked in full speed, and he felt as if his heart was beating five hundred times a minute. His pores had opened fully, and from his hairline to the pits of his arms, down the crack of his ass, sweat was pouring into his silk socks and wing tip shoes.

Once he reached the top of the stairs, he realized the lines leading up to the checkpoints were extremely long but seemed to be moving at a good pace. Of the three lines, he guessed the middle one was the shortest, so he joined the line behind a little gray-haired woman. Her colorless locks rolled in waves of curls. On the top of her head, kind of cocked to the side, she wore a hairpin, which resembled a small black top hat. Accordingly, she wore a smart black suit jacket with tails, and a matching long flowing pleated skirt. Her dry British accent reminded him of Audrey Hepburn in *My Fair Lady*.

Andre could hear his heart reverberating like a subwoofer.

He was certain that anyone looking at him would surely notice the tremors in his hands and the apparent quiver in his knees.

He tried to calm his mind by using some techniques he had learned as a child. Gradually, some of his fear subsided. Closely, he watched the TSA agents in their sharply creased gray uniforms as he stepped up and placed his things on the conveyor belt. The metal detector screamed with indictment as he passed through it side-ways. A TSA agent approached him from the left with an electronic wand in his right hand. The man studied Andre, and then waved the instrument up and down in front of his midsection. After a simple request to remove his belt and walk through once more, he was off once again in search of Gate C-22.

As he dodged oncoming travelers, Andre reflected back on the agent just before he cleared him to pass through the metal detector the second time. He seemed to stare at him with a sense of familiar-ity. He then noticed the man holding the wand gave an agent on the far side of the room a nod, which led to his prompt disappearance into a back room. He would chalk it up to coincidence, but he knew it would be naive to do so.

In the distance, the young man could see his gate only a few hundred feet away when he heard a voice over the loudspeaker say, "Now boarding, flight 4307 to Columbus, Ohio, at Gate C-22."

Walking up to his gate, he watched everyone scrambling to gain his or her place in line. Merging into the back of the line, he noticed a couple of small children just a few places ahead of him in line making funny faces at him behind their mother's quite portly back. The children waved and smiled as if they knew him. Looking at her ample mass, he gave thanks to God that he did not have to lug this extra weight around every day.

Andre's tension began to ease as he saw the speed at which the line was moving. In no time at all, he was at the front of the line about to hand his boarding pass to the woman at the gate when he was suddenly approached from all sides by TSA agents, led by the man who had just scanned him with the metal detector.

"Mr. Webster, would you please step out of line and follow me? We have some discrepancies with your identification that we need you to clarify for us," the TSA agent said as he pointed in the direction which he wanted Andre to walk. Moments later in a cramped twelve-by-twelve room, which reeked of cigarettes and tuna fish, Andre sat with two TSA agents. One stood silently, while the other began to batter him with a barrage of questions.

Across from him, in front of a mirror, which took up more than half of the east wall, stood Ivan Kempernick. Kempernick wore a tight-fitting gray Hugo Boss suit with an extra starched white shirt, fully buttoned with no tie. He was a handsome stone of a man with wide muscular shoulders and well-defined biceps attached to long stringy forearms, giving the man extremely long arms for his height. He stood with one foot resting on the folding chair across the table. Even with his boots displaying a four-inch heel off the edge of the chair, he barely measured four feet, nine inches tall. His diminutive size had forced him to overcompensate at every task he endeavored since he was kid in the sixth grade. In time, it made him a relentless, competitive monster.

Now at the age of thirty-two, he was the federal security director at one of the largest airports in the country. He strived for self-vindication in a life of being bullied by being an asshole to every person who had the guile to attempt to get away with something in his airport.

"Look, dickhead, we have been on to you since you waddled up to the ticket counter. Who are you, really? We know that you are not Milo Webster because our department has had the real Milo under investigation for the past eight months," Ivan said as he walked over and attempted to look down at Andre. "At best, you are a second-rate, punk-ass fill-in!" he shouted before he poked him in the back of his head with his tiny index finger.

Ivan grabbed Andre by the shoulder and attempted to turn him around when his fingers sank into the synthetic skin all the way down to his actual shoulder. Kempernick's facial expression drew a blank shortly, then his thin lips turned into a hook when he realized that the man was not really obese but wearing padding or some kind of suit.

"Stand up and take off all of your clothes," Kempernick instructed the man sitting in front of him.

"What?" Andre questioned.

"You heard me, you fat bitch. I said stand up and remove all of your clothes unless you want us to do it for you. Johnson over there loves a good strip search, don't you, Johnson?" Ivan asked as he pulled upward on the man's lapel, forcing him to stand.

With nerves of steel, Andre stood up and began to remove each article of clothing until he stood in just his Joe Boxers, white tube socks, and anatomically incorrect tan fat-man bodysuit.

"Holy shit! What do we have here, Johnson?" Kempernick asked as he slowly circled the man in his custody.

"I've seen this before!" the agent snorted and threw his suspect up against the wall.

"Where is the dope?" he said as he tugged at the neckline of the suit, pulling Andre down to the floor.

"What dope? I did this as a dare," Andre said as he looked up. "A friend of mine in college bet me three hundred dollars that I wouldn't take a flight somewhere wearing this suit. I have family in Ohio, so I thought it was a good way to get paid to go see my family."

Andre began reaching back, struggling to unhook the tiny connector on the back of the neck.

"Well, how do you explain this ID when we know that Milo Webster has been transporting narcotics back to the East Coast on a regular basis for the past eight months?" Kempernick asked, showing his frustration. "There has to be dope! Johnson, you know what to do. I want a thorough cavity search conducted on this doofus, and I'll break down and explore every stinking square inch of this smelly-ass suit."

Four hours later, Andre sat exhausted and shivering, chained to a cold metal bench with just his boxers and socks while all his belongings were scattered across the floor randomly. The purple suit pants lay inside out on top of the silk Pierre Cardin jacket in the same condition. Next to it, partially on the floor, partially on the cigarette-burn-covered table, lay the fat suit. Hanging on the far edge of the table primed to fall to the floor rested his wallet with all of its guts strewn across the table trailing off to the floor.

The door hinges screeched for oil as the two TSA agents entered the room. Both were trailed by a lagging stench of cigarette tobacco.

"Mr. Brown, your info checks out. It appears that you are who you say you are. I can't believe you were stupid enough to think that you could slide through our security with this sloppy costume and this second-rate fake California identification card. You are lucky we don't lock your punk ass down for having a forged ID card! It's a good thing for you that I've got bigger fish to fry today," Agent Kempernick said as he reached into his pocket, pulled out a set of keys, bent over, and unlocked Andre's handcuff and told him to get his shit and get out before he changed his mind.

"We will be in touch, dick wad. We still have some questions regarding where you got the ID," the aggressive agent said as he held the door open and began tapping on it with the wedding band on his ring finger impatiently.

Andre began collecting his things as quickly as he could, but when he reached for the fat suit, Agent Johnson waved his pointer finger and head from side to side simultaneously. With perfect timing, Kempernick said they would be keeping it for evidence. The young man attempted to hold up the size 52 waist with one hand and place everything back in his wallet with the other. In haste, he failed to see his California Lottery ticket on the floor hidden in the shadow of the table's leg.

Andre quickly hustled out of the door with his wallet in hand and jacket under his arm, when Ivan reached out to him and said, "I probably shouldn't say anything, but you don't seem like a bad guy. So, I'm going give you a little heads-up. You should be more careful of who you hang out with because someone tried to set you up today," the agent said as he stood with his long arms appearing to extend past his knees.

"What do you mean?" Andre asked.

"We were warned to be on the lookout for the real Milo Webster today because he would be carrying five kilos of dope. Apparently, you're a little smarter than someone gave you credit for being. I'm just saying that doesn't seem like a friend or a good business partner to me. Does it to you?" Agent Kempernick said before quickly tapping his pointer finger to his temple. He then turned and walked away, disappearing through a door at the end of the narrow hallway.

Andre exited through the door at the opposite end of the hallway and immediately found a restroom so he could try to fix his clothing situation as best he could while he figured out what he would do next. Moments later in the bathroom, he tucked the monstrous jacket into his backpack and began rolling the waist of the sizable slacks down three or four times, then tied the enormous belt around the base of the roll and rolled the silk pants one more time over the belt. He then finished buttoning the four-X dress shirt, strapped on his backpack, and made a beeline for the train station.

Even with everything on his mind, Andre found time to marvel at how fresh and pristine the Metro train was, until he scanned the car and realized he was one of only five riders in his entire car. Being only in its second year of service, he guessed many people still did not realize how conveniently it connected Los Angeles to the Antelope Valley. Staring out the window of the moving train, reality set in. He had to do something. He could not let Dollar get away with this. First, he had Corn killed, and now he had tried to get him arrested.

As he watched the city descend into the background and the rolling hills extended north to the San Fernando Valley, Andre flashed back to two nights ago when he had the out-of-body experience. He recalled seeing Wanda Fleming sitting on her stoop smoking a cigarette as he floated over his rooftop. When he awoke from the OBE, he eased out of the bed, careful not to wake Eileen, got dressed, and slipped out to ask Wanda about the promise she had made him. After she assured him that she had meant every word she had said, he asked her if she would be interested in making five thousand dollars. Ten minutes later, Andre had gone through his plan and asked Wanda what she thought. She slowly shook her head back and forth and formed a disgusting, sour look on her face.

"What's wrong, don't you like the plan?" Andre questioned.

Still with the sick look on her face, Wanda spoke up and said, "I think it's a good plan, Dre. But it could use a little tweaking."

"Well, what would you do different?"

"I would take my kids with me. Now, hold on before you go judging me. I don't think anyone would suspect a mother with two little girls to be transporting drugs. That's just my opinion. I could be wrong," the large woman said to him, smiled, and placed her hands on her voluptuous hips.

"I would never ask you to take your kids with you. In fact, I'd probably suggest the opposite. But if that's how you want to do it, I'm sure I could get you a couple of kids' tickets as well."

Still zoning out, he flashed forward to the early morning. Andre recalled how refreshing the cool air was on his suffocating skin when he stepped outside for the first time after donning the suit. It was then that he slid over to Wanda's to drop off the money for her tickets and the five kilos of dope. To his surprise, he found Wanda leaning out the door in a beautiful white-flower dress, smoking a cigarette. Just inside the door, he saw the girls dressed and ready to go, sitting at the breakfast table, eating big bowls of Cheerios.

Snapping back to the present, Andre looked at his watch and guessed that Wanda was more than halfway to Columbus by now. He only hoped that the drop went without a hitch because he had problems of his own to worry about on this end.

The subtle rock of the train combined with the soft lighting in the car created a relaxing setting for the tired young man. He struggled to maintain focus to work out a plan to take down Donnie. If it were not for the occasional screech of the metal breaks on the steel wheels every time the engineer approached a sharp curve, Andre would have already lost wakefulness.

Andre knew that he stood no chance in a fistfight. After all, Donnie was an Army Ranger, trained in hand-to-hand combat. He also knew that his teammate was well armed at both of his homes. On a couple of different occasions, he had seen firearms. At his party, Donnie had shown him an AR-15 with an extended clip, not to mention the Remington pump shotgun he had sitting on his coffee table the first time he and Corn had gone to his house on Beech Street. If he were going to use violence, it would have to be done in stealth. And if it was going to be done in stealth, he had the perfect tool for the job.

It was nearly noon when the train pulled into the station. Andre rushed off the train in search of the information booth. Ten minutes later, he found himself waiting in the designated area to catch the Twentieth Street East bus. The back of the bus reeked of diesel fluid. It was so strong that he, like those before him, was forced to move up toward the front. Leaning against the window, he planned to go home and get his mom's .32 two-shot Derringer with the pearl handle that she kept under her mattress. From there, he would make his way over to Donnie's house on Beech Street. It was about fifteen blocks. He figured that if he ran a block, walked a block, he could be over there in about ten minutes. Andre hoped that Donnie was not there when he arrived, so he could force Latice to leave. Then, he would lie and wait on the other side of the door in the darkness, wait for him to enter, then he would send both chambers into the back of his head.

Andre exited the bus, running at full speed down the block toward their apartment. With little effort, he cleared the four steps, which greeted the porch, slid through the doorway, and entered his key into its lock.

Within moments, he had changed clothes and was racing down the street at full speed. Occasionally, the young man would look back in hopes that he would see the bus coming, but he had no such luck.

With every jolting step, the Derringer struggled to be free, bouncing its way down the sidewalk. Staring up at the crosswalk as he sprinted across the street, Andre wished he had worn some tighter pants to better contain the palm-size gun.

The closer he got to Beech Street, the more anxious he became. Inside, an internal conflict raged between the archetypes on his shoulders. He had never killed anyone and was not sure he could bring himself to do it. Unless, of course, it was a matter of life and death. Instinctively, he knew that it was wrong to take another's life.

However, he then heard a voice in his head say, "This is a matter of life and death."

Indeed, it was.

As he turned left and hurried past the Beech Street Liquor, he noticed a funeral procession headed by a police officer on a *CHIPs* motorcycle with its blue and red lights flashing as it made its way down Beech toward Avenue I. Two blocks later, the tail of the procession eased its way out into the street, cutting in front of him at Stanton and McCarthy funeral home.

Two blocks away from Donnie's house on J-8, he had already begun to scan up the block for either of Donnie's cars. Silently, he prayed that he was not home yet. His palms felt wringing wet, and every nerve jittered anxiously. With each step, his heartbeat quickened. He was not sure, but he thought that his pace had slowed and his steps had grown smaller.

On edge, he nearly panicked when a gray sedan with dark tinted windows slowed down in front of him and the window began to roll down slowly. Paranoid Andre stepped back, ready to dive behind the closest car at any quick movement. Once the window was three-quarters down, he could see the passengers behind the dark windows, and it made him chuckle to see that it was three little white-haired ladies who had gotten turned around, looking for Lancaster Boulevard.

The comical encounter settled his spastic nerves a touch, allowing the young man to regroup and rethink his plan. As soon as he reached the corner, he crossed the street, inspecting the block carefully, and he continued straight then jogged to the alley and made a left, intending to enter the property from the backyard. Two houses from Donnie's place, he stopped, closed his eyes, and started breathing in and out deeply for a few seconds before he continued.

Andre's plan depended on Red remembering him if she was patrolling the backyard. He stood at the back fence, quietly calling the dog to him. After about thirty seconds he assumed that the dog must be in the house. Quietly, he shimmied up the corner of the fence directly behind the garage. He then let himself down easily, bracing himself between the fence and the concrete building at his back.

With his right hand, Andre removed the Derringer from his front pocket and released the safety with his thumb. As quietly as he could, he dashed up to the back of the house, palming the pistol in his right hand. With the stealth of a cat burglar, he gently pulled the handle of the sliding door. When it refused to budge, Andre placed the tiny weapon back in his pocket and quickly vanished around the left side of the house where he tiptoed to peek into the window of the master bedroom, but he couldn't see anything because of the huge headboard blocking the window, and on top of that the windows were locked, so he edged back across the patio and made his way past the window to the guest restroom. As he did, he could hear a low whimpering whine. It almost sounded like a baby crying. He was not sure, but he guessed it was Red locked in the bathroom. As he eased around the right side of the house, he turned around to make sure that no nosy neighbors were watching him. When he was sure that he was not being watched, he crept up beside the living room window. He could not see anyone, but he could hear the blaring television clearly from where he stood.

Lightly lifting up on the window, Andre heard it click; the window was open. Once again, he peeked through the windowpane, making sure no one was in the room. As soon as he lifted the window, he heard a shot ring out. It was quickly followed by another shot. In a panic, Andre began shouting.

"Latice! Latice, are you in there?" he screamed through the window.

Then he ran around to the front, jumped over the banister, and began pounding on the door.

"Open the door!" Andre screamed. Almost as a second thought, he attempted the doorknob. To his surprise, it easily turned with a twist of his wrist.

He figured it was too late to try to be quiet now as he reached into his pocket, pulled out the miniature firearm, and pushed the door open.

"Come out, I know you're in there," he said as the words just charged out of his mouth as if he was the police in an old 1950s movie. In the bathroom, Red was going crazy, barking and repeatedly throwing herself into the door. It sounded like she was now trying to chew her way through the door. Andre hurried over to the master bedroom door and kneeled beside it with his weapon ready, like he had seen in so many movies. With his left hand, he pushed the door halfway open, waited a second, then ducked his head in real quick and pulled it back just as quickly.

Andre lowered his position and uncocked the Derringer. He placed the weapon back on safety and back in his pocket as he stood up and walked into the bedroom where he found Latice hunched over, holding the nine-millimeter pistol Donnie had told her about weeks ago.

Latice stood, slouched forward at the foot of the bed, crying with her left hand over her mouth and the pistol in the other with her index finger still on the trigger.

At the other end of the bed sat a dead Donnie Pickens stripped down to only his "kiss me" boxers. Donnie was handcuffed to his queen-size headboard. Each arm was attached with military-issued handcuffs to its adjoining post. He had a three-quarter-inch bullet hole right in the middle of his forehead and another one right in the center of his chest. Donnie's eyes were still looking forward at Latice in total disbelief that she was about to shoot him. He had never seen it coming. He thought she was really going to slip into something a little more comfortable.

Andre slowly walked over to Latice, kneeled down, and picked up Donnie's white T-shirt from off the floor. He stood up, placed one arm around Latice. And with his other, he placed the shirt over Latice's hand and removed her hand from the gun. He then picked it up with the shirt and began to wipe it down as thoroughly as he could. When he finished wiping it down, he set the nine millimeter on the floor beside the bed, grabbed his sister by the hand, and led her toward the back door. Running past the bathroom, Andre noticed that Red had chewed a hole nearly big enough to fit her head through.

He reached for the doorknob and then drew his hand back quickly. He looked around for something to open the door with, and it hit him. All the places he had touched when he was attempting to break into the house. He looked at Latice to give her instructions, but she was still in shock or something. Andre grabbed her firmly by the shoulders and shook her, causing her head to snap back.

"Snap out of it!" he shouted.

"I need you to wake up and get your shit together. I want you to grab anything with your name on it and anything you need. Then go out the back gate, head down the alley, and make a left on J-8. I'll catch up to you. Once you get a couple blocks from here, don't run. Now, grab your stuff and take off! I'm right behind you."

As soon as he saw her heading down the alley, he turned his attention to the chomping sound. He could hear Red chewing threw the bathroom door. Andre took a second and peeked around the corner at the door. The dog's snout was protruding through the bathroom door. Its mouth was gushing with blood, and toothpick-size daggers were jutting out of the canine's gums. Red's eyes were glazed over with rabid rage. Andre grabbed a dish towel and began to quickly wipe down everything he had touched inside as well as outside the house. He guessed it had been nearly five minutes since the shots had been fired. He assumed that one of the neighbors had called the police.

For a second, the young man wondered if Donnie had any cash stashed somewhere, but then realized he did not have time to search with police coming and the crazed dog eating through the bathroom door. Andre took one last look, then darted out the back door and down the alley. Andre caught up with his sister about five blocks away. In the background, he could hear police sirens screaming just a couple of blocks away. The two took a roundabout way to Avenue I where they waited twenty minutes for a bus to take them home.

In the aisle seat of a nearly empty bus, Andre stared at his sister as she gazed out the window.

"Why did you do it?" Andre whispered to Latice.

"Because he was an asshole who deserved it!" she said as she turned around and faced her brother. "I hated what he did to Corn. I liked your friend a lot. Besides that, he reminded me of my dead ex-husband," she said and laughed.

Momentarily, her eyes had glazed over with a familiar look he had just seen in another crazed female.

For the next ten minutes, Andre sat quietly and tried to recall where Latice had been for the past seven years.

EPILOGUE

A few days later on a cool rainy day which actually resembled autumn, Andre met with Wanda Fleming to collect the money she had received from Donnie's connect in Ohio. The appalling conditions in which the family was living both disgusted and saddened Andre, so much so that he made his neighbor a deal. He bargained that he would split the $120,000, which she had returned with equally if she promised to clean herself up and get some help. He gave her the five thousand dollars he had promised her and told her to check into rehab. He gave her a hug and told her to come see him when she got released, and he would give her the rest of her money.

Later that evening, the family was sitting in the living room watching the news as they finished eating dinner. Andre was talking to his mother about maybe going into law when a California Lottery commercial came on, congratulating the newest lottery millionaire from yesterday's drawing. To Andre's surprise, it was a very familiar face. Before the announcer could even say his name, Andre shouted out, "Ivan Kempernick, well, I'll be—"

"You had better watch your mouth, boy," his mother said as she sat up in her seat, smacked the young man on his leg.

Latice turned around, looked at Andre, and asked how he knew the winner's name.

"It's a long story, but he was the NSA agent that processed me at LAX the other day," Andre said, shaking his head with eyes that looked on the verge of watering.

"That was my lottery ticket! They must have taken it when they went through my things… That's messed up. I can't believe it," Andre said while still shaking his head, looking at the floor.

"It's going to be okay, baby. There is a lottery drawing every week," she said with a smile as she placed her arm around her sobbing son.